On

Thin

Ice

BY

DAISY EGAN

This book is part of a series called The Redwood University Series.

This book is the first in the series.

Daisy Egan

First published in Great Britain by Daisy Egan, 2024

Printed and bounded in the UK.

Daisy Egan

To all the girls whose love of ice hockey

came from hockey romance books…

Me too.

PLAYLIST

Don't Rush (Explicit) | Young T & Bugsey	3:28
Play Play | J Hus (feat. Burna Boy)	3:25
Charmer | N-Dubz	3:08
RUNAWAY | Nino Uptown	2:40
Love Me Like You | Little Mix	3:18
I GUESS I'M IN LOVE | Clinton Kane	3:24
My Way | Timbaland & Anna Margo	2:56
Sprinter | Dave & Central Cee	3:49
Ice Ice Baby | Vanilla Ice	4:32
Stuck with U | Ariana Grande & Justin Bieber	3:49
No Favours | Mowgs & Nino Uptown	3:05
Twilight | Cover Drive	3:28
No Worries | Nino Uptown	2:48
Lose Me | Nino Uptown	2:48
Low | Flo Rida (feat. T-Pain)	3:51
So High | Mist (feat. Fredo)	2:43
Fine Girl | ZIEZIE	2:46

Daisy Egan

Content Warning:

This book is intended for adult readers only.

It contains mature themes and sexually explicit content that is not

suitable for readers younger than 18 years old.

Chapter 1

Sean

"Taylor, what the fuck are you doing?" Coach screams from the edge of the rink.

To be totally honest, I don't know what I'm doing, all I know is that my head is most definitely not in the game today. My teammates fly across the ice past me, the puck bouncing between them. The stadium is pumping with tension, the team we're playing today are wiping the floor with us and as much as I hate to admit this, it's mainly because of me. Since the second my skates hit the ice today I've not been able to keep my eyes on the game because they've been fixated on something else. The curly haired, sexy brunette that sits with her legs crossed in the penalty box, picking her nails and scrolling on her phone looking entirely uninterested in the excruciatingly tense game that's going on in front of her.

I'm a ladies man I'll admit and I mostly let my dick lead all of my decisions, but after last night I thought my horny ass would be satisfied at least for 24 hours. I tend to stick to a one night, one girl rule, it prevents any complicated feelings or expectations. Almost all of the girls I sleep with want more from me, they want to be the one to change my fuck boy ways but I've always known that I'll change when the time is right, and that time most definitely hasn't come yet, I'll know when it does. I respect the fuck out of women though make no mistake, I love women, but I've only really ever had any interest in their bodies. The second they start talking about themselves is the same second I need them to make a swift exit through my bedroom door.

I've only been at Redwood for three months but I've managed to fuck my way through almost every girl on campus…ok that may be an exaggeration but I get a *lot* of sex. Last night was the craziest of my life, I had three girls all over me after the game. Three blondes with legs that went directly to heaven were touching me and flirting with me at the bar we all went to post game to celebrate our win. To be honest I got kind of pissed off that they wouldn't leave me alone to celebrate with my boys so I took all three of them back to our shared house just off campus and fucked them all, one after the other. I won't pretend I wasn't fucking exhausted afterwards, the three of them probably had the time of their life but all I could think off when they left was sleep.

The girl in the penalty box tonight though is something else entirely, she's a fucking rocket. I keep skating past the box purely to get a closer look at her. She's small, a lot smaller than me which isn't hard because I'm pushing 6-foot-4. Her long, chocolate brown curls hang over her shoulder and her green eyes are soft and uninterested, but I can see a lingering fire beneath the surface.

I hope she's a feisty one, they're my favourite.

"Focus man, you're throwing us off." Kyle nudges me into the plexiglass when the ref blows the whistle to signal the end of the second period.

My eyes are still hooked on *her* though, I watch as she stands and turns to leave. *Fuck, her ass is incredible, I can't wait to get my hands on that later.*

"I *am* focused." I say, brushing my face with my gloved hand as I watch the sexy thing saunter through the crowd towards the corridor that leads to the locker rooms.

Kyle snorts a disbelieving laugh. "I mean focus on the game, not on Callie's ass."

"Callie? That's her name?"

"Yeah man, that's her name, now erase it from your memory and keep your head on what's happening here. We need to win this game and we're having to work extra hard because you're too busy drooling over a girl that you'll never have."

That's got my attention.

I lift my eyes from the delicious curve of Callie's swaying ass to look at Kyle. "Never have? You're crazy man, I'll have her if I want her."

Kyle shakes his head with a smirk. "You're dreaming. You know who she is right?"

"No, but I'm about to find out." I say under my breath. I bat him away with my now glove free hand and skate off the ice towards the locker rooms. I'm sweating like a whore in a church and I need to piss, but more importantly, I need to find that girl.

My plan wasn't exactly planning the way I wanted it to and I ended up back on the ice before I was able to locate the mysterious, sexy, rocket of a woman that I now know as Callie. I force myself to take my eyes off her and concentrate on the game, we really need this win to get us out of the relegation zone and back to our usual status.

Coach is screaming at all of us from the side of the rink, he gave us a heavy pep talk — it was actually more like a verbal ass whooping — during the break. We deserved it, we're playing shit tonight. My team is usually like a well oiled machine, working perfectly in sync with each other and battering our opponents, but tonight I'm letting the side down. I know this and yet I can't stop. I literally can't tear my eyes away from Callie, her tight stomach through the thin material of her bodysuit, the swell of her perfect tits, the way her thick curls bounce as she moves. She seems totally disinterested in the game itself and I find my curiosity growing by the second. It's the third period now so I only have twenty minutes to make a quick decision, is this game my priority right now? It should be, I am the captain after all, but I think my dick has taken over at this point. The longer I look at Callie the more I start to panic that she'll leave after the game before I get a chance to talk to her. I need to take her home with me tonight, I *need* to see what's under those clothes.

I make a snap decision, zipping across the ice and shoving my skate under one of the defensemen's legs, sending him tumbling onto his stomach. I wait for the sound that will determine my fate and I hope I've done enough to be sent to the sin bin, which is exactly where I want to be right now. The high pitched sound of the whistle has my stomach jumping with triumph, but I keep my face neutral as the ref directs me to the penalty box.

Fuck yes!

Kyle is shaking his head at me from his spot in goal, reading my mind as usual and knowing that my plan worked. He's trying to hold back his smile but he's failing miserably. I've left my guys a man down for the next five minutes and I know that's shitty of me, but we're one nil up at this point so the chances of us taking this win are pretty good. I can spare five minutes of my precious time to speak to this sexy bombshell, who by the way, doesn't even glance in my direction when I fall down onto the bench next to her.

Oh my god, she's even better up close. Her creamy skin dips along her collarbone, lifting and falling as she breathes a sigh of boredom.

Callie might just be the most beautiful thing I've ever seen in my entire life. Her chocolate curls fall down, dancing across her jaw and accentuating the light sprinkling of freckles that decorate her cheek bones. Her eyes are bright when she finally looks up at me, the emerald pools drinking me in and making me ache to slap my lips onto her's. Then her gaze hardens when she sees who's sitting next to her and the tiger behind those sexy, green eyes sharpens it's claws.

This is going to be a fuck load of fun, I can feel it in my bones.

Daisy Egan

Chapter 2

Callie

If there's one thing I know about hockey players, it's that they stink. I don't mean metaphorically, I mean they literally stink to high heavens. The amount of sweat that pours out of them during a game is enough to fill the Thames. I should know, I've been around them since I was little.

James Burch, also known as head coach of the men's ice hockey team at Redwood University also has another nickname he likes to go by, Dad. Yes, my dad is the men's hockey coach at the university that I attend for gymnastics. The sport is my entire life, has been since I was four years old and almost every decision I make is to further my chances of making a success of myself.

Redwood University sits about half a mile from the road, surrounded by green and cocooned away from the rest of the world, or so it seems when you're there. It's miles from anywhere, the nearest city being London with it's hustle and bustle, which is incredibly ironic considering all you can hear after dark at the university is the incessant tapping of laptop keys from students who have missed their deadlines and the squawking of unknown animals in the forests that line the property.

I love sports, not just gymnastics but it's where my natural flare was as a child. Dad wanted me to do something, anything that was athletic as he used to be a hockey player himself. As hurtful as it is to say, I think he was disappointed to find out he was having a daughter, it's natural for him to want to pass down his hockey genes to someone, but it certainly wasn't me. I can barely stay upright on the ice so I avoid it at all costs. My dad has drilled it into me from the moment I said my first word that being successful is what life is all about. My parents never had any other children, so Christmases and family events are quiet, but it's the way it's always been and it's the way I like it. My mind is a constant buzz of deadlines, competitions and training, so going home is pretty much the only time I'm able to fully switch off from the stress of university life. Don't get me wrong I love it here, my dad has been planning for my time here since I did my first cartwheel and I have to say I'm glad he saved every penny for the first twenty years of my life to make sure I could get a place. I met my best friend here too, Molly Crawford, we were paired in a dorm together two years ago and the click between us was instant. She's 100 miles per hour all day, everyday and I'm about 10 miles per hour behind her, so we make for a perfect pair. Anais then joined our dorm room 18 months ago, not long after she started at Redwood, she's a gymnast on my team too so we have a lot in common. The girls on my team and Molly are pretty much the only people I'm willing to give up my time for here, everyone else pretty much pisses me off, especially my dad's hockey boys. That's why I'm wondering how I ended up where I am right now. In the penalty box at a hockey game, my dad screaming profanities from the plexiglass and waving his arms in the air. I used to come and watch the games all the time with Molly, but I've been so busy with competitions since we came back from summer break that I've not made the time to come and watch any games. Like I said, I'm awful on the ice, but watching hockey and playing hockey are two different things entirely.

As I sit, picking at my finger nails and half watching the game, the sensation of warmth rolls over my skin when a huge wave of heat brushes past me and lands on his ass, right next to me in the sin bin. I twist my neck reluctantly, not wanting to engage for even a millisecond with whichever player has been sent off the ice. He's bound to be mad, frustrated at being sent off for something he'll be sure he didn't do. When I look up at the dimple-faced, smiling hunk of muscle I see it's Sean Taylor.

Why god, why did it have to be Sean Taylor?

He's the most annoying of them all, captain of the team since he joined the university three months ago he's already made himself known to every single female that comes within a mile of him. The cocky smile spread across his rugged face right now proves that. I watch as his gaze turns sultry and he drags his caramel eyes down, prowling over my skin and making me shiver.

Don't get me wrong, he's hot as balls, but I'm not the type of girl to jump into bed with any guy who shows me an ounce of attention. I prefer to be in a relationship, I like the stability and feeling like someone is committed to me and only me. Not that *that* worked out for me the last time.

My ex-boyfriend Joel is a football player here, we were together for just over a year when he dumped me last week. He said I was constantly in a bad mood, always had an attitude with him and he could never do anything to please me. I can't help it though, it's just the way I am and as much as I love being in a relationship I refuse to change myself for any man.

Sean is still fluttering his eyes across my body, his gaze lingering on the low neckline of my sleek, black, bodysuit as he digs his teeth into his bottom lip. The whistle snaps his attention back to the game and I sigh with relief to think he won't bother me anymore with his perverted looks and eye fucking. But of course I'm never that lucky, and when I turn my head back in his direction he captures my eyes with his.

If he wasn't so heartbreakingly good looking it would be easier to be rude to him, it's obvious why girls are literally falling at his feet. He's huge, about a foot taller than me and I'm 5-foot-4 on a good day. His short, dark curls accentuate the hardness of his jaw line and the discreet coating of shadowy stubble that blankets his face is screaming for me to reach out and brush my fingers against it. But unfortunately for Sean Taylor he's also the most irritating, arrogant asshole on the whole hockey team. He knows he's hot and I think if you asked him he'd tell you he's the hottest person he's ever seen. There's nothing I hate more than a guy who thinks he's god's gift to women.

He's still looking at me like I'm his favourite snack, not saying a word and it's making me want to reach over and slap the smug grin off his gorgeous face. He finally clears his throat and I realise that I'm staring at his mouth, the pink of his lips tempting me in accompanied by his deliciously sexy dimples and extremely arrogant grin. Absolutely not, I will never be seen dead going home with a guy like him, like I said I don't do hook ups anyway and even if I did I'd have better taste than a walking ad for chlamydia like Sean Taylor.

"Hey," He says, his swampy eyes trapping me for a split second before I remember who I'm sitting next to.

As tempting as it is to be rude to this giant hunk of arrogance, I decide to try and be civil, hoping his time in here with me goes quickly so I can go back to my scrolling and nail picking.

I sigh, full of boredom and indifference. "What you in for?"

Daisy Egan

"It's not prison," He snickers and I turn back to my phone. He has to be annoying the second he opens his mouth doesn't he?

My obvious disinterest in him clearly has him confused. I don't think a girl has ever been less interested in him than I am. Like I said, he's painfully hot, but his 'I'm the king of the rink' attitude overrides his hotness the second he opens his mouth.

"It's hockey prison." I say, still not looking at him.

He barks a laugh. "I was sentenced to 5 minutes for tripping, which is bullshit because I didn't even trip him."

There's the 'I didn't do it' mantra that I was waiting for.

"Actually," he says, twisting his whole body towards mine and I purposefully shuffle further away from him down the bench. "I did trip him, I tripped him on purpose so I could get sent in here."

"You purposefully got a penalty?" I ask, his shit eating grin glowing back at me. "Wow, what a shitty captain you are leaving your boys a man down for 5 whole minutes."

His smile widens further and my stomach does a backflip. "I wanted to talk to you." He grins, caramel eyes flitting across my freckled cheek bones.

There he goes again with the arrogance, I'm sick of hockey boys thinking just because they're tall, painfully handsome and sexy that girls will automatically drop their pants. I'm not denying that most of the hockey team are fine as hell, Sean Taylor being at least ten times hotter than the rest of them, but that doesn't mean I'm going to dive into bed with him, begging him to give me the pleasure of his dick for one night.

"Yeah, ok, look, the smooth talking isn't going to work on me, so save your breath. Unfortunately for you I'm immune to your boyish charms." I let out an aggravated sigh, letting my irritation for him get the better of me. His eyes float between mine, washing with a sparkle of excitement mixed with the absolute confusion that any girl couldn't want him.

"There's nothing boyish about what I want to do to you." He smirks, a devilish grin spreading across his cheeks.

A flabbergasted scoff leaves my lips before I can stop it and Sean's face changes. "You're really living up to the whole fuck boy, sleaze bag, man whore image that I already have of you."

I twist my body completely away from his and check the clock on the scoreboard. Still two and a half minutes of torture left in here with this buffoon of a man whilst he desperately tries to claw his way into my pants. I keep my eyes on the game for a few seconds, but Sean never takes his sparkling gaze off the side of my face. He's so fucking annoying.

"What?" I spit, catching him by surprise and watching as his eyebrows shoot up into his hairline.

"Woah tiger," He laughs, the cocky smile never leaving his face. He doesn't try to hide the fact that his eyes keep falling to my tits.

I brush the uncontrollable mane of curls over my shoulder and cross one leg over the other with a huff, turning away from him again and ignoring him completely.

"So, are you enjoying the game? You don't seem to be actually watching it." He says and I continue to ignore him. I can hear the smile in his voice, like he's enjoying this game of cat and mouse between us. Little does he know that this mouse is like a cheetah and can outrun his flirty pursuit no problem. "You must have paid a lot of money to sit here during a game like this."

"Ha," I scoff and reluctantly meet his cocky smile. "Pay for this? You must be joking."

"Well, you must be a big fan to be sat in the penalty box, bet you're starstruck meeting me aren't you?"

Urgh, this man is insufferable.

"You're not going to stop talking to me are you?"

A slow smile crosses his face. "No,"

I let out a loud, impatient sigh. "The fact you don't know that I'm your coach's daughter just proves how self absorbed you really are."

"There's no way you're Coach's daughter, I would have seen you around before. And trust me, there's not a chance in hell I would have laid eyes on you and not taken you home with me." He coos, leaning closer.

His woodsy aftershave is deliciously manly and I fight back the drool that wants to escape. No way is this asshole going to get to me that easily.

"Wow, your head is so big we can barely fit in this box together." I huff and he barks a laugh, leaning back against the bench, arms folded behind his head. "You know a lot of the guys on your team are hot, you're not the only one."

"Ha!" He sits up, pointing his finger at me playfully. "You think I'm hot."

I roll my eyes. "Well, I'm not blind Taylor."

He laughs again. Why does this fuck head laugh at me constantly? It's like he's hating the fact that I have no interest in him, but revelling it in at the same time.

"So now that we've established that we're both hot as fuck, are you coming home with me after the game?"

Now it's my turn to laugh, albeit dryly. "You don't even know my name you pig!"

He stands to his feet, the seconds ticking by as his time in the sin bin comes to an end, thank god.

"Yes, I do Callie." He sings, thirty-seconds left before he can go back on the ice and stop irritating the shit out of me.

I roll my eyes and fold my arms across my chest again. "I'm not impressed by you Taylor, now get back on the ice and do your job."

His eyes flicker to the timer on the scoreboard. 20 seconds.

"Will you come home with me after the game if I score a goal for you?" He asks, jutting his bottom lip out and making puppy eyes at me.

"I'll think about it." *I most definitely will not, think about it.*

He fist bumps the air and winks at me, before sliding back out onto the ice and flying towards the goal. Lewis smashes the puck to Sean, he glides across the ice effortlessly, weaving through the opposing team and whacking the puck flying. It whips past the left side of the goalie's head and within seconds of Sean hitting the ice, he's scored the winning goal. With only minutes left of the game it's almost certain that Redwood have taken this one, and when his teammates clamber off him, releasing him from their bear hugs, he looks straight at me. He points his hockey stick directly at me and throws me a dazzling smile. My vagina does a little dance and I metaphorically slap her around the face. I can't let him get to me like this, he's interested in one thing and one thing only. And that thing is something I can't give him.

Chapter 3

Sean

Thank fuck for that, I'm so glad that game is over. My poor dick couldn't take the torture of staring at Callie any longer, the poor guy needs relief. Her face was a picture when I pointed my stick at her, her cheeks glowing pink as she sunk lower in her seat, hiding from everyone's staring eyes and mouthing insults at me. I thought for a second there that my usual charms really weren't working on her, which is something I'm not accustomed to and don't wish to experience. My cock leapt with joy when I scored that goal, imagining all the things I can to do to Callie tonight.

I take a slow jog towards the hallway, exiting the rink after my teammates and letting the crowd's loud cheers muffle when the door falls closed.

Callie is walking alongside our coach, the soft curve of her spine begging me to run my fingers down it. Her thick curls sway with her as she walks and when coach turns left and enters the locker rooms I run to catch up to her.

"I'll be ready in 15 minutes, wait here for me." I whisper into her curls and her head flies around to face me.

Oh man, she smells so good, like pineapple and mango.

She purses her pouty lips and tips her head at me, her thick lashes fluttering. "And why would I do that?"

I hear snickers from my teammates who are loitering behind me, listening to their captain being sass mouthed by this fierce little firecracker.

"I scored a goal for you, now I get to take you home, that was the deal." I say, my heart picking up speed as I watch her eyes sparkle with delight.

"Deal's off Captain." She smirks and spins around, strutting towards the exit.

My mouth has fallen open and I'm not sure whether to laugh or cry. My dick is definitely crying right now, agonisingly desperate to see how she feels.

"What?" I choke, hearing my boys hooting with laughter behind me.

"I'm sorry to disappoint you but I have no interest in being another notch on your bedpost and I don't do casual sex." She says over her shoulder, not even bothering to turn her head fully to look at me as she batters me with rejection.

"Can I have your number then?" I blurt out.

My teammates fall silent behind me, their snickering stopping abruptly. When I flick my head around to look at them their faces are stunned in silence. It's not a secret that I don't ever ask for girls numbers, I don't need them. I don't make a habit of seeing women on repeat but Callie turning me down makes me want her even more, I'm willing to do almost anything to make her want me back.

She fully turns around now, just as she reaches the doors. "Sean Taylor wants my number?"

I smile, showcasing my panty dropping dimples and hoping my charm is slowly bringing her around. "I'll admit I don't usually ask women for their numbers, but for you I'll make an exception."

"Awe, that's so sweet." She says, smiling sarcastically and yanking at the door to leave.

I panic. "Is that a maybe?" I yell after her and she freezes in the now open doorway.

"Like I said, I don't do causal sex big boy, sorry to crush your dreams." The door swings closed behind her and she's gone, her mind bending scent filling the corridor and making me woozy with need. I don't know how I feel about this game we're now playing, I literally never get rejected by women, if anything I'm usually the one with the pick of the bunch. This is like a punch to my ego, but I also feel a competitive fire lighting inside of me. She's made herself a challenge and I fucking love to win. I already wanted her, the minute I saw her sitting in the penalty box with her soft curls falling over one shoulder, her beautiful green eyes bright but fiery at the same time and her delicious ass when she swished away during the break. But hearing her tell me no just makes me all the more desperate to win her over.

I don't make it home until 8pm and my legs are wobbly with exhaustion when I throw my bag down onto my bedroom floor. I'm really lucky to be living here in this huge house-share with my teammates but sometimes I crave alone time, like real alone time. Lewis, Nick, Kyle and I rent a house together just off campus along a quiet country road. The outside of the house really doesn't do justice to the inside, especially since the bedrooms here are more like their own luxury apartments. The four of us share the price of rent and food, but with me being from a family with cash to spare I like to chip in a little more where I can.

My parents are high flying lawyers, working in London in an office building that was designed and created specifically for their company. They're always put together, both of them in matching suit trousers and hair immaculately tamed, but don't be fooled by their appearances. They're two of the kindest, most level headed, loving people I've ever had the pleasure of knowing. There's nothing they wouldn't do for my sister Lois and I growing up and they're still a constant support for us both. My sister is two years younger than me and is here on a gymnastics scholarship, whilst I managed to bag one of the few hockey scholarships they offer here. When I told my parents I wanted to come to Redwood University to play hockey I was worried they'd be disappointed, that they'd want me to go into some sort of business like their's. But my mum's face lit up and she pulled me into a hug, reassuring me that I could do whatever makes me happy. Lois received the same reaction when she told them she'd been offered a full scholarship for gymnastics here. My parents really are amazing people, consistent and always present for me and my sister whenever we need them.

"What the fuck was that out there today?" Kyle's voice yanks me out of my daydream and I let myself fall back onto my king sized mattress. Kyle stands in the doorway, his arms folded and his body leaning against my doorframe. His grin is lazy and knowing, he's one of my best friends and I know for a fact that he has already deciphered exactly what was wrong with me on the ice today.

My teammates know what I'm like and they accept it, Kyle and Nick also being pretty much addicted to women the same way I am but I will admit, of the three of us I get the most attention. When the three of us have girls in our rooms at the same time the house sounds like some sort of orgy is taking place. I feel for Lewis though, he wants a relationship, craves more than just sex and after his messy breakup with his ex he's been pretty much wallowing. He outright refuses to take my advice and hook up with someone else to help him get over Grace, although I guess I don't blame him for ignoring me, what do I know about getting over a girlfriend? I've never had one.

Kyle flails his arms, his blonde hair shaking back and forth as he waits for an answer from me.

"You know what that was." I smile, letting my mind wander back to it's Callie induced coma.

"You're one crazy fucker you know that?" Kyle laughs, pushing off from the door and starting to close it behind him.

"Hey, hold on I need to ask you something." I call after him and he pokes his chiselled jaw around my half closed door.

"Is it Callie related?"

"Maybe…" I muse, trying not to smile.

He stifles a laugh. "What the fuck has gotten into you? You spoke to her once and you're obsessed."

To be clear, I don't know what has gotten into me. I just really fucking want this girl, more than I think I've ever wanted anyone before.

"Is she single?" I say, peering up at Kyle from where he's sat himself beside me on the edge of the bed.

"Yeah, only since last week. Honestly though man I think you're wasting your time with her, she's stubborn so if she's telling you no, it's most likely always going to be a no."

"We'll see about that."

It's like everyone's goal here is purely to spur me on, to make me even more desperate for a taste of her.

Kyle launches one of my many pillows at my head and leaves the room with a loud bout of laughter.

"I wasn't finished with my questions!" I shout as he disappears from sight.

"I was!" He yells back, laughter still rippling his voice.

I lay back again, grabbing my phone from my pocket and typing her name into Facebook. It doesn't take me long to find her profile and as I scroll through her pictures I realise she's a gymnast like my sister Lois. I bet they know each other.

After about half an hour of social media stalking I click 'Add friend' on her profile. Within seconds the button goes back to blue, indicating that she rejected my friend request. I fight the playful smile that pulls at my lips and click, 'Add friend' again. When she hasn't responded in thirty-seconds I click my lock screen shut and close my eyes. As fun as this game with her is I'm so fucking tired I could pass out, today's been full speed and I only got five hours of sleep last night. When we got to the rink this morning there was water leaking from our gym where we do all of our weight training and warm up shit. We weight train at least once a day so if that shitty gym is flooded we're going to have a huge problem on our hands.

Just as I feel my ever buzzing brain starting to switch off I hear a ping from my phone. I squint my eyes, peeling them open only a crack to read the message on my screen.

Callie Burch:

'Stop friend requesting me, stalker.'

My face lights up with a triumphant grin. I don't care if she's calling me names, getting pissed at me or wanting to rip my head off. Any sort of attention from this beauty is good attention and the more she talks to me, the more likely that I'll eventually get her to drop her pants and give in. My god, I need a night with this woman, maybe even more than one.

Chapter 4

Callie

"Callie I don't know how many times I need to repeat myself this morning, have you gone deaf?"

I wish I had, if I have to hear Ellen yell my name across the gym one more time I might stab white hot pokers into my ears.

"Straighten your legs on that walkover or I'm going to come over there and tape wooden boards to them!" She yells, throwing her hands in the air before turning back to where Lois hangs sheepishly on the bar.

My beam routine is fucking awful this season, I don't know what's wrong with me but I just can't get the hang of it. I have all the skills under my belt, beam is my strongest piece but for some infuriating reason I just can't nail this routine. To be honest I'm screwing up all of my routines this season, I'm sure Ellen manufactured the most difficult routines possible just so she can watch me crumble. But I'm nothing if not determined so I try once more. Training is almost over and I can't wait to get home tonight, get into my comfiest PJs and sit on the couch with Molly eating our body weight in cookie dough flavoured ice cream.

I straighten my arms above my head, shuffling my feet on the beam before launching myself forwards. My legs travel over my head and my feet hit the beam again one by one. The momentum is too strong though, I misjudged it again and soon my feet land on the huge mat below the beam with a crash that echoes through the gym. I hear Ellen sigh loudly from across the room and I know I'm in for it again.

I'm used to being yelled at, my whole life I've been subjected to screaming and yelling in the gym. You don't become successful at gymnastics without being constantly criticised and told your doing things wrong. That doesn't mean it doesn't drain the life out of you though.

"Right! All of you on the floor now, we're stretching before we finish." Ellen huffs and the rest of my teammates make their way over to our huge floor area.

I'm so grateful for the team I have here, there's not one of them I don't like or get along with. Actually that would be a little bit of a lie, there's always Sofia, bitching about her boyfriend or telling us all were doing things wrong in our routines. I don't know why she doesn't just focus on her own shit, it would make the whole gym a lot more pleasant to be in. The rest of my girls though, Lois, Anais and Jennifer are great to work with and I always feel at ease when we are competing in team events.

Obviously Ellen makes me go first for stretching, I swear that woman made me captain of the team solely so she'd have a reason to pick on me. I sit down into a front split, my good leg first of course and Ellen quickly lifts my back leg, stretching my muscles and making me grit my teeth together. I can hear her counting under her breath whilst my teammates sit in a line watching, waiting for their turn in the torture chamber. As she reaches my sixtieth second of pain, the gym door swings open, squeaking and dragging all of our eyes in the direction of the sound. A crowd of huge, topless men filter into the gym, my dad trailing behind them. Normally twelve hunky, gorgeous, shirtless men all swarming into our gym would be like a dream, but these particular men are the bane of my existence. One in particular, who finds me immediately and overpowers me with his Hollywood smile. I roll my eyes which only makes Sean titter and nudge his shoulder into Kyle's, gesturing towards me like I'm a zoo animal.

"Can I help you gentlemen?" Ellen squawks, lifting her eyebrows so high I almost lose them in her hairline.

I'm still sitting in my splits, much more comfortable now Ellen's talons are off me and she's focusing on the greek god looking giants who have just interrupted our training session. My eyes fight not to look at Sean, but the warmth that settles between my thighs wins this particular battle and I spare one more glance his way. His bottom lip is pulled between his teeth and his swampy eyes are winding all over my body. I suddenly feel very exposed in my crop top and gym shorts, I'll admit they're so tight they're practically painted on, but they need to be for this kind of sport. I'm just grateful I chose not to wear a leotard today. He spots me looking at him when his eyes rise up from my chest and he grins brightly again.

Those fucking dimples. Why are they so irresistible?

My dad shoves his way through the sea of hockey players and comes to the front of the group, before throwing me a quick, forced smile.

"Our gym is flooded again so I'm afraid we'll be using your floor for the foreseeable future." He sighs and my brain almost explodes out of my skull.

This isn't the first time we've been in this shitty situation, the hockey team have a small gym area off the side of the rink that they use for weight training. The fucking thing has already flooded once this year and we were stuck with them using our floor everyday for an hour, eating up our training time. Like I said earlier, my routines this season are dog shit and the last thing any of us need is for sweaty, stinking hockey players to be parading around shirtless in our gym, soaking up our precious time that could be used perfecting our routines before competitions start.

I groan loudly, slapping my hands down on the ground. "Are you fucking serious?"

"Language Callie!" My dad snaps, fisting his hips and trying to seem authoritative.

"I'm sorry Dad, but this is bullshit." I groan, snapping up from my splits and rising to my feet.

I'm so done with this year already, we've only been back at university for a few weeks and already the entire year has pretty much gone to shit.

My teammates watch as I make my way towards the door in a sulk. Sean moves to the right slightly, purposefully wedging himself between Kyle and Nick so I have to pass through the middle of them to exit. The closer I get the more defined his torso looks, the ridged planes of his stomach make my vagina excited again and I silently tell her to calm the fuck down, she's not getting any action from that man whore, over my dead body. He's not making it easier for me to stay strong willed though when he comes into the gym looking like *that*. He's grinning from ear to ear again, as usual and the closer I get to him the more obvious it is that my resolve at hating him is faltering. Don't get me wrong I do hate him for needing to have his dick wet at all times, but why does he have to be such a sex magnet?

I huff. "Urgh, why do you have to be so hot? It's a shame you're an irritating asshole." I grumble at him, slapping at Sean and Kyle's bare chests and making a gap between them that I can squeeze through. The second the back of my hand hits Sean's stomach I hear him groan and his palm lands where mine just was against his skin.

"She touched me." He moans and I hear Kyle cackle.

"You ok there man?" He says, patting Sean's shoulder in mock condolence.

I turn my face just before I reach the door and see Sean cupping his dick.

"No, I'm not ok, I have a raging boner now." He groans, running his hand down his face and continuing to cup his ever hardening dick.

I let an arrogant smile flicker across my own face as I slip through the exit, it feels nice to be the one turning him on. I know he thinks I'm attractive, he's made than abundantly clear but seeing him weak with no sign of the cocky smirk he wears is very fulfilling for me.

"Is it weird that I find her even sexier when she's mad?" Is the last thing I hear Sean's muffled voice say through the gym door before I make my way into the changing rooms, a grin of my own overtaking my face.

Chapter 5

Sean

"I think you need to chill out with this whole stalking Callie mission you've started." Kyle titters as the two of us spot each other during our weight session.

The gymnasium here is pretty fucking huge, considering my sister Lois has been at the university for three months just as I have, I've never been in here before. Wish I would have come down and paid her a visit, I could have been balls deep in Callie right now if I'd started my 'get into Callie's pants' project three months ago.

"I literally can't stop Ky, I don't know what the fuck has gotten into me, but I like it."

"You just like the chase that's your problem." He swats at my arm as we swap around and he lays down in front of me, positioning his body before he reaches for the weight above his head.

"You know when she first turned me down yesterday, I thought it was the chase that excited me too, but now I'm not so sure. I mean yeah, she's so go damn fuckable I could come in my pants just looking at her, but I'm not sure that's all it is that's drawing me in. I kind of like the fact that she hates me." A laugh rumbles in my throat and Kyle lets out a harsh breath.

"Fuck me, you're going soft for this girl. You know you only met her yesterday right?"

"I know and my brain has been able to think of literally nothing else since then." I groan, yanking my fingers through the pillow of curls that rests on my head.

Kyle stands up, wiping his sweaty palm against his shorts. "Just be careful is all I'm saying, if you do get your way with her you don't want Coach finding out."

I bark a dry laugh. "Don't worry about that, I'm sneaky as shit. I've had to be, living in a house with three guys."

"You don't think we hear you with a new girl every weekend? Your walls are paper thin man." Kyle taunts, jabbing me in the chest with a balled up fist.

I yank my t-shirt over my head, I can't fucking wait to get out of here and go home. All I want to do right now is eat an entire tub of ice cream and watch some shitty movie in bed. Maybe piss Callie off a bit too by sending her countless messages on Facebook.

"Maybe that's all about to change." I mutter, swinging my bag over my shoulder.

"You'll never change." Kyle titters, his blonde hair bobbing as he slips his feet into his trainers.

I nod robotically. "For the right woman I will."

My evening isn't exactly going as planned. I know I'm only 23 but surely I should be able to just snuggle up in bed and watch a shitty movie and eat my ice cream like a teenage girl occasionally. When I get home the house is already pretty crowded, it's not a party exactly, more of a get together with the team. We've had a busy few weeks since we came back from summer break and we've not had much down time. I groan internally though at the thought of not being able to have the relaxing, post training evening I wanted. We have another game tomorrow and I can't be fucked for a night of loud music and drinking.

Nick hands me a beer and I reluctantly take it, lifting the glass bottle to my lips and letting the alcohol burn my throat as it travels down to my stomach. I'm not really a drinker, my grandfather was a drunk and he abused my mum as a kid so I don't like to associate myself with the devil's liquid. I'll drink sometimes with my team after a big win, or occasionally use the stuff to numb me after a shitty game, but apart from that I tend to avoid it at all costs.

The first thing I notice when I scan the room are the three blondes from the other night, one of them draped over Lewis as he uncomfortably tries to prise her manicured nails off the collar of his shirt. The other two are sitting on Nick's lap, practically undressing him in the living room. Normally I'd be envious, wanting some of the leggy blondes for myself, especially after I saw what they could do the other night. But every time I try to mentally undress them, Callie's beautiful, glowing face comes into my mind and distracts me from anything else. I sigh, reaching for another beer and convincing myself I'll be going upstairs to bed after this drink, I really am exhausted and I need sleep.

It's Saturday tomorrow but hockey doesn't stop on the weekends and we have another important game in the afternoon. I know I'm the captain but I'm definitely more on board for breaks and rests than the rest of my team, they'll want to be in the gym or on the ice all morning before our game.

When I put my beer down on the side, lifting my eyes back to the crowded living room I see one of the blondes staring at me, walking towards me with her sultry gaze, suggesting everything I would normally be looking for. I have no fucking clue what any of their names were, I didn't bother to ask, I couldn't give less of a fuck.

"Hi you," she coos, her bright blue eyes tracking down my large frame as she runs her hands down my stomach. "Wanna continue the fun from the other night?"

I can't be arsed with this shit right now. "No, not tonight sorry," I say, lazily throwing my empty bottle into the bin and slithering out of her grip. I make my way up the stairs and Nick calls after me, "Where you going Taylor? We're just getting started down here." He winks and gestures to the blonde who is now pouting from my rejection.

"I'm done, crashing for the night," I lift my arm in a half assed wave and trudge up the stairs to my room.

I've only just locked the door when I hear a light tap on the wood, I swing it open and see that fucking girl again, smiling at me suggestively.

Fucking hell, can she not take a hint?

"What do you want?" I say sharply and she looks hurt again. I can't find it in me to care though, not after I already told her I wasn't interested.

"I thought maybe we could hang out…" She whispers, looking down at the ground and shuffling her heeled feet.

I take a deep breath, digging deep in the unused part of my brain for the right words to not hurt her feelings. "Look, I'm not trying to be an asshole but I'm seriously not interested, the other night was fun sure, but it's done with." I try to close the door on her but she wedges the sparkled toe of her stiletto between the wood and the door frame.

Ok now she's really starting to piss me off.

"Move your fucking foot, now." I growl and her eyes narrow.

"You're such a prick. You think you can just use me the other night and now pretend like I don't exist? Jerk." She hisses, sauntering off down the hall and shoving past Kyle as he ascends the stairs.

He catches my eye and confusion floods his vision. "Thought you were only interested in Callie now? Didn't take you long to go back to your old ways." He tuts jokingly and pushes his way into my room.

"I didn't fucking touch her, trust me. She came up here begging for a ride on my dick and I told her I wasn't interested."

Kyle's face is twisted into an indecipherable expression, I'm not sure if he's pleasantly surprised at me sticking to my word or disgusted that I turned down a hot girl.

"Seeing as you've made yourself at home," I say, watching as Kyle takes a seat on my chair, leaning back and sipping at his beer. "You can make yourself useful and answer more of my Callie related questions."

Kyle's beer nearly sprays across the room as he fights to swallow his mouthful. "*More* questions? What am I, her mother?"

"Come to think of it, how do you know so much about my girl?"

"Your girl?" Kyle lifts his eyebrows. "You're delusional man, she'll never have sex with you."

"What makes you so sure?" I say, whipping my t-shirt over my head and laying back on my bed.

"Well, for starters, she's already rejected you, more than once." He smirks and I momentarily want to smack him. Callie will come around, I'm going to *make* her want me like I want her. "And secondly she's got a vendetta against us hockey players. She kind of has a soft spot for me though." Kyle grins and I want to smack him for a second time.

"Answer my question dickhead, how do you know her so well?" I try to ignore what he said about Callie having a soft spot for him, surely she would have fucked him by now if she was attracted to him.

"She comes to all the joint parties that we have with the gymnastics team at weekends, you know, the ones you never want to come to?" He sips his beer again.

"Well, I would have fucking come if I'd known she was there. Why didn't you tell me that my sister has a sexy captain?"

He chuckles. "Thought you got enough pussy already, save some for the rest of us."

My stomach lurches as I swallow the brick that's made it's way into my throat. "You haven't fucked her have you?"

Kyle snickers and watches the red fury creep up my neck. I'm jealous, fucking jealous. I've never been jealous in my life and now the mere thought of Callie wanting Kyle but not me is making red blur my vision.

"No, I haven't fucked her." He laughs and stands up to leave. "There's a party tomorrow at Mac's place, you should come."

As much as little Jamie Macdonald pisses me off, if there's somewhere Callie is going to be then I'll be there too without having to be asked twice.

Mac is a left winger on our team, he's the youngest of us all and he's a fucking irritation to say the least. He's about 5-foot nothing and brags about his sex life like he doesn't picture his own grandma when he beats his meat. The guy pisses me off, but if Callie is going to this party

tomorrow it will be a chance for me to see her relaxed, outside of the gym
or the hockey games which she apparently finds 'boring'.

"Oh I'll be there." I say as Kyle lets my bedroom door swing closed
behind him.

Chapter 6

Callie

"Come on, pleeeease!" Molly gets down on her knees in front of me and pouts her bottom lip.

I sigh. "Get off your knees, knob head."

"I will when you agree." She smirks, yanking playfully at my legs, her blonde waves shaking with her head. Molly is my best friend, has been since we moved into this dorm together but my god she can be annoying.

"Fine." I huff, crossing my arms over as she stands and yanks me into a hug.

"Thank you, thank you, thank you!" She sings and I wriggle away from her.

"But you're not coming to the party afterwards." I point a warning finger at her and she puts her hands up in surrender.

"I won't even ask." She flashes me a bright smile and runs into her bedroom to get ready. If we're going to make this damn hockey game on time we need to leave in ten minutes.

Molly, unlike me, loves hockey and used to play as a child. She's a runner now and is the best on her team here at Redwood, I've watched her run and I'm not exaggerating when I say the girl looks like she's flying. Her feet barely touch the ground when she runs and it's the thing that makes her happiest in the world, except for me of course. She came home after practice today and told me there was a hockey game this afternoon, I told her I didn't give a shit and she slapped me around the back of the head. This lead to us rolling around on the carpet together, fighting playfully like we were in some sort of cheap porn movie. She then proceeded to beg me to get tickets from my dad so we could go and watch the game. There's also a party at Jamie Macdonald's house after the game, which is the usual routine. The gymnastics team and the hockey team often have joint parties, we train in the same building so it kind of makes sense as we all know each other. I wouldn't normally be so opposed to going to watch a hockey game, I don't love them like Molly does but I can enjoy it occasionally. The only problem with going tonight is I now have a stalker by the name of Sean Taylor, also known as Redwood's hockey team captain. As soon as I got home last night I had countless Facebook messages from him, I know he's just trying to get into my pants and I get it, I know I'm attractive. I don't have a problem in that department, I work hard for my body and I'm proud of it, but I don't give it away to just anyone. I've made it clear to him that I'm not looking for a hook up with the biggest playboy in our university, but it doesn't seem to be sinking into his thick skull. Even if I was up for some casual sex, the last person I would choose to engage in said sex with would be Sean Taylor. He's the most irritating, big headed asshole I've ever had the displeasure of meeting and for some unknown reason he's set his sights on me.

"Ready?" Molly says, emerging from her bedroom sporting a Redwood hockey jersey and spinning around to showcase her golden waves that reach all the way down her back.

"You make me cringe." I roll my eyes and grab my jacket, not bothering to change out of my jeans and tank top.

She swings her arm over my shoulder and presses her cheek to mine. "I love you too Cal."

The stadium is pretty packed when we arrive and we shuffle our way through the crowd to our seats just above the penalty box. My dad saves the seats for us every game, hoping I'll decide to come and watch his boys play. Don't get me wrong, hockey is a great game to watch if you like adrenaline, it's fast paced and there's constantly something happening on the ice, but I don't get the same thrill from it as my dad and Molly do. Molly grabs a handful of sugary popcorn and shoves her fist into her mouth, chewing happily.

"This is going to be such a good game Cal. Redwood and Preston are arch enemies so there's bound to be endless fighting today, which I fucking live for." She groans dramatically, grabbing another handful of popcorn and ramming it straight into her lipgloss covered mouth. "Oh god, they're so sexy."

I twist my head, turning my attention back to the ice and away from Molly's hamster cheeks that are now bursting at the seams with popcorn. The guys emerge from the tunnel and slip onto the ice one by one, each of them looking fine as hell. My subconscious mind is searching for him and I want to punish myself for even wanting a smidge of his attention, but I can't help it. When Sean launches himself onto the ice, following the track of his teammates and skating in a circle around the rink I watch his eyes lift up to the stands where Molly and I sit. He's looking for someone, my

stomach jumps to think he might be looking for me, then I remember the
man has never held interest in one woman for more than an hour in his
entire life before moving onto the next one. I'm sure he's forgotten I exist
by now, I fucking hope he has anyway, the pig headed arsehole.

He glides across the ice, skating in an 's' shape before dropping down to
stretch. He bends his knees and gets down on the ice, stretching his legs
and keeping his chocolate eyes flitting around the stadium. When he
comes up empty I watch him skate over to Kyle and whisper something in
his ear. Molly hasn't noticed my eyes following Sean, she's too busy
singing along to the music that pumps through the arena as both teams
complete their warm up skate. Sean and Kyle are still whispering to each
other and after a few seconds Kyle points directly at me, drawing not only
Sean's attention but some of the other guys in the team too. Thank god
Molly is too drunk on her second cocktail of the night to stop singing
along and actually pay attention to the fact that half of the hockey team are
staring at me. Before I can turn a dark shade of red Sean lifts his gloved
hand to his mouth, and blows me a kiss.

The fucker blows me a *kiss* in front of everyone.

I want to die of embarrassment, but I don't want the man whore himself
thinking he's getting to me. I can't let him get to me.

So I do the only thing I can think to do, I lift my middle finger and direct it
straight at him, which only widens the smug grin that was already
plastered across his handsome face. His toothy grin is blinding as his
caramel eyes lock mine in place and I have to fight to break his invisible
hold on me.

Luckily Sean doesn't stare at me the entire game, but every time the ref blows the whistle his eyes catch mine immediately and his face widens into that shit eating grin that's come to live in my head rent free. During the third period Redwood are two-nil up and the Preston boys are getting more and more aggressive on the ice. They're constantly bashing our boys into the plexiglass and sneakily tripping and jabbing at them with their skates. Like Molly said earlier, they are arch enemies and the whole stadium can feel the heavy tension and growing violence filling the air as the timer moves towards the end of the game. The second the ref blows the whistle to signal the end of the game, the captain of the Preston boys launches at Sean. Sean is known for fighting during games so he was likely prepared and hoping one of the Preston boys would give him the fight he was waiting for. The two of them whip their helmets off and start hitting each other, and all I can think of is, why does Sean have to be so hot for no reason? My heart jumps into my throat as I watch them land punch after punch on each other and I can't decide if I'm turned on or worried for Sean's beautiful face to be ruined.

Molly is loving it, whooping and shouting, "Go on Sean, smack him!" When my dad and the refs finally break the two of them up I see Sean's face is bloody, a small gash across his cheek which he wipes with his jersey. My dad escorts him off the ice whilst Molly and I stand to leave. I'm trying to be sneaky, glancing Sean's way and hoping Molly doesn't spot me, god knows the girl will have twenty-thousand questions to ask if she sees me eyeing up the one and only Sean Taylor. Luckily my best friend is now three cocktails and a large popcorn down so she simply saunters ahead of me out of the stadium, not even glancing back to see if I'm following. I let myself look one more time towards Sean and see that my dad has an ice pack on his face. My dad looks mad, he's cursing at him, I can tell. As if he can feel me staring, Sean looks up at me, his eyes softer than I've ever seen them and he gives me a quick nod as I scurry out of the stadium.

Fuck, how could he tell I was worried about him? I don't want to him to think I give a shit because I don't...Ok, maybe I do a little but I don't want to. God how do I stop his charm from seeping it's way into my pours and making me want to do something I know I'll regret?

Chapter 7

Sean

"Jesus Christ…" I whisper under my breath as Callie comes into view. She saunters down the stairs of Mac's house, the music blaring and making the walls jump to the beat. She's wearing all black, her mini skirt looking like it's sewn onto her skin, dipping just under the curve of her ass and making me itchy to reach out and grab a handful of it. Her top is tight too, fitting like a glove and showcasing her perfect chest. Her thick curls cascade down her back, swishing with her as she takes each step at a time, her heels clicking and making her legs look long and sultry. A slap on the back of my shoulder pulls my eyes away from Callie.

"Think you're drooling there man, not a good look." Kyle says, breathing a heavy laugh and bringing his frosty beer glass to his lips.

"I swear I've had a wet dream exactly like this." I groan, shaking out the dark curls that sit on my head.

Kyle titters next to me and yanks my arm towards a group that has congregated around the kitchen island. Of course my eyes are on Callie immediately, who leans her hip into the counter and sips at some fruity concoction. She's chatting with the group, they're having a debate about some shit, I don't know and I don't care. I wrap my huge arm around her chest and rub my other fist on the crown on her head like she's five years old. She scowls up at me and then shoves me with all her might, which is the might of a mouse.

"Get off me Sean! Why do you have to be so fucking annoying? Is it your new hobby now or something?" She runs her fingers through her hair, shaking out her chocolate curls.

I grin, booping her nose and earning another slap on the arm. "I think it *is* my new hobby, I'm enjoying it."

"Yeah well I'm not, so can you piss off and annoy someone else please? There's some girls over there that I'm sure would love to go upstairs with you, keep you busy and out of my way for a while."

She spins around, facing away from me and continuing her conversation with Lewis and the others. Does she not understand what's going on here? I don't want any other girl, I want her. I'm so far from interested in other girls it's actually worrying me, I'm losing my touch.

I lean down to her ear, her hair tickling my nose. "Never going to happen tiger, it's you that I want."

Her green eyes catch mine over her shoulder and I see her falter for just a second, before the familiar scowl returns and she spins back to Lewis.

God, I love this game we're playing.

After a few hours of watching my friends drink themselves stupid and pretty much just staring at every detail of Callie's body, I decide I'm done being sober. I wasn't planning on drinking tonight, we have a day off from training and games tomorrow so I thought I could get shit done, you know, be productive and all that. But I need some sort of anaesthesia for my dick, every time I look at Callie he jumps for joy like he's getting some tonight, he's not and we both know it. I don't know if I've ever gone this long without sex and I'm not sure how much longer I can wait. But the kicker is, no other girls are doing it for me right now. Even the thought of taking some random girl upstairs and fucking her just isn't exciting me like it usually would. One drink, that will be enough to blur my mind a little and make this evening pass by more easily.

As I make my way into the huge, open plan kitchen, making a beeline for the array of alcohol that's scattered all over the countertops, I see Mac. He's stuck to the spot, fixated on something and when I follow his line of vision I spot the girl who's quickly taken over my mind. Mac is staring at her ass, pulling his bottom lip between his teeth and readjusting his junk like a teenage boy who's never seen a sexy woman before.

Fucking pervert.

I grab the back of his collar, yanking him back towards me and making him stumble.

"Hey Mac, keep looking at my girl's ass like that and I'll have to break your fucking neck." I growl into his ear.

The little fucker is so annoying most of the time anyway but watching him fantasise about what's under Callie's clothes the same way I do makes me consider acts of violence that I never have before.

He turns around and breathes a stuttered sigh. "Oh shit, sorry Cap, didn't realise you two were a thing."

"Well, now you know, keep your eyes off what's mine." I say, slithering past him and moving across the large expanse of kitchen towards Callie. Fuck the drink, I don't want other guys staring at her like that, like they want a piece.

I snake my arm around her tight waist and kiss the crown of her head as Mac slinks away with a frown. She knows it's me before she looks up, I can tell by the way she stiffens under my touch and I wait for her to shove me away again, but she doesn't.

Instead I'm greeted with an eye roll and a muttered, "Fuck off Sean," but she doesn't wriggle out of my grip. My chest tightens and my dick does a dance at the realisation that she might actually be warming up to me. Maybe I can get a kiss from her tonight…fuck me what I wouldn't do to get a taste of her soft lips. The same lips that are moving seductively right now, continuing her conversation with Anais, Kyle and Nick, whilst pretending her heart isn't beating 100 miles per hour with my hand wrapped around her middle. If she thinks I can't tell the way her body reacts to me then she's crazy, I feel her pulse quicken and the air thicken between us every time I'm near her.

I eventually remove my arm from Callie's waist and join in with the conversation, receiving a knowing wink from Kyle as his eyes track my arm where I let it rest possessively on the island behind Callie.

"I'm not fucking telling you her name so just back off." Nick groans as Kyle continues to tease him about this new, mysterious girl he's been secretly seeing.

"Come on, just tell us, is she blonde?" I snicker, pressing my palm into his shoulder.

He shakes his head. "Brunette, actually," He smiles and I let out a belly laugh at seeing him blush like that over a girl.

Nick is a lot like Kyle and I, we don't usually go further than a one night stand with women, but it seems like me, Nick has become infatuated by this mystery girl. Maybe we're all growing up.

"I thought you hockey boys only date blondes." Callie says, lifting her almost empty glass to her pouty lips, lips I would die to suck into my mouth right now.

"Nah, that's a myth," I muse and she turns to me. "We only date 5-foot-4, sassy mouthed girls who think they're better than us. You fit any of that criteria?" I grin and she rolls her eyes at me.

"You don't date anyone Sean Taylor, you just fuck and chuck."

"I think I'd like to date you Callie Burch." I whisper, still grinning at her. I see her emerald eyes flicker to my lips before she blinks, trying to hide the fact she wants me, I know she does.

"Hey, did Pelker's skate cut your stomach earlier? Coach said something in the locker rooms about you needing to ice your stomach as well as that gash across your face." Nick interrupts my unspoken moment with Callie and it takes me a moment to remember what the fuck he just said. My mind is on some sort of hallucinogenic drug when she's around me and I can't fucking think straight.

"Erm, yeah I did cut my stomach but it's not that bad. It's probably healing up already." I say, lifting the hem of my t-shirt and showing Nick the long, but thin gash that slices through the centre of my hard stomach. Callie groans beside me and I flick my eyes to her face. It's twisted into a painful expression and a flash of panic hits me in the chest, is she hurt or something?

"What's wrong?" I say, letting my t-shirt fall back down to cover my stomach.

She gives me her signature scowl. "Can you stop showing me your sexy body? I'm trying so hard to resist you here and you're not making it any easier for me."

A loud laugh explodes from me and Kyle at the same time.

"I think someone is wavering..." He says, smirking at Callie whilst she narrows her eyes even further at both of us.

"Never," She states, clenching her thighs together and making my dick instantly hard with need. "I might be finding it hard to resist his hot body but he makes it easier for me every time he opens his mouth and words come out."

A smirk covers my face. "I can use my mouth to make you happy if you want, wanna go upstairs now and I'll show you?"

She scoffs, flicking her hair. "You wish I was that easy Taylor." She saunters away and I watch her with a satisfied grin on my face. She can deny it all she wants, but she's definitely wavering.

"Why is she playing so hard to get? I know she wants me." I say to Anais who is also watching Callie make her way up the narrow staircase of Mac's huge house share.

Anais snickers. "She's not *playing* hard to get, she is hard to get. She only broke up with her boyfriend a week ago and she doesn't do hook ups. I've known her for almost two years now and not once has she had a one night stand."

I sigh, I guess I'll compromise then, if that's what it's going to take to get what I want.

"I guess I could break my 'no dating' rule to win her over. If I'm going to see anyone more than once it's going to be her. There's just something about her, I just can't...I can't stay away." I muse as Callie's sexy thighs disappear out of view at the top of the staircase.

Anais tips the last few drops of her drink to her mouth and tries to hide her smug smile. I think I'm already ready to give up the fight, Callie has made it pretty clear that's she's not going to be the one to give in easily. She says she doesn't want to hook up, so maybe I could take her on a date instead? The idea alone makes me shiver with equal parts excitement at being around her and also complete and utter panic. I've never dated anyone before, it's unknown territory for me and if I'm being honest it scares the shit out of me. But I think I need to put my big boys pants on and accept that I really fucking like this girl and I think it goes past just sex.

Wow, I think I *am* growing up.

Chapter 8

Callie

A few minutes of silence is all I need, my head is thumping from the music, not helped by the sloshing of alcohol that I knowingly added to the mix. But of course, I won't be granted that moment of silence because my stalker is in the house with me and he practically follows my every move at this point. Considering I've only really known Sean for a few days he sure does act like he's obsessed with me.

"You ok?" His deep voice interrupts my peaceful silence from the doorway of the random bedroom I've made myself at home in.

I grumble. "I was until you came in and bothered me."

That just makes him laugh and he moves to sit beside me, his manly scent invading my senses and making me wet again. For fuck's sake, what is wrong with me? I'm like a horny teenager around him.

"Why do you hate me so much? You barely even know me." He says, his hand clenching the bedsheets between our thighs.

"And yet you've managed to make an enemy out of me, well done Captain." I chuckle and he sighs. I lift my eyes from where they rest in my lap and look at his face, it's softer than usual, the arrogance invisible and clouded by something else that I can't decipher.

"I don't hate you Sean, you just irritate me, and this cat and mouse chase you've started isn't going to end well, trust me."

He twists his body to face mine, our knees brushing off each other. "No Callie, you trust me." He pauses, fighting an internal battle with himself. After a silent beat of contemplation he blurts, "Let me take you out on a date."

What the fuck?

"You don't date Sean. I don't want to go out with you to then have sex with you at the end of the night and have you pretend like I don't exist the next day." I huff, feeling irritated again and folding my arms across my body, pushing my chest up. His eyes immediately fall to my tits, but I pretend not to notice, I've gotten used to him looking at me like I'm a snack.

"I just asked you out on a date, I wouldn't have done that if I didn't want to, trust me."

"That's the thing though," I sigh, "I don't trust you, I don't trust anyone."

He lays his hand gently on my thigh and I stiffen under his touch again.

"You can trust me Callie, I swear. I know I like to fuck around but I'm not a tin man, I have a heart in here." He pounds a fist against his chest and smiles softly. "I can be good, I promise."

I swat his hand off my thigh and stand up in a panic. "Woah, I don't need to see that side of you. Please don't show me that side of you."

"Why?" He chuckles, his dark curls brushing against his forehead. "I'm not all mouth you know." He pats his solid chest again.

"Yeah well I don't need to know about it, just makes resisting you even harder."

He stands up from the bed and moves towards me. "Stop resisting me then."

"I can't." I mutter, a warmth flooding my chest when he brushes his fingertips along my forearms, watching as the goosebumps follow his touch.

I whip away from him after a lingering moment of contact between us and I can tell from the sparkle in his caramel eyes that he wants to grab me, pull me back to him and smash our lips together. I want that too, but I don't want to want it.

"I just have too much going on right now Sean. I'm buried deep in coursework that is way past it's deadline, I have competitions coming up and a coach that constantly yells at me when I'm trying my best. I can't add a guy into the mix right now, especially one that will most definitely be done with me after a quick fuck."

He ignores my last comment and goes back to the yelling, like it's bothering him. "Ellen yells at you all the time?" He says, keeping the distance that I created between us.

I nod sadly. "Yeah, and as much as I hate to admit it, it really bothers me. I'm kind of sad really, I pretty much live for people's praise at this point."

"That's good to know." He muses and I look up at him, my eyes full of suspicion.

"Why?" I fist my hip and lean against the doorframe.

He grins. "I'll remember to tell you what a good girl you are when I'm fucking your sassy little mouth."

Oh. My. God.

I gulp loudly, then try to hide it. I feel my eyes brighten at the thought of Sean doing anything to me than involves us being naked. But, before I let my vagina take over, I force my spine to straighten and flounce out of the room.

"Fuck off Sean!" I yell over my shoulder and the satisfied smile that covers my face makes me want to kill myself. Why is it so easy for him to make me squirm? I kind of love it.

I can't hold it in any longer and the moment I get home I'm word vomiting all over my best friend, telling her everything I've been trying to hide for the last few days.

"Oh my fucking god, Sean Taylor wants you? What are you doing here? You should be in his bed, letting him make you feel fucking incredible!" She squeals, jumping all over the dorm with childish excitement.

I wish I could share it with her, but as much as Sean fucking me senseless excites me, I can't let him. I don't want to deal with the consequences after, him avoiding me and watching the other girls who will be draped all over him. I would want to rip my eyeballs out. This is the exact reason that I keep my walls firmly up, especially with people like Sean and I can feel him climbing them, peering over and trying to figure out a way in. I'm terrified that if he does, I won't be able to get him back out again.

"I can't Mol, you know I don't do that, that's your thing not mine." I groan, falling back onto the sofa and letting Molly yank my heels off my sore feet.

Molly is a hook up kind of girl, she usually sticks to one guy at a time, having casual sex with them for a few months before moving onto the next one. But relationships? They're a no go for her, we're pretty much total opposites when it comes to dating.

She laughs. "Then let me fuck him if you don't want to."

"I do want to, I just know that he'll want nothing to do with me afterwards and I can't deal with that. I've tried it before and I know it fucking hurts."

Molly pulls me lazily to my feet and hugs me tight. "You said he asked you on a date though, maybe he wants more than just sex."

"I just don't trust him Mol, I can't trust him not to hurt me." I sigh, running my fingers though her blonde tresses as she squeezes me tighter.

"I know you felt fucked over by Joel, I know it hurt, what he did but it doesn't mean every guy is the same Cal, you have to let someone in at some point." She kisses my forehead.

"Not yet, I'm not ready." I mutter, padding barefoot towards my bedroom. When I get there I plug my phone into the charger and a message pings through on my lock screen.

Sean Taylor:

'I meant what I said tonight Cal, give me a chance to earn your trust. I promise I won't hurt you.'

Chapter 9

Sean

I've tried to get Callie's attention all week since the party, but she's clearly doing everything she can to avoid me. She didn't reply to my message the night of the party and everyday when my teammates and I come into the gym to do weights she scuttles out, keeping her head down and eyes away from me. I know she scared to get into anything with me and how can I blame her? I know I have a bad reputation and it's my own fault for fucking around with so many girls I've lost count. But I don't know how else to make her see that I actually like her and I don't think this is just about the chase anymore like it was when I met her.

Everyday I've left little notes in her locker, telling her how badly I want her, begging her to give me a chance and telling her how god damn beautiful she is. I know she's been reading them, because every time I go to put a new note in her locker the one from the previous day is gone. She's done well to avoid me all week, but by the time Thursday rolls around I'm done with her little game of hide and seek. Anais told me yesterday that Callie stays late on a Thursday evening to practice her routines when the gym is empty, we don't have weight training today so she won't be on alert, expecting me to come in and performing her usual disappearing act.

I leave the rink and head upstairs to the second floor, still sweaty from a day of training and drills. When I arrive at the gym it's silent, eerily silent and I momentarily panic that she somehow found out about my plan to ambush her and she's already left. Then I hear a muffled, frustrated grunt coming from inside, so I push the doors open and watch Callie flick her head in my direction when the squeak of the door draws her attention. Her eyes widen when she sees me and I can almost hear her heart hammering from across the gym.

"You should really lock the door when you're in here alone, any weirdo could come in." I say, watching as she jumps back up onto the beam.

"Huh," She barks a dry, sarcastic laugh. "Like you, you mean?"

I guess I deserve that, I have just snuck in here to catch her when she's made it clear that she doesn't want to talk to me.

I watch as she lines her body up on the beam, shifting her feet into position and throwing her body backwards into the air. My breath catches in my throat as she lands safely back on her feet, breathing a sigh of relief that's accompanied by my own. She jumps down from the beam and crosses the gym towards where I stand at the lockers.

"What are you doing here Sean?" She huffs, twisting her locker door open and watching as another one of my notes floats to the ground. She heaves a sigh and picks it up, I left it for her yesterday and I watch a tiny tint of pink seep into her cheeks when she reads it.

I grip her hand in mine and twist her around to face me. "I told you, I want you Callie and I'm not going to stop until you agree to go out with me."

She sighs with frustration and yanks her hand out of mine. "And I told *you*, I don't trust you." She drags her hair tie down her long ponytail and flicks her hair over her shoulder.

Daisy Egan

"I'm going to shower." I mumble and turn towards the door.

"Good for you," She huffs and I leave the gym wondering what the fuck I'm supposed to do now.

I really thought after our talk upstairs at the party last weekend that I was making some progress with her, breaking down those walls that she's fighting to keep up. But the anger in her bright green eyes just now makes me think she's rebuilt every brick that I took down, filling in the gaps with extra strong cement and making them even studier than before, specifically to keep me out.

I get into the shower, letting the hot water soothe my aching muscles after a long day of training on the ice and close my eyes. I need a plan, a next move, something to help me get through to this fireball of a woman and make her see that I'm not going to fuck her over.

Just as I feel my shoulders start to relax under the warm spray I hear a muffled knock on the locker room door. I poke my head around the shower curtain and listen, when I hear the door open softly.

"Sean?" I hear Callie call tentatively.

"Yeah?" I yell back, immediately turning the water off and wondering that the fuck has changed in the last five minutes that she now wants to talk to me.

Callie opens the door wider and I can hear her voice more clearly now.

"Are you nearly done in there? Ellen has locked the women's locker room and I desperately need a shower before I leave."

I ruffle my wet hair and grab my towel from the hook. "Yeah, I've just turned the water off so give me five minutes and I'll be done." I wrap the towel around my waist and step onto the cold floor. "You can wait in here if you want but I am naked."

I hear her curse under her breath and then say, "Yeah, I think I'll just wait out here."

I smile to myself at the knowledge that she thinks she'll be tempted in here with me, maybe those bricks aren't so sturdy after all.

I come out of the shower, into the main changing area and start to dry myself. I'm still naked and Callie has been waiting outside all of two minutes when she bursts into the locker room and slams the door closed, rising on her toes and peering out of the tiny peephole in the centre of the door. I freeze, watching her and confusion floods my brain, what the fuck is she doing? She looks panicked, I can see her chest rising and falling from behind before she breathes a sigh of relief and lets her feet fall flat on the ground again. A chuckle slips out from my throat and Callie stiffens, like she forgot I was in here, she spins around to face me and slaps her hands over her eyes when she realises I'm still naked.

"Oh my god," She groans, her hands completely shielding her eyes from my body as she stumbles back against the door.

I laugh quietly. "I did tell you I was naked in here."

"I know," she says, eyes still covered. "But I just saw my ex coming down the hallway with another girl and there was no way I was having *that* conversation right now."

I smile to myself as Callie's eyes are still covered. "Wanna have this conversation instead?" She makes a slither of a gap through her fingers and peers out at me with one eye, keeping it firmly directed towards my face. "You're trying not to look at my dick aren't you?" I tease and she lets her hands fall to her sides, exposing the pink tint to her freckled cheeks.

"Naturally," She breathes, spinning back around to face the door.

My dick is so happy to see her, especially since he's not folded away in my trousers, fighting to break out and wave hello to her like usual. I'm certainly not lacking in self confidence, having girls constantly throwing themselves at you will do that to a man.

"I know it's big, you don't have to pretend like you're not impressed." I muse, feeling my head grow ten times.

She scoffs, still facing the door. "You're disgusting, and I've seen better."

Ouch, maybe my ego is more easily bruised than I thought.

"Like who?" I say, trying to push the images of anyone else's dick inside Callie but mine.

She laughs dryly. "None of your business fuck boy, now can you hurry up and get some clothes on so I can shower in peace?"

As tempting as it is to keep teasing her I know she's getting frustrated, so I pull my trousers up my legs, tucking the big guy away again and apologising to him that he's still not getting any tonight. I pull my t-shirt down and grab my bag, moving towards the door where Callie has her head pinned, determined not to see my naked body.

"I know you want me Callie, you don't have to keep fighting it, I know you think I'm sexy." I whisper into her hair with my chest pressed against her back. Her breathing catches as usual before she covers it up with a scoff and wriggles away from me. "Was that a 'I'm dying to give in and let you fuck me' scoff or a 'No, I don't want you' scoff?" I tease and she folds her arms.

"The second one," She purses her lips at me and I'm fucking itching to suck them into my mouth. I pause for a moment, watching her chest rise a little faster under my stare.

"Huh, you know you almost had me convinced for a second there." I smile and the frustration builds behind her emerald pools again.

"You might possibly be the most pig headed, egotistical prick I've ever met." She spits, which makes me crack another grin.

I reach out and leave a pat-pat on her ass. "Touché," I say and yank the locker room door open, leaving Callie wide eyed and probably horny from my ass grope.

I've been dying to feel her ass in my hand since the moment I met her and it felt even better than I'd ever imagined. It was hard to leave it at a pat and not just grab hold of it and lift her to my waist, kissing her so hard she forgets how to breathe.

But I guess I can save that for another day.

Chapter 10

Callie

It's Friday thank god, which means I have a day off from training. The problem is that all I want to do is get fucked into Sean's mattress now, he has left me in a near constant horny state with no way of satisfaction. I have a special friend that I keep in my drawer but for the last week it's just not be satisfying me the way I'm craving. I let myself lie in this morning, which I almost never do, but Molly offered to go out and get us some breakfast so I took her up on the offer and stayed in bed until 10am. I've been trying to study since midday but I just can't focus, my mind keeps going back to Sean's miraculous body yesterday. I know I shouldn't have looked, I'm just making life more difficult for myself but I couldn't help it. He stood there, completely bare looking like he was carved from stone and my brain just wouldn't let me look away. I did keep my eyes away from his dick though, knowing for a fact if I looked at that I would have to have it, I'm not known for my strong willpower so I try not to tempt myself any more than necessary. I kept my eyes firmly on his rock hard chest and rugged, yet boyishly handsome face, plus I couldn't keep my gaze from landing on his dimples. *Those fucking dimples.* However, since then I've been practically dripping from the inside of my thighs, desperate for some sort of relief.

By 5pm I'm squirming in my seat at the kitchen island, trying desperately to focus on my coursework and tapping away on my laptop. The words I'm typing aren't even making sense, I can't concentrate when all of my blood is between my legs right now. Molly is under a blanket on the sofa behind me, watching a trashy reality show that she constantly begs me to watch with her and Anais is at the opposite side of the island, cramming fruit into a blender. I slam my laptop shut and jump down from the bar stool I've been sat on for the last three hours, my ass is numb and I stretch my arms above my head.

"Anyone want a smoothie?" Anais says, licking the purple mixture from her fingers.

Molly jumps up from the sofa. "Oh yes please, I'll have one. I need an energy boost before my evening run."

The girl runs competitively and even when she's supposed to be resting, all she wants to do is run, she's like a dopamine addict but I guess I'm one to talk, I love the rush of flying through the air too.

"I'm good," I say, shaking my head but smiling at Anais with gratitude. "I think I'm gonna take a quick nap."

I walk down the hallway and round the corner to my room, letting the door click shut behind me and making sure to slide the lock into place. I don't need any distractions, I just need a huge, relief filled orgasm and then I'll feel better. I don't need Sean with his smug face and painfully beautiful grin…God, he's so annoying. I lay back and yank my shorts down to my ankles, reaching down and letting my cold fingers explore. It doesn't take long for the heavy orgasm to build and just as I'm about to come it vanishes, like it ran away and took every ounce of my patience with it.

"Fuck," I mutter under my breath and pick up the pace with my fingers. I circle my clit and before I can stop it, Sean's face fills my mind. His deep voice calling me a good girl and causing the orgasm to quickly pick up speed. The more I try to force him out of my mind, the more intense my images of him become. Now I'm imagining his face between my thighs, his tongue tracing the outline of my clit and sucking it between his lips as I come all over his face. Before I know it I'm coming, my back arching off the bed and Sean's name leaving my lips on a muffled cry.

That might have been the best self inflicted orgasm of my life, and it was so needed.

I let my body come back down to earth like a deflating balloon before I clean myself up in my bathroom and pull my shorts back up my legs. I know I still have a shit load of coursework to do and now I have no excuse not to get on with it. I swing open my bedroom door and without lifting my head, step into a wall of muscle. When I look up I see Sean's arrogant grin staring back at me, his eyes full of gloating.

"Fucking hell Sean! What the hell are you doing here, sneaking around like a creep? How did you even get in here?" I smack his chest with both hands and his smile widens. This whole stalking thing is going too far, now he's in my fucking dorm.

"Molly let me in." *Sneaky bitch.* "You were just making yourself come weren't you?" He whispers, moving closer to me.

I'm speechless from his question, how the hell does he know what I was doing in there? How long was he out here listening? There's only about a foot between us in this narrow hallway and I can smell his fucking woodsy aftershave again, the one that makes me weak in the knees.

I put on my big girl pants and square up to him a little, my hands on my hips. "Maybe, what's it to you?"

A deep chuckle rumbles in his throat. "You said my name." He whispers, his breath so close I can taste him on my tongue.

Oh fuck.

"You imagined it." I say, but the wobble in my voice proves him right without me needing to say another word.

He moves closer again, our chests touching. "I definitely didn't."

"Why are you even standing outside my door listening? That's so pervy and you shouldn't even be in my dorm, what do you want?" I make my voice a little louder but it doesn't take more than a millisecond for Sean to take my breath away again.

His hand flies around my throat and pushes me gently back against the wall, his body pressed up against mine. He brings his lips to hover above my mouth and I force a hard swallow, my heart involuntarily stuttering in my chest.

"Do you need me to fuck you Callie? Because I'm fucking desperate to." He coos, his huge hand still resting on my collar bone.

I feel the heat creep into my cheeks, coating my ears and neck as it goes. I don't want to let him win like this, why is it so easy for him to make me feel weak?

He runs his hand down my chest, over my hardened nipples and curses under his breath, letting his hand rest there for a moment before continuing his path down my stomach. When he reaches the waistband of my shorts my breathing really falters and I can't hide the anticipation in my stomach when he dips his fingers below the elastic.

"Are you still wet for me?" He whispers, his lips still inches from mine. The second his warm finger pushes inside of me my legs almost crumble. "Fuck Cal." He curses, letting his forehead fall onto mine as he explores the soaking mess in between my thighs. I let out a moan as he adds a second finger, pushing deeper inside of me and using his free hand to hold my waist so I don't crumple to the ground like a wet piece of paper. "Callie! Do you wanna get a takeout for dinner with me and Anais?" Molly yells from the living room and reality crashes onto me like a ton of bricks.

I shove Sean away from me and his back lands softly against the wall on the opposite side of the hallway. The fucker is smirking, bringing his fingers to his lips and sucking the moisture from them with a delicious grin on his face. My mouth is open, watching him and feeling more turned on than ever before.

Fuck him for doing that to me.

"Coming!" I shout to Molly and Sean smiles wider.

"Again? Thought the image of my handsome face already made you come once today?" He chuckles deeply and I thump his chest, moving behind him and pushing his huge frame down the hallway towards the front door. When we finally make it to the living room Molly and Anais are both huddled up on the sofa, flicking through takeout menus. They barely look up at us when Sean and I enter the room and I attempt to steer him towards the door undetected, which of course fails miserably.

"Wanna stay for food Sean?" Molly smiles and I want to stab her. I try to, with my eyes, but that girl can almost never take a hint.

"No," I pipe up, "he needs to go home, he's busy."

"I don't need to g—" He starts but I grab his hand and drag him to the front door with me.

I swing the heavy wooden door open and gesture for him to leave, he's still holding onto my hand and when he looks down at our joined fingers and smiles I rip my hand away from his.

"Bye Sean," I say, pulling the door slightly closed behind me and blocking my friends from seeing Sean's annoyingly beautiful grin.

"Oh no you don't." He says, pushing the door back open and stepping into me. He grabs my ass with both hands, lifting me off the ground to his height and peppering kisses all over my cheeks before I can stop him.

Then he puts me back on the ground and gives my ass another pat-pat, for good measure before leaving me standing in the doorway gobsmacked. That man is so fucking brazen it's not surprising he gets his own way so often.

I point at Molly when I spin back around to face them. "I will kill you." She simply shrugs and smiles brightly. "He's cute."

Anais laughs too and I look around for something to throw at them both.

"He may be cute, but he's also a fucking irritation who won't take no for an answer." I groan, resting my head in my hands, my elbows on the kitchen counter.

Molly barks a laugh. "Why would you ever *want* to say no to that god of a man?"

I lift my head, glaring at her and she widens her puppy dog eyes, throwing her hands up in front of her and surrendering. Good choice Mol, I'm not in the mood for games today, not after that encounter.

I wanted to make myself come, give myself some relief and instead I'm now left even more turned on than I was before my orgasm. All because of that annoyingly sexy, man child that won't stop torturing me with his killer dimples and disgustingly hot body.

Chapter 11

Sean

Molly Crawford has quickly become my second favourite woman after her sexy, brunette best friend.

I went over to their dorm yesterday, looking for advice on how to win Callie over and Molly graciously supplied me with top secret information about her best friend. Molly suggested I go to the farm across the road from Redwood, there are apparently some strawberries there — homegrown and all that shit — that Callie loves. Molly warned me that they're very expensive, but little does she know, money is pretty much unlimited for me. I ask my parents to send me some money and they do, without question or concern on what I'm spending it on. I'm actually really fucking good at saving though so I didn't need to ask them for money for some strawberries, that could have been embarrassing, don't want them to think I'm going soft.

I pull up outside the green building at Redwood at around 6pm. It's the building shared by the hockey team and the gymnastics team, our rink being on the ground floor and the gymnasium on the second. I have my strawberries in a brown paper bag, hidden from Callie's view when she sees me enter the gym. Anais graciously told me yesterday that training finishes at 6pm, but that Callie was planning to stay late again to practice her routines. Luckily, the girls know their captain well and when I close the door gently behind me she looks up from where she sits in the centre of the huge, springy gymnasium floor.

"Oh, you again… Are you ever going to leave me alone?" She sighs, rising to her feet and showcasing her slim figure.

I shrug. "No, I don't think so."

She huffs but pads over to me regardless and is eyeing my paper bag immediately. "What's in there?" She says, peering in before I snatch it out of her eye line.

"Ah, ah, ah," I say, wagging my finger at her and lifting my eyebrows. "Say please and I might show you."

The familiar red frustration creeps up her neck and she folds her arms across her chest. I give in to her so easily, it's pathetic really but I can't help myself.

"Ok fine, come here." I gesture for her to sit on the bench in front of the lockers with me.

She sighs like she's going to say no and flounce off to the locker rooms, but instead she quickly unfolds her arms and sits next to me. Her eyes light up like a child on Christmas morning when I open the bag and she peers inside.

I smile at her childlike happiness. "They're your favourite right?"

She nods, reaching inside and producing a shiny, ruby red strawberry. "How did you know?"

I tap my nose and wink. "I have my sources."

"You mean you harassed my best friend for information about me? Weirdo,"

She's smiling though, bringing the perfectly ripe strawberry to her lips and taking a bite. Her eyes fall closed and she moans with delight.

"Mmmm, that's so fucking good," She chews delicately, savouring every morsel.

Is it bad that she's turning me on right now? I can't help but imagine her moaning like that when I fuck her. I've got her here in a good mood, I've brought her something she loves so now is probably the most she's ever liked me. I see an opportunity and I'm taking it.

"Can I have a taste?" I say, smiling weakly at her even though my heart is picking up speed.

She rolls her eyes but extends her arm, holding the half eaten strawberry out to me. Why am I so fucking nervous? This is it, and if she rejects me now then I'll take it like a champ.

No, I won't, I'll be totally crushed, but it's now or never.

She's still holding the strawberry out to me, confusion knotting her eyebrows together. "Well, do you want a taste or not?" She says, shaking the strawberry at me.

Come on Sean, just do it.

I shove her hand to the side. "I wasn't talking about the strawberry." I smash my lips onto her's and clearly take her by surprise. She's only stiff for a second though before she relaxes into the kiss, her hands landing on my jaw.

I wish I could deny the way everything explodes when our lips finally meet. I'd love to say nothing changed and I knew in that moment that I *was* just lust, just sex that I wanted from her.

But that would be a lie.

Fucking hell her lips taste incredible. The sweet strawberry still on her tongue combined with her usual fruity smell is intoxicating. *She's* intoxicating and I can't stop. Before I know it she's in my lap, straddling my waist with her fingers tangled in my curls, yanking me closer to her. I'm groping her ass and the heated air between us is ignited into flames. I suck her bottom lip into my mouth and she moans. My dick responds immediately, thinking he's been summoned.

I've kissed more girls than I can count, but the way Callie's lips mould with mine, like they were made for me, makes me sick to my stomach with anticipation.

As much as Callie seems into this kiss, I don't think she's going to let me fuck her tonight. The strange thing is, I don't know if I even want to. Of course I want to feel every inch of her body, fuck her until she can't walk and leave my fingerprints all over her, but I don't think tonight is the right time for that.

After a few minutes the kiss slows down, deepens and I'm hyper aware of the fact that our tongues are swiping at each other so softly it's making my stomach gape with an emotion I've never felt before.

When we eventually pull away, the two of us fighting to inhale as much oxygen as possible and bring our heart rates down, Callie stands up from my lap. She smooths her hair and clears her throat before looking at me again. Her lips are swollen, pink and delicious, and I wonder how I ever stopped kissing her.

"I knew you secretly liked me." I say, standing to my feet and grabbing my bag.

This fucking stupid smile won't get off my face. I'm so happy right now I could burst. For fuck's sake Sean, get a grip, it was only a kiss. *Yeah, a kiss with Callie!*

She sounds her usual scoff. "I really don't."

"Ok baby, whatever you say." I snicker. I have a plan up my sleeve, now I've tasted her I need more, I'm desperate for more and I'm going to get it.

"Urgh!" She fake gags and I laugh deep in my chest. "Don't. Call. Me. That." She says, with a jab to my chest on each word.

I cup her face in my hands and smack a kiss on her swollen lips before leaving. I head straight for the women's locker rooms, my master plan in action and sit down on one of the benches, waiting for Callie.

She strolls in about ten minutes later and almost falls over when she sees me sitting there with my signature grin plastered all over my face.

She skids to a stop. "What the hell are you doing in here?"

"I knew you were nearly finished so I waited for you." I shrug, standing up and towering over her tiny frame. *Man, I just want to fuck her all over this room.*

"Well, can you please fuck off and annoy someone else for a change? I need to shower."

I shake my head, my dark curls moving with me. "That can wait, I need more of you."

I grab the back of her soft thighs and hoist her up to my waist, her legs circling me instinctively as my lips find her's again. She's like a drug and I'm most definitely an addict. She kisses me back, letting her usual sass melt away and I know she'll be falling at her knees in a moment when my plan comes into action. I walk us over to the other side of the room and place her carefully onto the marble countertop in front of the sink, still kissing the crap out of her. I reach for the hem of her shorts and she untangles her lips from mine, stopping my hand from moving any lower as her eyes darken with warning.

"I'm not having sex with you Sean." She says, her hands on top of mine, preventing me from undressing her.

I nod. "I know, just let me make you feel good."

I get on my knees, pulling her shorts down to her ankles and admiring the sight in front of me. Her pussy is gleaming with moisture, just for me, and I nearly crack and beg her to let me fuck her. But I manage to hold my own, running my hands over her milky thighs and dipping my head between her legs. She's hot and pulsing for me to give her the pleasure that she needs. I watch Callie's head drop back and her breathing become deep and airy. She's moaning before I have even touched her and when I let my tongue ghost over her clit she almost suffocates me. Her hands land in my hair and she pushes my face deeper into her, making me chuckle against her swollen bud. I suck it into my mouth, tasting every drop of her on my tongue and revelling at seeing her like this.

I've thought about making her come so many times, seeing her vulnerable and completely raw in front of me, when her usually hard exterior prevents me from seeing the real her. She's repeatedly cursing my name under her breath and when her back arches I taste her sweetness on my tongue, dipping into her pussy and collecting every last drop of her. I grip her thighs as they shake with intense pleasure and I gently lick her clit, soothing the burn that my sucking caused. I stand up, wiping the moisture off my chin with the back of my sleeve and pulling her shorts back up her legs. She hasn't said anything, she looks dazed, like she doesn't know how I managed to win her over like that and let me make her come. I lift her down from the countertop and place her to the ground, she quickly moves away from me, still not saying a word. She heads for the showers without so much as a backwards glance in my direction so I take that as my cue to leave. I won't push her past her breaking point, she let me get much further with her tonight than ever before. So instead, I text her the minute I'm out of the building and back in my car.

Sean Taylor:
'I want to see you tomorrow.'

She texts back almost immediately.

Callie Burch:
'I have training tomorrow,"

Then she adds some more.

'And you're annoying.'

I smile so fucking widely it hurts. Why do I love that I can piss her off and turn her on at the same time so easily? And why is it so addictive? Why is *she* so addictive?

Chapter 12

Callie

I don't know how that happened, but I think I need to just accept that I want him. I wish so much that I didn't want him but I do. Only physically of course, he still irritates the shit out of me almost every second of the day, but why is he so painfully sexy? I'm on the brink of waving my 'no casual sex' rule for this 6-foot-4, excruciatingly charming playboy. What the fuck is wrong with me? I never thought I was this weak. I'm still not buying the whole 'I want to date you' nonsense, Sean Taylor doesn't date and I don't see why I would be the girl to change that. The woman that he's going to marry one day will be drowning in money just like him and she'll probably be a 5-foot-11 blonde with legs that go straight to the sky. Basically, the opposite of me...

I'm trying so hard to focus on my routines lately, it's all I can think about — when I'm not thinking about Sean's tongue all over me — but it's not making much of a difference to the quality of those routines. I have a competition coming up and I'm about ready to rip my limbs off one by one for not co-operating with me. My legs just won't do as I ask them to and

when I attempt my final tumble of the night and land on my ass — *again!*
— I groan loudly and smack my hands to my face.

"What the fuck is wrong with me?" I yell at myself, sitting on the ground
and crossing my legs.

It feels like there's a blockage in my brain, stopping the usual smooth
connection between the instructions my brain is screeching and my limbs.
I'm staring off into space, contemplating just laying down on this gym
floor and wallowing in self pity when I hear the gym door creak open. I
can smell him before I even break my vacant stare, his scent overpowering
me as usual and making me instantly needy for him.

"You thinking about that orgasm I gave you yesterday?" He says and I can
hear the smirk in his voice. *There's the usual arrogance I was waiting for.*
I grin with malice. "I faked it."

I stand to my feet and pad across the floor area, determined to try my
tumble once more before I leave and go back to the dorm. Molly is waiting
for me with a tub of ice cream the size of my head and one of my favourite
movies.

Sean's airy laugh interrupts my train of thought. "Baby, I tasted it, there
was nothing fake about it."

I glare at him and lift my arms above my head, ready to let the adrenaline
take over and try to land this fucking awful tumble again. "Stop calling me
baby, Taylor, I'm not your baby."

He grins. "You will be."

I turn my head, ignoring his beautiful, annoying face and sprinting forward
across the floor. I throw myself into my tumble, trying to keep track of the
floor below me as I twist, planting my feet on the ground at last.

"Fuck yes." I shout, punching my fists in the air and jumping for joy. I've been trying to land that tumble for weeks and have only managed it a handful of times. Ellen is insistent that it needs to be in the routine, even though I clearly haven't cracked it yet. I hate her sometimes.

Sean is watching me with wide, sparkling eyes, full of pride and I feel my chest tighten.

He picks my bag up from the floor and gestures for me to come to him. "Come on, let's go, the table is booked for 7pm."

"What?" I say, fisting my hip and watching his face twist into a knowing smile. Why does he smile so much? Every time I see it I want to eat him up like a cookie.

"Our date," He says, grabbing my hand and pulling me out of the gym with him towards the locker rooms. He hangs my bag gently off my shoulder and leans down to kiss me, it's so gentle and soft it almost takes my knees out. I lift up on my tiptoes, deepening the kiss.

"Umm," I sigh, as Sean lifts my body up to his, my legs encircling his wide torso. The kiss is still slow, soft and meaningful and I find myself unsure on what the fuck to do next. I know what I want to do, I want to give him a chance, to let him prove that I can trust him. But I'm still terrified, his reputation exists for a reason, he created it himself with his fuck boy ways. Seeing this side of him, this gentle, puppy dog side of him is stirring up an internal battle in my chest.

I eventually wriggle down his body, letting my bare feet land on the cold ground. I take a breath, deciding which side of the battle is going to win today. "Sean, I don't think it's a good idea us going on a date."

"I think it's a great idea." He says, running his thumbs along my jaw line. His eyes are still soft and swimming with hope. I fucking hate it.

"I'm not sure I'm ready to put my trust in you yet." I let my eyes drop to the ground and he instantly pulls my chin back up.

"Let's stop playing this game now Cal, I was enjoying it at first, but you and I both know that this isn't about sex. Please give me a chance, I've never done the relationship thing before so I'll admit I might need some help, but I want to try...with you." His eyes are pleading with me, the swampy chocolate flitting between my lips and my own uncertain gaze. "I know you want to trust me."

I swallow hard to stop the tears that are gathering in my eyes. "I'm scared." I squeak and Sean lifts my chin with this thumb again.

"What do you mean?" He says, his warm eyes melting me.

I swallow again, clearing the remaining tears from my throat. "I do want to trust you. You're the most infuriating man I've ever met but there's something about you that draws me in." His signature grin spreads across his face. "I'm scared though, to put my heart on the line after last time."

His lips find mine, gentle and tender again and the urge to just climb inside his coat and let him hold me is gnawing at my insides.

"Baby your heart is safe with me, consider me your own personal safe. I'll lock your heart in my chest with my own, if you'll let me." He cups my face again, his huge hands soft as they caress my cheeks. "I know I've never done this relationship thing before but I'll be so good at it, if you just let me try. Please let me try." His eyes are still swimming with hope and I don't know what else to do with his words but nod.

His forehead lands on mine and he takes a long breath. "Really? You'll let me try?" He whispers and I lift my head away from his, throwing him another fleeting nod.

Daisy Egan

"This isn't a relationship though Sean. I'm still not 100 percent convinced that you won't get bored of me once we have sex, but I'm willing to give you a chance."

His eyes flash with hurt for a second before he nods knowingly. "Ok, that's fair…So, are you my girlfriend now?" He smiles, so soft and hopeful it makes me almost blurt out a yes.

"No, I'm not your girlfriend, we're just dating, taking things slow ok?" I press my palms to his chest and feel the heat of his skin through his shirt.

He bobs his head, contemplating. "Slow…I can do that." He smiles and smacks a kiss to my jaw. "Come on, let's go out for dinner."

Chapter 13

Sean

I never wanted my life to be centred around anyone but myself, but it's too late. My whole life is about her, when I can see her, when I can touch her. I find myself counting down the seconds until I can hold her again, smell her hair and feel her breath against my lips before I kiss her. I just can't get enough. Hearing her agree to give me a chance set off fireworks in my chest, I'm so glad I was finally able to crack her. Not in the way I had originally intended, getting her into bed isn't even a concern of mine anymore, I just want to be around her all the time.

We arrive at the restaurant just before 7pm, it's a miracle Callie was able to get ready quick enough after we spent at least ten minutes just sucking each other's faces off outside the locker room. We're seated at our table quickly and I step behind Callie to pull her chair out, earning myself an eye roll. I shake my head and guide her into the seat with a smile, that she certainly doesn't return. She's scowling at me when I sit in my own chair opposite her, her arms folded and lips pursed.

Fuck, she turns me on.

When the waiter approaches our table seconds later it's like a switch is flipped inside of Callie and a bright smile softens her features. I want that smile for myself, I don't like her looking at this waiter guy with a smile like that. Is this what real jealousy feels like?

I reach across the table as Callie orders her drink and grab her hand from where it rests in front of her. I enclose her small hand inside my own large one and I watch as her eyes flicker to mine for a moment. I grip her hand tightly, waiting for her to pull away but she doesn't. The waiter takes my order too and leaves us alone whilst he collects our drinks from the bar.

"What was that all about? You're turning green." She teases, but I can tell she likes that I'm jealous, she's enjoying this, a little too much for my liking.

I lean back, letting go of her hand. "Don't know what you're talking about."

Our food is incredible, the two of us eating like we've not had a bite for two weeks. The food might be excellent but it sure doesn't satisfy the hunger I have for the fiery brunette sitting opposite me.

Slow Sean, she said we need to take things slow.

The conversation is light between us for the most part, both of us talking about our families and when the conversation moves over to Callie's dad I see her eyes darken a little and her shoulders tense.

"My dad's a hard man, as I'm sure you know." She says, fiddling with her fingers. "He's always been hard on me, I feel like I need to be talented at what I do to earn his love and attention."

My heart shatters instantly when her face crumples. "Baby don't say that, I'm sure that's not true." I reach for her hand again and she lets me take it.

She smirks. "Don't call me that." Then she drops her hand from mine and leans back against her chair. "I don't even know why I'm telling you all of this deep shit."

"Because you know I listen to you." I say, sipping at the last few drops of my coke.

She barks a sarcastic laugh. "Yeah, when you want something."

Ouch.

"That's not fair, I've made it clear that I'm interested in more than just your pussy haven't I?"

She nods and purses her lips again. "Uh huh, you know how to talk the talk, that's for sure."

"You're still not convinced?" I tip my head towards her and she smiles.

"I'll show you soon enough. Just wait until I give you the best fuck of your life, let you sleepover at my house and then make you breakfast in the morning."

She gleams at me, then lets her face drop to hide it. God, I'm obsessed with every little bit of her.

The waiter drops the bill onto our table after a while and I watch in disbelief as Callie reaches into her bag and takes her purse out.

It's my turn to scoff today. "What the hell do you think you're doing with that thing?"

"I'm paying for my own food." She warns and I sit up straighter.

"Like hell you are!" I grab the receipt off the table and stand up, leaving Callie seething as I walk up to the bar to pay for our food. She's fucking crazy if she thinks I'm letting her pay, I'm trying my damn hardest to prove myself to her here.

When I turn back to our table she's gone, and I can't help but laugh to think she's throwing a strop outside because I wouldn't let her pay for her own food. When I exit through the huge glass doors I see her, leaning back against the wall, her face like thunder.

She sees me and flashes me an eye roll. "You're not the boss of me Sean."

"I know," I laugh, laying my palms on her waist. "but I am a gentleman, and there's no fucking way I'm asking you out on a date to let you pay for your own food."

She grumbles something I don't understand and swats my hand away when I try to lace my fingers through her's. She starts towards my car and I follow behind her, watching her curvy ass sway as she moves, looking like a wet dream.

"Excuse me…" A quiet voice says from behind me and I turn around, tearing my eyes off Callie's ass. There's a girl around my age, shuffling her feet uncomfortably and looking me up and down.

"Sorry to bother you but I just wanted to say I love watching you play hockey, you're amazing on the ice." She smiles, looking like a mouse with her timid eyes and tiny features.

"Oh, yeah thanks that's really nice of you." I say, checking over my shoulder and not being able to see where the fuck Callie has gone.

The girl clears her throat as my own starts to close up, where the fuck did she go?

"Could I maybe have your number?" She says, watching as my eyes float around the car park looking for Callie.

"Are you kidding? I'm right here." Callie's cold voice comes from my side and I turn to see her possessively nestling herself into the side of my chest. The girl freezes and looks like she's being burnt alive by Callie's stare.

"Oh sorry, are you his girlfriend?"

Callie huffs. "Well, n—"

"Yes, she is." I interject, cutting of Callie's denial of our relationship. I know she said she's not my girlfriend — yet — but this stranger doesn't need to know that.

The girl gasps quietly and steps back. "Oh sorry I had no idea. I'll just go then, it was nice to meet you."

I nod once at her and watch her scuttle away from Callie's fiery gaze. I spin around to face her and smile widely as the green tinge fades from her cheeks.

"Looks like it's your turn to evolve into a green monster baby." I chuckle, flopping my arm over her shoulder and pulling her back into my side. I like feeling her body against mine, she fits me like a jigsaw puzzle.

"Whatever," She huffs, shoving my arm off her and storming to the passenger side before yanking the door open and climbing in.

I get in beside her and let the engine rumble to life, reaching over and gripping her bare thigh in my palm. She's wearing a satin dress that lands midway down her legs, giving me a handful of her soft thighs to grab at. Her skin is deliciously creamy and smooth and I run my hands up and down it as we drive back across town to her dorm. We don't say a lot, just small bits of chit chat here and there before Callie's phone pings and she reaches into her bag.

"Oh, well that's just great." She groans, locking her phone and shoving it back into her bag.

I look at her, then back to the road. "What's up?"

She brushes her curls off her face and sinks lower in her seat, crossing her arms over her chest.

"Molly and Anais have gone to a club for the night and I hate being home alone." She grumbles, watching my fingers draw patterns on her creamy thigh.

I hesitate, should I ask her to stay at mine? Or is that not taking it slow enough? I don't know how to navigate this dating stuff, I've never done it before and I'm scared of messing it up.

I clear my throat and sit up taller. "Do you erm…do you maybe want to stay at my house tonight?" I shuffle in my seat, forcing myself not to look at her beautiful face for fear of what I might see in her eyes.

"Is that ok? Are you sure you don't mind?" She says, sitting up, her eyes bright.

Well, I wasn't expecting that reaction.

"Yeah, yeah I'm sure." I say, trying to hold back the triumphant smile that's threatening to break free.

I have to really control myself tonight, no funny business that's going to push her away from me when I've managed to get her so close. Come on Sean, you can do this, you can spend a whole night with her and not have sex. It will be easy…ok maybe not easy but I know I can do it. My motivation is too high to mess this up when she's finally agreed to give me a chance.

Chapter 14

Sean

The house that I share with Nick, Lewis and Kyle is fucking huge and Callie's eyes widen involuntarily when we pull up outside. I watch, amused as she fights to close her gaping mouth.

"Hey," She says, putting her hand on my arm as I start to get out of the car. "Is anyone else here?"

My face twists in confusion. "I'm not sure…why, is it a problem if they are?"

She shakes her dark curls and grabs her bag. "No, I just don't want it getting around that I'm sleeping over at Sean Taylor's house."

I laugh deep in my throat. "Oh, you're embarrassed of me?"

"Hardly," She scoffs and heads for the front door, me following like a puppy behind her. She doesn't wait for me to open the door for her, she just walks straight in and makes her way up the stairs. I stand in the hallway for a second, in shock at her confidence, she clearly didn't spot Lewis curled up on the sofa either playing on his Xbox. But more importantly he didn't spot her, due to the fact he has his headset on and is currently screaming profanities at the poor fucker on the other end of it. I trail up the stairs behind her and watch as she pushes open my bedroom door.

"How did you know this was my room?" I say, dropping my bag and coat to the ground.

She shrugs. "It smells like you."

Ok, what the fuck was that little flip that my heart just did?

She takes off her jacket and sits herself on the edge of my bed, bending down to unstrap her heels. I move towards her, dropping to the ground and unbuckling them for her, kissing each of her creamy thighs as I go.

"I'll get you something to wear to bed." I murmur as I stand up, leaving a light kiss on her temple.

"Don't look," she says, her eyes flickering with anxiety. "While I undress I mean."

I knew exactly what she meant and I don't want to agree, I want to see her, but we're building trust here, so I simply nod and turn around. I really want to watch her slip out of her dress and stand there looking exquisite like she does. But instead I throw a t-shirt of mine over my head, still facing away from her temptingly delicious body.

"You can sleep in that." I say, forcing a swallow as my throat tightens along with my jeans at the thought of her behind me right now, in only her underwear.

When I hear the mattress creak I assume the coast is clear and I spin around again, pulling my jeans down my thighs and stepping out of them. I lift my t-shirt over my head too, watching Callie's throat constrict as her eyes track down my stomach and land at the ever growing bulge in my extra tight boxers. She's climbed into my king sized bed and has the duvet pulled up to her chest, it makes her look even tinier than usual as she sits right in the centre. I clamber in beside her, lifting my arm and gesturing for her to move into my side and let me hold her. She shuffles over, a little stiff and I know she's nervous, we are both half naked and in bed together. But there's nothing more to this night, she's just starting to trust me and I'm determined to keep building it brick by brick until neither of us can escape. I grab for the remote that sits on the bedside table, I lean over her and hear as her breath catches in her throat at the proximity of our semi-naked bodies. I can sense exactly what she's feeling right now, the scorching heat of electricity between us, the unstoppable sexual tension that grows every time I'm near her.

"I'm not ready to have sex with you yet." She blurts, as my back hits the headboard and I resume my upright position.

Her head is down as she plays nervously with a loose thread on my duvet cover. I tuck her curls behind her ear so I can see her face again. She stares up at me through thick lashes, her usually bright eyes darkening with caution.

I smile softly. "I know, I wasn't expecting anything tonight. We can just cuddle and watch a movie."

She sighs and I feel the weight of unwanted expectation fall from her shoulders.

"Ok," she breathes, "I just didn't want you thinking anything was going to happen tonight."

I grip her chin and lift it, forcing her eyes to meet mine. "I didn't invite you to stay so I could get into your pants Callie, I know you're not ready yet. I said I'd earn your trust and me trying to fuck you any chance I get — as much as I want to," I flash her a cheeky grin and her mouth tempts her to smile back. "Isn't going to achieve what I want here. I want you to trust me before we do anything that we can't take back and I know you're not there yet."

Her eyes change as she listens to my words, every single one of them true and I'm desperate for her to believe what I say.

"I'll wait as long as I need to, I'm in no rush." I say, kissing the dusting of freckles on her cheek lightly and releasing her chin from my grip. She doesn't look away from me though and I watch the disbelief filter in, followed by something I can't decipher.

Before I have a chance to say anything else she wraps her arms around my neck and pulls my lips down to her's. I suffocate in her fruity taste, her tongue teasing mine, hot and wet and I almost bust in my boxers right then. She flips the duvet off us and climbs into my lap, straddling my thighs and pressing her warm, beating pussy right against my semi hard cock. Our lips haven't parted even for a moment since she grabbed me and pulled my mouth onto her's.

There's an alarm blaring inside my head though, as amazing and fucking electric as this is, I don't want her to do something she's going to regret. I grab her ass in my palm, groping and squeezing the cushiony flesh, making her groan wildly into my mouth. My hands run up her bare back under the thin material of my t-shirt, her skin burning with desire. I don't know how to stop this, I don't want to stop this but I know that I should.

"Callie," I say between sucking on her lips and her teeth digging into mine. "What are you doing?"

Her breath is airy, so fucking sexy when she says against my mouth, "Changing my mind."

Fuck me, what am I supposed to say to that?

Her hands are tight in my brown curls, passionately yanking my mouth to her, cementing our lips together. I'm still kissing her when I feel her run her fingers under the elastic of my boxers. My cock jumps for joy, he thinks he's finally getting some tonight from the only girl who's been able to make him hard since the day I met her.

"Are you sure?" I pant, my swollen lips brushing against her's as I make another desperate attempt to dissuade her from having sex with me. I think I must have completely lost my mind to be trying to stop her from doing this, when this was all I wanted from the beginning. But things have changed, at least in my mind.

She sighs and cups my face between her hands, brushing our noses together. "Yes, I'm sure."

But my brain is still battling, trying to get through and win this fight. I know Callie can easily break me on this, there's no way I'm going to stop her when her hands are in places I've always dreamed of them being. But at least I can say I fought to the death.

"Callie…wait," I say, gripping her hips and sliding her down my thighs a little, away from my aching cock. "I thought we were taking this slow, and this doesn't feel very slow."

She fists her hips, showing me the little tiger in her that I love. "You don't want to have sex with me?"

Oh. My. God.

I groan, burying my face behind my hands. "Oh course I do, I really fucking want to but I don't want to ruin this progress that we're making." Then a wide grin takes over her face before she shuffles back up my legs again, our chests pressed against each other. I wrap my arms around her waist and haul her closer.

"We *are* taking things slow, we're getting to know each other and spending time together. But I can't fucking wait any longer, I'm so damn turned on by you and it's making me insane." She whispers, her mouth hovering over mine as I struggle for words, any more words to make her think this through again. I come up with absolutely nothing though before her lips are against my ear, her warm breath tickling me. "I need you to fuck me Sean."

Ok, I give up.

I don't need to hear another word before I smash our mouths together again. Our lips are everywhere, sucking and nipping at each other, but it's not enough. I flip our bodies and lay her down on the bed, slipping my t-shirt over her head and tossing it to the ground behind me. She's wearing a bright pink lingerie set, the lace barely covering all the parts of her I've been dying to see. I stand up, admiring her every curve and the soft, creamy skin that follows them before pushing my thumbs under the elastic of my boxers. I'm fighting with them, she's made me so damn horny it's a battle to get them down my legs. Callie props herself up on her elbows when my dick bounces out, saying hello to her.

She gulps hard, her throat bobbing and I know I'm in for a treat.

Chapter 15

Callie

"Wow, that is one pretty dick." I say, eyes wide and lips moist. "I can see why everyone wanted a ride on that thing."

Sean grins with pride, fisting his cock in his hand. "I know."

I purse my lips at him and sit up straight. "And you ruined it."

"No," His eyes crease with panic, "no I didn't, I still get to have sex with you right?"

Imagine if Sean's big head ruined this moment, the moment I was finally admitting out loud that I wanted him.

"Sean, that's not fitting inside me," I swallow again, my eyes still wide as I watch him run his hand up and down his painfully hard dick.

A smirk covers his entire face, eyebrows rising with arrogance. "Thought you'd seen bigger?"

I roll my eyes and then cross one bare leg over the other. "Maybe I underestimated you a little…or a lot. I mean how big is that thing?" I'm still mesmerised by his hand movements and I momentarily want to beg him to switch with me, to let me wrap my hands around him and send him into orbit.

"9.3 inches," He grins, flashing his teeth at me as I lick my lips and gulp hard again.

I want to taste him.

"9.3?" I purse my lips at him and his eyes capture them, looking like he's dying to suck them into his mouth again. "You measured it?" I let out a throaty laugh and flick my hair back over my shoulder.

"If you had a sword this big wouldn't you measure it?"

"Ha," I bark, "still full of yourself I see."

"You'll be full of me too in a minute, now lay down."

I press my palm to his chest as he stalks towards me. "Hold on," I stand up, shoving him down to sit on the edge of the bed. "Let's see if it fits in my mouth first."

I watch as his face pales and his Adam's apple bobs in his tight throat. I know exactly how to get to him and I fucking love it. A thin trail of hair leads me to his erection, the sheer size of it is intimidating to say the least and I take a breath, preparing myself to choke on his cock. I'll do it though, I don't care if it kills me at this point, I need to have a taste. Sean's chest is heaving as he watches my hot tongue take a lap up his throbbing dick.

"Oh fuck," His head falls back and his muscles ripple as he grips my hair in his fist. I press a kiss to the tip, lifting my eyes to his, wanting more than anything to please him.

His caramel eyes are dark with desire, his taught fist gripping the bed sheets beside him and ripping them from the corner of the mattress as he tries desperately to push down his orgasm.

I let his cock leave my lips with a pop. "You ok there champ?"

"Do I look ok?" He breathes, raking a hand through his thick waves. "My cock is in your mouth."

It's my turn to grin. "I normally suck at this but I'll try my best." I cackle, throwing my head back and looking up at Sean. His eyes are sparkling, soft as he watches me laughing at my own joke.

"Did you just make a dick joke?" He asks, his face creasing into a sexy smile as he suppresses his laugh.

"Depends," I say, wrapping my hand around his rock hard erection that's jutting out towards my face. "Was it funny?" I open my mouth and let his tip brush against my tongue.

His jagged breath breaks the air between us. "There's nothing funny about you kneeling in front of me with your pretty mouth open like that."

My lips turn into a smile and I take his entire cock into my mouth, letting it hit the back of my throat.

"Oh shit," Sean curses, his hand tightening at the nape of my neck. The twinge of pain as he yanks at my hair is drowned by the warmth of his aching cock down my throat. "No, no I can't." He pulls me away, letting his dick fall out of my mouth and bob happily in front of me. "Get up, I'm going to come in five-seconds of you doing that."

I get to my feet, wiping the moisture from my lips and collecting my now tangled curls, letting them fall down my back.

"Get on the bed, beautiful, it's my turn." His crooked smile is so sexy I almost combust. I do as he says and lay down on my back as he prowls towards me like a predator. He positions his naked body on top of me and gently wiggles my thong down my legs before reaching under my back and unclipping my bra with one hand.

"I don't even want to know how you can do that so quickly." I murmur, chasing his lips and pressing them to my own. "Please don't break me in half."

He kisses my lips softly, letting his tongue linger against mine for a beat before sucking my bottom lip into his mouth. He looks down between our bodies, admiring my shape and darting his tongue out to wet his lips.

"God Callie, you have no idea how I feel right now," He almost whispers. "I want to be everywhere but I don't know how." He shuffles down my body so his face is in line with my chest, he sucks my nipple between his lips and I arch my back, groaning from the teasing pleasure.

"Choose your position Captain." I say, as my nipple pops from his mouth and he smiles up at me seductively. "Are you going left wing?" I point to my left nipple and he lets out a deep chuckle. "Or, centre?" I pick up his huge hand and splay it across my lower stomach. "Or...goal?" I tease, pushing his hand down, over the warm skin of my stomach and letting him land on my pussy.

There's that crooked, dimpled smile again, he looks between my thighs and swallows hard. "I'm number 1 goal scorer for Redwood you know that right?"

I scoff. "Didn't know that actually, I know you find it hard to believe this but I'm actually *not* obsessed with you."

"Hmm," He muses, still staring at my glistening pussy as it begs him to do something, anything. "Well, I'm obsessed with *you*." He says, finally looking back at me, his chocolate eyes are wide with need. "And I'm going to score a shit load of goals for you tonight."

He dips his head and I forget where the hell I am, who I am, what my name is, everything. His tongue makes a trail up my clit, the pressure causing my back to snap up off the bed again. My hands are tight in his hair as I practically grind against his face, desperate for more. His hot tongue lashes up and down, tasting me, devouring me like a starving man would. He groans with delight into my pussy, circling my clit with his tongue before sucking the throbbing bud into his mouth. That's it, I'm a mess and I cry out his name, yanking his hair harder and forcing his face as deep between my thighs as possible. My body shakes with pleasure and my eyes sting with tears, the orgasm sweeps over me, washing me away completely. Sean grips my thighs tight, letting his lips ghost over my pussy as it releases my orgasm onto his tongue. He leaves light kisses all over my skin on his way back up to my face. The sweat is sticking my hair to the back of my neck and I shuffle under Sean's huge frame.

"You ready?" He says, sucking my collar bone, causing the skin to turn purple.

I nod. "I think so."

I'm still coming down from my orgasm so my head is kind of light right now, which is likely a good thing because his dick is looming over my pussy and it's fucking intimidating.

But I want it, I want it so bad, I'm so ready to be respectfully railed into his mattress tonight.

"I'll be gentle," He mumbles against my lips. "I promise. Just tell me to stop if it gets too much ok?"

I nod again and gulp loudly, scrunching my eyes slightly and waiting for him to fill me like a cream doughnut. He presses himself into me extra slowly and I know even with my eyes closed that he's watching my face for any sign of pain or distress. I release a curse under my breath as Sean pushes into me further, almost completely filling me.

My god he feels like heaven and hell stirred together in a deathly concoction.

"You doing ok?" He says, tucking his face into my neck and sucking at my skin like a hungry baby.

I take a jittery breath. "Depends what you define as ok…"

I feel his hot breath against me as he chuckles into my neck, before lifting his head again to look into my hazy eyes. "Still in one piece?"

I nod robotically. "For now…but I want you to fuck me like you hate me, so I might not be in one piece for long."

His eyes widen and ghost over my freckled cheeks, gliding down to my lips and his bottom one comes between his teeth.

He brushes his lips against mine and whispers, "I could never hate you, but I can pretend just for tonight."

I smile and lift my face, smashing our lips together again and he begins to thrust into me. Fucking hell the tightness is making me dizzy. But I don't want him to stop, ever.

"Fuck Callie baby, you're so tight." He breathes, planting sloppy kisses all over my neck and collar bone.

He's so big, stretching me past my usual capacity and it's then that I realise he's inside me, without a barrier of protection between us.

"Sean," I grip his rocklike shoulders, still adjusting to his size. "You don't have a condom on."

"Shit," He pulls out of me, causing a pulsing ache inside where he once was. "I wasn't even thinking." He rubs the back of his neck and scans the room. "I don't know if I have any here."

I reach out and grab his biceps, pulling him back to me. "What are you doing? Put it back in."

His expression is puzzled. "I thought you wanted me to suit up."

"I didn't say that…are you clean though?"

"I've never gone in bare before Callie, I just lose my head when I'm with you, I get caught up in the moment and don't think about what I'm doing." He groans, teasing my clit with the moist head of his pulsing dick. "I get regular checks though, I'm clean, I promise." He whispers, nudging my jaw and planting his open lips against the crook of my neck.

"Umm…" I murmur happily before my breath is snatched from me as Sean pushes his cock into me, filling me so deeply I can feel him in my stomach. He hits me with one punishing thrust after another before stopping again, staying nestled inside me and swiping his tongue against my bottom lip, coaxing my mouth open to allow him in for exploration. He pulls out of me, his cock bobbing with happiness as he flips me over. My ass is pointing right at him, my pussy glistening with need as he pushes into me slowly again.

"Oh god Sean," My muffled screams spur him on, making him thrust harder and faster. "You're so big I…I can't…" I stutter, my body feeling like it's about to crack down the centre.

He pulls my chest up from the mattress, pinning my back against his sweaty torso. He nibbles at my ear, leaving purple marks all down my neck. I groan so loudly that Sean reaches around and covers my mouth with his palm for a moment.

"That's it baby, tighten that pretty pussy around me and make me come." He growls into my ear and removes his hand from my mouth. I squeeze myself around him and my name leaves his lips on a curse.

"I'm gonna come Sean, oh fuck don't stop." I moan, my voice so throaty and tight I don't recognise it as he massages my nipples with rough fingers.

Sean shakes his head. "I've wanted to fuck you for ages Callie don't you dare come until I tell you to." He slows his pace, going torturously slow and purposely teasing me, stealing my orgasm away.

I want to punch him in the face so badly right now.

He must see the fiery frustration in my eyes when I pull away from him and turn onto my back again, yanking his body on top of mine.

"Fuck you Sean, let me come!" I hiss and grab his cock in my hand, bringing it to my opening and sliding it back inside my achingly empty pussy.

I see his eyes roll back and I know he's forcing his own orgasm down into the pit of his stomach, he's not ready for this be over yet and neither am I, but I'm desperate to come all over him.

He keeps his pace slow, watching me get more and more mad. "You come when I tell you to come. Who do you belong to Callie?"

Fuck, I hate him sometimes.

I dig my nails into his shoulders, biting my bottom lip so hard I taste blood on my tongue. I still haven't answered him so he stops moving entirely and I almost explode.

"You! You!" I gasp, giving up the fight for domination this time. He can dominate me all he wants to when his cock is inside me, I'll do whatever he wants. He pumps into me, cupping my face between his huge hands and leaving a trail of open mouthed kisses along my jaw line. My back arches off the bed and I cry out his name, clawing at his back and wrapping my slippery thighs around his solid torso, keeping his cock buried deep inside me as I orgasm. I can feel as his own orgasm starts to peak and I consider teasing him too, making him desperate but I don't think I have it in me after he's made me come twice tonight, I'm spent.

I can feel the fire lighting in the pit of my stomach and Sean moans against my lips, "Oh fuck, I'm gonna come baby." He continues his pace and just before the orgasm can shoot out of him he grabs me from the bed. "Get on your knees Callie."

I don't hesitate, eager to have his stickiness all over my tongue I immediately fall to the ground. I crouch below him and stick out my tongue. His eyes are small, squeezing tight as he fists his cock hard and fast. My dark hair is wild and sticking to my neck, my wet tongue waiting to taste him.

"Oh fuck, you're such a good girl." He groans, draining his cock and painting my face in his warm come. "That's easily the sexist thing I've ever seen."

I lick my lips and use his t-shirt that lies in a crumpled pile on the floor to wipe my face clean before standing up to put my underwear back on. The moment it's over the panic sets in, the worry I was squashing beneath the overpowering desire to have a piece of Sean Taylor for myself. But now I'm reminded that I would only ever have one piece of him, because the entirety of him isn't up for grabs and likely never will be. I can't believe I gave in so easily, I'm embarrassed of myself. I know Sean can feel this immediate tension between us, filling the air and weighing us both down. I feel from behind me as he starts to panic, like he knows that I might be regretting what we just did.

His rouged hands reach for me, turning my body towards him and pulling me to his chest. "Hey, you ok?"

I nod and rake my hair back into a ponytail, before pulling my thong up my legs and turning around so he can clip my bra for me. I'm sure he's never clipped a bra up before, he's only well practiced at unclipping as many as possible. I can feel my head taking over again, the horny side of my brain having done her part and now she's off to bed, letting my logic take over.

The problem is, Sean knows me too well already and his brown eyes are swampy with worry, it's hurting but I don't know how to fix it for him, or for me.

Chapter 16

Callie

Sean snakes his arm around my waist and turns me back around to face him, his eyes are creased with concern and it's making me want to throw up. I don't want to hurt him, but I'm scared now we've done the one thing I was putting off. It's fear on my part, fear of rejection now that I've given him what he wanted from me since the very beginning. I'm trying to trust him, really I am, but whenever a sliver of light pokes through, showing me the real him, I'm reminded of his past and the way he's always treated women. I'm terrified of being tossed aside again, like with Joel, he decided he was done with me and that was that, until recently of course. It fucking stung, worse than anything I'd ever experienced and I can't go through it again, I just can't.

"Callie, are you sure you're ok? You don't regret having sex with me do you?" The pain and worry that's creasing his handsome face is stabbing a hole through my chest.

I shake my head, a loose curl falling onto my forehead from my ponytail. "No, I don't regret it. I just feel like now we're a ticking time bomb and I'm going to be holding my breath, waiting for you to get bored with me." He cups my face in his huge hands, running his thumbs along my jaw. "Baby…" His eyes hold a thousand words that he doesn't know how to say, but somehow I find comfort in them. "Look, we've had sex, which *is* what I wanted from the start. But I'm still here and I *still* want you." He coos, leaving one kiss on each of my cheeks before releasing me. "Let's watch a movie or something, we can cuddle and I'll make you breakfast in the morning like I promised."

I nod my head and whisper, "Ok." Which is all I can force out right now. I don't know how my life has done such a 180 in the last few weeks. When I first met Sean properly in the penalty box I thought he was a man whore who wanted nothing more than to sneak his way into my pants. I think that's what he thought about himself too, I don't think he even realised he was capable of wanting anything more from a girl than just sex. At first his infatuation with me was just a love of the game, the thrill of the chase and he was so taken aback that any girl could reject him that it made him want me even more. But the consistency this man put in to try and win me over is pretty admirable if I may say so. I know I can be grumpy and foul mouthed at times, but it's honestly just my tried and tested defence mechanism to ensure nobody can hurt me. Sean has somehow found a gap in my ginormous brick walls and scrambled his way in without me even having chance to notice an intruder.

Sean is rifling through his top drawer, pulling out a clean pair of black, extra tight boxers which show off his exquisite package. I grab the t-shirt from the ground that was whipped off my body, leaving me exposed before Sean and I let ourselves go like wild animals. I smile as his familiar smell fills my nose from the worn out t-shirt in my hand. I start to look for the opening to put it over my head, but before I have chance to cover myself his bedroom door swings open.

"Hey man, do you have that glove I let you bor—" Kyle skids to a stop, his eyes flickering between Sean and I, who are both still half naked. It wouldn't take a genius to work out what's going on here and I instantly point my finger at him, my eyes a glare with warning.

"Not. A. Word." I hiss, watching as his pupils widen and then crease with a proud smile.

Sean is lying back on his bed, his arms folded behind his head looking extremely content with himself right now. The man has no shame.

Kyle shakes his head with a grin. "He finally won you over then?"

I look at Sean, who's face is plastered with that fucking arrogant smile as usual. He's just watching the interaction unfold, not bothering to defend me to his best friend. Look, I don't particularly care what people think of me but I don't need the entire hockey team thinking I'm that easy to get into bed.

I yank Sean's t-shirt over my head and pull my curls out of the neckline. "Not exactly, he's on trial, we're taking things slow for now." I mutter, grabbing my stuff from my bag.

"Looks slow to me…" Kyle laughs and winks at Sean who's now watching me gather my things.

Sean clears his throat and rises onto his elbows, his movie star stomach contracting and giving me butterflies. "My dick isn't on trial though, she's already in love with him, just have to make her fall in love with *me* now." He smiles and I consider throwing my deodorant at his head. Instead I decide to be mature and just glare at him, metaphorically stabbing him with my pupils.

I head into Sean's bathroom and leave the door ajar, letting the FOMO control me and not wanting to miss any part of their private conversation.

Kyle's slightly muffled voice breaks the silence first. "Have you been drinking tonight? Does Callie need a ride home?"

I hear the mattress squeak and Sean's large feet pad across his bedroom towards the TV stand. "Nah, she's not going home." He says, so nonchalantly that I don't know what to do with myself.

I'm supposed to be getting my makeup off my face, brushing my teeth etc, but all I can do is press my ear to the door as discreetly as possible and listen to what the hell he's going to say next.

"Where's she going then? I can take her if you can't drive." Kyle says, confusion lacing his tone.

Sean sits back on the bed, the mattress squeaking again. "She's not going anywhere, she's staying here tonight."

I hear the TV click on, the crackling sound of animated voices creating a blanket over the conversation I'm dying to listen to.

Kyle stutters, "What? She's staying here? Like, sleeping over?" He's as shocked as I was when Sean invited me to stay, we all get it, he's not a sleepover sort of guy.

I wasn't hinting for an invite when I told him that I don't like staying at the dorm by myself, I was worried about Joel turning up when I don't have Molly's backup to get rid of him. I've been keeping something from Sean because I haven't felt like there's been a right time to tell him and now we've had sex everything is ten times more complicated than it was before.

"Yeah, like sleeping over." Sean says with confidence and I hear Kyle gasp under this breath. The TV is now only a quiet hum in the background as Sean waits for me to return so we can watch a movie together.

Kyle chuckles low in his throat. "Ok, well shit maybe you really do like her. You never do sleepovers."

"Yeah, I really fucking like her man, like I don't know what to do with myself. I've never done sleepovers before, but I'll do them for her." Sean whispers and my heart grows a pair of wings and leaves my body.

Oh god, I feel like this is going to end in tears.

We watched approximately twenty-minutes of the movie before my fingers were skating around Sean's pretty dick again. I don't know what's gotten into me but I just couldn't help myself, and of course Mr sex maniac was more than happy to participate in round two. After we had sex again — and yes it was just as good as the first time — we fell asleep, the TV still blaring as Sean's arms tangled themselves around my body, pulling me back to his chest. This man held me all night long and not in a sexual way either, he didn't sink his hand between my thighs or try to grope me. His large hand lay splayed out across my lower stomach for almost the whole night as I drifted in and out of sleep. Occasionally he skimmed down my waist and gave my bare thigh a comforting squeeze, which only made my brain even foggier with confusion. I don't know what the hell I'm supposed to do now, he's been so amazing, so caring and patient with me. But the nagging anxiety, the overbearing worry about him getting bored with me and craving his old lifestyle still has me in chains. I give up trying to sleep at around 7am, Sean's face is buried in my neck and his breath is laced with vanilla as I twist my head to plant a quick kiss on his nose. I swing my legs over the edge of the bed, sliding out of his grasp and padding towards my bag that's laying on his bedroom floor. That's the moment when I make the mistake of checking my phone, I just wanted to see if Molly and Anais got home safe last night, but instead I'm greeted with ten new messages from my ex-boyfriend, Joel. He's been texting me for a few days now, begging me to talk to him, saying he wants me back and he misses me. Telling me he loves me, which is the one that hurts the most and he knows it, that's why he's using it against me. I haven't told anyone about Joel wanting me back, not Molly, not Anais or Lois and definitely not Sean. I don't know how he'd react but I don't want to find out. I don't know what I want right now, I'm really starting to like Sean and I can feel my trust for him stacking higher and higher, but Joel and I have history and the feelings I had for him are still buried in there somewhere. I got so caught up in Sean last night, allowing my attraction to him to blind me, making me forget about my current predicament of two men pulling me in two different directions. I think I need space, time to think about what the hell I'm supposed to do with myself.

I grab my things from my bag and head into Sean's bathroom, checking over my shoulder to make sure he's still sound asleep on the bed.

Chapter 17

Sean

"Callie?" I groan, sweeping my arm across the warm but empty bed sheet beside me. I crack open one eye, scanning the room but I don't see her. Fuck, did she duck out on me this morning? I know she was stressed last night, anxiety clouding her mind after she gave herself to me. She's still scared, utterly terrified really that I'm going to toss her aside, but she couldn't be more wrong. Now I've seen every side of her I'm even more obsessed and the chance of me getting bored with her and changing my mind about what I want is laughable. I just wish she could read my thoughts sometimes, see how I see her, how I feel when I look at her beautiful green eyes and her wild yet soft curls. I know it's actually me who's in dangerous territory here, falling hard for a girl who doesn't know if she can trust me, doesn't know if she can give herself to me fully. My heart is in her hands right now, waiting to be cradled or crushed.

I sit up, my stomach fluttering with worry as I realise she's definitely not here, but then I spot her clothes in the corner of the room and hear the toilet flush in my bathroom.

I breathe a sigh of relief. "Thank fuck,"

The bathroom door opens and Callie emerges, her hair perfectly brushed and hanging loosely down her back, her jeans so tight they're hugging my favourite parts of her and all I can do is stare. Then the disappointment floods me when I realise she's dressed and I wanted to fuck her again this morning before we have to leave for training, or cuddle the shit out of her, I don't care which. All I know is I can't get enough of this girl.

"Oh, come on we didn't need to be up yet," I moan, scratching my head.

"We could have cuddled for longer, or fucked again whichever you prefer." She's collecting her things from the ground, her dress from last night hanging over her arm as she anxiously stuffs everything into her bag.

She sighs and I feel the weight of it from across the room. "Sean, I have to go."

What? No, I don't want her to go, not yet, I'm not ready to say goodbye to her.

I clamber out of bed, my feet slipping on the laminate floor as I reach for her. Her eyes are planted firmly on the ground and she refuses to look at me, her chocolate curls creating a curtain over her face.

"No, you're not leaving now. I'm making you breakfast remember?" I sound like a whiny idiot, but I don't want her to go and I know she's pulling away from me again, her fear taking over what she knows is good for her. I *can* be good for her, for us.

My hands are gripping her biceps as she stares at the floor, shuffling her feet like she doesn't know how to navigate this. I don't know how to either, I've never done this shit before, never wanted a girl past one night and now here I am begging her to stay. I have a feeling she's still going to leave anyway though.

"I just…I need to go home." She mutters, but makes no move to slink away from me. My fingers trail up her arms to bracket her jaw between my hands. I pull her face up to look at me, forcing her eyes to meet mine and that's when I see it there, sparkling behind the emerald of her irises. The fear, the uncertainty that I want to pull out of her but I don't know how. I pull her bottom lip down with my thumb, admiring the way her breath stutters as I lean down to kiss her. Our lips are so soft as they move against each other, slow and steady.

"What's going on?" I say as I break the kiss. "Why are you being cold with me?"

Her face crumples slightly under my scrutiny and I rub the lines away with my thumbs, still cupping her cheeks in my hands.

"We shouldn't have had sex last night." She whispers and my heart plummets to the bottom of my stomach. My hands fall from her face and I take a step back which makes her drop her eyes to the ground again.

I scrub my hand down my face. "I tried to stop you Callie, three times I tried to stop you but you wanted me. I wasn't going to keep fighting when I've wanted you so badly since the moment we met."

She rakes her hand through her curls and lifts her eyes to mine again, letting them harden a little as she controls the wobbling of her bottom lip. I know she's trying not to let her emotions out, I wish she would though so I'd know how deep her feelings for me run. Are they just surface level? Did last night make her realise she actually doesn't like me, she's just attracted to me physically? God, I want to know what's running around inside her head right now.

"That's the thing though isn't it?" She blows out a breath, "You wanted me for sex since the moment we met. I didn't even start to like you as a person until recently and I don't do things this way around." She hoists her bag up her shoulder and moves towards my bedroom door. "I do feelings first, then sex."

She shoves her feet into her heels, not even bothering to strap them and I know she's already mentally got one foot out of my door right now. I follow her movements though, planting myself in front of the bedroom door and grabbing her wrist.

"Are you seriously telling me you don't have *any* feelings for me?" I say, my heart pleading me to stop torturing myself and just let her go. The quicker she goes, the quicker I can start to get over her. *But I don't want to get over her, I want to keep her.*

She takes another jittery inhale. "I have to go."

She snakes her body around mine as I scan the floor for a pair of joggers, sliding them on and stumbling out of my room and down the stairs after her. I catch her elbow as she reaches the front door and I see my three roommates in the living room, watching us out of the corner of my eye. Normally I'd tell them to fuck off and mind their own business but I'm too focused on the beautiful brunette that's trying to run away from me.

"Callie please don't do this, there's no reason for you to leave right now." I beg, my eyes darting between her hand on the door knob and her feet, worried she's going to just dart out the front door and I won't be able to catch her.

She groans and presses her fingers into her temple like she has a headache. "I'm sorry Sean, but you and I both know this isn't going to end well, we're just playing with fire here and someone's going to get burnt."

"That's bullshit Callie!" I'm yelling now, not knowing how else to stop her from doing this, from ending whatever the fuck this is between us. "I want to change for you, I've told you that, I just need you to give me a chance."

Her eyes soften now and she rests her warm hand on my shoulder. "I don't want you to change who you are for me Sean, that's not fair on either of us."

"This *is* who I am. That other guy who fucks around and doesn't give a shit about anyone but himself that's not me, not really. I like who I am when I'm with you."

I take a glance to my right, my friends' eyes are all ricocheting off Callie and I, watching me pour my heart out to her. On a normal day I'd care, not wanting them to see me vulnerable like this but the only thing I care about now is the girl in front of me, what she thinks. Nobody else's opinion matters right now.

"I like who you are when you're with me too." She drops her hand from my shoulder and lets it hang at her side. "But there's still another side to you and you can't just block it out, pretend it doesn't exist. Fucking a constant conveyor belt of girls is what you do Sean, it's what you've always done and there's no reason for you to change now."

"There is a reason…you."

Her face drops and her lip trembles again, I just want to grab it to stop it from making my heart ache.

"I think we need to figure things out on our own." She whispers, pulling her hair over one shoulder and looking at the front door again. I know she's going to bolt so I hold her jaw in my hands, pulling her face to mine.

"No, no," I murmur, planting my mouth on her's, relishing in the way our lips fit together like a puzzle. Her hands find the nape of my neck, pulling me down to her and forcing the kiss to travel deeper. The feeling of her lips on mine is already imprinted into my fucking bones, I don't think there's any deeper it can go. I haul her to my chest with one arm wrapped around her tight waist, leaving another lingering kiss on her soft lips. She pulls away from me and I see a tear travelling down her cheek as she throws me one last broken look. She yanks at the front door and scurries down the path to where an Uber waits for her. She doesn't look back as she practically throws herself into the back seat and the car takes off down the road, leaving me standing on the doorstep, topless and speechless. I pad back into the house, slamming the door behind me and drawing the attention back of the three nosey fuckers who are sitting on the couch. She's actually gone, she said we should figure things out on our own, but I don't want to do anything on my own, not now I've seen what it's like to be with her. I don't like the thought of being alone anymore, which is funny because that's all I've ever wanted, to be alone and not have to consider anyone but myself. I grab the nearest thing to my hand which happens to be the ceramic bowl on the side table by the front door and throw it across the room, cursing loudly as it smashes into the marble counter and the pieces clatter to the floor. My head feels like it's on fire, my chest tight and my heart constricting inside. I want to just rip it out and stamp it into the ground, stop it from ever feeling anything again.

"You ok man?" Kyle says, getting up from the sofa and walking across the huge expanse of living room towards me. I don't have anything to say to him, I have no words to give anyone right now. I don't know how the fuck I'm supposed to feel but I can't pretend to be ok when I'm not, I'm far from it.

I start to trudge up the stairs, my head spinning with questions, why did she leave like that? This can't just be about not trusting me, not after last night. It was special, I know that's corny but it's true. I've never felt that

way after having sex with a girl and I know Callie felt something too, she
can deny it all she wants but she's not fooling me.

Nick clears his throat from where he's sprawled out on the coach and I
look up at him. "You fucked her last night didn't you?"

I stop on the stairs, letting my chin fall to my chest. "Yeah, I did and now
she wants nothing to do with me."

"Oh how the tables have turned." Nick chuckles and my hard eyes find his.
"Shut your fucking mouth or I'll come over there and crush your
windpipe." I growl, continuing up the stairs and away from his smug,
fucking face. I love my guys, but sometimes Nick can be such a fucking
unfeeling arsehole. The guy wouldn't know love if it bit him in the balls.
Love? The word sounds weird even in my head, but it kind of fits. I know
it's really fucking quick but I don't do slow in any aspect of my life, not on
the ice, not in the bedroom. I think I could love Callie… screw that, I
could *definitely* love that girl. I just need to make her see, I can't just let
her walk away from me, from us.

Chapter 18

Callie

"Callie, door!" Anais' high pitched yell breaks through the peaceful silence of the dorm room.

"Can you get it? I'm busy." I groan, flopping over onto my back like a dead fish.

I'm not busy, not even a little bit. I'm lying on my bed doing nothing but staring into the open space above my head like I've done for the last two days.

"My nails are wet!" She yells again and I heave a sigh, swinging my half numb legs over the edge of the bed and plodding out of my bedroom and down the hall.

I look like a jumble sale threw up on me, Sean's huge sweatpants hanging off my hips purely because I feel like I can't breathe unless I have his scent rammed up my nose at all times. I miss that annoying man who closely resembles sex on legs, I miss him so much but I just can't drag myself out of this pit of despair that I voluntarily launched myself into. I want to have him, he said I could have him, all of him but I just don't think life is that simple. He sees things so black and white but he's never been in a relationship before, which in turn means he's never been hurt by one. He doesn't fully understand my worries, the trauma response to having your heartbroken before but he's being so incredibly patient with me it's making the ache in my heart seep even deeper. It's only been two days and he's shown up at my door each one of those days, begging Molly or Anais to persuade me to talk to him. He should know by now that I'm not easily swayed by people, apart from him of course. Sean could ask me to launch myself off a ten story building with him and I'd likely consider it. He's brought me roses everyday too and my favourite strawberries, the ones that won him his first kiss with me. Not that I had much of a choice, he shoved that strawberry out of his way and pounced on me. That kiss quite literally changed everything, for both of us.

As I pass Anais' open bedroom door I point a finger at her. "You're lucky you're one of the only people on this earth that I actually like."

She blows me a kiss, blowing a strand of auburn hair out of her face, her nails bright pink and shining wet.

I yank open the door, expecting it to be Molly having forgotten her key like she does at least once per week, but to my utter horror it's not Molly. It's heaven and hell combined.

"Heeey!" My mum throws her arms out wide, shimmying her chest and causing her collection of necklaces to clatter together. I don't need a mirror to tell you what my face looks like right now, my eyes are popping out of my skull and they immediately zoom into my dad's face as he stands, hands in his pockets and face coated in indifference, behind my mum. I smooth my tangled mess of curls, not that it will make much of a difference to the absolute mess I am right now.

"Oh, honey you look like shit, come here." She wraps me in a tight hug, sniffing my hair and holding it out like it's a dead animal. It probably looks like one sleeping on top of my head. "What the hell's going on?"

Daisy Egan

I shuffle my feet and pull Sean's sweats up my hips. "I don't want to talk about it."

Mum blows past me like a gust of wind and heads straight for the kitchen, a bag of goodies hanging from her thin arm. I don't want to look at her too hard, don't want to notice the small changes in her already frail body since I last saw her over a month ago. Her hair is still shaved, the dark shadow across her skull where her curls, identical to mine used to flow from. The cancer took all of that away from her, the hair, the muscle and fat on her bones. But it couldn't take her light, the sunshine that radiates brightly from her smile and her piercing green eyes.

My dad saunters into my dorm, hands in his pockets like he has not a care in the world. He's not fooling me though, I know he's stressed to fuck about my mum. He likes to hide behind a hard front, pretend like nothing bothers him and he's not emotionally affected by things, but I know him better than that. I guess I inherited that trait from him, if not any of my physical looks.

"Thanks for the heads up," I hiss at him, keeping my mum out of earshot. "You could have warned me you two were dropping by."

"I've been calling you for two days and you don't answer your phone!" He hisses back, both of us keeping our voices hushed but laced with equal annoyance at each other. Dad and I aren't exactly close, but I respect the hell out of him and aim to please him as much as I can.

I sigh. "Sorry, I've been a bit distracted."

"I brought ingredients for spaghetti bolognaise, your favourite Cal!" Mum sings from the kitchen counter as she unloads a bag full of food. My dad falls back into the living room chair and turns on the TV, making himself at home in a place he rarely visits, even though he works at this university.

Seeing his only daughter has never been a priority of his, he'd much rather be on the ice all day with his adopted hockey sons.

"I hope you're cooking, because I'm certainly not." I say over my mum's shoulder, peering into the never ending bag of food she's emptying onto my marble counter. She nods quickly, her excitement flowing from her and momentarily making me feel a wash of calm for the first time in two days. The woman loves to cook, experimenting with food and creating so many scary combinations throughout my childhood. It was her thing, combining random ingredients and hoping they would taste good. News flash, they rarely did, but I always loved her enthusiasm all the same.

"Just heading out Cal!" Anais says, stuffing shit into her handbag, before looking up and seeing I have unexpected company. "Oh sorry, I didn't realise anyone was here."

"Wanna stay for dinner honey?" My mum says, her eyebrows lifting on her forehead.

Anais smiles gingerly. "No, thanks though, just meeting a friend."

My mum waves her out the door and I throw her a 'please help me' look, which only makes her laugh as she lets the front door fall closed behind her. I love my parents make no mistake, but spending an awkward dinner with the two of them when I look like a bag of shit isn't something I'm in the mood for. I haven't wanted to talk to anyone or really do anything besides going to the gym and coming home since I last saw Sean. And I don't plan on changing that, not yet anyway.

We eat dinner in near silence, my dad and I do anyway, my mum yaps about nonsense the entire time. I clear my plate, having not had much of an appetite in the last couple of days and enjoying some normal food that didn't come from a takeout box.

My dad clears his throat and shoves his barstool back against the lino floor. "I better head off in a minute, I have to be at the rink in twenty and I can't be late today. My boys have been slacking lately and they need all the extra ice time they can get, especially Taylor," my throat closes on the mention of his name, my heart thumping hard as my eyes spring up to my dad's face. "He's been grinding my gears for the last few days, I don't know what's gotten into that boy." He points at my mum as he shrugs his jacket over his arms. "You, don't be late to the rink or I'll leave without you." He plants a firm kiss on her temple and gives my shoulder a squeeze as he passes me, disappearing through the front door.

My mum's hands land on the island with purpose. "Right, movie time baby."

I roll my eyes when she can't see and collect up our plates as she dives onto the sofa like an excitable child, scrolling through Netflix to find the cheesiest movie possible I assume. I don't know if I can stomach watching any kind of romance, but I can't break her heart either so I guess I'll suck it up for tonight.

'She's The Man' is the movie my mum picks, one of our all time favourites when we need a laugh and that's the kind of medicine I'm looking for, but I just can't find it, the usual humour inside me. And when a scene that normally has the two of us rolling around the sofa clutching our stomachs doesn't so much as pull a chuckle from me, my mum pauses the movie and turns her body towards mine. Her bright eyes are swimming with confusion and suspicion.

"What's going on with you honey? You've got bags the size of big ben hanging under your eyes, your hair is ratty as hell and what's with the extra large, man sized sweatpants?"

I huff and shakes my curls out. "Just struggling a bit recently,"

She tucks a loose curl behind my ear. "Tell Mummy all about it."

"Please don't call yourself that." I scrunch my nose and she laughs heartily before taking my hand.

"No but seriously honey, you've always talked to me about everything, so come on, spill."

Oh god, I feel the water works bursting behind my eyes.

"Honestly?" I squeak. She nods and the first tear falls down my cheek. "I feel like my heart is breaking."

Mum pulls me into her, cradling me close to her chest like I'm still a small child. "Who broke it?" She whispers into my dark tresses, brushing them back over my shoulder as I cling to her small body. I always worry that if I squeeze her too hard she'll shatter like glass.

I lift my face from her shoulder, a wet patch left on her t-shirt from my tears. "This guy…he's literally perfect in every way except one thing that my head just won't seem to let me get over."

"Sean Taylor?" She says casually and I swallow hard, wondering whether to lie.

I stutter, "What? No—"

She holds her hand up to me, stopping me. "You're a shitty liar. I saw the way your face changed when your dad mentioned him earlier."

Tears spring from my eyes again and the flood gates well and truly open, pouring down my face and soaking both my mum and my clothes as they splatter. She reaches for my other hand, covering them both with her own warm ones.

"I think I'm falling in love with him and I don't know how to stop it." I cry, slapping the tears away from my skin.

My mum swipes a few drops off my cheeks with her thumbs. "Why do you need to stop it?" I shrug, finding it harder with each day that goes by to answer that question myself. "Look, I know a bit about heartbreak sweetheart, let me give you a piece of advice." She leans closer, "If it's right, it will all come together and if not, you'll heal from it."

"That simple?" I say, my voice still stumbling through the remaining tears. She nods once. "That simple baby." She kisses my temple and stands up from the sofa. "Now, I better go before your dad throws a temper tantrum because I'm two minutes late." She rolls her eyes playfully and heads for the door, my hand in her's as she pulls me behind her.

I put my other hand on her shoulder when she yanks open the front door. "You're ok...aren't you Mum? Chemo is still going ok and everything?" My mum flaps her hands through the air and turns away from me, one foot already in the hallway, making her escape. "Yeah, yeah I'm fine. You know me, grab life by the balls and all that." She floats down the hallway, waving a hand behind her. "See you at Christmas honey, love you!"

"Love you too!" I yell after her, before closing myself away in my igloo again, away from the world.

Daisy Egan

Chapter 19

Sean

Callie is avoiding me, like really fucking avoiding me. She's even been planning when she's in the gym around our weight training schedule so she doesn't have to run into me. When she ran out on me four days ago I sat in my bedroom coming up with a plan to make her see that this can work. I know her fears are warranted, I've given her no reason to believe that I've changed for her when it was me who created the fuck boy narrative in the first place. I tried to stop her when she wanted to have sex with me, I told her I was worried she'd regret it and it seems like that's exactly what's happened. The irony of this whole situation is that Callie was so anxious about me throwing her to the side like a used napkin after we had sex and that's exactly what she's doing to me. The worst part about this whole thing is that I feel like shit without her, all I want is to see her beautiful face, to talk to her and work out a way to fix this so I can keep her. I'll do literally anything to be able to keep her.

It's been four days of her avoiding every text I send, every call I make. I've even gone to her dorm with flowers — white roses to be exact — and her favourite strawberries every day since she ran out on me, but she's still refusing to talk to me. I don't know if I did something that made her scared or if she just never built any trust in me after all. But I really felt like I could see a change in her, in both of us. I mean god I look in the mirror right now and have no idea who is staring back at me. Sean Taylor, renowned play boy turned mopey asshole over a girl who fucked him then chucked him. Talk about karma.

I'm probably at the last place on the entire face on the planet that I want to be right now. The only place I want to be being 9.3 inches deep inside Callie. But that's not going to happen is it?

My car rolls to a quiet stop at the edge of my parents' obnoxiously huge property. I stick my hand out of the window and press the buzzer, listening to it ring out a couple of times before Lois' smug voice travels through the speaker.

"Hey fuck boy, I bet Dad twenty quid that you wouldn't show up, so you owe me twenty quid." She chimes and I roll my eyes, ignoring her.

The gate finally whirs open and I hit the accelerator again, slowly moving up the driveway and rolling to a stop next to Lois' car. I let my head fall into my hands once before opening the door and stepping out. I really can't be fucked for this today, a family dinner is usually enjoyable for me, I'm a very sociable person and love my family to pieces. But right now it feels like there's a gaping hole in my chest and no one in this house can fill it for me. My social battery is low too, needing to be filled by one curly haired, fiery brunette who currently would rather develop scurvy from never leaving her dorm, than talk to me.

Lois leaps on me the second I step through the front door. "Awe, I knew you missed me." She grins at me, her deep dimples mirroring mine. Not that they're out today, they've not seen the light of day since four days ago when Callie left me, taking my happiness with her.

I shove her off me. "I see you all the time." I grunt, kicking my shoes off and padding towards the kitchen where the smell of sizzling meat is floating from.

Lois trails behind me like an annoying Chihuahua nipping at my ankles. She definitely didn't inherit Dad's tall gene like I did, she's even shorter than Callie.

Callie.

I need to stop thinking about her or I won't make it through this fucking dinner.

"Yeah but you pretend like I don't exist." She scoffs from behind me just as I reach the kitchen door, I swing it open and the hot air hits me directly between the eyes.

I bark a dry laugh. "I wish that you didn't."

"Hi Sean! Oh I missed you." My mum comes bounding over, arms outstretched towards me just as Lois reaches up and pinches my bicep.

"Ow! No pinching, you little shit." I hiss, nudging her into the kitchen island that almost takes up the whole room. The kitchen ironically being the smallest room in the whole house, it's the room my mum spends most of her time in when she's not in the office. My parents spent just under 3 million pounds on this house, with it's vast expanse of land and it's regal, winding staircase. The funny thing is the pair of them spend less time in it than ever before, both of them working their fingers to the bone everyday, travelling an hour into London and never leaving their office before 8pm. Mum wraps me in a tight hug, her familiar, homely smell giving me a moment of peace and comfort in her arms. "You don't call us enough

anymore, or answer your phone when we call. We miss you." My mum
sticks out her bottom lip and Dad comes behind me, slinging one arm over
my shoulder.

"Leave the boy alone Judith he's a busy man." He ruffles my hair like I'm
five years old and grabs a potato from the tray. They're still spitting and he
curses at the scolding heat as he pops it into his mouth and chews happily.

"Your sister actually answers her phone when we call." Mum huffs and
Lois throws me an arrogant smirk.

I sigh and follow after my dad, launching a potato in the air and catching it
in my open mouth. "Sorry Mum, I've just been a bit out of sorts lately."

Lois snorts. "Yeah we can see that, you look like a bag of dicks."

"Lois!" My parents shriek in unison, Mum throwing a tea towel across the
room at my sister.

Lois throws her hands in the air as I glare at her. "What? He does! Look at
his beard." She scratches the dark coating of stubble that's appeared on my
face after four days of not shaving. I swat her little hand away and move
towards the dining room. "You look like father Christmas with that thing
sprouting out of your face." She cackles and I turn to her as I reach the
adjoining doors.

"Will you fuck off?"

"Jesus Christ!" My dad says, his mouth opening to let out the billowing
steam from his second roast potato. "We send you two off to university
with impeccable manners and you both come back with potty mouths."

Dinner goes by relatively quick, I pretty much inhale my food, having not
had my mum's home cooking for about four months now. I'm cutting into

my last piece of steak when Mum clears her throat and my stomach clenches. She only ever does that when she has something awkward or uncomfortable to bring up.

"So," She starts and I pop my last piece of steak into my mouth. *Big mistake.* "Who's this girl you've been seeing?"

My steak almost flies across the room when I start to choke. Of all the things I thought she was going to ask, that would have been so far down my list it would have been invisible.

"I haven't been seeing anyone." I croak, my throat tightening at the lie coming from my lips. I take a sip of water, then another one, trying to clear the bubble that's expanded in my windpipe.

Lois barks a laugh and I turn to face her. "Sean? Seeing someone for more than one night? The mere thought of it nearly made him choke to death."

If I had something to throw at her right now I would seriously consider it. I go quiet, not knowing how else to deal with a situation like this with everyone's eyes on me, assessing me like they're trying to decipher morse code.

"You ok honey?" Mum says, looking at me through her lashes as she tips her glass of ruby wine to her lips, temporarily staining them.

I push my chair back, scraping it across the marble flooring. "You know what I actually feel a bit sick. Think I'll just go and lie down in my room for a bit."

"Sean, I can—"

"Mum, it's fine honestly. I just need to lie down." I cut her off and leave the room before anyone else can say a word and head upstairs to my old bedroom.

Daisy Egan

I don't know how long passes, half an hour, an hour maybe before a soft tap sounds on my door. I can smell Mum's perfume from here, the light lavender smell that she's carried with her since I was a child. I'm glad she's never wanted to switch up the perfume choice, this one brings me so much comfort the moment it hits my nostrils. My mum's face appears around the door, concern etched deep into her eyebrows, I've never been a good liar and I think now, with my heart literally living outside of my body I'm even worse at hiding things. My mum's a great people reader too, even strangers, so as you can imagine she reads Lois and I like we're copies of her own personal biography. I force a half smile onto my face for her sake as she crosses the room to get to me, my arms rest behind my head as I stretch my long body out across the king sized bed. The mattress dips as she sits beside me and a sympathetic smile lines her mouth.

"I know something is hurting you." She says, her voice draped in sadness. I can't look at her, if I do I might give away the last tiny pieces of myself that I have left. "You might be a big, 6-foot-4, 23 year old man now, but you were my baby once and I know you."

I sigh. "Yeah, I guess I'm just kind of a mess at the moment." My eyes are still fixated on my lap as I sit upright, crossing my legs over each other. Mum's hand lands on my knee. "It is a girl isn't it? I was right."

I finally take a glance at her face, the laughter lines drawing my attention as I think about the happy marriage she has. I want that one day, I never thought I did but now there's nothing I think I want more.

"How did you even know?" I mutter, watching her face soften when she sees the pain hiding behind my eyes.

She smiles gently. "I called your house the other day and Kyle answered, said you were on a date."

Thinking about my date with Callie creates a sloshing wave in my stomach, the memory of her electric touch lingering on my skin, the tightness of her perfect pussy wrapped around me. But more importantly when she lay her head on my chest and fell asleep, when I wrapped my entire body around her's, nestling into her neck and inhaling her fruity smell. Then, when she ran out of the door in the morning, leaving me there alone.

"Oh yeah...that," I say, letting my misty gaze travel back down to my jean clad lap.

"I've never seen you like this before, over a girl."

I take a deep breath and try to hold back, but the words tumble off my lips like word vomit. "She's not just *a* girl, she's *the* fucking girl Mum and I don't know how to make her see that she can trust me. She knows what I've been like with women and because of that she's too damn scared to give me a real chance, and how can I blame her? She's right about all of it." I feel a single tear prickle at my eyelids and I sniff it harshly back. My god, I really am going soft for this girl, Kyle was right.

My mum's head falls, giving my knee a loving squeeze before she exhales a sharp puff.

"Look sweetheart, I know this is hard to hear... but you can't *make* someone trust you. You just have to build it bit by bit and show her how much you care about her."

"I've been going to her dorm everyday, taking her flowers and her favourite strawberries." I sigh, scrubbing a hand down my face. "She won't talk to me though, doesn't want to see me."

Mum takes both of my huge hands in her tiny ones, the contrast dragging a snicker up my throat.

"She'll come around Sean," the certainty in her eyes makes this whole thing seem simple. "If she's right for you and you for her, then she'll come around, trust me."

I do, I trust my mum more than anyone else in this world but now my brain is floating above my body. Am I being too soft about all of this? Maybe I should just barge my way into Callie's dorm and force her to talk to me.

No, that would never work, she's too stubborn, she'd just pull back even further. I'll go and try again tonight on my way home, take her flowers and strawberries and maybe, just maybe I can convince her to hear me out.

Chapter 20

Sean

I always thought for sure it would take a huge event or some crazy fate for me to find the woman who would make me want to change, to commit to her and only her. But, it didn't. Callie just fell into my life in the most unexpected way possible and since the moment I set my eyes on her I could feel a magnetic pull. I can feel it now, as I stand outside her dorm room for the fourth day in a row, a weighty bunch of white roses tucked under my arm and a bag in my other hand containing an extra large punnet of her favourite strawberries. My mum's words are buried deep in my chest, pumping away with the organ I wasn't sure was even working until I met Callie. I came straight here from my parents' house, the light fading behind the clouds as I drove, thinking about all the different ways I could persuade her to talk to me today. The light padding of footsteps approaches the closed, red door and I hold my breath, hoping it's the girl I'm missing so badly. It's familiar creak lifts my attention from the ground and Molly's sympathetic face looks back at me, a pained smile creasing her forehead. Her blonde waves swing over her shoulder as her eyes grow soft. "Hi Sean,"

"Can I talk to her?" I say, my mind already telling me the answer to my own question. I've asked to talk to her everyday, and everyday she's refused.

Molly sighs. "Well, it's been a no for the last four days but I can go and ask her anyway."

"Thanks Mol," I smile, but it's forced. I don't feel like I have anything to smile about right now, not without her. It's like the ray of sunshine that was a constant in my life since I met her has been snatched away from me. Now I'm left with nothing but darkness and frost.

I can hear Callie's murmured voice snap, "I said no." at Molly, before her best friend returns to me at the door with her face twisted into a scowl.

"I'm sorry Sean, it's a no again," she huffs, "and she nearly bit my fucking head off for asking."

I hand the bunch of roses to Molly, their comforting scent floating in the air between us.

White roses are my mum's favourite and my dad would always get her a huge bouquet of them for birthdays and anniversaries. My parents' love for each other is something I'm desperate to emulate in my own life, it's so pure and comfortable. I didn't think I needed anyone to love until I met Callie, now it's literally all I need.

"Give her these please, and tell her I miss her." I say, handing her the bag of strawberries too before shoving my icy hands into my pockets and turning to leave.

"Sean," Molly calls after me and I turn back to face her. "For what it's worth I have tried to convince her to talk to you about what's going on in her head." She sighs and I can see the protective best friend behind her eyes. "The thing you have to understand about Callie is, she's fucking terrified of letting her guard down with anyone. She let her guard down with Joel and that ended in a shit storm. She barely lets me inside her head and I'm her best friend." Molly takes a step into the hallway, pulling the door almost closed behind her. I'm guessing she doesn't want Callie to hear any of this, to hear Molly being totally honest about her deepest feelings.

"Callie has built this solid wall of protection around herself so that nobody can hurt her. She's scared that you've found a way in, but she'll never admit that."

I lean back against the wall in the glossy, white hallway of the dorms, digesting every word that Molly said and stitching it to my brain so I never forget it. How can I show Callie that she doesn't need to be scared with me? I know I can be what she needs, because the thing is, we need each other equally. I need her to show me how to do this relationship thing, how to navigate the hard times and she needs me to show her how it feels to be loved so deeply it's in every crevice of your bones. I know I can do that for her, love her how she deserves.

"Thanks Molly, can you just tell her something for me please?" She nods, gathering her long, blonde hair and hanging it over one shoulder. "Tell her I'm not going to give up on her, I want her so much and I'll keep coming here every day for the rest of the year if that's what it takes."

Molly's face crumples and she sniffs back a tear. "Oh my god, you're so cute." She looks back over her shoulder and gestures to me with her palm. "Come on, come in."

"I thought Callie said—" I start and Molly interjects with a dismissive wave of her hand.

"Forget what Callie said, that girl doesn't know what's good for her." She smiles and grabs my forearm, leading me through the kitchen where she lays my gifts on the island and we round the corner to stand just outside Callie's half open door. I know it sounds crazy, but it's like I can feel her heart beating from here, like we're tied together by an invisible string.

Molly's palm lands flat on my torso, stopping me from getting any closer to Callie's bedroom door. "Wait here, I'm going to try and talk to her again, hopefully she doesn't rip my head off this time." She whispers, rolling her eyes and darting into Callie's room, leaving the door cracked open so I can hear every word that's being said.

"Come on Cal, he's really trying here. I mean for fuck's sake Joel never once bought you flowers and you were together for over a year. You should really give Sean a chance, it's obvious how much he likes you." Molly sighs, and I hear Callie return with her own.

"I had sex with him." Callie blurts out and my eyes widen. She obviously hadn't told her best friend that we slept together, is that bad? I feel like girls usually tell their best friends things like that.

I hear Molly choke on her own saliva. "Ok, hold on, back the fuck up… when did this happen?"

"The other night!" Callie's voice has gone up two decibels. "When I ran out on him and it's all your fault!"

"*My* fault?" Molly gasps and I push my ear closer to the crack in the open door.

"Yes, your fault. You told him to bring me those strawberries and then I let him kiss me, and then I let him take me on a date and when he said I could stay at his place we got into his bedroom and we were alone together and I just couldn't resist!" She groans, fighting to get her breath back after her

Daisy Egan

rambling. "He took me out for a really nice dinner that he wouldn't let me pay for, then he said I could stay over at his place when he found out you and Anais were out and I didn't like staying alone. He even promised to make me breakfast in the morning, but I didn't stick around long enough to let him." She groans again and I hear her shove her face into a pillow.

There's a moment of silence behind the door and I hold my breath, waiting for one of them to speak again. My mind is swirling with thoughts, none of them coherent.

"Why didn't you stay then?" Molly says, her voice quieter and milder than before.

Callie's muffled voice comes through the pillow she's stuffed her face into. "I don't want to tell you."

Molly sighs deeply. "Ok, well I'm not seeing any negatives here…"

"That's the problem," Callie says, "I can't see any negatives either, I'm desperately trying to find them but I can't." She takes a breath. "The only thing I'm worried about is my dad finding out, but he doesn't pay enough attention to my life to figure it out on his own."

I can't believe what I'm hearing, she doesn't see any negatives with me? I'm not sure whether to be even more confused or ecstatic. If she has no negatives to being with me then why has she been avoiding me for days?

"The other thing is," Callie continues, shuffling and making her mattress creak. "I know he's been a ladies' man in the past, but he really is pulling out all the stops to prove to me that he wants to change. He wants to change for *me* Mol, how can I resist that?"

Molly sighs deeply and I hear the mattress squeak again as Molly gets to her feet.

"You don't need to resist him," Molly says, swinging open the door to reveal me standing there like a gameshow prize. "He's here and he wants you, so stop being a princess and talk to him."

Callie's face is like a horror show, she doesn't know where to look. Our eyes meet and I can feel the pain in her's, mirroring mine and I'm almost certain that she's missed me like I've missed her. I need her to talk to me, to tell me what's holding her back from me and maybe then we can figure out a way through this storm.

Chapter 21

Callie

It's him, he's here, standing in my doorway and staring me with those eyes, those fucking caramel eyes that live in the deepest part of my chest. I stand to my feet in shock, watching Molly scuttle out of my bedroom door like the traitor that she is. Sean moves towards me but maintains at least two feet of space.

"Molly, you bitch!" I shout over his shoulder towards my half open door. I hear her cackle like an evil genius from the kitchen. "Just doing what's best for you, and what's best for you is Sean Taylor!" She yells back and I turn my attention back to the only person I've been able to think about for the past four days.

"Hey," He says quietly, his eyes pinning me to the spot.

"Hi," I whisper, my feet shuffling uncomfortably below me. I don't know how to drag my voice up from my throat.

He clears his throat and rubs the back of his neck. "Are you...ok?"

"No," I say without hesitation. "Are you?" I already know he's not, from the deep bags under his eyes to the grown out dark stubble across his jawline.

"Not even close." He mumbles, running a hand through the bundle of messy waves that rest on his head. "I've missed you Cal, I've missed you so much these past few days."

I sniff back the tears that are attempting to escape down my cheeks and shuffle my feet again. I want to just dive into his arms and let him have me, let him have all of me but the fear is still holding me hostage. The knowledge that I've not been totally honest with him is eating me alive at the same time.

"Tell me how I can fix this Callie, I promise I can fix it." He pleads, his eyes crinkling with desperation.

God, I feel like my heart is going to crack down the centre looking at him like that. I tried so hard to offend him for a while, to put him off me and make him see that I didn't like him. But now, seeing him hurting like this is making me contemplate pouring poison directly into my eyeballs so I don't have to watch his face collapse like that.

I sniff, holding back the tears that I know are inevitably going to fall soon. "You didn't do anything wrong Sean, in fact you did everything right."

"Tell me what made you run out on me then. I thought we were making progress and then you left me there, after I all but got on my knees and begged you not to go."

I want to scream at him that he's right and I don't know what's wrong with me, but I don't.

"I'm sorry I did that, it was shitty of me and I'm sorry for avoiding you since then, it's just what I do when I get scared, I run." I let my face fall, keeping my eyes off his.

"You don't need to be scared Callie, and I'm not mad at you for leaving, I just want to know why." He inches closer to me, our bodies now about a foot away from each other and I can feel the heat drawing me to him. "You just told Molly that you don't see any negatives to being with me and you can see how hard I'm trying to prove that I want to change for you, yet you're still holding me at arms length." He sighs and his shoulders slump. "You were so worried about me losing interest in you after we had sex and then you totally flipped the switch and wanted nothing to do with *me*."

He looks so defeated, so hurt and the moisture falls from my eyes before I can stop it. Sean finds my face again and when he sees the tears tracking down my cheeks he takes one stride towards me and cups my face in his warm hands. His thumbs are rough in the most comforting way, the way they run along my cheekbones and his warm, concerned eyes dip down to meet mine.

"Talk to me baby, tell me truthfully what's holding you back." His voice is like fresh coffee, smooth and warm, his vanilla laced breath tickling my nose and tempting me to kiss him. All I've wanted to do for the last four days was kiss that man.

I let out a heavy breath. "I told you we shouldn't have had sex. It was a mistake, I wasn't emotionally ready and I let myself have you when I shouldn't have." I take another breath, my shoulder lifting and falling weakly. "Because I'll never have you, not really and that's what scares me Sean can't you see that?"

His grip on my face tightens and his nose brushes against mine, increasing the taste of his breath on my tongue. "You can have me Callie, you can have all of me."

"There's always a part of you I won't have, the part that will be satisfied with me for a while and then will start to miss the game, miss taking a new girl home every night and the excitement of that." My lips part on a jagged breath again and Sean takes his hands off my face. "I can't give you variety Sean, I'm trying to make you see that."

He throws his hands in the air and blows out a sharp puff of exasperation at me. "I don't want fucking variety Callie! I've had variety my whole adult life and I'm so damn bored of it. I'm a big boy now and I'm craving more, ever since we met and you told me to go and fuck myself I've wanted more. You've changed something in me Callie and I want you, just you." He steps closer to me again, pulling me to his chest, his arm snaked around my waist. "I want you every day and every night and there's nothing you can say to make that not true." He ends his rant in a whisper, the passion draining from his voice and transforming into a plea again.

I want to say yes, he can have me and that's the end of it, easy, but life isn't always like that. I have to tell him about Joel, this isn't fair on him.

"Joel wants me back." I blurt as his hands drop from my waist again, shock and confusion making a haze float across his eyes.

"What? Since when?" He says, forehead crinkling with worry and betrayal. I feel an enormous pang of guilt for keeping this from him, but when the hell was I supposed to tell him? On our date? Or maybe just after we had sex for the first time? No, there was no way I could have told him then.

I look down, guilt crawling all over my skin like spiders. "He's been texting me, asking me to forgive him, to give him another chance. He's been saying that he misses me and that…" I look up to Sean's face, the crumpled worry now replaced with what can only be described as utter panic. "He loves me."

Sean runs a heavy hand over his dark stubble. "Do you miss him? L-love him?" His voice is strained with gut wrenching pain as he forces the L word off his tongue. His chocolate eyes burn into mine and I can't even blink, I'm stuck to the spot, my feet refusing to budge when my head tells them to run, run away from this terrifying conversation. Flecks of my pink nail varnish float to the ground as I scratch and pick at it nervously before slowly shaking my head. What am I thinking? Of course I don't love Joel anymore, the feelings I once had for him are buried deep in the back of my mind but there's no chance of them resurfacing, they're firmly anchored down.

I inhale quietly. "I didn't know how I felt or what I wanted last week, that's another reason I was so confused after we had sex." Sean's face has softened a little, the realisation that I don't love Joel anymore and am purely trying to explain my erratic and downright cold behaviour towards him. "My head's been swimming Sean, and I think I'm at a point where I'd rather drown than carry on treading water like this, fighting over what I want and what I think I *should* want."

Sean's still staring at me, his face changing expression with each new word that comes out of my mouth, like he doesn't know how he should react. This could force him the other way, make him realise that I'm more effort than I'm worth and he'd rather a life without me in it. I've been dishonest with him and I have to admit, if it was the other way around it's more than likely I would have told him never to talk to me again.

"I'm sorry I didn't tell you," I whisper, stepping towards him and closing the gap between us. "I just didn't know how to and I wasn't sure what I wanted, then we had sex and I felt awful like…like I was leading you on." My eyes fall to the ground again, my nail varnish following it as I pick at it anxiously. I can't even look at his face, not now everything is out in the open. I know what's going to happen, what *should* happen. Sean should tell me I was wrong to keep something like that from him, that I shouldn't have slept with him and that he never wants to see me again. That's what should happen, but of course Sean is like a real life, huge, muscular angel. So instead, what comes off his lips is much softer and gentler. "I understand Cal," I look up then, that being the last sentence I expected to hear him say. "I mean of course I wish you'd have told me, but I understand why you didn't." His hands find my waist, resting against my cold skin and warming it with his touch. "I know we've only been taking this 'slow' for like a week," He finger quotes the air, smiling bashfully and I let out a teary chuckle. The truth is we've never been slow, not since the second we locked eyes for the first time in that penalty box. "But I can feel myself changing. All I've done is think about you since we slept together and I'm not exaggerating when I say I've *never* thought about a girl after we've had sex. Can we try this relationship thing properly? Please Cal, I know what I want."

He takes my jaw in his hands, running his thumbs along my cheeks and I let my eyes flutter closed. I want to say hell yes, let's crack this thing wide open and just jump, but the fear still has me in it's grip and I can't work out for the life of me how to wriggle free. I think I need his help.

"I don't know Sean, I'm reluctant to give myself fully to someone again after last time." His face dips and his lips brush against mine, floating and making my knees weak, the urge to smash my lips onto his is lighting a fire in the pit of my stomach.

"Do you want Joel back?" He whispers, his sweet breath warming my lips, his scratchy stubble brushing my chin.

I shake my head. "I thought maybe I did…but I don't. The way he treated me wasn't right and I don't want that again."

"Do you want me?" He says, lifting his head and towering over me as usual, one arm still snaked around my waist. "I hope you do because I'm afraid you're stuck with me." He attempts a smile but it's weak and I know he needs to hear the words, that I want him and only him.

I wrap my arms around his solid torso and rest my chin on his chest, looking up into the depths of his swampy eyes. "I think I'm starting to love being stuck with you."

His face relaxes, the lines on his forehead vanishing and he blows out a breath laced with relief. "Thank god," He sighs, his nose brushes mine as he tips his head down, our foreheads touching.

Sean pushes the hair from my face and whispers, "I really want to kiss you, can I?"

My head bobs eagerly in a nod and I yank his face down to mine, our mouths colliding in a hot and breathy kiss. His tongue swipes against mine and I grab a fistful of his jacket in each hand to keep me on my feet, rising up on my tiptoes to increase the ferocity between our lips.

"I love the way you make me feel Sean, I don't think anyone has ever treated me the way you do." I say against his parted lips, letting my heals fall back to the ground and making me a whole foot shorter than him again.

His blinding grin spreads across his dimpled cheeks and he scoops me off the ground, lifting me to his level with both arms trapping my waist. He leaves a few open mouthed kisses on my neck as I bury my face into his, inhaling ever drop of his delicious scent. I can feel him still smiling against my neck before he pulls back, still holding me against him, my feet an entire foot away from the ground.

Daisy Egan

"So, you're my girlfriend now right? Or am I supposed to ask you properly? I don't know how any of this works Cal, you have to help me." He places me gently to my feet and I laugh, lacing our fingers together as he rubs the back of his neck nervously with his other hand. I still find it weird seeing him like this, all the arrogance out of sight and the real Sean showing his vulnerable side, just for me.

"I mean, you can get down on one knee if you want and ask me t—" My words are stopped in their tracks when Sean lowers himself to the ground, one knee out in front of him like he's proposing. "I was joking." I say, watching as a smirk widens his face.

"Callie Burch, will you please do me the honour of being my girlfriend?" He coos, his hand holding mine and a sharp laugh bursts from my lips.

"You really should stop picking your nails." He raises an eyebrow, eyeing my half eaten fingernails.

"You should really stop taking everything I say so literally."

"So? Will you?" He smiles, his dimples deepening.

How the hell am I supposed to say no to that face?

I do like to fuck with him though, so the first word that comes out of my mouth is, "No."

His face falls. "No?"

"Joking," I bark another laugh and he throws me over his shoulder, slam dunking me onto my bed. His lips find my stomach first, he lifts my t-shirt and peppers tiny kisses all over my skin, making a pathway up to my collarbone and neck before I'm shivering all over.

He hums with satisfaction into my neck and whispers, "Take your clothes off."

I laugh and shove him off me. "Absolutely not, Molly is in the other room." I swing my feet over the edge of my bed, standing up and grabbing my phone from the dresser.

Sean moves behind me, his warmth cocooning me as his hands grip my hips and he peers over my shoulder.

"Is he still contacting you?" He says, sucking my earlobe between his lips. I nod. "He keeps texting me and saying he's going to come here so we can talk, even though I've told him there's nothing to talk about. He's not getting the hint."

Sean swipes the phone from my hand, over my head and spins away from me. "Let me call him."

"What? No, Sean you—"

But it's too late, he's scrolling, then tapping, then pressing my phone to his ear. I clamber onto my bed and jump on his back, the weight of me barley causing his body to move when I collide with him. I reach around, snatching at my phone and cursing at him, until Joel's deep voice comes through the phone and I freeze, clinging to Sean's back like a chimp.

"Callie? Thank god you called me I was starting to think—"

"It's not Callie." Sean growls, his shoulders tensing under my grip.

I bury my face into his shoulder blades, shaking my head. I need to hear what he says to Joel but I'm also shitting myself at what he's going to say to Joel. This is 100 percent a no win situation but I'm dying to see how it plays out.

"Sean Taylor? Is that you? What the fuck are you doing with my girl's phone?" Joel's voice is a little jittery on the other end of the line and Sean cracks his neck from side to side, red hot possession climbing up his neck.

Something resembling a protective rumble rolls up Sean's throat. "Don't
ever call her that again, she's not your girl anymore, she's mine." I hoist
myself up Sean's back, wrapping my arms around his neck and nestling
my nose into his shoulder. "She doesn't want you, she wants me, so back
the fuck off and don't contact her again."

"I-I-I don't know what the hell you're talking about, she—"

Sean cuts him off again. "Let me make this easy for you man, don't ever
contact her again or I'll come over and snap your puny legs in half…
alright?" He doesn't give Joel a chance to respond before he hits the red
button and pockets my phone.

"God you're such a dick, that was unnecessary." I groan, slipping down his
back and landing on my feet with a soft thud.

Sean sits on the edge of my bed and rakes his hair back. "It was necessary
Cal, he needed to know that your mine and I don't share."

"You sure used to be good at sharing your dick with everyone on campus."
I fold my arms over my chest and jut my hip out the side. Sean lifts his
chin, that crooked grin plastered across his face as he reaches his arms out
and hauls me to him. I stand between his open knees, still pursing my lips
at him whilst his runs his hands down my back.

"Yeah well, I don't share *you*."

I climb onto his lap, my legs straddling his hips. "I don't want to fall in
love with you." I moan, pushing my fingers through his thick hair and he
nudges my nose with his.

"Well, unfortunately for you I'm balancing on the edge right now and you
best believe if I fall I'm taking you down with me."

Chapter 22

Sean

I've been away for just over a week now, competitions swamping my schedule and my mind, tearing me away from the girl who now rules my every thought. I miss her, having not seen her for 9 days now, I can't pretend I'm not struggling with withdrawal. She's like a drug and I'm her biggest addict. We're due back from two weeks of competitions on Saturday and I'm constantly thinking about spending the whole weekend wrapped around Callie, touching her at all times, I love touching her. My dick is missing her too, that's why when I call her tonight I have one very specific request.

"I need a photo of you Callie." I say, the phone balancing precariously between my shoulder and my ear as I fight with my sock.
"Hello to you too," She snickers, the sound of her silky voice sends my cock rocketing behind my jeans. I huff and rip my sock off the end of my foot, giving up that particular one handed fight whilst I talk to my girl.
"Hey baby, I miss you. I need a photo of you."
"Why?"

"I can't keeping jerking off to mental images of you, I need something to look at." I sit on the edge of the sofa next to Kyle as he batters his Xbox remote, muttering curses under his breath.

Callie huffs a laugh. "Oh, you want a naughty picture?" Her voice takes on a sultry tone and I have to adjust my junk.

I nod, even though she can't see me. "I mean, I could definitely still make myself come to a picture of you fully clothed, but where's the fun in that?"

"Ok, hold on," She says and I hear her start padding barefoot across her dorm.

My eyes widen and I shift on the sofa, the sword in my trousers digging into my leg uncomfortably. "You're doing it now? Oh my god,"

Ping!

I pull the phone away from my ear, putting Callie on speaker and opening her message. "Sweet Jesus," I breathe, smashing the phone screen against my chest to hide it. "Callie, what the fuck?"

I can hear the smile in her voice. "Is that good enough?"

"Good enough?" I gape, looking at the photo again, turning the phone away from Kyle's wandering eye.

Callie is standing in her bathroom, one leg crossed over the other as she leans back against the sink. She's wearing absolutely nothing, not even a scrap of material in sight and I can't fucking look away. My cock is throbbing, fighting to get home and live inside her for the entire weekend. "Erm…yeah, baby…that's…wow, I miss you." I stutter like a fucking idiot, scrubbing my hand across my jaw, still staring at the photo of my girl, looking like a fucking angel.

Kyle leans across towards me. "Let me see."

I shove him hard and scramble off the sofa, almost falling flat on my ass as I clamp my hand over my phone, hiding Callie's body from Kyle's eyes. "You know I'd have to gauge your eyes out if you saw her like that right?" Kyle barks a laugh and Callie clears her throat on the other end of the phone, drawing my attention back to her. "Sorry baby, Kyle's just being certifiably insane over here. Please come and save me."

"I have to go Sean, I have training in the morning and I'm so fucking tired from the competition today." She sounds tired, really tired and I know she's having a hard time with her routines right now, she keeps telling me how no matter how hard she tries she just can't get the hang of them. I know it's totally draining her mentally and physically. Even so, she smashed the competition today, the team event was their strongest and they managed to come second which was a surprise to everyone when my sister fell off beam twice and Anais took a fall on bars. Lois has been a gymnast since she was a child but I've never really cared to learn anything about the sport, until this fiery brunette came along and consumed me, I want to know everything about her. Even though I know she's exhausted tonight after a long day she still stripped off her clothes and made me a happy boy with that photo. God, I love h—

Shit! My head is getting way ahead of me, thinking crazy things like that when we've only been dating for a month. I am crazy right? It's not normal to think you might be in love with someone after a month together? I don't fucking know what I'm doing with this relationship stuff, even though Callie has helped me a lot when I've been feeling uneasy, like a rookie. It's hard for me to be bad, or unpracticed at anything, I'm pretty much good at everything I do. I'm a weapon on the ice and with the ladies, but wanting someone as bad as I want Callie is total uncharted territory for me and I don't know what I'm doing with myself.

My blades glide to a stop next to Nick, my chest battering him into the plexiglass and earning a hard jab in my right shoulder as he smirks at me. Only 4 days left until I can go home to my girl, I can't fucking wait to see her, smell her, kiss her. She doesn't know this yet but we are spending the entire weekend in bed, naked.

"Stop daydreaming Taylor, you're losing it." Coach passes me, slapping a palm down on the back of my shoulder and making his way off the ice. I'm glad he can't read my thoughts, images of his naked daughter swirling through my mind.

We've been training since 8am this morning, it's now 2pm and I'm fucking exhausted. I've been making good use of the photo Callie sent me everyday, the guys and I are sharing a hotel room though so I've had to be mindful of that. I can't help but let her name leave my lips on a curse every time I come now, my dick takes over my brain and I can think of nothing but her.

Nick grunts beside me as he yanks his gloves off his hands, the red, icy skin underneath causing him to wince when he curls them into fists. "I know Callie is super fucking hot but she's kind of a bitch, I don't know what you see in her past her pussy."

This fucking guy never knows when to shut up.

My brow furrows and I grab the back of his jersey, leaning into his ear. "First of all, call my girl a bitch again and you'll be seeing the inside of a hospital." I watch his smirk widen, he loves fucking with me, watching me lose my shit. "Second of all," I take a breath, letting the protective anger fizzle out. "I'm scared shitless of her, but I think that's what keeps me coming back. It's like I'm scared of her but I like it, keeps me on my toes you know?" I step off the ice, following after Nick and walking towards the locker rooms, the sweat dripping down the back of my neck. "All the other girls I could have are always fawning all over me, desperate for my attention but Callie is the opposite." I let a coy smile cross my face before I squash it down, watching as Nick drops his trousers. "She tells me how much I irritate her at least once per day and I fucking love it. Maybe I'm fucked in the head." I cover my eyes with one hand. "Put that fucking thing away."

"Jealous that it's bigger than yours?" Nick grins, swinging his hips and making his dick dance before wrapping a towel around his waist.

"Anyway, maybe you are fucked in the head or maybe…" he grins and throws his arm around my shoulders. "You're falling in love with her."

I drop my trousers too, admiring the muscle hanging between my legs, I can't fucking wait to put him to good use in 4 days.

"I already know I'm falling in love with her, but I can't tell her that yet can I? Isn't it way too soon?" I grumble, lifting my jersey over my head and grabbing a towel from my locker. "I feel like such a fucking rookie at all this relationship stuff, I never know if I'm being too keen or not keen enough."

Nick yanks back the shower curtain and I step into the cubicle next to him, the hot water creates a cloud of fog around us. "Maybe talk to Lewis about it, he's done the relationship thing before."

"Yeah, good idea man." I say, letting the water flow over my face, the warmth softening my tense muscles.

I need to figure out how to navigate this stuff and I think Lewis might be the perfect person to help me smooth out the confusion that's rolling my brain into a ball and bouncing it around inside my skull. The funny thing is I know exactly how I feel, it's not my feelings towards Callie that are confusing me, it's what to do with them.

Chapter 23

Callie

It's finally Friday, just one day to go until my new favourite person comes home and I can spend the weekend strapped to his chest, never moving more than a few centimetres away from him. I really miss him, more than I'd like to admit but the phone calls and video chats we've been having every day since he left just aren't enough anymore. I need to actually touch him, to lie with him and have his huge arms wrapped around me so I can bury my face in his mind bending smell.

When I got home last night Molly practically tackled me to the living room floor and made me solemnly swear to stay home all day with her today watching romance movies and eating ice cream in our PJs. Ellen gave us a rare Friday off because our gym is being prepared for a competition tomorrow, thank fuck it's not a competition I have to participate in. The freshman have a practice comp before the real shit starts for them next year, the poor little fish dealing with big bad Ellen on a Friday and Saturday back to back. I feel bad for them because I've dealt with her wrath all fucking week and she's been in an extra bad mood so I'm even more mentally drained than usual. Molly should have known I wouldn't need convincing, I've always been a PJ day kind of girl. Probably because I spend most of my life now either naked and squashed under a huge, dimple faced hockey player or sucked into a pair of way too tight gym shorts. Since I agreed to give Sean a real chance, to be his girlfriend, I feel like my lightbulb has been relit. If you'd have told me two months ago that Sean Taylor would be my boyfriend I'd have either laughed in your face or swung at you with a baseball bat. But he's seriously been the one thing I never knew I needed, he makes every part of my life better, except when he has to go away and I'm left missing him. Like right now, he's been gone for 13 days, due back tomorrow thank god because I need that 6-foot-4 slab of warm muscle to put a very specific part of his body inside me ASAP, before I implode.

The credits role across the screen and I lift my stiff body off the sofa and out of the sea of blankets that cocoon me, Molly and Anais. I gallop across the living room towards our tiny kitchen, my stomach is painfully tight but I can't stop eating, maybe my period is due or something. I grab a few more snacks and fall back onto the sofa between my friends who are huddled against the cushions. Molly's gazelle like legs tangle with mine as she spreads out and groans at the stiffness of her muscles. The three of us have barely moved since this morning and it's almost 9pm already, we've ordered a takeout, eaten our body weight in ice cream and watched at least four romance movies. I'm draped in Sean's wardrobe, his grey sweatpants swallowing me whole and his hockey hoodie reaching down to my knees as they quake from the bitter cold in here. Our dorm currently resembles a fucking ice box, the heating having been broken for the last six hours as engineers flocked into the basement to try and fix it. I personally think they should all find a new career, my toes are still frozen as I wiggle them, trying to bring them back to life.

"I miss Sean." I huff, bringing the collar of his hoodie up over my nose and mouth. "Especially right now when I'm freezing my ass off and his body is twice the size of mine. Plus he's always hot, he's like my own personal hot water bottle." I snicker and scratch at the bun that closely resembles a bird's nest on top of my head, before yanking it out and raking my hand through my curls. When I look back up at Molly she's smiling brightly at me, her blue eyes twinkling with something I can't decipher. "What?" I say, my cheeks washing with pink as she gives me a knowing look.

She lets her gaze drift over my reddening cheeks before landing back on my eyes. "You grin like a Cheshire Cat when you talk about him."

My cheeks flush even more, so I look down at my lap, pulling my lip between my teeth and fiddling with a loose thread on Sean's hoodie. "So?"

"Oh my god, are you falling for him?" She gapes, sitting up straight and pulling her blonde waves over one shoulder.

A sound somewhere between a snort and a scoff falls from my lips. "No," I'm not even convincing myself with that half arsed lie.

Anais jumps up from the sofa and squeals, Molly joining her like they're a pair of teenagers at a Justin Bieber concert.

"Oh my fucking god you're really falling for him!" Molly shrieks and I grab the nearest empty ice cream container and throw it lazily at her and Anais. Before I have chance to fight back the two of them grab my ankles and pull me onto the living room carpet, landing on top of my painfully full stomach and bear hugging me so I can no longer breathe.

Anais squeals, "You're in love! This is so great!"

I wriggle under them and they finally relent, pulling me up to sit cross legged with them on the carpeted floor.

"I'm not in love, I'm in like." I grumble, pulling Sean's hood up and tugging on the strings, making the material close in on my face.

Molly lifts a sculpted brow at me. "That's not a thing, especially not for you Miss all or nothing,"

I wish she wasn't right, I'd love if she wasn't right, but I'm pretty sure the bitch is right.

By 11pm the three of us are like blocks of ice, huddled on the sofa together finishing our last movie of the night before heading to bed. Anais and I have been roped into going to the gym to help the freshmen tomorrow in preparation for their practice competition so I need my sleep, especially if I'm expected to handle Ellen and her ferocity again. There's a light tap on our door and our heads all swivel simultaneously, our foreheads creasing in confusion. I stand up, cracking my back as I go and shuffling across the room in my two sizes too big socks.

"Did you order more food Mol?" I say and she shakes her blonde head.

"At 11pm? No,"

I pull on the doorknob, rubbing my tired eyes and hauling the front door open. Sean's beautiful smile greets me, his dimples deep in his cheeks and the grin he flashes me blinding. And his smell, oh my god it's everywhere, in every pore of my body the second I open the door. His huge frame makes me feel tiny as I stutter, looking for the words I don't know if I can find.

"What...what are you doing here?" I gasp, blinking way too many times and holding onto the doorframe to stop my knees from giving up on me.

Sean's smile cracks open wider. "I couldn't wait until tomorrow, I hope that's ok." He hauls me into him, lifting me to his waist as my legs circle his hard torso.

"It's more than ok," I breathe into his neck, inhaling every drop of his woodsy smell and crushing myself to him as hard as possible. He cups my ass in his hand and tightens the other one around my back, holding my body against his.

"I missed you." I whisper, pressing soft, sleepy kisses against his neck. He sighs. "God, I missed *you* baby." He prises me off him, placing me to my feet and letting his caramel eyes trail down my body. I look like a jumble sale threw up on me, nothing I'm wearing fits and the size of his clothes is dragging me down, making me look even smaller than usual. His eyebrow rises up his face and his expression shifts into a shit eating grin. "Are you wearing my clothes?"

"Yeah, it's fucking freezing in here… and I like the way you smell." I smile, burying the tint of pink coating my cheeks behind my loose curls. Sean's hand moves to bracket my jaw, tucking my hair behind my ear and pressing his warm lips to mine. The heat spreads down from my lips, lighting a fire through my chest all the way down to my frostbitten toes. I shiver when his arms snake around my waist as his tongue swipes lightly over my bottom lip. Molly clears her throat and I suddenly remember that we're not alone.

"Get a room please." She laughs, nudging Anais into joining her taunting. I snap my head around to face her, keeping my palms flat on Sean's chest. "Fine, we will." I throw her a sarcastic smirk and lace my fingers through Sean's, guiding him into my dorm and kicking the door shut behind us.

He's bobbing up and down like a puppy, letting me pull him towards my bedroom, he knows what's coming, we both do.

"Keep the noise down!" Molly yells after us, earning a muted snicker from us both as we reach my bedroom door.

Sean yells back, "Not a chance! She's going to be screaming my name all night long!"

I grab the back of his jacket and yank him inside, dragging it down his shoulders and undressing him like a ken doll. He's fumbling with his hoodie that's draped over my body, pulling it over my head and throwing it to the ground as he steps out of his jeans. He dives on me, making me squeal as he whips my sweatpants off in one smooth motion, nipping at my inner thighs as he makes his way up.

"I'm not gonna last long Cal, you know that right?" His tongue presses against my hot skin, just under the aching bud that's been craving him for two weeks. "I dreamed of this every night I was away, just being able to touch you, feel you, taste you." His rough hands run up my thighs and he looks up at me through thick lashes, his warm tongue lightly flickering against my clit, making me squirm. "We're going to take it slow tonight, I just want to feel every little bit of you." He climbs back up my body and kisses me, his lips warm and hungry.

He really does take it slow, sliding inside me and thrusting cautiously, feeling every inch like he said. And I feel every inch of him too, when he eventually flips me back onto the mattress, my back sinking into it, he lets his face hover over mine. I can see in his eyes that there are words floating behind them that he doesn't quite know how to say yet, but that's ok, I can drink them in just by looking at him. His sharp jaw, his tight, rippled stomach, his fucking dimples. God, I'm in so deep with him I don't think there's any chance of me climbing back out now.

"I really fucking like you Callie, like I don't know what to do with myself when I'm away from you. Am I supposed to tell you that?" He groans, rubbing the nape of his neck anxiously. His cock is still inside me as I chuckle back at him, cupping his chin in my hand.

"Yeah, you can tell me that. I really like you too, I missed you so much whilst you were away." I wrap my legs around his hips and tug him to me, pushing him deeper inside me and cursing with pleasure as he begins thrusting again. He's hungry, starving for me and me for him. He trails sloppy kisses up my neck and across my jaw as I come undone around him, arching my back and sinking my nails into his taut biceps.

"Oh shit, I'm gonna come. Can I...can I come inside you?" He brings his face back to mine, brown eyes flickering with uncertainty. I nod and he exhales deeply, sucking my lips between his and letting his tongue explore my mouth as he comes, my name leaving his lips on a pained groan. He's never come inside me before, he's never asked to, he just always pulls out but I'm on the pill so I don't see a reason to deny us both.

As we lay there sweaty and panting, Sean scoops me up with his arm and hauls me into his side, smacking a kiss to my temple as our bodies stick together.

"There's a party at your house tomorrow right?" I say, tipping my face up to look at him.

He leaves a tiny kiss on my nose and nods. "Yeah, you're coming aren't you?" He cups my cheek, thumb tracing my freckles. "If you don't want to then I'll come here and we can spend some time alone."

"Of course I'm coming, I'd never miss a party Taylor, do you know me at all?"

He flashes me a bright smile and pulls me closer, bumping our noses together affectionately.

He sighs. "You're never going to get rid of me you know that? Like there's no fucking way I'm ever leaving you alone now."

I purse my lips, trying to halt the smile that's taking over my face. "Does that mean you're staying here tonight?"

He nods and pulls my body on top of his, his firm torso surprisingly comfortable to lie on. "I'm thinking about just moving in."

I bark a laugh. "You barely fit in my bed, you monster." I roll away from him to the other side of the bed, intending to get dressed but Sean's huge hands grab hold of my bare hips and pull me right back to him.

"Oh no you don't." He murmurs, his palm closing over my collarbone as he plants wet kisses on the back of my shoulders and neck, his arms enclosing me to his chest. "You're staying here with me until tomorrow morning."

That's fine with me. I've decided, there's no place I'd rather be than right here.

Chapter 24

Sean

"Fuck," I mutter under my breath, straining to open my eyes and find the source of that fucking irritating noise that dragged me out of the best sleep I've had in two weeks. I spent the night wrapped around Callie's naked body and honestly I feel like I'm waking up on a cloud. I swipe an arm across the mattress searching for her blindly and dragging her back to my chest when I locate her bare stomach. I grab my still ringing phone from under my pillow and answer it gruffly, making no effort to hide my distaste to whoever is on the other end of the phone for waking me from my Callie filled slumber.

"What?" I spit, keeping my eyes closed and breathing into the crook of Callie's neck.

"Sean Taylor, do you have a girlfriend now?"

Shit.

I've been avoiding all of my mum's calls since I saw her about a month ago. She's been desperate for me to get a girlfriend and settle down with one woman for ages and I could tell by the texts she's sent me over the last few weeks that she somehow knows I managed to win Callie over. I swear she calls my house purely to get inside information about me from Kyle, that fucker tells her everything.

"You would tell me right? You'd tell your mum if you managed to win over the girl you were pining over when you last saw me?" She says, hope and trepidation lacing her tone.

I huff. "No, I wouldn't tell you because you'd get all excited and quite frankly I'd want to kill you."

"Oh my god you do! You won her over didn't you?" She squeals and I lift the phone from my ear, wincing at the volume of her voice when I only woke up precisely 7 seconds ago.

"Like that." I groan, reluctantly pulling my arm out from under Callie and sitting up straight against the headboard. My girl stirs and flips over to face me, her hands searching for me in her sleep. I take her small hand in mine and twine our fingers together.

"Sorry, sorry," My mum says, sniffing back tears of excitement.

I smack my hand to my forehead in disbelief, this woman is crazy, she's holding back tears because her 23 year old son is only having sex with one woman for the first time in his life.

"I won't get ahead of myself." She says.

I groan and scratch my chin. "I feel like you're already planning mine and Callie's wedding."

"Let me see a picture of her, pretty please, make your mummy happy." She says and I can hear her pouting her lip even though I can't see her. It's clear where I got my flare for the dramatics.

I sigh and put my phone on speaker, flicking through the many photos I now have of Callie on my phone. The picture she sent me whilst I was away flashes onto my screen and I have to bite my fist to stop the horny groan that wants to escape.

Daisy Egan

"You want a picture of her fully clothed or naked? I have both." I grin, swiping across to a more appropriate photo of my girl.

My mum scoffs with disgust, which only serves to widen my smirk. "Sean Taylor!"

That's the second time she's full named me during this phone call, usually I'd be scared of this tiny woman with a big attitude but luckily I've got an even spicier version snuggled up to my side right now. So I tap send and a photo of Callie, her dark curls cascading down her back, her jeans hugging her perfect ass and her smile so bright it hurts my chest, comes through on my mum's phone. I know when she's received it because she audibly gasps.

"Oh my god, she's beautiful." She gawks, I hear her repeatedly gasping under her breath as she assesses the photo of Callie.

I breathe a laugh. "I'll take your surprise as a compliment rather than an insult to my taste in women."

I know my taste in women is impeccable, I bagged Callie didn't I? And she's the most beautiful woman I've ever laid my eyes on.

She snorts dramatically. "It's not your taste in women I'm concerned about, it's the fact that a woman *that* beautiful has agreed to give you a chance." Her voice twists into a stern version of it's usual chirpy nature. "Don't, mess this up Sean."

I sigh and look down at Callie, her features soft with sleep as she nuzzles her face into my side. "I won't Mum, I swear. I think that I...I think I love her."

My mum tries to swallow her shriek of delight but it still almost deafens me, Callie stirs next to me wriggling against my side, her warm skin running up my stomach as she strokes her palm up my abs.

Daisy Egan

"Sean? Who are you talking to?" She murmurs and my Mum literally screams with joy right into my eardrum.

"Oh my god is that her? Let me speak to her Sean please I—"

"Ok, I'm hanging up." I say, pressing the red button and silencing my mother before she spontaneously combusts.

I shuffle my body down so I'm face to face with my baby, planting a hard kiss to her freckled cheek as she peers at me through sleepy eyes.

"We need to leave for training soon, it's already 9:30." I say into her mane of hair as she stretches beside me.

Her eyes widen and she jumps out of bed. "Oh shit, how is it so late? I won't be ready on time." She grabs a towel from the floor of her bedroom and wraps it around herself as she skips around the room in a panic.

I sit up too, swinging my legs over the edge of the bed, just in time to catch her elbow as she tries to leave the room in a flurry.

"Hey, it doesn't matter if we're a bit late. We could have another five minutes in bed." I smirk and she breathes a light laugh.

"No, we can't be late, you know what Ellen is like and she's been in a foul mood all week, I don't need to be irritating her any more than necessary. Plus I'm helping out with the freshmen today, not training."

I stare at her blankly, lifting my eyes from where they rest on her tits. I just want to suck her taut nipple into my mouth and drag my tongue all over her body. "Sorry baby I didn't listen to a word you just said."

She rolls her eyes in the way I love, the feisty side of her showing itself for a moment before she flicks me between the eyes, earning a sharp, "Ow!" From me as she swishes out of the room.

I have to admit she's right about being late, Coach will give me more shit than it's worth if I rock up more than ten-seconds after he wants me there.

We better not show up together either or Callie's dad might get suspicious
and that's the last thing either of us need.

"How do you know if you're in love?" I say to Lewis as he lifts the weight
off my chest where it almost crushes me. The guy is at least four inches
shorter than me but he's built like a bull.

I've been watching Callie from across the gym all morning as she helps set
up for the freshmen competition tomorrow. I can't stop wondering if my
feelings for her will ever settle, or if they'll just keep multiplying every
day like they have been since we met.

Lewis chuckles beside me as we switch places. "Ahh, you've been
infected I see…"

"Well, I'm not sure," that's bullshit, I've never been so sure about anything
in my life but I need someone else to confirm it for me. "How would I
know?"

Lewis lies back on the bench, taking the weight on his arms and pressing it
up and down with ease. "Easy," he grunts, setting it back on the stand after
five reps. "What's the first thing you think about when you wake up in the
morning?"

"Hockey," I say after a beat of hesitation. Lewis cracks a smile and shakes
his head at me, his chestnut waves moving with him.

"Liar," He says, smirking at me as he gestures for me to get back on the
bench.

I lie down and take the weight from him, pressing it to the sky. "Ok, her,"
"And the last thing you think about when you fall asleep at night?"

"Her again," I grunt, giving him the weight and sitting up, rubbing my hand over my jaw.

"You're in love man, plain and simple." He murmurs and my eyes fall on Callie again, she's watching me too this time and I notice a smile pulling at her lips when she catches my eye.

"Can I tell her that though? Or is it too soon?" I mutter, still holding eye contact with my girl before she shifts her gaze to one of the younger gymnasts who's asking her for help with something.

Lewis shrugs beside me. "Depends, do you think she feels the same way?" I turn back away from Callie and start to collect my things, stuffing my clothes into my gym bag and contemplating everything that's happened between us over the last couple of months. Does she love me? I'm not sure yet, maybe that means she's not quite there.

"I'm not sure if she's there yet." I say as Lewis and I head to the locker rooms, towels hanging over our forearms. Lewis, pushes open the door and I spot Kyle sitting on the bench, his head buried in his phone screen.

"Maybe wait for her to say it first then." Lewis says, swinging his bag into a locker and heading for the showers.

"I hate this uncertainty, I know how I feel about her but I don't want to come on too strong and scare her off. I also don't want to hide my feelings, I feel like an idiot." I huff, following behind Lewis into the showers. I strip off my clothes and hang them on the hook outside my cubicle, stepping into the steaming water.

"You're not an idiot, you've just never been in love before. It's new man and you're learning, that's nothing to be ashamed of." Lewis says, his voice slightly raised so I can hear him through the splatter of water and the shower curtain between us. "She's the first girl you've ever loved, she'll be ecstatic to hear that when the time is right."

A light laugh rumbles in my throat. "She'll be the only girl I ever love I can guarantee you that, because there's no way I'm ever losing her."

Chapter 25

Callie

I thought I'd get out unscathed today, considering the fact I was only supposed to be 'helping out' the freshmen gymnasts, preparing them for their first practice competition tomorrow. Somehow I ended up on the bar, demonstrating something that Ellen requested of me when my hands weren't adequately chalked up, leaving me with a gaping rip in the centre of my palm. It hurts like a motherfucker and the entire drive to Sean's after practice all I can think of is dousing it in freezing water to cool the burning skin. There's a party tonight at Sean's house and I can't fucking wait to get drunk off my face so I can forget about the competitions I have coming up next week that I'm far from ready for. When I pull up outside I don't bother to knock, I spend a hell of a lot of time here and the guys don't mind me just walking in unannounced. Although I did get instant karma for that once when I walked through Sean's front door and found Kyle naked on the couch, balls deep inside some random puck bunny. He of course thought it was hilarious, but I've struggled to look at him the same way since. I accidentally use my bad hand to twist the doorknob and curse at myself under my breath before shoving the door open with my foot. Kyle, Lewis and Nick are all on the couch, shovelling something into their mouths whilst they drool over some half naked girl on the TV screen. I go

straight to the kitchen, dropping my bag from my shoulder in the hallway
and turning on the cold tap before sticking my palm under it.

"Ah fuck!" I yell, gaining the turning of three heads in my direction from
the couch. The horny zombies soon turn back to their movie when they see
I don't have any limbs hanging off or anything.

Sean's loud footsteps descend the stairs, having heard me yelling in pain.

"What's wrong baby?"

I twist my neck to look at him, he has those grey sweats on that I was
wearing whilst he was away, they look much hotter on him. The deep v
shape leading down to his impressive package catches my eye as he tucks
his hands into his pockets, the sweats shifting lower on his hips.

"I have a really bad rip," I say, squeezing my hand into a fist and wincing
as the raw skin contracts. "I need to clean it but it's painful as shit."

Sean reaches across me and tears off a piece of kitchen towel, damping it
under the cold water as Kyle brushes past him on his way to the fridge. He
gives my shoulder a squeeze as he leaves the kitchen again, arms full with
beers and popcorn.

"Here, let me do it." Sean reaches for my hand but I put my balled up fist
behind my back, snatching the wet towel from him with my other hand.

"Let me look after you." He says sternly and I'm automatically turned on, I
love when he gets bossy with me.

I scowl at him. "No, I look after myself, I always have."

"You don't need to anymore." He reaches around my body, snatching the
wet towel out of my balled up fist and polluting my lungs with his manly
aroma.

His fingers dig into my hips and he lifts me off my feet. My ass lands on
the kitchen counter and the zombies on the couch turn their heads to see

what's happening. I fold my arms over my chest and purse my lips when Sean sinks his hands into my thighs and brings his face closer, his minty breath tickling my tongue.

"Sit your pretty ass on there and let me clean your hand." He whispers, pulling my hand towards him and prising my fist open.

I'm not finished fighting yet though so I snatch it away from him. "No, I don't need y—"

He smacks a hard kiss against my lips, silencing me and splaying his hand across my back, pulling my chest to his. "Callie," he sighs, pressing another lighter kiss to my flushed lips. "Just shut up for once and let me take care of you."

I try to scowl but my cheeks betray me and turn a light shade of pink as I slap the back of my hand into his, allowing him to clean my gaping wound.

He smiles triumphantly and kisses my warm cheek. "Good girl,"

Oh god.

My pussy is all excited now, hearing those two magic words and thinking she's about to get some…maybe she is. Sean's eyes find mine, swimming with confusion as I clench my thighs together and suck my bottom lip into my mouth, trying to calm the warmth that's spreading down my inner thighs.

His eyebrows knit together as he watches me squirm on the counter. "What?"

"Nothing," I shake my curls, one falling over my eyes as I watch his large fingers gripping my wrist, the other hand gently dabbing at my rip. Why am I so turned on right now?

He glides his damp hand up my thigh, reaching the hem of my shorts. "Are you…?" He dips his fingers below the hem, into my thong and ghosts them over my sopping clit. "Oh fuck," He mutters, pulling his hand out and leaning into my ear so his eavesdropping friends don't hear. "Is that because I called you a good girl?" His voice is so sexy, raspy and deep and I just want to climb him.

I nod fast. "Can you help me with that?" I tilt my head, gesturing to the heat radiating from the apex of my thighs.

His eyes darken with a sparkle and he twists a lock of my hair around his finger. "Get upstairs now."

Sean's hands are covering my waist, lifting me off the counter and dropping me to my feet before his palm lands with a clap on my ass. I run up the stairs, Sean following behind me, his loud footsteps banging up the staircase before I swing open his bedroom door and throw myself back onto his bed.

He really does help me with my situation, yanking my shorts down my legs and feasting on my pussy like a starving man would. He makes me come, twice on his tongue and when he's done I'm panting, gasping for breath. He runs his warm hand up my bare stomach and leaves a tight kiss on my parted lips.

"You can pay me back later." He winks and strolls into his bathroom to shower, ready for the party that starts in an hour.

I needed that orgasm, this man pretty much has me in a constant state of horniness, always waiting for the next time he'll make me feel fucking incredible.

When Sean emerges less than 10 minutes later he's naked, my favourite part of his body hanging between his legs, begging me to just stick out my tongue for a taste.

I think I may have an unhealthy obsession with him.

He watches my eyes as they follow him across the room, shaking his head as a cocky smirk spreads across his face. He takes my black dress from his wardrobe and throws it at me, gesturing for me to go and change before people start arriving. I stand up from the bed with a huff and salute him playfully before trapping myself in his bathroom for the next half an hour, taking a hot shower, taming my mane of curls and covering my face in makeup. When I step out of the bathroom Sean has left the bedroom, his expensive aftershave still filling the room and making my pussy excited again. I adjust my black thong and twist my body in front of the mirror, admiring the backless, thigh length dress I'm wearing. I step into my sparkly heels, giving me an extra four inches of height, making it even easier for me to pull Sean in for a kiss the second I get my ass down those stairs. I take one last look in the mirror, ruffling my hair and tapping my lipgloss stained lips before pushing open Sean's bedroom door and descending the stairs.

Chapter 26

Sean

The music has started pumping, rocking the house back and forth as people start arriving. The gymnastics team are always here first, Lois being quicker than usual to find me in the sea of people so she can attempt to piss me off within five minutes of arriving. Callie still hasn't come downstairs so I wait for Lois, Jennifer and Anais to vacate the corridor and find their seats in the living room before I make my way over to the stairs. Before I even get there I hear the click clacking of her heels and when I look up I have to blink, at least five times to make sure what I'm seeing isn't a hallucination.

"Wow, you…you look beautiful." I gape, watching my girl take one step at a time down the staircase. She looks like she painted that dress on, stitching it to her skin for a perfect fit. I meet her at the bottom step, her face almost equal with mine as her heels and the step give her more height than usual. "You always look beautiful but I'm sure you get sick of hearing me say it."

She shrugs and plants her manicured hands on my shoulders. "I like hearing it."

I run my hands up her bare back, the dress swooping down where her spine curves. "Good," I lift her off the bottom step, putting her on the ground and bracketing her jaw. "Because I like telling you how beautiful you are." I press our lips together for a beat then grab her hand and lead her into the kitchen, pouring us both a drink.

Only half an hour passes by before my stomach is grumbling again, I know I'm a bottomless pit but I'm even hungrier than usual, considering I ate Callie's pussy before coming downstairs a couple of hours ago. I think I might need more of that later.

I get up from the sofa, brushing past Kyle and making my way to the kitchen for the third time tonight and piling my plate with pizza. The house is pretty packed now, gymnasts, hockey players and everyone in between crowding the living room, kitchen and hallway. The only part of the house that we make off limits is upstairs, none of us need to be finding some horny freshmen fucking on our beds when we go up there later.

When I get back to the couch, letting myself fall down next to Nick and starting to shove a huge slice of pepperoni covered pizza into my mouth, I feel a warm breath against my ear.

"Do you ever stop eating?" Callie whispers and I turn my head slightly, brushing my lips against her warm cheek. Her perfume is strong, intoxicating and I don't know if it's the alcohol but I'm drooling as her scent washes over me.

I've not spoken to her much tonight, just watched her from across the room, dancing, swishing to the music with her friends and losing herself for once, letting her hair down. I love to see her like that, relaxed and not as highly strung as she usually is when training is getting on top of her. I know she wants to get drunk tonight, I can already smell the heavy alcohol on her breath as she leans into my ear.

I shake my head, pizza still making it's way down my throat and into my growling stomach. "No…and I'll be wanting dessert soon too." I wink and she lets her eyes flicker around the room, making sure my sister doesn't spot us before dropping a light kiss to my jaw and starting to saunter away. God, that dress is something else, as much as I'm a fan though it's the creamy skin underneath that I want to see. I'll have to rip it off her soon and fix the shredded fabric later. I grab her wrist before she can get too far away from me and pull her closer, making her sit on the edge of the couch next to me.

"I don't like hiding this from Lois, I want everyone to know you're mine." I say, my hand hovering next to her bare thigh. I want to grab it, feel her baby soft skin on my palm but I know she's already panicking from the way she keeps looking over her shoulder. Lois couldn't be more fucking clueless, she's past drunk already and dancing with Anais, grinding against her and shaking her dark waves back and forth, eyes closed as she lets the music take over her body.

Callie shuffles next to me, laying her hand over mine. "I know, I'm just worried about what she'll think of me."

"Ouch," I say, chuckling quietly and watching our fingers intertwine where they rest on the sofa.

"I don't mean it like that," she says, tightening her hand around mine and giving me a reassuring squeeze. "I just don't want her thinking that her captain is some sort of puck bunny all of a sudden."

I lean closer, watching Lois sway with the music over Callie's shoulder. I leave a kiss in her hair, her dark curls tickling my nose.

"It's ok, we can keep it a secret… for now." I watch her eyes soften as she looks down at our hands. "I guess we'll have to tell your dad at some point too."

Her head snaps up, eyes wide with horror. "Woah, steady on there Captain."

I huff a laugh, lifting her hand to my mouth and leaving an lingering kiss on her soft skin, tasting her perfume on my tongue. She stands up, straightening her dress and raking a hand through her hair before swishing away, looking at me once over her shoulder as she goes.

"Any pizza left man, or did you inhale it all already?" Nick bumps my shoulder when he stands up from his seat next to me.

I nod and point to the kitchen. "Left one slice just for you." I smile, mouth crammed with pizza again.

I watch over my shoulder as Nick makes his way to the kitchen counter. Callie is grabbing something too, another drink I think or maybe two, I don't know. I'm distracted again by her smooth skin, the way her spine curves and leads down to that perky ass that I want to grab. Nick says something to her, gesturing towards the lemonade bottle that sits next to her arm on the other side of the counter. I see her emerald eyes flash up to his for a moment, then they roll in that sassy way they always do and her face twists in disgust. She takes a drink in each hand, flicking her head and causing her curls to fall down her back before she brushes past Nick and leaves him with a face creased with confusion. I let my chin fall to my chest, stifling my laugh as Nick falls back down beside me on the couch. "Your girl's in a mood," He mutters, shoving a slice of cheese pizza into his mouth and wiping the sauce off his lips with the back of his hand. The guy eats like a fucking animal.

I look over at my baby, she's laughing with Lois, her hand on her shoulder as she hands her another drink.

"Nah," I say, pointing at my girl. "She's good, she just doesn't like you." I'm trying not to laugh, honestly I am, but watching a tiny girl like Callie put Nick in his place is just too fucking funny. He could do with someone taking him down a peg or two, the man's ego is almost as big as mine… almost.

He huffs again and takes another bite. "Why, what did I do?"

"You're a fuck boy."

"So were you before you met her and she likes *you*." He scoffs and folds his crust, cramming it into his mouth and chewing hard.

My laugh slips out before I can stop it, the couch dipping as Kyle lands beside me. "Yeah, she likes me now, but trust me, I fucking knew about it when she didn't."

"Who are you kidding?" Kyle pipes up from my left side. "She still doesn't like you."

I nudge his shoulder with mine, his drink lapping up the side of his glass and wetting his hand.

"You're probably right, I think she just puts up with me at this point." I chuckle, hauling myself up from the couch and heading to the bathroom for a piss.

I know what I just said isn't true, I know Callie likes me, she told me last night that she likes me as much as I like her. I remember distinctly because my heart tried to burst through my rib cage when she said it.

Chapter 27

Callie

I'm pretty drunk right now and I know it's my own fault but I needed the alcohol tonight. I have a busy couple of weeks coming up with competitions and other shit that I'm less than prepared for and I was fully planning to ease the pain with as many drinks as I could pour down my throat tonight. It's been about an hour since I last talked to Sean but I've felt his eyes following me around the room most of the night. I love that he watches me, I've never had anyone want me as badly as he does and it makes my heart flutter uncontrollably every time I accidentally catch his eye.

I decide to ditch my heels on my way to my favourite room in the house, the one with the alcohol.

Ok maybe it's my second favourite, after Sean's bedroom of course.

I see him get to his feet as I pass him, his bright eyes fix on my ass as I move across the floor, his footsteps covering mine as he follows me to the kitchen. My bare feet pad across the kitchen floor before I reach for the vodka, pouring a generous amount into my now empty glass. I feel Sean's presence behind me, his tall, looming frame shadowing over me and making me feel tiny as usual.

His warm breath hits my neck. "Put that down."

I spin around to face him and hit his dimpled face with a scowl. "Don't tell me what to do Taylor." I'm feeling extra sassy tonight, the vodka sloshing through my bloodstream and creating a wave of attitude that I suddenly want to drown him with.

"I think you've had enough now Cal." He sighs, warm eyes melting into mine. "I know you're just trying to numb your anxiety about your competitions next week but you need to stop now, it's enough." His voice is velvety in my ears, soft and gentle.

I love when he's like that with me, pulling out his warm, fuzzy side and giving me all of it on a plate. I just want to pounce on him like a tiger, devouring every inch of him when he treats me this way, like he's afraid of breaking me with his words alone.

What comes out of my mouth doesn't reflect that though.

"Sorry, are you my dad?" I spit, lifting the glass to my lips and letting the burn run down my throat.

Sean runs his hand down his face, scratching at his jaw for a moment before I lift the glass to my mouth again. His eyes darken and before the devil's nectar can touch my lips he whisks my glass away, tipping the contents down the plughole. The red I see behind my eyes can't be normal and I'm going to blame the alcohol for the way I behave towards Sean right now. I know he cares about me, but how dare he read me like a fucking book and then take my drink away like I'm a child? Forget pouncing on him, devouring every inch of him. I'm going to fucking tear him to pieces.

"You're drunk baby, no more." He coos, bracketing my jaw with his cold hands and I smash my palms against his chest, barely moving him but it felt good all the same.

I shake his hands off my face. "Go and fuck yourself Sean!"

I march past him, arms across my chest but he doesn't let me get far. He snakes his arm around my middle and yanks me back to him, holding me tight against his body, his comforting warmth coupled with his familiar smell making me forget why I'm so mad at him.

"Don't." He warns, the usual bright, caramel flecks in his eyes darkening to an espresso.

I pull my bottom lip between my teeth and fight not to let my gaze slip to his lips. But I fail miserably and his face instantly softens, melting as he stares at my mouth.

"Kiss me." He murmurs, leaning closer and suffocating me in his heavy presence. "You haven't kissed me all night."

I flick my head over my shoulder. "Lois might see."

He holds my chin between his thumb and forefinger, pulling my attention back to him. "Let her see, I couldn't give less of a fuck. I'm gonna kiss my girl whenever and wherever I want." He coos and my knees falter, I could blame the alcohol for that too…but I won't.

Sean's lips are on mine before I have chance to muster up another protest, and once I feel how hungrily he kisses me I don't care who sees anymore. I almost climb his body like a tree, tightening my fist in his hair and smashing our mouths together repeatedly, not caring that I can barely draw in a breath. He tastes like beer and I lap up every drop with my tongue when it hits his. I have no idea how long I'm wrapped up in Sean, the way he holds me against him, the way his tongue explores my mouth like this is the last time he'll ever kiss me, like he needs to memorise every crevice of me.

After god knows how long I feel a light tap on my shoulder, followed by a muttered curse. I break my lips apart from Sean's and see a very drunk

Lois holding onto the kitchen counter next to me, her eyes droopy and her body swaying like she's on a fairground ride.

"Careful Cal," she slurs, "he's probably got chlamydia all over him, make sure he wraps it before you get hot and sweaty." She chuckles, her Sean-like dimples appearing deep in her cheeks.

Wow, she's seriously shit faced.

Sean clears his throat and holds my waist with one strong hand, tucking me into his side. "Actually Lo, Callie is my girlfriend."

Lois blinks more times than I can count, a wash of disbelief making her face pale. Her eyes move between us a few times, flickering over Sean's hand placement on my waist before she throws her head back in laughter. Her eyes crease and she holds her stomach, wagging a pointer finger at us both as her eyes flood with tears.

"You two are hilarious!" She waves us off and stumbles back towards the couch, drink in hand.

Thank god she's not in her right mind.

Sean pulls me back around to face him and dips his face to mine. "See?" He nudges my nose with his own lovingly. "I told you she wouldn't care." I sigh with irritation. "She's drunk, it doesn't count." I slam my hands against Sean's solid chest, scrunching my eyebrows at him. Why did he have to do that when I told him I didn't want Lois knowing about us? The man is so infuriating, I want to rip his balls off sometimes.

Don't think it, don't think it, don't think it.

But then I'd have nothing to play with.

I thought it.

He grips my wrists as my palms attack his torso again. "Stop being a naughty girl or I'll have to punish you." He half groans, half growls.

My thighs are suddenly stuck together, my lip between my teeth again and my eyes glued to his. How does he flick that switch in me so easily?

"Is that a threat or a promise?" I whisper, tiptoeing up to breathe against his ear. I see the shiver roll over him before I feel his hands on my hips in a bruising hold.

His lips ghost over the shell of my ear. "Which one do you want it to be?" Now it's my turn to shiver, a ripple running from my ears to my toes as Sean brings his face back to mine, dipping his head and running his thumb along my bottom lip. I literally can't take my eyes off his.

"A promise," I breathe, my heart pounding against my rib cage.

Sean's eyes flash over his shoulder before he tugs at my elbow. "Come on," he says, dragging me towards the stairs.

"Now?" I gape, watching my teammates collapsing onto the couch in the living room, finally giving up the fight to stay on their feet after drinking their collective weight in alcohol.

I resist a little, keeping my anxious eyes on everyone in the living room. I down know why I'm so worried, most of them are too drunk to notice a tornado ripping through the house.

Sean halts and turns to me, our hands intertwined as we reach the bottom of the stairs. "Yes, now, you think you can turn me on like that and then make me wait?"

I rip my hand from his and clap my palm across the back of his head. "I can do what I want."

He turns around, face cracked into a crooked grin that splits his face in two, dimples out in full force as he wiggles his eyebrows at me.

"Wow, you're extra feisty today baby." He folds his body in half, tipping his chest below my hips and hoisting me over his shoulder. I don't bother to fight him, I'm desperate to let him rip this dress off me anyway and as much as I love to make him work for it I think the vodka has taken the real fight out of me tonight.

Sean bursts through his bedroom door, dropping his chest and making me land on the bed with a soft thud. His king sized mattress swallows me and I spread my arms and legs like I'm making a snow angel. I hear him laugh but my eyes are closed, letting my alcohol laced blood sink straight to the middle of my thighs. When he climbs over me, creating a shadow across my face I feel his warm skin covering me. He's naked, I can feel it. Without opening my eyes I tilt my head to the side and gain another titter from Sean, he knows exactly what I'm asking for and he doesn't hesitate to sink his face into my neck. He sucks at my skin, wetting and nipping at it as his makes his way down towards the neckline of my dress.

"Now these," he says, pulling my dress down and burying his face between my breasts. "These are my favourite." He shuffles down further, pulling my dress with him and whipping it off me so I'm naked too. "Actually, scrap that," he coos, tipping his head down between my open thighs. "This is my favourite."

I finally peel my eyes open, watching him transfixed as he sucks at my pussy, groaning with delight as my back arches off the bed without my permission. Before I have chance to come he scampers up my body like a monkey and presses himself into me without warning. I gasp, writhing at the size of him and clawing at his tight back, digging my manicured nails into his muscles. I clamp my legs around his torso, begging him to drive deeper into me as he kisses me desperately.

"Oh fuck," I hiss, grabbing Sean's face and smashing his lips onto mine. He kisses me like I'm the only thing he'll ever need and I feel my legs start to shake with my impending orgasm. Sean pulls out of me and flips us over so I'm on my knees, my pussy waiting, begging for him to fill me again. He lowers his face and I feel his beer laced breath against my clit. "You look fucking incredible." He murmurs, before sucking the throbbing bud between his lips and taking me over the edge. He fills me again, making me scream his name into the mattress, forcing my face down to drown out my pleasure filled shrieks.

"I want to come inside you again baby." He pants, fisting my hair and wrapping it around his hand, pulling my chest up from the mattress so our bodies stick together. "Can I?" He whispers into my ear, twisting my nipple between his fingers.

I nod, shaking with intense pleasure again as Sean's thrusts become deeper and sloppier. I know he's close so I reach back, holding the nape of his neck and twisting my face to kiss him. All I have to do is run my tongue along his bottom lip and he collapses on top of me, cursing my name under his breath as the orgasm crashes over him.

He rolls off me after a moment and I stand up, watching his come run down the inside of my thighs.

He groans and I turn to face him. "Why is that so fucking hot?"

His face is pained, his quickly deflating cock in his hand like he's waiting for round two. I purse my lips, smirking at him and saying nothing as I head for his bathroom to clean myself up.

Chapter 28

Sean

"You're staying over tonight right?" I say, glancing up at the dark haired beauty that stands naked, tapping a finger to her red painted lips as she looks in the mirror. Her lipstick is mostly worn away from the starved kisses I stole from her earlier but she pouts her delicious mouth and attempts to salvage it anyway.

She twists her body, leaning back against the wall and stretching out her tight stomach. "Do you *want* me to stay over?"

I nod, gulping as I trace her milky curves with my eyes. "Of course I do, I always want you with me."

Her face pales a little and she brings her manicured nail to her lips, nibbling on the varnish and I watch her gaze fall to the carpet. I take a few long strides across my bedroom to reach her, planting my hands on her bare hips and dipping my face into her curtain of curls.

"What's wrong?" I murmur, hoisting her chin up and lifting her emerald eyes from where they anxiously rest on the ground.

The second her gaze fixes on mine she blurts, "I'm scared," then her shaky hands hold onto my biceps like she's clinging to the edge of an unstable cliff edge.

"Of what?" I whisper, tucking a loose curl behind her ear.

She sighs deeply and her eyes turn melty as she captures mine. "That this is it. That we're forever."

Woah, I wasn't expecting her to say that, but honestly, she's hit the nail on the head.

I push down the smile that wants to lift my lips and instead deepen my gaze, holding Callie's jaw in my palms and forcing her to look at me. "Me too," I breathe, rubbing my thumbs rhythmically across the splattering of freckles on her cheekbones. "Because I'm certain that we are, and that's fucking terrifying." My lips part on a chuckle and Callie's face gains back some of it's usual pastel pink colour. "But we'll be scared together baby, this shit is new to both of us. I don't want to brag but," her eyes flicker to mine, gaining me a roll filled with attitude. "I don't think you ever felt this way about Joel."

I think I'm right…god I hope I'm right.

"You're right." She sighs. *Thank fuck for that.* "I never did and I think that's why I'm so scared. I thought I knew the relationship game really well but the way I feel about you is just…it's different."

"Good different?" I murmur, raking my fingers through her thick tresses, a smile creeping onto my face before I can stop it. She nods, a shy smile lifting her lips and my entire face cracks open and blinds her. I love when she's open about her feelings towards me, it's rare that she expresses her emotions with words so when she talks like this with me, so open and vulnerable I feel like I'm looking through a window into her soul. It's fucking addicting.

I slide my hands down to her hips and pull her naked body to my chest, our warm skin colliding and making my chest flutter. "I'm a catch aren't I?

A weapon on and off the ice." I lift a taught bicep and squeeze, admiring as the muscle strains against my skin.

When my eyes fall back to Callie her fist is on her hip, eyebrows pulled together. "You're on thin ice Taylor." *I love when she tells me off.* My dimples deepen further and I smack my lips against Callie's jaw, feeling the goosebumps ripple everywhere my open mouth touches. I feel her shoulders relax as my hands run over them, down her bare back, heading for her ass. I cup both cheeks in my hands, giving her perfect ass a hard squeeze and hauling her into me. She only gives me a few seconds to hold her to me, just staring at her pouty lips and daydreaming about sucking them into my mouth before she shoves at my chest, brushing past me and grabbing her dress from the floor. She slips it over her head, shaking out her curls and turning back to face me as I stand there, still naked and watching her every move, mesmerised. I think I could watch her stare at a wall and never get bored.

"Speaking of ice…" she smirks, smoothing her dress over the curve of her ass and turning to look at her open back in the mirror. "You have a game on Tuesday right?" I nod, clearing my throat but remaining silent, hypnotised by watching her move. "I'm gonna come and watch."

"Thank god," I say, finally picking up the bundle of boxers on the ground and pulling them up my legs, hiding my deflated cock. "I always play better when I know you're watching." I catch Callie's sneaky smile that she tries to hide by turning away from me.

"That reminds me," I continue, unraveling my jeans and hoisting them up my legs. "I need a hair tie from you, to wear around my wrist when I play."

Callie spins back around, padding closer, her bare feet sinking into the carpeted floor. "Why?" She says, head tilted in confusion.

"For good luck, you're my lucky charm." I smile, throwing her a wink and earning myself yet another eye roll.

Callie drops to her knees, sticking her ass in the air and rummaging under my bed. She pulls out a handbag, popping the button and rifling around inside for a moment before triumphantly holding up a black hair tie. She gets to her feet, moving into me and securing it around my wrist. I tilt my face down, crushing my mouth to her's for a beat and whispering a, "Thank you," against her soft lips.

"Hey, I hope you don't think I'm really fucking nosey for asking this but…" Her wary eyes capture mine and I nod for her to continue. "How much did it cost for you to come to Redwood? I know your parents are rich but it must have cost a fortune to send you and Lois here."

That's not at all where I thought she was going with that. I was expecting a question about how old I was when I lost my virginity. Or how many girls have I slept with, something along those lines but money is never really something we've talked about. Callie is fully aware that my parents are high flying lawyers with their own business in London. Our conversation about family never really went past where our parents live and where we grew up. Callie had a few choice inquires about why her ass started burning when she sat in my car, that's how my parents came up. She wanted to know how a 23 year old hockey player who doesn't currently have a side job managed to afford such a new car with instantly heating seats. I told her that my parents bought it for me as a birthday gift last year and that's how their overflowing bank accounts came into the conversation.

"Well, it cost a lot when I was at Preston while I waited for my space to open up here. Redwood was always my first choice university especially because they offered me a full scholarship, so now it costs nothing." I shrug, raking a hand through my curls and covering my stomach with a t-shirt.

Callie's face drops, her mossy green eyes following. "I didn't know you were on a full scholarship...I'd have killed for one."

I let out a light chuckle. "Don't be so entitled Cal, we all know your dad pulled some strings to get you into Redwood. Bit of a coincidence you were then made captain of the gymnastics team too." I laugh, half joking, half serious.

I know Callie is talented, I've seen her body move in that impossible way it does through the air like a bird. The way she springs across the floor like her spine is made of rubber bands and the way she twists and turns with such precision. She's impressive to say the least. But of course with her dad having been the head hockey coach here for almost ten years, she must have seen the advantages of that. I'm sure he did his best to talk to all the right people, ensuring his only daughter got a place at the most sought after sports university in the country.

When I look back at Callie her mouth has fallen open, eyebrows high with disbelief. "*I'm* entitled?" She shrieks, flailing her arms in the air. "You're the one with two millionaire parents and yet here you are on a full scholarship that someone else could have had!" She's really yelling now, finger pointing at me aggressively, her cheeks flooding red with anger. This isn't like the normal attitude she throws at me, this isn't just a black cat with it's claws out, ready to swipe at me. This is real, bubbling, volcanic anger and I'm not sure how to play it, I don't think I've ever seen Callie truly mad like this. She's pretty fucking terrifying I won't lie.

"It's not my fault I'm talented." I say, and immediately regret it when Callie scrunches her hands in her hair, yanking at the roots with brimming frustration.

She blows out an exasperated breath and releases her curls. "Do you know my dad had to save almost my whole life for me to be able to come here? He gave up so much to get me where I am today." Her voice has mellowed a little, the red seeping out of her cheeks and down her neck, warming the purple welts I left there earlier.

"What about your mum?" I say, watching her face crumple slightly and again, regretting ever opening my big mouth.

I've asked about Callie's mum before and she always seems to skate around any mention of her, I know her parents are still together as Coach often mentions his wife and you can't miss the wedding ring attached to his finger. Callie has always been more than happy to talk about her childhood, all the happy memories and experiences but as soon as her mum is brought into the conversation she does a u-turn and changes direction.

She heaves a weighty sigh. "I don't want to talk about her."

Don't push her Sean, she's clearly upset.

"Why not?" Is what flies out of my mouth before I can stop it. My intrusive tendencies will get me in trouble one day I know but I've always pushed Callie to her limits, there's no use stopping now.

I see her usually bright eyes turn a murky colour as they mist over and she tips her head down so I can no longer analyse her.

"Just leave it Sean." Her voice has transformed into a whisper, the warning still creeping it's way through her hard tone.

But of course, I don't heed the warning, I never have with her.

"No Callie, I won't just leave it, tell me."

"My mum has cancer!" She snaps, waving her hands in the air as if to say, 'happy now?' The answer is no, I'm not happy, not even a little bit. Why didn't she ever tell me this? I could have been there for her, she's been holding it together, trying to be strong on her own and I fucking hate that. My heart hates it too, looking at her crumpled face, the lines in her forehead as she sniffs back tears and the thought of her crying alone whilst she dealt with her mum's illness. All the while I was going about my day having no idea of the internal battle she was facing without me.

"She had it a year ago," she sniffs, "we thought she was ok now but, it's come back and it's worse than the last time. She says she's ok but I know she's not, she just insists on wearing a brave face all the time. I'm sure she does it for my sake." Her voice cracks with pain at the end and I want to fall to my knees at her feet, hug her warm thighs and tell her everything will be ok. But I can't do that, it wouldn't be fair to lie to her when I can't be sure everything *will* be ok.

Instead I opt for, "Baby I'm sorry, I didn't know." She smacks my hands away when I reach for her, wanting to scoop her up and hug her so tight she forgets about everything. "Come here."

She shakes her head at me. "No Sean, go away."

"I wasn't asking." I say, grabbing her by the waist and dragging her to me. I lift her off the ground, my arms wrapping around her body like tree trunks. She instantly buries her face into my neck and her arms circle around me as I feel the moisture seep into my t-shirt.

"Let me hold you, please." I whisper into her mane of curls and she brings her thighs up to enclose my waist, tightening around me as she hoists herself up my body, sobbing into my shoulder.

She's given in, allowing me to comfort her, to be her anchor when her own is floating away. I love when she's like this, totally raw and vulnerable with me, letting me see the deepest parts of her.

I squeeze her tight. "Shhh, baby it's ok." *It's not though is it?* My inner voice screams at me not to give her false hope, to tell her things that aren't true just to comfort her in this moment. If there's one person in this world she can rely on to always be honest with her not matter what, I want it to be me.

"It's not ok Sean," she sniffs, her voice watery and unsteady. "She's going to die, I'm sure of it." Her face sinks back into my neck, the slippery skin there coated in her tears.

I take a breath, pulling on the big boy pants that I don't want to wear, but know I have to, for her. I'd do literally anything for her and I refuse to lie. "I can't tell you that's not going to happen." I murmur and feel her body tighten like a koala around mine, clinging for dear life. "But whatever happens I've got you ok? I promise I've got you."

Her wailing cuts through my chest, piercing a hole directly through my heart and making me want to keel over in pain. I drop to my knees, still holding her to me like we're superglued together.

I don't know how long we stay there, me gently rocking my girl back and forth and whispering, "It's ok baby," in her ear on repeat until her stuttered sobs finally cease. She peels her body off mine and I finally get a look at her face, her rosy cheeks and her puffy eyes. My t-shirt is quite literally soaked with tears, the cotton sticking to my skin where my baby's puddle of misery has spread across my shoulder. I can almost feel the weight float away from her shoulders at having shared that with me and let out all the pain she's likely been carrying around on her back for god knows how long. Callie fans her face, trying to cool her burning skin as I run my thumbs along her under eyes, wiping away the smudge of mascara.

I stand up, taking her hands and bringing her with me. "Wanna just stay up here for the rest of the night and cuddle?" I whisper, dropping my forehead to her's and breathing her in.

She shakes her head, her curls brushing over my jawline. "No, I need another drink. The mental breakdown plus the mind bending sex has sobered me up."

I stifle a titter and follow her out of my bedroom like the obsessed puppy that I am.

Chapter 29

Sean

The ping of my phone distracts me for a moment as I follow Callie down the stairs and back to the party. I lift it from my pocket, reading the passive aggressive message from my mum about why I haven't answered any of her repeated phone calls, when I bump into Callie's back.

"Shit, sorry baby." I mutter, grabbing her hips to stop me from knocking her flying forwards.

She's just staring, her body frozen like a block of ice and when I slide my hands up her biceps I feel her trembling.

I immediately move around her, creating a shadow over her face and blocking her wide eyed gaze from whatever it's locked on. "What's wrong?"

She lifts a trembling finger and points over my shoulder. "Joel...Joel is... he's here. Why, why is he here Sean?"

I twist my neck, tightening my grip on Callie's arms and pulling her into my side as I scan the downstairs for Joel. When my eyes land on him he's laughing without a care in the world, lifting his beer bottle to his lips and jabbing an elbow into Nick's stomach.

Nick. That fucker.

"I'm so sorry Cal, I told Nick not to invite him when he mentioned it a few days ago." I cup her face but she circles my wrists with her delicate fingers, releasing her face from my protective grasp.

Her eyes are still wide with fear, trembling hands grip my t-shirt in her small fist, pulling my body across to cover her's.

"I don't want him to see me, I can't deal with him tonight." She whispers in defeat and I turn back to face her, still concealing her tiny frame behind my huge one. "I think one mental breakdown is enough for one night."

I drop a kiss to her temple. "He can't do anything here baby, don't worry."

"I *am* worried Sean, I know how manipulative he can be." She sighs, scraping her curls back into a bunch.

"Yeah well, I'm here, so he won't do shit." I growl, looking over my shoulder at Joel's smug face again.

Nick's such a fucking arsehole for inviting the football team tonight, after I specifically told him not to. There's a good chance he'll be feeling my fist against his jaw at some point in the next week if he doesn't stop pulling stupid shit like this. Joel follows Nick across the room, landing with a soft thud on the couch that faces away from the kitchen, so I drag Callie behind me towards the island.

We manage to avoid Joel for another hour, hovering in the kitchen, me constantly checking over my shoulder to watch his every breath incase he decides to come over here. I'm pretty sure he hasn't spotted Callie or me considering we've barely moved from our spot since he got here. I've tried to steal as many kisses from her as possible but before she allows herself to get lost in me she breaks our lips apart and her worried eyes flicker back to Joel. I've been holding my piss for almost a solid hour now and I'm at the point where I'm squirming on the spot, grabbing at my crotch in discomfort.

"Callie I've really got to piss, come with me." I reach for her wrist and she allows me to hold it as she takes another sip of her drink.

She was right, the sex and the crying really did sober her up and it's like she started from scratch when we came back downstairs. She's by no means drunk right now, but I know she's hoping the liquid courage will aid her if Joel does set his eyes on her tonight.

She shakes her head, letting her emerald eyes land on mine. "It's ok, I'll be fine here for a minute while you go."

I don't want to leave her alone, I really don't want to leave her alone but I know better than to fight Callie on something once she's made up her mind.

I give her a quick nod and hold my lips to her cheek for a moment before scurrying off to the downstairs bathroom before my piss escapes and creates a puddle on the floor. I can hear the bustle from inside the bathroom, groaning with intense relief when I release a shower of piss over the toilet bowl, tipping my head back and releasing a breathy sigh.

"What the fuck was that phone call Callie? You're with Sean Taylor now? Are you fucking stupid?" I hear a muffled voice spit from the kitchen.

The bathroom door and where I left Callie standing are within a few metres of each other and now the music has died down I can hear everything.

"Fuck, he moves fast." I mutter, fumbling to zip up my jeans and dashing back out the bathroom, not even bothering to wash my hands. I guess Joel had spotted us loitering in the kitchen after all and was just waiting for his moment to pounce on my girl the second she was left alone.

I hear a grunt from Callie before she shrieks, "Let go of my arm Joel!"

I crash out of the bathroom and grab my girl from behind, sliding her body behind me and releasing her from Joel's bruising grip on her forearm. My brain is foggy, red mist circling my every thought and making me want to do nothing but smash this guys skull with my foot like a pumpkin. Instead my palms collide with his chest, pushing him back and making him almost trip over his own feet before he catches himself on the kitchen island behind him.

A sound between a snarl and a growl rolls up my throat. "Put your hands on her again and see what happens."

I know everyone's eyes are now on us, the commotion drawing in the drama loving assholes but I couldn't care less in this moment.

Joel's lips flicker with a knowing smirk as his eyes roll down my body. I have at least four inches on him and I know by the tiny gulp — that he thinks I don't see — that he's at least a little intimated by me.

"You'll be done with her soon anyway and then she'll be begging me to fuck her again." He mutters, murky eyes searching for Callie as she keeps herself hidden behind me, her wall of protection.

I bark a laugh, ready to crush his pathetic little daydream about ever touching my girl again but she beats me to it, moving around my body and crushing her back against my chest.

"Your dick is tiny Joel, get over yourself." She snarls and I snake my arms around her tight stomach, holding her securely against me and letting a proud grin split my face.

You tell him baby.

"Fucking slut," Joel whispers under his breath as Callie attempts to drag me back towards the stairs, leaving this pathetic weasel alone in the kitchen. I roll my neck and spin back around to face him, stepping into his space and blocking his line of vision.

I tip my face down to his. "Sorry I didn't quite catch that, could you repeat what you just said a little louder?" I say with contempt, my tone laced with patronising aggression.

"I said," he stands taller, pretending like his eyes don't keep falling to my balled up fist that rests against my leg. "She's a fucking slu—"

I don't give him chance to finish that word before my solid fists lands on his jaw, connecting with his nose soon after and sending him crashing into the island. He lands, like a crumpled mess on the floor, gripping his nose and looking up at me like I'm a crazed murderer. I certainly would consider murder after hearing him use such a derogatory word to describe my beautiful girl. The laughable part is that she couldn't be further from a slut, it took me a hell of a lot of begging and persuading just to get her on a date with me, she made me work even harder to get a taste of her heavenly pussy.

I grab the collar of Joel's stupid, fucking preppy shirt and haul him outside, almost lifting his feet off the floor as he continues to hold his nose in place. He groans in pain as I launch him onto the front lawn, watching him scramble to his feet and back away from me like he's an injured gazelle and I'm the monstrous lion who's hunting him. I slam the front door, not taking notice when it rattles the entire house from the force of my slam. I point a warning finger at Nick who's eyes are bulging out of his head from where he sits on the couch, Lewis gaping on his left and Kyle's prideful smirk on the right.

"He doesn't set foot in this fucking house again do you hear me?" I bellow and Nick nods, any sign of his usual arrogance disappearing into thin air. My eyes immediately scan the kitchen for Callie, her small frame leaning against the kitchen counter looking less than surprised by my outburst. I think she's the only one who could have predicted that I'd break Joel's nose over a comment like that, as when I approach her she simply rises on her toes and kisses the frown that's pulling down on my mouth.

"Let me see your arm where he grabbed you." I say quietly, lifting her forearm and examining the red fingerprint that's made it's home on her skin.

I don't fucking like that one bit, it's making me sick to my stomach to see another man's handprints on her. I'm the only one who gets to leave my mark on her body, she's mine and only mine. The protective, possessive monster rears it's head again and I yank her into me, swallowing her with my body and inhaling the scent of her coconut shampoo, forcing the burning anger to dissipate from my chest. I need to focus on her, making sure she's ok, not on that fucking waste of oxygen that thinks he still owns her. I drop urgent kisses all over her bare shoulders, her neck, her freckled cheeks and she hums with comfort ridden happiness.

"I'm ok Sean, really I am." She whispers as my lips detach from her neck. I bury my face in her shoulder, lifting her from the ground and bringing her to my height. "Don't say you're ok."

"But I am," she protests, curling her fingers into the wisps at the nape of my neck. "I promise." She whispers, her warm breath tickling the shell of my ear and making me shiver. "Thank you for doing that for me."

I pull my face out of her warm neck and catch her eyes with mine.

"Anytime,"

I plant a soft but possessive kiss on her pink lips and sigh as her tongue gently traces the length of my bottom lip.

Callie could so easily ruin me, make me fall in love with her and then break my heart. But I'd let her, if it meant I got even five minutes of her love, I'd let her fucking destroy me.

Chapter 30

Callie

The hockey team are no longer using our floor for their weight training, their gym was fixed about three weeks ago, the weak water pipe that continued to burst was replaced and there have been no problems since. As much as I love being around Sean — and I really do — I can't say I wasn't relieved to hear the hockey team would no longer be stealing our precious training time. My routines have improved slightly, I've been working my ass off trying to perfect them since competition season has started and I finally feel like I'm getting somewhere. Don't get me wrong they're far from gold medal standard but I've been scoring pretty well in my competitions considering these routines were the bane of my existence only a couple of months ago. Sean tells me how proud he is of me when I come home from a weekend of competitions and it makes my heart skip a beat every time those words leave his lips. I miss him insurmountably when I'm away, even though it's only for two days it feels like I'm missing an arm without him. When I come home to him he rubs my sore thighs and massages my back before devouring my pussy like he hasn't eaten in weeks. I know I'm falling in love with him and I fear I'm in so deep now there's absolutely no way I'll escape without having my heart broken in the process.

But I try to squash that thought down as I leave the gym after a long day of training, it's unusual for me to finish before Sean so today it's my turn to meet him at the rink. He's been waiting outside the gym for me everyday after training, driving me either home to my dorm or to his place where I stay the night at least three times per week and more often than not if I'm not staying at his place he's staying at mine. We're rarely apart, already reliant on each other's presence like oxygen. This relationship between us feels like it's rocketed so fast, going from me hating him one minute to teetering on the edge of love the next. But in the exact opposite way I feel like I've known that man my entire life, like he's always been there, waiting to fill that gap in my heart that only he can fit inside.

I won't tell him that though, I don't need to boost his already oversized ego.

I push open the double doors and the cold air hits me square in the face, making my eyes sting, water filling them as I make my way towards the edge of the rink. My dad has already left and the guys are just putting a few cones and other random hockey shit away that I have no knowledge or interest in. I lean my elbows on the side of the rink, watching Kyle and Sean play fighting like children and stifling my laugh. I love seeing Sean happy, it's my favourite hit of endorphins watching him in a state of playfulness like he is right now with his best friend. After a moment of them tackling each other, arms wrapping around each other's heads and loud bellowing laughter coming from the two of them as they wrestle each other to the edge of the ice, Lewis catches me watching and throws me a shrug accompanied with an eye roll as if to say, 'Children.' I nod back, acknowledging that I am very much in agreement, these 6-foot tall, 23 year old men are still very much children in adult bodies, but I kind of love it all the same. Sean soon spots me and glides across the rink, my smile growing wider the closer he gets. His chocolate curls are wild when he ruffles them with his icy hand, his brown eyes melting into me as he gets closer and my heart flutters as usual. Plus, he never looks hotter than when he's all kitted up in his hockey gear. My heartbeat settles between my thighs as Sean clashes with the half wall that I'm leaning on and dips his face to kiss me warmly.

"Hi beautiful girl," He whispers, planting a wet kiss on my cheek before spraying the back of his sweaty neck with his water bottle, cooling his hot skin. God, he's making me blush.

I stretch a sarcastic smile across my quickly reddening face. "Hi arrogant arsehole,"

Sean puts his water bottle down and smirks at me, letting his arms hang over the wall and dangle by my hips. Our faces are centimetres apart and I can taste his minty breath on my lips as the icy air creates clouds between us.

"Oh good," he snickers, "I was hoping you'd be in one of those moods today. We're going for a skate together before we leave." Sean ducks down behind the wall as my eyes widen and my throat tightens. I can't skate to save my life, I've always been a disappointment to my father's hockey genes considering I can barely stay upright on a pair of skates.

When he reappears he's holding a pair of white ice skates, dangling them from his hand and flashing me a shit eating grin. He knows I can't say no to his gorgeous face, his dimpled cheeks and his sexy caramel eyes, the man knows how to get his own way with me. I could never give up the fight that easily though, I can't let him think he's won just yet.

Daisy Egan

I fold my arms across my chest and jut my hip out to the side. "No, we're not. I can't skate Sean."

"Consider it a trust exercise." He muses, lightly placing one hand on the curve of my spine as he leans close to my face again.

All the other guys have left the rink now so it's just the two of us in this huge place and it's daunting as fuck to think about getting on the ice with Sean and completely embarrassing myself. The truth is I'm scared, terrified even because I know I'm no good at skating and every memory I have of it as a child includes my dad getting frustrated at my lack of natural talent on the ice. I always felt like a disappointment and the last person on earth I want to disappoint now is Sean Taylor.

Wow, never imagined a crazy thought like that would ever enter my mind. I'm not done with the sass just yet though. "You want me to trust you not to let me fall on that death rink?" I taunt but Sean's face softens a little, the smile fading and being quickly replaced with a serious look.

He slings the skates over his shoulder and holds my waist in his hands, squeezing it reassuringly. "I'd never let you fall…" His eyes capture me in their depth and he tilts his head down, lips brushing against mine. "Never," Then his lips connect with mine so softly it almost sends me to my knees.

"Sean, I'm not—" I start to argue again, still not wanting to back down of doing this terrifying thing and having to really trust a guy I'm not sure I'm 100 percent ready to embarrass myself in front of yet.

But Sean presses his finger to my lips, halting my resistance. "Baby, it wasn't an option."

I'm speechless, as much as my instinct is to continue to argue with him, the way he's taking control of me like that is so fucking hot I want to just burst into flames. So I huff, but takes the skates from his outstretched hand and sit down on the bench to put them on. I slip my feet into them, the unfamiliar stiffness and wobble when I place the blades on the ground is making my stomach slosh with anxiety.

Sean won't let me fall, I know he won't.

"Good girl," He says, his voice smooth and reassuring as he pats his thigh, offering to tie my skates for me.

I'm too fucking nervous to argue now, so I land my blade on his thigh and watch as a arrogant and triumphant smile creeps onto his face. He loves bossing me around and I love it too, the worst part is the fucker knows it. He holds his hands out to me, helping me to my feet and onto the slippery death rink. My legs are shaking, trembling with nerves as I take a couple of steps, digging my nails into Sean's biceps as he guides me, gliding backwards like it's the easiest thing in the world. I'm sure it is for Mr I'm good at everything. God, he still annoys the shit out of me.

How can someone so painfully attractive also be good at everything they try, even being someone's boyfriend which they've never done before? As if he can read my every thought he cracks a bright smile, picking up our pace across the ice. I can't pretend this isn't a little thrilling, being upright and sliding so smoothly across the slick ice, Sean's hands holding my waist tightly, making me feel safe and secure in his grasp.

"See, I told you I wouldn't let you fall." He grins, lovingly giving my waist a small squeeze.

I bark a laugh and then my heart drops into my ass when I wobble a little. "There's still time."

He purses his lips, forcing his own laugh back down his throat. "Do you trust me more now?"

"Yes," I answer too fast, not giving my brain time to think out a sarcastic answer like I usually would when every one of my brain cells is focused on not landing my ass on the freezing ice.

"Maybe…" I correct myself but it's too late.

Sean's arrogant grin is cracking his face wide open and before I have chance to fight him he bends down and throws my body over his shoulder, spinning us in a circle. I scream and pound his back with my fists, all the while trying not to piss my pants from laughing so hard. I hate to admit it, but it's actually been fun skating with Sean. Maybe I only thought I hated the ice so much because every experience I've had with it had heavily featured my dad yelling at me.

Sean drops me gently to my feet off the side of the rink and moves behind me, making his way off the ice too. I bend down to untie my skates and I hear a groan roll up Sean's throat. When I lift my head his fist is in his mouth and his muddy brown eyes are glued firmly to my ass.

"Can I help you?" I tease, watching as his eyes grow wider and his teeth dig further into his curled up hand.

He blows out a sharp breath. "Your ass is fucking exquisite."

"Yeah, I know." I smirk, pulling my already aching feet from my skates and standing back on solid ground.

Sean still has his skates on which means he's even taller than usual and he's quite literally a giant towering over me right now. My vagina does a dance, licking her lips and imagining how great she's going to be treated tonight, like most nights.

Sean leans down to my ear. "I'm going to fucking ruin you later." He whispers, causing a tiny whimper of anticipated pleasure to escape from my lips. He smirks again, loving the way his words affect me before smacking a fleeting kiss to my jaw and walking down the hallway towards the locker rooms.

My god, it's like my arousal switch is constantly on around him and I don't know how to switch the damn thing off.

Chapter 31

Sean

"Can we have some music on in here for once? It's like driving with my grandma." Callie grumbles, twiddling the knobs on my radio and then giving up with a sigh.

The radio is the one thing that lets my car down, the soft leather heated seats, the tan interior, the automated parking is all well and good, but having no radio is a bit of a shit one at times. I rummage in my pocket, lifting my ass off the warmth of my seat and sliding my phone from the tight front pocket of my jeans, frisbeeing it onto Callie's lap.

"Here, plug my phone in and choose something. I will warn you though," I reach over and squeeze her thigh. "My music isn't to most people's taste."

She rolls her eyes in the way I love and sighs. "Nothing about you is to most people's taste. Apart from your—"

"Dick," I jump in, finishing her sentence for her and earning myself a slap on the back of the head.

"I was going to say," she continues, her tone laced with familiar irritation. "charismatic personality." Callie huffs a laugh and I join her, lacing my fingers through her's as she selects a song from my playlist and sets the phone down under the radio.

When Luke Combs' 'When It Rains It Pours' blasts through the speaker
I'm surprised, thinking she'd choose a much more popular song to play
first. I love country music, it's no secret for people who know me, but I
never play music when Callie is in my car. All I want to do when she's
around me is talk to her about anything and everything. I've picked her up
from training every night for the last month and having not seen her all day
I have to put on my detective hat and find out everything there is to know
about her day, what she did, who she spoke to, how she felt etc. It's not a
controlling thing, it's just that I'm clearly totally obsessed with this girl and
I'm on a constant chase to learn everything about her. I let my hand relax
over her thigh and give it a gentle rub, sinking my fingers into her baby
soft skin and letting the music flow through me. This kind of music always
made me happy as a child, it was the one good memory I have of the
summer, having a break from hockey and driving down to the coast to
spend the week with my family. We'd swim in the ocean, go for fabulous
dinners in fancy restaurants and Lois and I would eat until we were sick.
My parents would always have a country playlist ready for the six hour
drive and Lois and I would sing along in the back before falling asleep
with our faces plastered against the windows.

The chorus of the song soon begins and when Callie's angelic voice starts
singing along word for word I'm dragged out of my trip down memory
lane and land back in the present with a thump. Callie knows all the words
to this song, her voice is like a lullaby, soft and sweet in my ears as she
leans her head back and lets herself get lost in the music. I try not to stare
at her in disbelief, really I do. I try to focus on the road ahead but I can't.
How the fuck does she know this song? There's no way she likes country

music too, it's so niche here and I don't think I've ever met anybody who likes the same kind of music I do. This woman is my fucking soulmate.

Callie turns to me after a moment, pausing her singing to ask, "What?" As I stare at her wide eyed.

I force a gulp. "Marry me." I croak and she furrows her brows, eyeing me suspiciously.

"Did you hit your head today?" She says and I let out a sharp laugh, wrapping her small hand inside my huge one and resting it in the dip between her thighs.

"How the hell do you know this song? I didn't peg you for a country girl Callie Burch."

"Don't judge a book by it's cover Sean, you'll get yourself in trouble." She taunts and my cock hardens in response.

He's constantly on alert around her anyway, never feeling satisfied unless he's buried 9.3 inches inside her wondrous pussy.

"My mum has always loved Luke Combs, she used to play him on repeat when I was a kid and it kind of became our thing as I grew up. She would take me on road trips when Dad was away coaching, it would be just the two of us and we'd sing until our lungs were aching." She smiles, eyes watery from the happy memories. "I miss those days with her, before she…" she looks up at me, sadness clouding her usually bright, mossy eyes. "Well, you know, before she got sick."

I suddenly feel the need to change the subject sharpish, I want to take her mind off this path of depression it's found itself on, so I rub my thumb across her bare thigh and turn the volume down slightly.

"Am I taking you home or are you staying at mine tonight?" I say, Callie lifts her head from where it droops and gifts me a light smile.

Daisy Egan

She sighs. "Take me home."

Oh, I didn't think she would want to be without me tonight. I never want to be without her.

"Ok…" I mutter, questioning myself now and wondering if I can actually read her at all. I thought for sure she'd want to stay with me tonight.

"Really?" I look over at her and her eyes narrow playfully.

"No, not really," Her breathy laugh makes my chest tight. "Why don't you just say that you want me to stay over at your house?"

The way the mood has lightened is a 'thank fuck' moment for me, just being able to drag her out of that sudden bout of sadness is something only I can do and the thought alone makes my heart beat quicken.

"Callie, I'd have you move in if it was my choice." I laugh, meaning every word but immediately wondering if I'm coming on too strong. I don't tend to stress about that too much anymore, I know how Callie feels about me and I'm not scared of being too much for her. But I still occasionally let my obsession with her make itself known and then spend a few hours worrying that she might change her mind about being with this love sick puppy and want to end things. But I should have more faith in her because her response leaves me speechless.

"Move in with you…do you mean that?" She whispers, eyelashes fluttering as she peers up at me.

I nod, trying to hide the lump in my throat as she bites the inside of her cheek, contemplating.

After a minute that felt like an hour she finally nods and says casually, "I'll think about it and get back to you."

I suck in my smile and lean over to kiss her forehead. "Ok baby, but remember I always get my own way."

There's that sexy eye roll that I love.

"I'll be getting my own way the second we step foot in your bedroom tonight Taylor, you wait and see." She flutters her eyelashes at me again, this time the flirty energy crashes over me like a tsunami.

I gulp hard. "What…what do you want me to do?"

She flashes me a sultry smile, then her eyes darken and she whispers, "I want you to choke me with your cock."

Oh my fucking god, I'm in for one hell of a night.

I practically drag Callie up the stairs the second we get back to my place, crashing through my bedroom door and undressing at the speed of light. Callie watches me amused, fisting her hip and pursing her sexy lips at me as I rip my clothes from my body. I march over to her, lifting her skin tight t-shirt over her curls and launching it over my shoulder. Her shorts go next, also flung over my shoulder and landing somewhere on my bedroom floor.

I point to the floor. "Get on your knees."

Callie swallows and licks her lips, anticipation burning behind her bright eyes before she drops to the ground in front of me. I fist my already painfully hard cock as Callie tilts her head back and gives me the perfect view of her moist, pink lips.

"Fuck my mouth and make me gag." She coos and I almost come all over her face right then. Her voice is raspy, full of need and it's so fucking sexy it hurts.

My eyes widen at her request. "What the hell has gotten into you today?"

"I just love—" She clamps her mouth shut and fights to keep her expression emotionless, but I know she's slipped up.

I twist her curls around my finger. "You love what?"

She shakes her head. "Nothing, just put your cock down my throat."

Sweet Jesus.

I don't need to be asked twice so I part her soft lips with my thumb and dip my erection inside her warm mouth.

"Oh my god," I groan as the moisture and the heat start the orgasm swirling in the pit of my stomach. But it's actually hard to focus on the physical pleasure after hearing the L word slip out of Callie's mouth so automatically like that. I know she loves me, she was going to say it, but I understand she's still wary, scared to completely let her guard down and that's ok. I can wait as long as she needs, but my heart gallops in my rib cage all the same, wanting to leap out of my body and makes it's home in her's.

She cups my balls in her small hand, massaging and pushing me closer to the edge. She licks slowly up my cock, teasing me as my head falls back and my hand roughly grips the hair at the nape of her neck, pushing my pulsating dick further into her hot, wet mouth.

"Jesus baby, you suck my cock so well." I stroke her face, running my thumb along the length of her jaw. "Good girl," The words leave my lips on something between a growl and a whimper.

Yes, this girl has me fucking whimpering.

She lets my cock fall out of her mouth with a pop and begins to run her fuck-able lips all the way up my shaft, licking, sucking and making me groan with desire. I part her lips again and a cocky smirk cracks her face as she watches me silently beg her for more, for relief preferably in the form of watching her swallow every last drop of my come. Her mouth opens for me again and I slip inside, revelling in the addictive way she takes my entire cock down her tight throat and totally milks me dry, swallowing my come and licking the residue from her juicy lips. I curse her name with a growl as she licks the last bead of come from my tip and wipes her mouth clean with the back of her hand. I help her to her feet and kiss her still wet lips, tasting myself on her tongue before leading her towards my king sized bed and lifting her from the ground, earning myself a high pitched squeal and battering of her hands against my chest. I launch her onto her back, watching my mattress swallow her tiny frame. God, I could just look at her all day. Her tight stomach, her soft, milky skin, the way her spine curves and trails down to the most perfect, grab-able ass to ever exist. Her perky tits with hard nipples in the centre, begging to be sucked between my lips, my tongue swirling over them. Then there's her face, that's a whole other masterpiece in itself. Her bright green eyes, the way they hold mine in that intense way like she's trying to speak through them. Her sharp jaw line and the splattering of tiny, honey brown freckles that coat her cheekbones, her thick eyelashes fanning against them as she blinks seductively at me, just watching me watch her. As my eyes finally land on her's I can see a sparkle behind them, a wondering, mesmerised look mixing with the usual fiery sass.

"Why are you looking at me like that?" She says delicately after a moment of silence between us.

I shake my head. "I just fucking love looking at you Cal, I could look at you all day."

Her mouth parts like she wants to say something, leaning up on her elbows, but instead she closes the gap between her lips and sighs as I start to move towards her, climbing onto the bed and covering her naked body with my own.

I kiss her jaw, sucking lightly on her skin and feeling her shiver beneath me. "Lie back now beautiful…" I lift my face to her's landing a firm kiss on her lips. "It's my turn to worship you."

Chapter 32

Callie

Sean made me come a total of three times last night, worshipping me as he promised he would and sending me into an orgasm induced sleep. Those orgasms are all I can think about this morning when I wake up to an empty bed and a note on Sean's pillow.

It reads:

'Gone to the rink baby, don't forget puck drop is at 12:30. Your seat is saved as usual princess.'

He adds a winking face to the end of his note, plus a heart with the letters C+S inside which makes me equal parts cringe and swoon. I flip my body over and stuff my face into Sean's pillow, soaking up every drop of his vanilla sweet smell and then swallowing the drool that pools in my mouth. I sweep a hand under my pillow for my phone, checking my messages and groaning when I see three from Ellen, saying she needs to talk to me urgently. I don't have training today so she can shove her urgent chat up her ass if she doesn't mind. My day is going to be spent cheering on my man at the rink then going out for drinks and proceeding to be respectfully railed into his mattress for the rest of the night. *Maybe I'm a sex addict now.*

Molly has also called me twelve times since last night so I tap on her number, watching as her contact photo appears on the screen. Her tongue is out, licking the ice cream that's clasped in her hand, her blonde waves flowing down her cheeks, eyes closed and a smile of childlike glee on her face. We had a weekend away together last year by the coast and spent the entire time eating ice cream and drinking cocktails, it was totally carefree. Come to think of it I'm not sure I've spent even one day like that since our trip last year. I barely get any time off and when I do all I want to do with it now is have my back rubbed and be smothered with kisses by my very own sex god hockey player. I still make time for my best friend of course, like right now as the phone rings out and I almost think she's not going to answer, but then her high pitched shriek comes flying through the speaker at me.

"Callie Burch!" *Uh-oh, I'm in trouble.* "Are we not friends anymore?" She squawks and I can picture her in the dorm right now. Hands on her hips, back against the kitchen counter as she throws crazy accusations at me, probably rolling her eyes as she does. If Anais is there she's sure to be rolling her eyes too, but at Molly's dramatics rather than at me for staying at my boyfriend's house for one night.

I push my laugh down my throat. "Yes, Molly Crawford we are still friends, best friends."

"Huh," she muses, "well, I would have thought a best friend would have answered at least one of my calls in the last twelve hours."

My laugh escapes before I can stop it. "I'm sorry Mol, I was busy being fucked into oblivion last night, couldn't really get to the phone."

Molly cackles like an evil genius. "I mean Sean Taylor *is* delicious, so I guess I forgive you."

"Wanna come to the game today? It's at 12:30 but I'm leaving in about half an hour. I can pick you up on the way?"

"Yes, yes, yes! I haven't been to a hockey game in forever. Ever since you started fucking the captain you've abandoned your best friend to watch the games alone, all so you can finger yourself when your boyfriend starts winking at you every time he scores a damn goal." I can hear the extra dramatic eye roll in her voice.

I hum in amusement and check the time. 11:10am, god I slept late this morning, I better get moving if I want to be on time to the game.

We make our way up the steps just behind the penalty box to find our seats, arms full of snacks that Molly insisted we needed. My coat pockets are stuffed with enough sweets to send us both into an instant sugar coma and when we sit down Molly plants an extra large Pepsi in my lap and begins sucking on her own straw.

"It's Preston again today right?" She asks, wriggling out of her coat and hanging it on the back of her chair. I nod, sipping on the ice cold drink and shoving my hands between my thighs to warm them. "I fucking love when we play Preston, there's always at least one fight and when I tell you I live for that shit…I mean I live for that shit."

I shake my head at her and hold back my laugh, attempting not to choke on my drink before placing it to the floor. I mean, Molly isn't wrong, there's something so hot about the way the guys fight on the ice, it's a major turn on. I've always loved to watch it but now I have Sean's beautiful face to think about and as much as it makes me horny watching him smash his fist into someone's nose on the ice, I also don't want him bruised when he comes home to me.

The guys start their warm ups, sliding across the ice effortlessly and battering puck after puck into the net at Kyle as he fights the repeated attacks. Sean scans the stands for me and when his eyes lock onto mine he skates over to the glass immediately, ignoring his teammates teasing when he blows me a kiss. They pat the back of his shoulder as they pass him, whispering taunting comments into his ear but the man isn't lacking confidence in any aspect of his life so he simply ignores them.

I wish I was more like him sometimes, able to not worry about what people think of me.

When I don't blow him a kiss back, rather flash him my middle finger and purse my lips, Sean curls his finger, gesturing for me to come to the edge of the ice. I get up reluctantly, not wanting to draw any extra attention to myself from the quickly filling stadium but Molly and Sean decide to team up and ruin my plan. Molly's hand lands against my ass with a slap as I stand up from my seat and make my way towards the steps to go down to the edge of the ice. A loud bang from the plexiglass grabs my attention and when I look down Sean's pointing a warning finger at Molly, eyes wide and teasing.

"Hey Crawford!" He yells and Molly playfully points her finger at herself, puppy dog eyes turned up to the max as she looks behind her like she has no idea who Molly Crawford is. "Don't fucking touch that ass, it's mine." I bury my face in my hands and scurry quickly towards where Sean is leaning over the wall at the edge of the ice. The second I'm within a metre of him he reaches for me, pulling me into the wall and smashing his lips against mine passionately, barely giving me chance to come up for air. I can feel people's eyes burning into me and I pray to god that one pair of them doesn't belong to my dad who's voice I can hear bellowing from the other side of the rink. I break the kiss after a minute and watch Sean's shit eating grin split his face before his eyes dance over my lips again and he leans closer.

I press my finger to his looming pout. "Nuh-uh big boy, you can have more later."

He bites his bottom lip and lifts his chocolate eyes to mine, stopping my heartbeat in the process. "Ok fine, I guess I better get back to," he throws a thumb over his shoulder, gesturing to his teammates who are still engrossed in their warm up, minus their captain. "that."

He smiles again and I curse him in my head for making my heart stutter so often. He holds his icy lips to my neck for a beat, arms cocooning me in a tight hug before flying back across the ice and making my thighs automatically clench together as I watch him. I scuttle back up to my seat and sink low in it, still feeling too many pairs of eyes on the back of my head.

"Now that," Molly gestures between Sean and I, "was hot." She smirks, wiggling her eyebrows at me and stuffing a handful of popcorn into her mouth, a few sweets poking out between her fingers.

I watch her in disgust. "Ew, you don't mix the two, like ever."

Molly kicks her heels up on the wall in front of us with a 'I don't give a shit because I'm iconic' shrug, just as the announcer asks all the players to leave the ice in preparation for the start of the game.

We're half way through the second period and Redwood are two nil up, Sean having scored both of those goals and pointed his stick at me obnoxiously every time. I thank god for the fact my dad has been too distracted with his other players to notice any of Sean's brazen attempts at flirting with me mid game. Molly has stuffed almost every kernel of popcorn into her mouth before the whistle blows again and we both watch wide eyed as Sean and another player take their helmets off and square up. I can see Sean's eyes darken and his hand grasps the other player's collar, yanking him closer and murmuring threats into his ear. Both of their faces are red with aggression and I can almost see the steam coming off them. The ref places a warning palm on both of their shoulders, muttering something and then backing away. He's allowing them to fight, which is common practice in hockey, as long as it's quick and clean. But I already know from the look in Sean's eyes that this fight will be anything but clean if he has his way, quick, yes, but not clean. Sean's never been one to fight clean, on or off the ice which he proved only a month ago when he smacked Joel at that party for calling me a slut. I have no idea what this fight is over, I was too busy daydreaming about Sean's tongue all over me later that I missed what provoked either of them. Sean's fist collides with the other guy's jaw first, making a piercing crack echo through the arena and everyone erupts. The crowd is shouting, bellowing even, as the two of them brawl, landing on the ice and throwing repeated punches towards each other. Sean is spitting something at the guy he's currently straddling, hissing something through gritted teeth and practically pinning the smaller guy beneath his heavy frame. Watching him evokes a ripple of heat to roll up my body, starting between my thighs of course and spreading up to my cheeks, heating them and making me blush.

This man can do anything he wants to me later and I mean *anything*.

The ref rips them apart after a couple more echoing smacks and splatters of blood hit the ice. Sean is still seething, I can feel his energy from here, the fiery anger emitting from him as he fights to get back to the battered player who's being carted off the ice by his coach. My dad's face can only be described as thunderous, eyebrows furrowed, deep lines in his forehead as he grabs the back of Sean's jersey and yanks him towards the edge of the rink. He's berating him, pointing fingers and spitting curses as he forces him down onto the bench. Sean quickly catches my eye and I pray my pink cheeks aren't visible from here. Our gazes crash and Sean's mouth twitches with a sly smile so I hit him back with my own.

Molly blows out a jagged breath next to me. "Jesus that was hot. I'm actually jealous that you get to go home with him tonight and let him fuck you until you can't walk." She groans and I let my laughter rip through me. She's not wrong, I am going to let him fucking break me later.

Chapter 33

Sean

"Sorry guys, but there was no way I was going to let Ryan fucking Pritchard talk about my girl like that and not smack him in the mouth." I breathe, rubbing a rough hand down my face, scratching at my dark stubbled jaw.

Kyle pats my back. "Don't worry man, we get it."

They don't get it though, none of them are in love, not like I am. Fucking obsessed would be a more accurate way of describing the way I feel towards Callie.

There are a few grumbles from my teammates as they fight with their jerseys and shorts, trying to strip off and head for the showers. I feel bad for fighting and getting myself shoved into the penalty box for five minutes, leaving my guys a man down but there was no way I could just do nothing. Ryan Pritchard has always been a fucking nuisance, a bit like Mac who hangs around us now, thinking he's some hot shot hockey player that all the girls want, when in reality he's a scrawny little runt who is just desperate to lose his virginity at the ripe age of 22. But I was willing to let bygones be bygones tonight.

Preston was my university before I came to Redwood so I'm very familiar with Pritch in more than one way. I'll admit I stole a girl from him one night at a party, she was eyeing me up whilst she sat on his lap and I knew he'd liked her for a while, but I was an asshole back then. Ok, *more* of an asshole. So I winked at her and that's all it took for her to trail behind me up the stairs and let me fuck her. I don't think Pritch has ever really forgiven me for that and that's why he started on Callie the second he saw me point my stick at her after my second goal.

"Wow, she's hot as fuck." He murmured as he skated behind me.

My head flew around, recognising his voice immediately. "Shut the fuck up Pritch."

He huffed a dirty laugh. "I heard Sean Taylor had finally got a girlfriend, but I guess you're still fucking some puck bunny on the side right?"

He's trying desperately to get a rise out of me, I have to try and contain the erupting volcano.

"Can I have a go with her whilst you're away fucking some other bitch?" He continued taunting me and I could feel the possessive, protective fire burning hotter inside the pit of my stomach.

I of course ended up throwing him to the ice, hissing in his ear, "Don't even let her face enter your brain again or you'll be watching it spill out all over this fucking ice."

He got to me, I'll admit that but when it comes to my girl there are no lengths I won't go to.

Callie

I watch Molly hop into her taxi, arms still cradling her half empty, extra large popcorn as she throws me a lazy wave with the other arm. I head back into the arena, making my way around the rink towards the hallway that leads to the locker rooms. Sean is usually pretty quick at hitting the showers and I don't tend to wait more than twenty minutes after a game for him to emerge, smelling like a fresh autumn breeze. There are still a few stragglers hanging around when I get to the hallway, pushing open the double doors and passing a middle aged couple who are quietly chatting as they lean against one wall. I flash them a coy smile and keep walking towards the entrance of the men's locker rooms when I hear a surprised and unsure voice call after me.

"Callie?" She says, her voice cautionary and oddly familiar.

I turn my head fast at the sound of my name. "Yeah?"

The woman's face splits into a bright grin, her dimples sending a wave of warmth directly to my chest. *Do I know her from somewhere? I really feel like I know her from somewhere.*

She smiles and clasps her hand to her mouth for a moment, shaking her head. "Wow," she starts, deep, brown eyes warm and inviting as she looks at me. "You're even more beautiful in person."

Ok, now I'm really confused.

I cock an eyebrow at her, keeping my face neutral, not wanting to offend this seemingly friendly woman who apparently knows me from somewhere. "Sorry, do I know y—?"

"Baby!" Sean's voice cuts through mine and I twist back to the men's locker room door, watching him bound towards me like the usual puppy dog he is before he skids to a stop, eyes locked on the couple who's gazes are flickering rapidly between the two of us.

The woman squeals and clasps her mouth again. "Oh my god he calls her baby!" She taps the back of her hand against her husband's chest and he grunts, rolling his eyes.

"Jesus Judith, you'll make the poor boy insecure." He grumbles, placing a palm on her shoulder to calm her incessant bouncing with joy.

"Ha!" She barks, her sculpted eyebrows lifting high on her forehead. "A son of yours, insecure?" She gestures back to Sean who is still frozen like a deer in the headlights. "His head's so big it's almost falling off his shoulders."

Sean finally clears his throat — thank god because mine has never been smaller. "What the hell are you two doing here?"

Sean's mum clamps her arms across her middle and juts a hip. "What, a mother can't come and watch her only son play hockey once in a while?" Sean rubs the nape of his neck nervously and his eyes fall onto me.

"You'd have known we were coming if you ever answered your phone." She scoffs, her tone dripping in motherly authority.

"Shit, sorry Mum, I've been a little busy lately." He mumbles, still rubbing at the back of his neck.

I want to reach out for him, wrap my hand in his and reassure him that it's ok. But my own heart is racing, Sean's parents being unexpectedly in front of me like this is utterly terrifying I can't lie. I need them to like me, it's so important to me that they approve of our relationship. But at the same time I know they're high flying lawyers, Sean has told me all about their lavish mansion and their huge, custom built office building in the centre of London, every detail of which makes me feel minuscule right now, like a tiny fish coming face to face with a pair of sharp toothed sharks.

But Sean's parents are far from scary when I truly look at them, their soft eyes that resemble Sean's so closely and their many laughter lines that scatter across their faces.

Sean's arm comes around my waist, pulling me gently into his side and planting a light kiss on my temple. "Mum, Dad, this is my Callie."

My Callie...oh god, why does he have to make my heart grow a pair of wings every time he opens his mouth?

Sean's mum smiles as she reaches for my shaky hands, taking them comfortingly in her's. "I've been so excited to meet you Callie." She beams, her own personal rays of sunshine splashing the room with colour and light. "I've wanted Sean to settle down and have a meaningful relationship with someone for so long."

"Oh," I say, butterflies racing through my bloodstream as I glance up at Sean, his face loving and prideful when his eyes meet mine. "He told you about me?"

Sean's mum and dad nod in unison and Sean's breath tickles my ear when he tips his face down. "She forced it out of me." He smirks, planting a delicate kiss behind my ear lobe.

Sean's mum claps her hands together with action. "Right, let's go for dinner tonight, so we can get to know Callie better."

"Ok," I nod, gifting them a shy smile. "That sounds nice."

Her face splits in two, mirroring the smile I've seen Sean display so many times before, she claps her hands together and sings, "We'll meet you at the restaurant at 6pm, I'll text you the address."

She begins marching away and Sean's dad simply shrugs his shoulders apologetically at us, patting his son's arm as he follows his wife out the doors into the bitter wind.

Sean grips my biceps and turns me into him instantly. "We don't have to go to dinner with them baby, I don't want you to be uncomfortable."

I shake my head, grateful for his concern. "No, it's ok, I want to go. They seem lovely."

Sean rolls his eyes, smile tipping his lips. "My mum is very excited about me having a girlfriend so I'm sorry in advance if she's over bearing."

"I think she's sweet," I pause, looking down and shuffling my feet. "Do… do you want to go to dinner with them?"

His hands slide down my arms, landing firmly on my waist and sinking his fingers in possessively. "Well, I was hoping to spend the rest of my day fucking you into my mattress." He smirks, caramel flecks dancing through his irises. "But I guess I could spare a few hours for my parents."

I breathe a laugh, burying my fingers in his curls. "You can fuck me into your mattress when we get home." His face creases with a wide smile, dipping his lips to kiss me tenderly. "You smashed it today by the way, and that fight." I make an 'o' with my fingers, clamping my lips together. "That was hot."

"Really?" He beams, hands trailing up my back, pulling me further into him so our chests are glued together. "I'll remember to smash someone's face in every time you're watching from now on."

I reach up, my face pulling into a frown as I run my fingers along his bruised jaw. "I wish your pretty face didn't get bashed up though."

"The other guy was the one covered in blood baby, which makes it a successful fight."

"What were you fighting about anyway?" I ask, hands flat against his chest and I feel immediately when his heartbeat picks up under my questioning. He shrugs, holding my wrists and lifting them up to his mouth, tickling my palms with soft kisses. "He just said something I didn't like."

My inner thighs tense at the softness of his touch, his warm lips on my skin and I know he's purposefully trying to distract me by turning me on. It's working.

I wriggle free and fist my hip. "Like what?" My tone is more serious now, more determined and I watch as Sean's expression falters, giving in almost instantly to me.

"You're not going to let this go are you?" He sighs and I shake my curls, one of them falling loose and tickling my cheek. I tuck it behind my ear and Sean runs a hand down his face, breathing deeply before he speaks again.

"He asked if he could have a go with you when I'm off fucking some random puck bunny." He murmurs, hands wringing anxiously before he steps into me again.

"Oh," Is all I can say, feeling like a baseball bat has assaulted my head as the insecure thoughts drain in, seeping into every crevice of my brain like they used to when I first started dating Sean.

I thought I trusted him more now and in lots of ways I do, but hearing someone else assume he's still fucking someone other than me on the side makes me question myself.

Sean's hands are gripping my shoulders roughly before I can let the crazed worries totally plague my mind. "You know I don't do that right?" He waits, but I don't look up or respond straight away so he lifts my face, forcing my worried eyes to clash with his. "Cal?" His voice is laced with panic.

I sigh deeply and throw him a hurried nod, watching the anxiety trickle out of his bright eyes and the warmth make it's way back in whilst he breathes a heavy sigh of relief. The truth is, deep down I know he's not cheating on me, the man is quite literally obsessed with me. We're together every moment that we can be and when we're not together he's constantly texting or calling me. My heart is telling me I have nothing to worry about, he's worked damn hard to earn my trust and I don't want to see him feeling deflated because he thinks his hard work and dedication to me has gotten him nowhere. Because it has, it really has changed things for us both and I do truly feel I can trust him with my whole being.

Our foreheads fall together and I can taste Sean's sweet breath on my tongue. "You're the only one I want Callie, you know that."

I do know that and that's the exact reason why I'm not going to let my insecurity about being enough for Sean drive me to a pit of despair like I might have a few months ago. I want today to be great, dinner with Sean's parents has to go well and I'm determined to make it.

Chapter 34

Sean

There was a space in my chest that I didn't even know was there before I met Callie, it wasn't making itself known because she wasn't in my life yet. My heart knew that she was the only one who could fill that hole, nobody else could fill the void I never knew I had until I met her. That's all I can think about in this exact moment as I watch her pull a baby pink cocktail dress up her legs and shape it to her delicious curves. She twists one way, then the other, facing the mirror and mentally scrutinising everything about herself whilst a barely there frown pulls down the corner of her mouth. I fucking hate it.

I get to my feet and hold her from behind. "Baby, stop analysing yourself."

"I can't help it," she huffs, turning in my arms, still trying to get a good look at her body so she can pick on every tiny detail in her mind. "I feel like my ass looks flat in this dress."

I almost choke on my own breath. "I'm sorry, what?" I twist her away from the mirror, her hands flat on my chest. "This ass?" I grab it with both hands and her face twists into a smile. I dip my face to her's so our lips brush off each other. "You, are so fucking beautiful it hurts." I whisper, my breath dancing across her tongue.

She gulps hard, darting her tongue out to wet her pillowy lips before she smashes them onto mine, inhaling deeply as I haul her up off the ground, squashing her against my suited chest. When I eventually release her mouth from my hungry grasp I place her heeled feet back to the ground and she audibly gasps when she takes in my outfit. I'm wearing a suit, not a particularly expensive one but it's pretty nice, formal enough for this evening of painful fine dining we're about to endure with my parents. Callie gulps hard for the second time today. "Wow," she pats my blazer clad chest, smoothing the material like I'm getting ready for my first day of school. "Jesus Christ Sean…"

I can feel the arrogance seeping onto my tongue, begging to be released but I know Callie's tone will change to one of a feisty nature if I say anything egotistical right now and I'm fucking loving the look on her face. Her eyes are round and bright as they coast over my body, trailing up from my toes back to my face.

She pulls her bottom lip into her mouth and shakes her head, her dark curls dancing with her. "Ok, I think this is the exact imagine I'd like to orgasm to for the rest of my life."

The laugh that rips through me is filled with love and adoration, watching this girl who owns every piece of my soul drool over me all because I'm dressed in a suit is making this day one of the best I've ever experienced. The irony is that she doesn't see how beautiful she is, she's fucking breathtaking right now as she stands there, pink satin clinging to her shape, her face painted like a supermodel and her curls hanging down her back, softer than usual and accentuating her honey coloured freckles. The truth is though that she's always fucking breathtaking, when she's just waking up in the morning, when she takes off her makeup and her skin is pinker than usual, when she's just out of the shower, hair wrapped in a towel and skin dripping as the steam follows her like a cloud. She's the most beautiful though when she's truly happy, the unfiltered, unburdened kind of happiness and not to blow my own trumpet here but I've only ever seen her in that state of beauty when she's with me.

I'd like to think I make her happy, I really hope I make her happy.

The entire car ride Callie is bobbing her leg up and down on repeat, staring out of the window and lacing our fingers together tightly as I rest my hand against her creamy thigh. I know she's nervous, on the verge of an anxiety induced meltdown might be the more accurate way to describe her right now. When my car squeals to a stop in the car park I turn off the engine and pull Callie's thumb from between her teeth. She's bitten the skin down to red, raw flesh and she winces when I suck it into my mouth, trying to cool the sting with my tongue.

"Don't be nervous baby, it will be ok." I murmur, one hand still holding her's and the other brushing lightly against her cheek.

"What if they don't like me Sean?" Her eyes flicker with worry as they bounce between mine. "I need them to like me."

I grip her face in my hands, trying to calm her heartbeat, I can hear it strumming against her collar bone. "Shhh, stop panicking Cal. I'm telling you it will be fine…do you trust me?" She nods immediately and I feel a kick in my chest, my heart fighting to escape and get to her. "They'll love you just as much as I do, I promise." I leave a barely there kiss on her shoulder and watch her chest stutter as she peers up at me for a beat. That's the moment I realise what I just said.

Daisy Egan

I can't believe I just said that, what a dickhead. I wish Callie was too
nervous to notice the words that just flew off my tongue before my brain
had a chance to catch up and tell me to stop. But I'm pretty sure by the way
her eyes are resting on her lap right now that she heard every word. I told
myself so many times that I wasn't going to tell Callie I loved her until I
was sure she was ready to say it back, and I'm still unsure if she's fully
there yet. I can wait for her to say it first, I just need to watch my tongue. I
lose my filter around her — not that I have much of one at the best of
times — and I just end up spilling my feelings like vomit onto her. But
telling this girl I'm in love with her needs to be at the right time and I need
her to be ready too.

Callie quickly composes herself and reaches for her door handle, shoving
the passenger door open which I then proceed to reach over her and slam
closed again. I get out my side, running around to her and opening the
door, holding her hand in mine as she steps out in that stunning outfit that's
making me want to bust a load into my pants every time I catch a glimpse
of her. She hasn't said a word about my accidental love confession, but as
we walk hand in hand towards the restaurant entrance she gives my hand a
hard squeeze and lets her head fall against my bicep. I feel like she's
telling me what I already knew, that she's not quite there yet, but she will
be, soon.

Chapter 35

Callie

I think my heart fell out of my ass when Sean said he loves me. I know it was a passing comment and I'm not even sure Sean realised that he'd said it, but the weight of those words falling off his tongue so casually made my heart shudder with pleasure. I really want to tell him that I love him too, that I feel everything he's feeling and I want him to know how much he means to me. But the words still feel stuck to the roof of my mouth, slowing melting away as each day goes by and I know I'll be absolutely certain when I'm ready, which isn't yet.

Dinner with Sean's parents is going well…I think. I'm still nervous as shit but they've both tried their best to put me at ease, keeping the conversation relaxed and making jokes to lighten the heavy weight of nerves that is hurting my shoulders.

My leg continues bobbing for a while before Sean's heavy palm lands on it, rubbing his thumb across my goose pimpled skin and whispering, "Just relax, it's ok."

God I wish I could tell him how much I love him.

After we've eaten, Judith leans back in her chair, cherry red wine leaving a residue on her lips when she tips the liquid to her mouth. "Well, I can't say Sean getting a girlfriend this early into his time at Redwood wasn't a plot twist." She titters, tipping her glass up again. "One I certainly didn't see coming."

Sean's warm breath tickles my ear when he leans down, fingers digging into my bare thigh. "You're the best plot twist I ever had."

My heart takes off again and I'm sure at this point it's left my body entirely and made it's home in his. I try not to smile, really I do but my face cracks without my permission and I reward Sean with a beam so bright it most likely blinds him.

"Yeah, it was a plot twist for me too, considering I had a different boyfriend at the start of this year." I murmur, sinking my claws into Sean's hand where it rests on my thigh under the cover of the table.

Sean scoffs loudly. "Yeah, he's probably one of the biggest pricks I've ever met…and I've met a lot of pricks in my life."

"Sean, I don't care for your choice of language." Judith says, throwing him a disciplinary look before she leans towards me across the table, using her wine glass to shield her mouth from the men. "I bet he was a prick though…he was wasn't he?"

I burst into laughter and feel my muscles relinquish their tensing for the first time all evening. Judith joins me, tittering and downing the last mouthful of ruby wine before shifting into a more comfortable position in her seat.

The restaurant is quickly becoming quieter as the dinner rush dissipates and the only people left are us and a few other tables of people having late night drinks to wind down. The quiet murmur of voices is like white noise, forcing my mind to stop it's whirring and overthinking.

"So," Judith starts again and Sean's dad rolls his eyes, a 'does she ever shut up?' Look in his twinkling eye when he flickers a smile at me. "Tell me all about your family Callie, I know your dad is Sean's coach."

I nod and take a quick sip of my wine. "Yeah, he is. We've never been particularly close but I do try my best to make him proud." Sean gives my thigh a reassuring squeeze and his cold lips find my bare shoulder. "I'm much closer to my mum, I'm an only child so the two of us spent massive amounts of time alone together when I was growing up, you know, with my dad travelling a lot for work."

"What does your mum do then? Does she live close by?" Judith asks totally innocently, but Sean and I tense up in unison.

I don't want to feel like I can never talk to people about my mum, it's just like an aching pain residing in my chest when I think about her looming fate.

I swallow the tears and clear my throat. "My mum isn't working right now, she—"

"Stop." Sean says, his arm coming around my shoulder, hauling me closer to him. "She doesn't want to talk about that Mum." His eyes are worried, his palm on my shoulder lightly like he thinks I might shatter into a million pieces if he holds me too tightly.

"It's ok," I tilt my face up to his, purposefully softening my eyes and holding his for a beat. "I don't mind." I nod as he releases me, his protective sizzle still lingering on my skin after his palm has left.

Sean's mum grabs his dad's arm and points at her son. "He's such a gentleman, are you sure he's yours Ken?"

Ken rolls his eyes again — I think him and I could be kindred spirits — and rubs a hand down his face, looking like a mirror image of his son.

Daisy Egan

"Jesus Christ, I can't win can I? When he used to fuck around with loads of women you used to say he was definitely mine!"

Judith stifles a laugh along with Sean and I. "Yeah well, now I'm not so sure." She snickers and I force my laugh down my throat.

After another hour and a half, plus a whole other bottle of wine between us all — minus Sean who is designated driver and refuses to touch a drop when he has me in his car — we finish off our last few sips. I tilt my glass to my lips, letting the last few droplets run down my throat, except one that escapes down my chin and lands in-between my breasts, trailing down towards the crevice of my cleavage.

"Shit," I murmur, reaching for a napkin, but before I can catch the droplet and wipe it away Sean's tight grip comes around my wrist.

He shakes his head and a sultry look clouds his chocolate eyes. "Don't. Anything that ends up between those is mine."

I watch him, speechless and utterly choked as he dips his face into my neckline and swipes the droplet of red wine away with his tongue. I try to hide my red cheeks when I look up at his parents again, fully expecting their faces to be white with shock and disgust, but instead I'm greeted with a tired eye roll from Judith and a wink in Sean's direction from Ken.

What the fuck is going on?

Instead of saying something, using my big girl words like the 21 year old woman I am, I opt for playing dumb instead, standing up from my chair like Sean didn't just practically suck my nipple in front of his parents, and getting my coat. Sean holds it out for me, an innocent grin spanning his dimpled face and I know in his cave man brain that he sees nothing wrong with what he just did. I on the other hand am currently suffering from mind numbing embarrassment as we walk outside to our cars and wave goodbye to Sean's parents.

The drive home is quiet, I'm quiet because I'm mad at him and I know he senses it because he tries to hold my hand and make conversation with me, but I am determined to stay in a sulk at least until we get home and I can let rip on him. When I do let my eyes fall onto Sean his face is tense with suppressed laughter, not with worry or anxiety like it ought to be, he's finding this shit funny. He's not going to be laughing though, not when we get home.

The second we step through the door my hand connects with the back of his head with a slap.

"Ow!" He spins around and looks at me, wide eyed and confused. "What the hell was that for?"

I jut my hip and look at him with fire burning behind my eyes, sarcasm filtering through as usual. "Sean Taylor, do you have a death wish?"

Sean rubs the back of his neck nervously and glances over to the living room where Kyle and Lewis are sat, their headsets covering their ears as they fight their cartoon men on the screen. I know they're listening to our argument though, I can tell by the way their shoulders straighten and they readjust their headphones, tilting them slightly to let the sounds of mine and Sean's voices through.

Sean holds his hands up. "I feel like whatever I say right now is going to be wrong, so why don't you just tell me what I did and I can fix it baby." *Urgh, this man is insufferable at times.*

"Don't you dare baby me, Taylor!" I'm raising my voice a little now, drawing even more attention from the earwigs on the couch. "You stuck your tongue between my tits in front of your parents!"

Kyle is the first to spin around, so fast his head almost falls off his shoulders. "I'm sorry, you did what?"

I nod at him, my eyebrows high on my forehead as I gesture for Sean to explain himself. His guilty eyes find Kyle, then me, then Lewis, desperately looking for help, but he's not going to find any, not from them. "You're mad about that?" He says and I gape at his stupidity, of course I'm fucking mad about that. "I thought it would make you want my cock when we got home."

I didn't think he could drive me any more insane that he usually does, but this takes the biscuit.

Kyle and Lewis quickly retreat to their game when I hit them between the eyes with a 'mind your own damn business' scowl and turn back to Sean, moving closer to him and lowering my voice an entire octave.

"Usually it would," I hiss, watching his confused eyes follow mine as they climb up his annoyingly beautiful face. "If your mum and dad weren't watching it happen."

He grins widely, the usual cockiness back. "They didn't mind."

"Yes, but I did Sean," I groan and rake my fingers through my curls with frustration. "You just love to embarrass me don't you?"

His face softens but he grips my waist tightly, shrugging. "Kind of," his grin splits his face, "you're so cute when you turn pink."

I bang my palms firmly against his chest and fold my arms, huffing and turning my face back to the living room, pretending to be interested in the mind numbing game the guys are playing. But Sean's arms quickly circle me, hauling me back into him and pressing a tight kiss to my lips before I can protest. *Not that I want to, I always want to kiss him, even when I'm mad.*

Daisy Egan

"You're my favourite person in the entire world." He murmurs against my lips and my annoyance with him melts into the carpet at my feet.

I try to keep hold of it as it fights against me, tugging at my heart strings when his deep dimples make themselves known again. It's so hard to be mad at that face. I try to huff and cross my arms again, shrugging out of his grip and taking a step back, frown still pulling my mouth down at the corners.

Sean sighs. "You still in a mood?" I nod, face like thunder. "Fine, you asked for it."

I watch as a devilish grin takes over his usually bright one and I see his muscles tense beneath his shirt as he begins to prowl towards me like an animal.

"Sean, no—" I start but it's too late, he has me flung over his shoulder like a sack of feathers quicker than I can blink.

He breathes a heavy laugh. "I guess I'll have to fuck the sass out of you then."

My thighs clench automatically and I relax over his shoulder, happy to let him fuck every fiery flame out of me until I crumple into a pile of ashes.

Chapter 36

Callie

He did indeed fuck the sass out of me…well, maybe not all of it. There's always a healthy amount of sarcastic venom running through my veins, ready to spit at Sean anytime he needs his ego taking down a peg or two. But when his dick is so deep inside me that it feels like it's protruding out of my stomach I don't care to sass him at all, that man can do whatever he wants to me.

I gather the scattering of clothes from the ground, holding up my brand new, pink cocktail dress and peering at Sean through the gaping hole in the centre of it. He tore it off my body so aggressively that he practically shredded the thing.

"Shit, sorry," he eyes me guiltily, "I'll get you a new one."

"You better." I point at him, warning behind the piercing of my eyes.

The truth is I don't really give a shit about the dress, it was worth having him tear it from my body like a starving man, eager to tuck into his favourite buffet.

I start to rummage through Sean's wardrobe, certain I left an outfit here last week. "Aha!" I hold up my jeans and turtleneck in victory and Sean grins in my direction, flashing me his deep dimples.

"Hold on," I lift the jumper to my nose, inhaling the heavy scent of lavender. "Did you wash these?"

He shrugs. "Yeah, so?"

I stare back at him wide eyed, mouth pretty much open for anything to fly in right now. I can't believe he washed my clothes, he's so fucking adorable sometimes.

"You good over there?" He snickers, standing up from the bed, my favourite part of him swaying as he moves towards me. "You're turning my favourite shade of pink again."

"I just...I can't believe you washed my clothes for me." I squeak.

Why is there an actual tear threatening to spill over right now?

Sean breathes a laugh and pulls me into him. "Baby, I only threw a jumper and a pair of jeans into a washing machine."

"You don't get it." I huff, wriggling away from him and slipping the turtleneck over my head.

Sean pulls my curls out of the neckline and grabs my jaw, forcing me to look at him. "Actually Cal, I do get it. I know you're not used to being looked after by anyone, Joel never did anything for you, so every tiny thing I do you think it's a big deal. But you better get used to it, because I have no intention of ever stopping."

"Why do you always do that?"

"Do what?" He smiles, running his thumb across my cheekbone.

I dip my head, looking at the ground. "Make my knees weak."

Sean barks a sharp laugh. "You're funny baby." He picks his boxers up off the ground and pulls them up his legs as I slip my jeans on. "I don't know why you're getting dressed anyway, you're not going anywhere."

Daisy Egan

I purse my lips and hold back the sarcasm I really want to fire at him. "You want me to stay over again? I haven't seen the inside of my dorm for almost a week, don't you want some alone time after today?"

Sean shakes his head, his dark locks bouncing. "No, never want alone time."

I sigh and smile at him, planting my hands on his golden chest. "You don't need me attached to your hip at all times, you were fine before you met me."

"No, no I wasn't fine." He lifts my chin with his finger, "Callie before you I was just me, and I never want to be just me again."

I think I may just want to crawl inside his skin and live there at this point.

"I need to go home," I almost whisper, "I haven't seen Molly for five days and it's likely she'll claw my eyes out when I do see her."

I wait for Sean to look disappointed, to ask me not to go home and to stay with him, but instead he says, "Ok then, let's go," and starts rummaging under his bed, pulling out an overnight back and cramming it with clothes. He's coming with me, of course he's coming with me.

A light laugh falls from my lips and Sean looks up from his seat on the carpet. "What?" He says, eyes clouded with confusion.

I shake my head, smiling lovingly at him. "Nothing, come on."

The door clicks open as I twist my key, the thing is nearly gathering dust I haven't used it in so long. Sean goes ahead of me, carrying mine and his bag and dropping them to the ground in the hallway. As I move around him I see Molly curled up under a blanket on the sofa, 'Real housewives of Cheshire' playing in the background as she taps away on her laptop. She barely looks up as we enter but quickly does a double take when she sees Sean's 6-foot-4 frame creating a shadow across our coffee table. I've been gone so long she assumed it was Anais, like it couldn't possibly be me entering my own dorm with the key I've had since I moved in.

Molly stands up, placing her laptop on the sofa and folding her arms. "Oh look, if it isn't the best friend stealer." She's aiming her daggers at Sean, icy pools making him shiver with fear.

Sean holds his hands up in innocence. "I'm sorry, please don't hurt me." Molly strides across the room towards us both, pointing a daring finger at Sean. "You're lucky you're hot." He plants a fleeting kiss on the crown of her head as she slides past him. "Ok, you're forgiven." She smiles, ensnaring me in a tight hug.

As her familiar peachy smell fills my nose I squeeze her harder, wanting to hold onto her forever. Molly has helped me through a lot since we met and I can never repay her for the support she gave me the first time my mum went through cancer treatment. She was my rock and now I have Sean too, I'm so fucking lucky.

Before I know what's happening next my feet are lifted off the floor along with Molly's as a pair of tree trunk arms wrap around us both.

"Group hug!" Sean sings, holding the two of us in the air like we weigh no more than one of his goose feather pillows.

With my arms still around Molly's neck I roll my eyes and whisper to her, "I'm sorry about him, he's like an overexcited toddler at times."

Molly twists her face to Sean and grins. "He's cute though, so it's ok."

Sean finally puts us back on the ground and I reach for my bag which he quickly swipes out of my hand. I roll my eyes, his chivalry not lost on me but starting to get on my nerves tonight as I head for my bedroom.

"You two better not have super loud sex like the last time you stayed here." Molly huffs as I round the corner and push open my bedroom door, leaving it open so I can eavesdrop on their conversation. I love to hear Sean talk about me when he doesn't know I'm listening.

I hear a loud laugh burst from Sean's mouth. "It's not my fault she's so noisy." *Ok I take it back, the man's a pig.* Molly snorts a laugh and Sean continues, "You know, when Callie and I have sex is the only time she does as I tell her to."

Molly fake gags loudly. "Ok, I really didn't need to know that…like I *really* didn't."

"She's such a good girl…" Sean teases and I hear a slap, followed by a loud, "Ow!" from Sean. I make a mental note to kiss my best friend's face several times later to thank her for keeping my man in check.

"Don't ever, say something like that to me again Sean Taylor or I will remove your balls from your body in your sleep." She warns and the sound of Sean's footsteps quickly follow, the sound getting closer before he steps into my bedroom looking like a frightened deer, locking the door behind him.

"She's scary," he breathes and I turn away to hide my proud smile. "She may even be scarier than you."

"Wanna find out how scary I am?" I twist back, darkening my eyes and purposefully dragging my eyes up his body until I find his throat, watching his heavy gulp. "Thought not."

I climb under my duvet around an hour later, Sean and I having stuffed our faces with Oreos and ice cream whilst watching a shitty film that I didn't

see the ending of because by that point Sean's tongue was down my throat.
He climbs in beside me and I move over, making a cold strip of mattress
apparent between us.

His eyes immediately look at the gap, then at me questioningly. "What are
you doing all the way over there?"

I decide to tease him, purely because it's fun and I haven't done it for a
while. "I want some space tonight." I turn over so I'm facing away from
him, but only a second later he's yanking me back across the bed,
wrapping his arm across my chest and trapping both my legs under one of
his.

"Fuck the space." He mutters into my neck, peppering repeated kisses
there and making me shiver.

I groan playfully. "God, you're so needy."

He squeezes me tighter, his body warm and comforting around mine. "I
know, I just have this uncontrollable need to be touching you at all times.
I'm sorry if it's annoying."

Great, now I feel like a bitch.

I twist in his tight grasp, turning over to face him. "It's not annoying, I've
just never had a guy want me like this, I'm not used to it."

He grips my chin between his fingers, pulling my eyes up to hold his.

"Well, get used to it, because we're endgame baby." He presses a delicate
kiss to my lips, shit eating grin following after and I bury my face into his
warm chest, floating into a dreamless sleep.

Chapter 37

Sean

I swipe my arm across Callie's mattress…cold. My eyes fly open and I search the room for her briefly before climbing out of bed, heels of my palms rubbing at my tired eyes. I drag the zip open on my overnight bag, digging around for the pair of grey sweatpants I packed last night before coming here and that's when I notice the murmured voices in the kitchen. Callie's dorm is pretty small, so you can almost always here every tiny noise from whatever room you're in. There are definitely three voices out there, Callie's, — of course, I'd know her voice anywhere — Molly's and I think Anais must be home too. The three of them haven't had any alone time together for at least a week before I came along and whisked their friend away to my lair for endless sex and cuddles. So, I decide to give them a minute to catch up before I go out there and kidnap my girl again. We both have a full day of training today so I was hoping to keep her in bed until the very last minute, but she obviously had other plans. To be fair to her, she's a monster when she hasn't had a coffee in the morning so I should probably be grateful that she's out there, sipping away at the liquid gold before I undoubtedly piss her off over nothing. I crack the bedroom door, taking a seat on Callie's velvet, pink dressing table chair and leaning back, gazing up at the fairy lights that hang loosely from her ceiling.

"Have you told your boyfriend you're in love with him yet?" Molly says and I hear a mug being placed down firmly with an echoed clang on the marble island.

Callie blows out a quiet breath and I'm immediately straining to hear every word she's about to say.

"No…" she mutters and I just know she's picking nervously at her fingernails. "But he said he loved me by accident yesterday."

Oh shit, I really thought she may have missed that. I should have known, that girl doesn't miss a thing.

Anais chimes in, "By accident?"

I hear as the three of them sip their coffees and I'm pushing down the breath that's sitting deep in my throat. I don't want to risk any tiny sound coming out and them catching me listening. Like I said, the walls in this dorm are made of paper or something and I desperately need to hear how this conversation pans out.

"He said it in passing but…" another deep breath from my girl before she sighs, "it felt right, hearing it coming from his mouth."

I hear a bar stool or two squeaking as they are pushed back across the tiled floor and I guess Callie's friends are moving closer to her, hugging and smothering her in their love like girls do.

Callie clears her throat and I can hear the bubble of tears in her voice. "He makes me so happy, like happier than I ever realised I could be. Going from being with a guy like Joel who degraded me and made me feel like I was never good enough for him. To Sean, who tells me I'm beautiful every damn day and makes me feel so safe and wanted, has made my heart literally double in size."

Daisy Egan

I'm a puddle. Melted into hot, molten liquid on Callie's bedroom carpet from her words.

Molly murmurs, "So tell him that, he needs to hear it."

I do, I do need to hear it, but not until my baby is ready to say it. I won't push her.

"I can't," Callie squeaks and I'm practically bouncing up and down at the bedroom door, desperate to get out there and listen more closely. "I do feel it, honestly I do but the words feel like they're stuck in my throat and my heart is forcing them to stay there. My body is trying to hold onto the last smidgen of vulnerability that I have left, I've given him every part of me and telling him I love him would mean he has my heart to break if he chooses to and I'm just not ready for that yet. I trust Sean, I mean that, I trust him with my whole being but it's like I'm still waiting for something to change between us. Maybe he'll get bored of me or decide this one woman thing isn't what he wants."

As if I could ever get bored of her, she's crazy.

The girl has me in a chokehold I swear to god, I'm almost panting as I listen to the conversation trickle off, Anais and Molly offering supportive and comforting words to my girl and my feet take me down the corridor before I ask them to. *Poker face Sean, you heard nothing.*

As I round the corner into the kitchen all three sets of eyes fix on me like I just walked in on something I shouldn't have. Little do they know I heard everything anyway but my lips are sealed for now.

"You three ok?" I say totally innocently as they all pull their faces back to their original shape.

Callie nods and I move towards her, ensnaring her in a hug from behind and tipping my face down to leave a rough kiss on the back of her neck. I watch the goosebumps rise where I made contact with her skin and my heart skips at the memory of her words only a moment ago.

She sinks her fingers into my biceps as they curl around her shoulders, holding me tightly to her and all I want to do is whisper, "Do you know how much I love you?" into her ear.

But instead I opt for, "Another coffee anyone?"

Callie

"Were you busy yesterday or did you just decide to ignore my text messages about needing an urgent meeting with you?" Ellen folds her arms passive aggressively and lifts her eyebrows high on her forehead.

I breathe a heavy sigh and turn away from her. "Both…"

"Callie, I don't find you funny," she huffs with exasperation. I don't know what she has to be exasperated about though, I'm the one treading water with these shitty routines, battling at each competition and barely keeping it together. I've managed to nab a few decent scores this season but I'm usually the highest scorer on the team, that's why I was made captain in the first place.

I pad across the floor, Ellen's annoyingly uniform footsteps following me to the beam where I mount and sit, legs hanging astride it.

"Are you going to let me talk now or just walk off in a sulk?" Ellen sighs, eyebrows still lost in her hairline.

"I'm not in a sulk, I just want to practice." I say, chalking my hands and getting ready to swing my legs behind me and start the routine from hell. Ellen clears her throat and I let my legs hang loose again, sighing loudly. "Yeah?"

"I don't care for your tone Callie, this is important." She waits for me to object but I'd rather get her rambling over with so I can ignore her for the rest of the day. "I'm changing your routines."

My breath catches in my throat and I croak, "You're what?"

Ellen nods with a hint of fake empathy for a second before hardening her features again. "The routines I gave you just aren't bringing in the scores I expect from you so I've decided to change them all."

"I…I can't…" I try to speak but my throat is tightening by the second, stopping the oxygen from seeping into my lungs and the sensation is causing the panic to build even more. She can't do this, she can't change my routines just when I'm getting to grips with them. I've only just managed to crack them enough so I can compete and get decent points for the team and now she's going to change them? Half way through the season? I swear this woman hates my guts.

I try to suck in a breath but my lungs fight against me, trying to suffocate me silently. Anais' hand lands on my shoulder and the sound around me turns muffled. Anais is shaking me, yelling something I can't hear properly. All I can think about is breathing, which I can't fucking do. I grab at my throat, clawing and trying to rip a hole in it so I can get even a tiny sliver of air into my now shrivelled up lungs.

"She's having a panic attack, I used to have them as a kid." I hear Lois fire out, the girls are around me, shaking me, their voices breathy with stress as they chant over and over again, telling me to breathe. I wish I could scream at them that I'm trying, I just can't open my throat enough to get any air in and my heart is pumping faster than ever, using up any oxygen I do have.

Daisy Egan

Anais' face is in front of mine, her eyes flickering with fear. "Get Sean!"
She yells, gesturing for Lois to run and fetch the only person I can bear to
think about right now.

Breathe Callie, breathe.

I try to talk myself out of this but it's not that easy apparently, I need
something…someone.

"My brother Sean?" Lois' muffled voice asks, confusion clouding her tone.
And why wouldn't she be confused, she has no idea that Sean is my
boyfriend and that we've been seeing each other for months now. Jesus,
my head is throbbing.

Anais sighs roughly. "Yes, just go and get him now!"

She's running out of patience just as quickly as I'm running out of air. I
don't know how I haven't passed out yet, having felt like I can't take a
proper breath for the last few minutes I was sure I'd be dead by now. I
suck in a couple of sharp gulps but they do nothing to dull the aching
tension in my chest as my own body suffocates me in panic. I close my
eyes, imagining Sean's voice in my head telling me to relax and breathe…
then, I really hear him. His voice is strained, panicked as he hauls my leg
over the beam and stands in-between my open thighs.

His hands are on my face, his voice muffled but steady as he begs, "Callie,
look at me!"

I peel my eyes open, sure that I'm imagining him being here or maybe I
have finally died and gone to a Sean filled heaven with ice cream and
endless sex. But his chocolate eyes find me and I realise I'm not dead, he's
really here, holding my face in his warm hands and breathing his
peppermint breath onto my lips.

"Hey, I'm here, it's ok." He murmurs as I continue to fight with the air around me, dragging it into my throat and trying to swallow it down. I shake my head, twisting my fingers into the curls at the nape of Sean's neck, feeling like I might float away at any moment.

Sean's damp forehead lands on mine softly and I force myself to hold his gaze. "Deep breaths baby, deep breaths." I try, pulling the air in and holding it there for a moment. "That's it," Sean says softly, "and again, in…and out." I do as he says, clawing the oxygen in and forcing it to stay, waiting inside my lungs before blowing it back out. "Good girl, that's it," I can feel my heartbeat slowing, my throat loosening and the sound around me coming back, the cotton wool in my ears dissolving and making the gym sound extra loud, even though everyone in it is dead silent apart from Sean, who is still coaxing me through deep breathing.

"Callie, I'm sorry, I didn't mean—" Ellen starts but Sean silences her with a threatening, protective glare.

"No," he hisses, "don't fucking talk to her." His eyes are red with rage and his hand tightens around my back as he moulds me to his chest. "This is your fault."

"Sean," I squeak, pulling his face back to mine with my still shaky hand. He leans his forehead on mine again and whispers, "It's ok baby, I'm here." I wrap my dangling legs around his middle, burying my face in his neck and letting him lift me up to his waist. "I can't do it Sean…I just…I can't." "I know," he says, his voice smooth and comforting like my morning coffee. "Don't worry, we're going home."

I snap my head up from his shoulder. "I can't go home I have to—" his finger lands on my rattling mouth, silencing me and forcing me to swallow the words I was about to say.

Daisy Egan

"We're going home Callie, this isn't good for you. Either you walk or I'll carry you…your choice."

He's not fucking around, I can tell by the way his face flattens, expressionless and authoritative.

I huff and shuffle down his body, letting him win this particular battle because the truth is I really want to go home and sleep. My brain is exhausted from the mental load I've been carrying and with a bomb like the one Ellen just dropped on me I don't think I can take anymore, not today anyway. Sean takes my hand and leads me across the gym to my locker where he punches in the code and collects my bag, swinging it over his shoulder.

"Erm, hold on." Lois snaps just before Sean and I reach the door to leave. "Care to explain what the hell is going on here?"

Sean beats me to a response. "Conversation for another time Lo," he pulls me out the door after him as I throw a 'I'm sorry I didn't tell you' frown at Lois.

I feel bad for keeping our relationship from her but she's one of my closest friends and I know she looks up at me as a captain. I never wanted her to see me differently or to think I've turned into some puck bunny. These are the times I wish I could be more like Sean, not care about people's opinions of me and just do what I want to do without fear of judgment. But I'm not like that and I don't think I ever will be.

Chapter 38

Sean

Callie launches her bag across my bedroom the minute we step foot inside, having been in a major sulk with me the whole way home. I know she didn't want to leave training, she gets stressed out when she doesn't have enough time to practice her routines but how the fuck could I have just gone back downstairs to the rink and carried on training after that? Seeing Callie in that state made my heart rise like bile up my throat, watching her try desperately to suck in a breath as she clawed at her neck will forever give me nightmares. Nightmares of losing her, of her having another panic attack and me not being there to fix it for her.

She sighs and falls to a sitting position on the edge of my bed, head in her hands. "I'm so grateful you helped me come down from whatever the fuck that was back there, but I needed to stay and practice."

"Whatever that was?" *I swear this girl is next level complacent at times.* "Callie you were having a panic attack!" My palm runs down my face, exhausted from the mentally draining morning I've already had. Hearing Callie admit to her friends that she's in love me and then watching her fight for her every breath has knocked the soul out of me.

She shakes her head, ponytail swinging with her. "It's not the first time that's happened and it won't be the last but I can't just leave the gym

Sean!" She's getting mad now, frustrated at me for forcing her to leave
when she didn't want to, but she doesn't get it. I'm not trying to control
her, I'm trying to protect her.

I blow out a sharp puff of air. "I was doing what's best for you, it's all I
ever try to do because I l—"

I stop, halting the word from escaping and watch as Callie's eyes flicker
with knowing, she's not stupid, she knows what I was about to say. When
I'm around her it's like my brain goes to sleep and my tongue just does
whatever the fuck it wants, spilling my secrets left, right and centre.

"You what?" She whispers and I consider just telling her right here, right
now but Lewis' words ring clear in my mind, reminding me why I wanted
to wait for her to say it first. She just told her best friend this morning that
she wasn't there yet and that's ok, it just serves as a reminder as to why I
need to keep my big mouth in check for a little while longer.

I look down at the ground, feeling the unfamiliar warmth seep into my
cheeks. "Nothing, I just want to protect you baby."

She heaves a sigh and stands up, pressing her body into mine and encasing
me in a soft hug. "I don't want to need you Sean." She murmurs into my
chest, her voice muffled by the fabric.

I drop a kiss to the crown of her head. "But you do and it's ok to need
me…because I need you too."

Her tender eyes peer up at me, her freckled cheek bones accentuated by the
bright light hanging from my ceiling above our heads. She looks so
fucking vulnerable right now and I'm not sure my heart can take it, I feel it
splintering as I look down at her, wanting nothing more than to spill my
love all over her and drown her in it.

"I want you…always." She whispers, tiptoeing to lay a light kiss on the point of my chin.

I dip my head and mould her lips with my own, nibbling gently on her bottom lip, electing a groan from deep in her throat. Jesus Christ, everything she does is so sexy.

"I want you too baby," I breathe into her mouth, running my swollen lips over her's and enjoying the way her throat tightens with a gulp. "I'll never get tired of this, of you."

I push her back onto the bed, her back sinking into my mattress and push my hand up her creamy thigh, dipping into the pulsing heat of her pussy. She's ready for me, as always, and I waste no time plunging two fingers into the tight, wet heaven between her thighs. Her back arches, body convulsing around me as I lean down and suck her pleading clit between my lips, watching her knuckles turn white as she grips the bedsheet. When she comes all over my tongue — the one I've been lapping up and down her clit for only minutes — I feel a warm sensation wash over me, tightening my chest and making my heart thump excitedly. I don't think I could love this girl any more if I tried.

Callie

I haven't been to training all week, Sean was spot on when he said I needed a break and practically forbade me from going to the gym after my panic attack. Ellen has sent me a string of texts over the past week asking if I'm coming back and the word sorry has actually been scattered through the onslaught of messages I've received, which shocked me as I don't think I've ever heard that woman admit when she's in the wrong. I've spent the majority of my time reading, completing some coursework on my laptop and spending time with Sean — when he's not stolen away from me to hit pucks. I've had a pretty relaxing week, just what I needed. He on the other hand has been drowning in games and training, the team having been on a losing streak and it's making Sean more stressed by the day. So when I get a text from him at 8pm saying they bagged the win tonight my face lights up without my permission. I haven't seen him today, I stayed at my dorm last night as I promised Molly we could have a movie night, Sean had training really early this morning so he begrudgingly let me sleep without him — his least favourite thing to let me do. When his victory texts pings onto my lock screen I shoot him a quick text back, knowing I'll be in his bedroom waiting for him when he gets back from his celebratory drinks with the boys tonight. I don't tell him that though, I'll just lay there, naked and waiting for him, watching as he swallows and immediately rearranges his cock. I'll never get bored of the way he looks at me.

Molly, Anais and I order a few pizzas, extra vegetables for me and Anais whilst Molly's pizza looks like the inside of a morgue. The girl loves meat pizza, extra bacon, extra beef, extra everything that comes from any kind of animal. I watch in awe as usual when she stuffs an entire slice into her open mouth, chewing and humming like a happy child. When the three of us are full enough that all we can do is lay back and groan, I pick up my phone again, one more text from Sean appears on my screen telling me he misses me and I smile lazily as I reply.

"Get a room," Anais laughs, holding her bulging stomach.

I roll my eyes and lock my phone, slipping it into my back pocket. "Don't be jealous girls, you'll have someone that wants you too one day."

The two of them throw me a middle finger and start to clear the coffee table of empty pizzas boxes and wine glasses. I check the time, 11:04pm. Shit, I better leave soon if I want to get to Sean's before he does.

"Actually," I start and the two of them look up at me, eyebrows high on both of their foreheads. "I'm going to stay at Sean's tonight."

Molly barks a cocky laugh and opens her palm to Anais. "Cough up, you owe me a tenner."

My mouth falls open as I watch my so called best friends exchange cash after betting on me to cave and go to my boyfriend's house for the night. They turn back to me, faces both turned up into devilish grins.

"Bitches," I mutter, making my way to my bedroom and grabbing an overnight bag, cramming it with essentials — plus Sean's favourite lingerie of mine — and leaving my dorm with a sarcastic wave towards my friends. Maybe I'd be mad at them for betting on me but they're right, I hate to admit how obsessed I am with Sean Taylor but the man has me in a chokehold.

I arrive at his place by midnight, the house is dark and still, not a light flickering in the window, not the usual sound of cartoon machine guns coming from the TV in the living room. I use my key to get in and whack up the thermostat, shivering as I ascend the stairs towards Sean's bedroom. The house is fucking freezing, the guys having been out all day training, but the minute I'm tucked under Sean's huge duvet I hum with delight, wriggling my toes and feeling my skin warm up. His smell is everywhere, coating his pillows and swirling all around the room. I inhale deeply, revelling in his woodsy, manly aftershave and counting the minutes until he comes home so I can cling to his body like a koala for the rest of the night.

Chapter 39

Sean

Thank god we won tonight, I couldn't have handled another loss after four in a row over the past week. The guys and I went straight to our favourite bar in town which is where we still are at midnight. The drinks have been flowing but I've been attempting to keep somewhat of a clear head tonight, some of my teammates can go nuts, downing ten pints of beer, plus shots and still wake up tomorrow ready to go. But I'm not like that at all, the drink goes straight into my blood stream and lives there rent free for at least two days afterwards, making my mind fogging and unclear. I'm not really in the mood to be out tonight anyway, I was hoping to head home and pick up my girl on the way but the boys had other plans and I couldn't bail as their captain. I agreed to come out for a few hours, which of course turned into five.

"Oh my god man you have to tell us about this girl now, it's been what… three months or something?" Kyle jeers, jabbing Nick in the shoulder and nearly knocking his beer flying.

Nick mutters under his breath, "Fuck off."

Kyle jabs at him again. "Come on, if she's ugly it's ok, we won't judge you."

"She's not fucking ugly," Nick turns his head towards Kyle's taunting eyes. "She's just none of your fucking business."

"Man," Kyle sighs, pointing his finger between Nick and I. "You two are pussy whipped now and I'm not enjoying it." He lifts his frosted beer to his lips, a trail of condensation making it's way down the glass and then down his bare arm. I intentionally knock Kyle's glass with my elbow, causing the golden liquid to lap up the side and soak his hand and his chin. I grin at him as he curses me under his breath, wiping the back of his hand across his dripping jaw.

"Fucking hell I was only joking, no need to waste perfectly good beer over it." His own shit eating grin spreads across his face as he watches me, before his gaze lands over my shoulder and his bright eyes widen in horror. I follow his line of vision and before I know what's happening a blonde with legs that go straight to heaven lands gently on my knee. I know her, I'm almost certain I've fucked her before and her spicy perfume is tightening my throat, making me cough.

"Hey Sean, wanna get out of here and go to my place for round two?" She drawls, clearly having been plied with alcohol tonight by her friends.

I don't even remember her name, I never made a habit of finding out anything about the girls I slept with...until Callie of course.

"Get off my knee." I hiss, trying to keep the attention away from my rowdy teammates. Kyle is still gawking with me, his eyes tracking her legs as they dangle down from where she perched herself in my lap.

The blonde's eyes narrow at me. "Why? You let me sit on your knee before."

"Do you need me to make you get off?" I growl, getting more pissed off now. Why can't some girls just take a fucking hint when it's practically smacking them right in the face?

She huffs but shuffles off me, rubbing her ass against my leg as her heels land back on the ground. The air around us immediately feels lighter now she's no longer touching me.

I twist my body to block Kyle's view of her, his eyes still wide. "Look, I have a girlfriend now so there's isn't going to be a round two." The blonde rolls her eyes and reaches for the collar of my shirt. I brush her hand away with the back of mine and darken my eyes with warning. "Politely fuck off now."

She folds her arms, her thick lashes brushing against her cheekbones as she closes her eyes and lets out a long huff, before sauntering away across the bar. When I turn back to Kyle his eyes are back to their normal size and the icy blue of them is burning into me as he grins.

"What?" I snap, downing the last of my beer and deciding right there and then that I'm heading home and calling my baby. I don't fucking like this shit anymore, I don't want to deal with random women fawning all over me.

Kyle's grin widens and his eyes sparkle with pride. "Good for you man, you're a loyal guy."

My best friend loves to berate me for being pussy whipped but when it comes to me being loyal to my girl I know he's actually filled with pride at how much I've changed since I met Callie.

I shrug, forcing the smile down. "Yeah well, when I have a girl like Callie at home I don't feel the need to look at other women. The appeal just isn't there like it used to be."

Kyle nods, gulping down his foamy beer and patting me once on the shoulder. I push back my bar stool and get up, rubbing my damp, icy hands on my jeans and declaring to my teammates that I'm heading home. A few of them groan but most of them are too far gone to give a shit, they simply nod and throw me a lazy wave.

I kick off my shoes the second I get inside my house, the darkness enclosing me and making me feel like a beady pair of eyes must be staring at me through the shroud of blackness. I make my way up the stairs, dragging my feet and pulling my phone out of my back pocket to text Callie. It's 1:24am right now so I'm sure she's sleeping, I want to hear her voice so badly but I don't want to wake her so I settle for a text. I hit send as I step through the door into my dark bedroom, a pinging sound making me jump and hit the light switch fast. As my eyes adjust to the sudden blinding light that spreads across the room I see a lump in the centre of my king sized bed. Callie sits up, her phone cradled in her palm as her eyes focus on me. Her brown curls cascade down her back as she sits taller, piercing green eyes boring into mine as I lay my hand on my chest and breathe a sigh of relief. For a second I thought some crazy fucker had broken into our house and was sleeping in my bed, but the sight of my girl laying under my duvet waiting for me is like a wave of happiness and relief mixed into one.

I blow out a sharp, relieved breath. "Fucking hell baby you scared me, I didn't know you'd be here."

"Yeah," she murmurs, so quietly I can barely hear her. "It was supposed to be a nice surprise."

Her eyes are soft and sad looking, her shoulders slumped and her gaze staying firmly on her lap as she speaks quietly like a mouse.

"Yeah, it is a nice surprise…" I say warily, like I'm walking across broken glass, watching my every step. I'm staring at her, her slow, steady breathing and her frowning lips. "What's wrong?" I say, sitting down on the edge of my bed and brushing my fingers along her forearm which she quickly jerks away from me.

"Don't touch me Sean," she snaps, the volume of her voice suddenly increasing and I immediately notice the sharpness in her tone that wasn't there a moment ago.

She shuffles across the bed, creating a blanket of space between us, the air becoming colder the farther away from me she moves. A sickening feeling embeds itself into the pit of my stomach as I watch her, eyes prickling with tears and the fiery green that I'm used to dulling with aching pain.

I open my mouth to speak but have to force the whispered words off my tongue. "What did I do?"

My heart is racing faster than ever as she swipes the screen on her phone and turns it towards me, the bright light glaring as my eyes adjust to the photo. The first thing I notice is the flash of blonde hair, then my own face as the photo of the leggy girl from earlier sitting on my lap stares back at me on Callie's phone screen. I choke on my breath as it tries to escape from my throat, realising exactly what that looks like and it's then that the puzzle pieces snap together like magnets. Callie's sad eyes look back at me expectantly, waiting for me to say something to clear up her plagued thoughts but my throat is closing up by the second.

"I was going to just leave and never speak to you again," she croaks through the bubble of tears in her throat. "But I'm trying to be more mature than that, so I need you to tell me what the fuck is going on."

"What is that?" I stutter, leaning in closer to look at the photo before Callie angrily snatches the phone away from my view.

I don't know why I said that, I know exactly what that photo is, I was in that bar only an hour ago when that girl approached me but why the hell does Callie have a photo of it?

Callie's emerald orbs darken and she scrunches her eyebrows together in angst. "You tell me Sean, because it looks like it's you with some random slut on your lap." She spits, the fierce anger clear but I can see the hurt hiding behind it, the raw pain she must be feeling thinking I betrayed her.

"That's not at all what happened, she came to our table and was all over me. I told her I had a girlfriend and I wasn't interested, then she left me alone." I ramble, trying to get the words out of my mouth as quickly as possible to reassure Callie and save her hurt feelings.

"You sure as hell look interested with her draped all over you like that." She murmurs, looking back down at her lap and breaking contact with me. She wipes at her watery eyes and the urge to reach out and hold her is making my hands itch.

I shake my head and shuffle closer to her. "Callie that's not what happened, you can ask Kyle, he was there." She sniffs again, forcing the tears to stay hovering inside her eyelids. "Who even sent you that photo?" I say, suddenly filled with suspicion. Who the fuck is trying to purposefully sabotage my relationship?

"I don't know, it was an unknown number…" She whispers, finally looking up at me with her soft, melty eyes that make me want to die.

I reach out for her and she lets me take her shaky hand in mine. "You can see what's going on here right? Someone is obviously trying to set me up, make it look like I cheated on you."

"You're not getting out of it that easily Sean." She pulls her hand out of my grip and sniffs harder this time, the tears breaking free and trailing silently down her cheeks.

That's it, I can't sit here and watch her cry like this.

"Baby, please don't cry." I grab her face in my hands and wipe her rolling tears away with my thumbs before she shakes my palms off her cheeks. "I promise I didn't do any—"

"I trusted you Sean!" She yells, water splattering all over my duvet where she sits. "I fucking trusted you and I don't trust anyone, you know that."

"I spent so long building your trust Cal, why would I want to ruin that now? I swear I didn't betray you baby, I could never. You mean fucking everything to me, absolutely everything!" I'm yelling now too, the desperation to fix this mess clawing it's way up my throat and out of my mouth.

Callie's feet land with a soft thud on my carpet and she starts to pull her jeans up her legs. "You know," she croaks, water still forming tracks down her face. "I never doubted your feelings for me until now."

My stomach flutters with panic as I watch her collecting her things. "Are you leaving?"

She nods once but doesn't look at me. "Yes, I am. I need some time to think."

Shit, she's serious. No, she can't go, I...I need her.

"Callie no, please don't go." I stutter, falling to my knees as she reaches the bedroom door. I cling to her legs, holding her to me and hugging her thighs like a scared child. "No Callie, you can't go, please don't." My own voice is pained, desperate, pleading with her. If she leaves tonight she might never come back to me...I can't even comprehend trying to live my life without her now.

I peer up at her and her gaze is equal parts shocked and aching with uncertainty. "What are you doing?" She says, her hands landing on my shoulders.

"Begging you not to leave me, you have to trust me on this. I can't lose you Cal, I just...I can't." I croak through a bubble of my own tears, the water in my eyes spilling over and Callie's green orbs widen with pain as she tracks it down my cheek.

"Stand up Sean," she whispers and I sniff hard, wiping away the moisture with the back of my hand.

She squeezes her eyes shut for a moment and then brackets my stubbled jaw with her delicate hands, pulling our foreheads together. I breathe in her heavenly smell, the scent that reminds me that I'm home, when I'm with her, I'm home.

"I promise I'll come back, I just need some space for tonight." Her voice is soft and warm when she speaks now, her breath tickling my lips as I lick away a remaining salty tear that lies there and swallow down any more that are threatening to escape.

Her thumbs find my under eyes like mine did her's only minutes ago and she wipes away any remaining moisture. "I'm not mad at you ok? I believe you when you say you didn't cheat on me, I...I trust you."

The words that fall from her tongue make my heart melt into a puddle behind my ribcage. I pull her chest to mine, hugging her tighter than I ever have before and sinking my still wet face into her neck.

"Just go home for tonight, but please come back to me tomorrow. I need you Callie, you're the only person I'll ever need." I say into her shoulder and I feel her arms squeeze tighter around my neck. I lift my face and hold her gaze, locking our eyes together and deciding if I should say what's on the tip of my tongue right now.

"I can't believe you still don't fully trust me after all this time." I sigh, "I've been there for you through so much and it kind of feels like you have one foot out of the door, waiting for me to fuck up." She lets her hands fall from my shoulders to hang by her side, letting out an exhausted sigh. "If you still don't trust me now, I'm not sure you ever will."

She blows a tired breath and then brings her eyes up to mine again. "It takes a hell of a lot for me to trust someone Sean, but I'm getting there I swear. And I do believe what you've told me tonight, like I said, I trust that you didn't do anything with that girl."

I nod and lean down to kiss her soft, pink lips, holding her mouth to mine for a long beat before releasing her and watching her leave my bedroom. As soon as I hear her engine roar to life and the sound dwindle away as she drives off toward her dorm I sink back on my mattress, rubbing my jaw and thinking about how this night did a 180 so fucking fast I feel like my feet haven't touched the ground.

I need to find out who the fuck set me up tonight and when I do, it's going to get messy.

Daisy Egan

Chapter 40

Callie

I don't know why the hell I doubted him, I should have known it was a set up or a misunderstanding like Sean said. He has worked so damn hard to earn my trust over the months we've been together and how do I repay his hard work? By doubting his loyalty to me at the very first hurdle we've faced. I feel like shit as I twist my key in the lock, letting myself into my dorm at just after 2am, trying to be as quiet as possible as I tiptoe down the hallway to my room. I push open my bedroom door, the emptiness of not having Sean with me sinking deep into my bones and making it's home there for the night. I'm desperate for sleep, my eyelids we're dropping dangerously on the drive over here and I feel immediate exhaustion the second my head hits the pillow. Before I let my eyes flutter closed and the heaven that is sleep take over, I shoot Sean a quick text.

Callie:

'I'm sorry I doubted you tonight, I should have known you'd never cheat on me. I see how hard you've worked to earn my trust and I promise you it's working. Please don't give up on me now.'

It's mere seconds before my phone pings in my hand and I read Sean's text with a smile.

Sean:

'I know baby, it's ok. You forget that I know you, better than anyone and that means I know when you're scared. You can always tell me how you feel and I'll always listen, no matter what, but don't close the door on me. If I ever upset you, tell me and I'll fix it, ok?'

Callie:

'I will, I promise. I'll call you in the morning.'

Sean:

'You better. I miss you already, call me as soon as you wake up.'

I fall asleep clutching my phone, Sean's words swirling through my mind and allowing me to drift into a peaceful sleep.

Sean

"Is that blonde still there?" I say the second Kyle picks up the phone, the noise of the bar in the background taking over his muffled voice.

He chuckles a drunk laugh. "Hello to you too."

"Focus Kyle, the blonde, is she still there?" I snap, not in the mood for his jokes after the night I've had. Someone manufactured this whole thing and I'm going to find out who.

He pauses before speaking again. "Yeah, she's in the corner with her friends, why?"

"Give her the phone."

"What?" Kyle squawks and I crack my neck from side to side, loosing my patience by the second.

"Give her the fucking phone Kyle." I hiss and I hear him curse at me under his breath before muttering something I can't hear to someone else.

I hear a girly sigh. "What do *you* want?"

"I need to know why you approached me tonight." I say, trying to keep my voice from wavering and letting the burst of anger fly out.

She sighs again. "Because I wanted sex."

She's an even worse liar than Callie.

"No," I grit my teeth, forcing the seething anger to calm. "That's not the only reason. Did someone tell you to approach me tonight?" *Silence.* "Tell me who it was." I hiss and I hear her heels click clacking across the laminate flooring of the bar. The music immediately muffles and I hear a door squeak closed.

"I didn't ask him why he wanted me to approach you ok? He said he'd buy me a drink so I just did what he wanted." She whispers, her tone tense and nervous.

I gulp hard, the anger fighting it's way up my throat. "Who was it?"

"Do you know Joel? Joel Steller?"

My heart beat kicks up a notch and I feel every muscle in my body go into fight mode hearing that arsehole's name. I hang up the phone without so much as a 'thank you,' but I don't care in this moment. All I know is I need to get over to Joel's dorm, right fucking now.

I don't even know how late it is when I get to the five story dorm building that Joel lives in, I only know this is his block because Callie mentioned that he insisted on being in the building nearest to the football field and having the number 48 on his door because it's his lucky number.

Fucking weirdo.

On my way up to the fourth floor in the lift I flex my fist, knowing it's about to get some action, preferably against Joel's face. I try to calm my ragged breath but I just can't, I've totally lost control and the closer I get to his door the more animalistic I become. I feel like a tiger protecting his cub right now, claws at the ready as I bang my fist against the door hard. The sound echoes through the deserted hallway but the door swings open fast, the smell of weed permeating the air around me as a cloud of smoke floats out of the door and down the hallway.

"What do you want?" The guy on the other side of the door slurs, his eyes have red rings around them and his irises are twice the size of a sober person's.

But I'm not here for him, the wide eyes of the guy I'm actually looking for lock onto mine from the living room and before he can blink I'm inside his dorm room. I grab him by the neck, smacking him into the wall and pressing my palm deep into his throat as he claws at my hand. The adrenaline is racing through my veins now and it's like I have superhuman strength as I hold him forcefully against the wall and lean into his face.

"What the fuck?" Joel yells, wiggling his legs and fighting to break out of my tightening grip on his throat.

I crack my neck, feeling the heat crawling up my skin. "You know what, I'm not even mad that you tried to set me up." I say, watching his face pale as the realisation of why I'm here sinks into his puny brain. "What I'm really fucking mad about, is that you made my baby cry, you made her doubt my feelings for her."

"I knew that fucking slut wouldn't keep her mouth shut." He pants, still clawing at the hand that's trapping his neck against the wall.

I sigh with contempt, ready to leave this fucking weasel with one last warning before I go. "Let me make this crystal clear for you, you'll never have Callie again. Doesn't matter what you do to me, how much you try to destroy my character, she'll never want you." I take my hand off his neck and he coughs, gripping it with his own sweaty hands and panting like he's been held under water and only just allowed up for air.

I turn to leave, Joel's friends are still wide eyed and silent as I reach the door. "Oh by the way," I say, turning my head back to look at Joel who's still holding his neck. "If you ever look twice at my girl again I'll break your neck." I shake my head with a dry chuckle, "Sorry that sounded like I was joking, I will actually break your neck." I say, eyes darkening as I watch him gulp hard. I leave, letting the door slam shut behind me and tap a quick text out to my girl for her to read when she wakes up.

Sean:

'It was Joel who tried to set me up tonight, but don't worry, I've handled it. Call me when you wake up.'

Daisy Egan

Chapter 41

Callie

I fly down the stairs into the entryway of my dorm and look out of the foggy glass into the pouring rain. The water is pelting down, bouncing off the concrete and making it almost impossible for me to make out where anything is outside. I pull open the door, hovering under the canopy that is sheltering me from the torrential rain as it batters the pavement and all of the cars in the lot. I'm peering, eyes squinting as I try to work out if Sean's car is here yet when I hear a door slam and see him jogging through the violent onslaught of rain towards me.

Why does he look so damn sexy just by existing?

He heaves a sigh of relief as he steps into the shelter that I'm standing under. "Hi,"

I give him a timid smile and blink up at him. "Hey,"

His huge arms wrap around my waist and haul me gently into him before he cocoons me in a comforting hug, breathing deeply into the warmth of my hair and humming with satisfaction. I link my arms around his neck and tiptoe to bury my face into his damp shoulder, his jacket is dripping with moisture from the heavy rain but I don't care, I just want him to hold me for a minute.

"Joel set me up last night, he asked that blonde to approach me and then took a photo. He wanted to make it look like I was cheating on you so that you'd end things with me." He murmurs into my neck and I pull away, wanting to look at his beautiful, dimpled face. The hurt is clear in his eyes like I knew it would be, the pain that I could believe he would ever do that to me.

I always knew Joel was an asshole, but this really takes the biscuit, and the worst part is that Joel was the one who ended things with me, not the other way around. It's like he's just mad that I found someone who actually treats me the way I deserve to be treated and now I'm out of reach for him. I sigh and scrape my hair over one shoulder. "He's such a prick, I'm sorry I doubted you last night."

He tucks one rogue curl behind my ear and I shiver at the way his finger lightly brushes against my collarbone. "It's alright baby, I know trusting me is hard for you." He breathes a weighty sigh, laced with exhaustion and deep defeat.

I feel like shit that I've made him think I don't trust him because I do, I just have an automated barrier always at the ready to snap down and protect myself from any sort of hurt. I have to try to explain this to him so he gets it, I don't want him to feel deflated, like his hard work is useless and I still doubt him at every hurdle.

"That's the thing though," Sean raises his head as I begin to explain. "It's not hard for me to trust you. I don't know what came over me last night, I should have known it wasn't what it looked like." I breathe, bracketing his jaw in my hands and running my thumbs across his dimples.

He quickly shakes his head and covers my hands with his own. "It's not your fault, if I'd have seen a photo like that I would have felt all the same things you did, betrayal, hurt—"

I cut him off by pressing our lips together, taking his breath away for a split second before he gains it back and cups my ass with both hands, squeezing gently and swiping away at my tongue with his. The heat of his mouth, the words he just said, the way this man understands everything that I'm feeling without me having to say it, all makes me more sure by the second that I'm deeply in love with him.

He pulls away with a deep gulp of air. "You know I'm trying right Cal? I'm really fucking trying to be good for you."

My forehead lands on his chest as he plants a lingering kiss in my hair. "I know, I see it. I see everything you do, it doesn't go unnoticed." He pulls my face up to look at him, brown eyes swimming with gratitude and love as he glues me to the spot with his intense, yet soft stare.

"Good," he smiles, dimples waving hello and making my knees weak. "I would do anything for you, do you know that? I would crawl over glass, walk through open flames, cut my own hand off." He laughs and I copy, sniffing back the tears of happiness listening to him declare his unwavering feelings for me. "I mean it, I'd do absolutely anything."

I gulp down the three words that are balancing on the precipice of my tongue and clear my throat, raking a hand through my wild curls and looking past Sean at the still pelting rain.

"I know the plan was to go for a scenic walk but..." I grimace as I watch the rain splatter against the ground, puddles spanning across the car park. "I'm not sure that's a good idea anymore."

Sean barks a laugh and turns to look at the cinematic storm that's quickly growing. "Why? Nothing wrong with a little rain," he turns back to me, teasing grin out in full force. "Or are you scared about your hair getting ruined?"

I smack his chest hard and shoot him an eye roll. "Let's just go for a drive instead."

"Oh yeah?" He wiggles his eyebrows at me, a laugh bursting through my lips as I look at his sparkling eyes, ideas of a sexual nature forming behind them — which by the way, I'm fully on board with.

"Yeah big boy, come on." I leave a pat-pat on his chest and take a tiny step out into the rain, ready to sprint across the lot to his car.

But before my foot can even make contact with the soaking ground Sean's arm snakes around my middle and yanks me back under the protection of the canopy.

"Have you lost your god damn mind Burch? I'm not going to let you get wet running to my car." He shrugs his jacket off, his only form of cover from the downpour and hovers it over my head. "The only time I want to see you soaking wet is when my face is between your thighs." He smirks and my body listens to his demand, pooling the moisture and radiating heat right from the very spot he just mentioned.

Sean's arm hooks under my ass and lifts me to his waist with one hand, jogging across the car park with me clinging to him under the protection of his jacket. He drops me on my ass into the passenger seat before running around and climbing in beside me. Miraculously, I'm totally dry, Sean on the other hand is dripping like a dog who just climbed out of the bath but that doesn't even slightly dull the breathtaking smile that's covering his entire face right now.

Daisy Egan

We must have been driving for at least an hour, chatting nonstop like we always do and listening to country music, singing together at the top of our lungs. Sean decides to pull over into the gravelly area of a country park that looks pretty deserted. I know where his mind is at the second I glance over at him, feeling the familiar tingling sensation as his eyes coast over my body hungrily. I dive over the centre console, landing with my legs straddling his lap and begin to attack his mouth with mine. His breath catches in his throat before he sighs happily and sucks my bottom lip between his teeth, nibbling gently and causing a wave of desperation to wash over me.

"This isn't what I," he peppers kisses down my neck, "had in mind when I said" he rubs his nose across my jaw, "let's park up."

Bullshit, this is precisely what he had in mind.

"Hmm," I hum as his tongue strokes the sensitive skin behind my ear, leaving goosebumps on every inch of skin it touches. "I think this is exactly what you had in mind. Plus, I've been horny since last night." When his soft lips collide with mine again I feel more desperate than ever to have him touch me, like *really* touch me. "It's kind of exciting you know, doing it in public."

Sean's fingers find my jeans zip and drag it down slowly, swiping his tongue against mine. "Hell yeah it is baby." He breathes, his voice so deep and sexy it's making my blood boil with desire.

His hand dips inside my underwear, the hot skin reacting immediately to even the slightest touch from him.

Daisy Egan

He slips a finger inside me and I clench around him, a moan along with a quiet, "Fuck," leaving his parted lips as he circles my clit with his thumb. Jesus Christ I'm not going to be able to contain myself for long, I can never get enough of him. My back is arched, my legs still straddling him as they begin to shake, the orgasm heavy in the pit of my stomach. I want to make this last, to hold onto the burning, pulsating need as long as possible but Sean has other ideas. He picks up his pace inside me, his finger dipping in and out fast, the heel of his palm slapping against my clit. As I throw my head back, panting and moaning, Sean's mouth locates my neck, sucking a trail of possessive swells up it.

Sean mutters a muffled, "My god," as he watches me, his fist between his teeth and his eyes bulging. "Come on my fingers Callie, right now.

I shake my head, eyes still screwed shut and neck craned backwards as I fight against my impending orgasm. "No, not yet Sean,"

His hand is on the base of my throat immediately, pulling my face back to his, eyes dark with dominance. "You fucking do as you're told," he growls, *Jesus, he's so hot,* "now be a good girl and come all over my hand." The two magic words are all it takes to push me toppling over the edge, the orgasm crashing into me and knocking the wind out of me completely. I cry out his name, grinding against his fingers and feeling the prickling moisture in my eyes as the intense pleasure rolls over me like a wave.

"You're so fucking pretty when you're coming all over me." Sean coos into my ear, his hot breath coasting over my skin and making me tremble. "I fucking worship you." He whispers, sucking my earlobe into his mouth and forcing me to collapse with pleasure filled exhaustion against his chest. When I manage to catch my breath and look up at Sean he's gleaming with pride like he just accomplished something impossible, which is hilarious to me because making me come is one of his more practiced hobbies.

I love when he looks at me like that, like I'm the only girl in the entire world.

I unfasten his jeans and he wriggles them down his thighs, his cock already rock hard and bobbing in front of me. I dip my head, running my tongue up it and feeling his legs tense under me before I take the head of his dick between my wet lips and suck gently.

"Fuck Callie, you're unbelievable." He groans, the back of his head hitting the head rest with a soft thump. "You won't be able to do that for long if you actually want me inside you." I smile around him and lap my tongue up his length one more time, leaving an open mouthed kiss on the end for good measure before adjusting myself above him. He grips my hips and slams me down, forcing me to take his entire length at once. I choke on my own breath as he lifts me again, pushing himself as deep into me as possible. I take over the rhythm, lifting and dropping onto him, watching his eyes roll back in his head and I know he's already close.

He looks down at our joined bodies, heaving a rough sigh and digging his fingers into my hips again. "Oh fuck yeah, that's it Callie, don't stop baby."

So I don't stop, I keep my pace, gripping his shoulders for support and revealing in the sight of him coming totally undone inside me. His head falls to my shoulder with a muttered curse of my name, arms circling my waist as he comes down from his high. I close my eyes too and let my head flop, burying it in his damp neck and feeling his thumping heartbeat next to my ear. I feel the warmth of his lips against my neck, running along my collarbone and sliding along my jawline before Sean lifts my chin with his finger and our lips meet for a long, soft kiss.

Chapter 42

Sean

"So," Callie says, landing back in the passenger seat and hiking her jeans up her legs, hiding the wet patch that's made itself known on her underwear. *Jesus, I swear I could fuck her again right now.* "It's less than two weeks until Christmas break and you haven't mentioned any plans yet."

I haven't mentioned any plans because I don't have any, my parents are away for two months and Lois is spending Christmas with her new friends. It would be great if I could lie to Callie, I know what's she's going to say, she won't want me spending Christmas alone but I want her to enjoy her break without worrying about me. The only problem is that this woman can read my thoughts without even looking at me and she'll know immediately if I lie to her.

So instead I opt for a nonchalant shrug. "That's because I don't have any plans baby." I try to avoid looking at her but her beautiful green eyes are like a magnet to me, so I reward myself with one peek and watch as her eyebrows scrunch together in confusion.

"What do you normally do for Christmas break?" She asks, shuffling back up on her chair and shaking out her bouncy curls.

"Well, normally I'd go to my parents' house but they're going to Italy for two months."

There's the eyebrow scrunch again, this time she's staring right at me though, assessing me. "Did they not invite you?" She mutters, twisting in her seat to lean back against the door, her body facing me.

I shuffle uncomfortably, having wanted to keep this piece of information to myself. I should have known she'd prise it out of me, woman's like a bloodhound.

"They did invite me..." I take another peek at her and her softened features make me want to curl up in a ball and die. I know what I'm about to say is going to turn her into a teary mess. "But I said no. I didn't want to be away from you for that long." My cheeks flush pink and I feel like a fucking child, how is it she has managed to make me blush twice now since we met?

Her warm palm lands on my thigh and she squeezes gently, sniffing hard and gulping down those tears I knew would spurt the minute I told her why I turned down the chance to spend two months in Italy.

She points her finger at me and twists her face into a warning glare. "Stop that now."

"Stop what?" I titter at her attempt to be stern, her tiny frame barely filling the passenger seat of my car.

"Being cute," she says, pursing her lips and trying to avoid joining me in bellowing laughter. "Will you go to Kyle's for Christmas Day then? His Mum lives only a couple of miles from campus right?"

Fuck, this is the part of the conversation I was hoping to avoid.

I shrug again, hoping to convince her I don't care about spending Christmas alone. The truth is I do care, I don't like being alone, especially not now I have Callie. All I want to do is be within a metre of her at all times, preferably touching her too. I know she loves me and she won't want me to be alone at Christmas but I can't let her ruin her own plans to spend time with her family. With her mum's condition worsening it's more important than ever that she goes home for Christmas and I'm not going to let her worry about me. I'm a big boy, I can look after myself.

"Sean," she says, nudging my shoulder and waiting for a response. *God this woman will be the death of me one day.*

"Nah I won't go to Kyle's, I'll just stay at the house." I murmur, keeping my expression as neutral as possible until Callie decides to choke on her own saliva and my eyes widen. I reach over to pat her back and she shrugs me off, sitting up straighter and lifting her eyebrows high on her forehead in horror.

"Alone?" She squeaks, "You'll stay at the house alone?"

She looks absolutely horrified at the idea of me spending Christmas alone, which I fully expected. Back in the days when she used to pretend like she hated me — all the while wanting to dive into whatever I was offering her — she would have rather eaten broken glass than shown me this side of her. The side I fell in love with, the way she cares so deeply about the people she loves and the way she'd make herself unhappy before she saw me unhappy.

I simply nod and her eyebrows shoot even further up into her hairline. "I'll be fine Cal, honestly." I pat her thigh and turn on the engine which Callie proceeds to reach across me and turn straight back off again. As hard as I try, she's not going to let me run away from this conversation.

"Absolutely not!" Callie shrieks and I purse my lips to contain my blinding smile. I just love the way she cares about me so much, nobody ever has before her.

I shake my head and let a tiny smile slip out. "Baby, I'm a big boy, I'll be ok on my own for a week."

She rolls her eyes in my favourite way and folds her arms over her chest, pushing up her cleavage and giving me an eye full. "No fucking way Sean, you can't do that, you're coming home with me."

Ok, she's officially lost her damn mind.

"What about Coach? Do you not think he'll figure out what's going on between us if I stay at their house with you for an entire week?"

She shrugs, any air of worry gone. "You know what? I don't even think I care anymore. He can know about us, I don't need to keep you a secret."

"Oh," I smile, heart thumping a 100 miles per hour. "That's how it is now?" I take her hand in mine and she scoffs but I can see the beam trying to break onto her freckled face.

"Yeah Taylor, that's how it is. I'm proud to have you, I don't need to hide it from anyone anymore."

"Oh shit ok," I smirk, smacking a kiss to her lips. "What about Lois?"

Callie's hand slides out of mine and she tuts, quietly muttering, "That's different. And anyway, I think she's pretty much figured it out herself after you came riding in like a knight in shining armour when I was having a panic attack."

"Has she mentioned anything to you, asked you about us?"

"No," she shrugs, "she's been pretty good at avoiding any mention of you during training."

"Does that bother you?" I say, running my thumb along her jaw and swallowing down the urge to suck her lips between mine again.

She shakes her head, curls bouncing. "No, I understand why she'd feel uncomfortable, that's why I wanted to avoid telling her."

"She'll get over it baby," I tuck a curl behind her ear, "just give her a bit of time to come to terms with it."

"Yeah, yeah I know, just kind of sucks that she's not talking to me much at the moment."

Note to self, tell Lois to stop being a bitch to my girl.

I feel like I've barely had chance to blink and it's already Christmas break, the light frost covers the ground and I have to walk like my legs are made of wood so I don't fall on my ass as I make my way to the car. My suitcase is trailing behind me, the door handles frozen as I yank them open, listening to the ice crack. I land in the driver's seat with a shaky huff, I don't know why I'm so nervous to spend Christmas break with Callie and her family. I mean, I'm very familiar with her dad — him being my coach and all — but I've never met her mum and I'm desperate to make a good impression on her. I have a taste of what Callie must have felt when she met my parents, makes sense now why she was trembling with nerves during our dinner with them. Also, the inevitable fact that Coach is going to find out that I've been seeing his daughter in secret for months, I'm totally uncertain of how he's going to take it and I know Callie isn't bothered about what he thinks anymore but I am. I'm by far his favourite guy on the team, that's why he made me Captain and I don't want that to change. However, in the same breath there's nothing I wouldn't give up to be with Callie, that includes my future hockey career.

I'm leaving at 7am this morning for what reason I don't know, other than the fact that I'm nervous as hell and I need to get to Callie as quickly as possible. As soon as I'm with her I know my nerves will vanish into thin air, seeing her smile makes my heart melt into a puddle and all other emotions evaporate. Callie went to her parents' house yesterday but I had to stay on campus for an award ceremony that the hockey team host at the end of each year. It was my first one and it's normally something I'd revel in, going up on stage and being the centre of attention but my mind could focus on nothing but the fluttering in my chest when I thought about spending the entire week at Callie's house.

The drive goes by way too quickly, although I'm almost certain I've been speeding the entire way, the country roads allowing me to press the accelerator to the ground and get to Callie as quick as I can. When I pull up on the side of the road — triple checking the address she sent me yesterday — I stare up at the house, the moss around the windows, the little picket fence and the thin layer of snow that blankets her front garden. This house looks like something out of a fairy tale, the chimney puffing out smoke and the thatched roof remaining me of the stories my mum read to me when I was a little boy. I know Callie's family don't have a lot of money but this place is breathtaking, like a story book house and I'm all of a sudden itching to get inside and sit by the open fire. I walk tentatively towards the front door, knowing already that I'll have to duck to get inside, the door is no more than 6 foot high and there's no way I won't have to crane my neck to fit under the snowy canopy. My hand shakes a little as I tap lightly on the door, praying my girl is standing right behind it, waiting for me to arrive. I hear a muffled call and the padding of footsteps before the door swings open and the one face I've been dying to see is in front of me, beaming. Callie pants and smiles widely at me like I'm the best thing she's ever seen and I'm sure my face is mirroring her's right now.

She reaches for my hand, pulling me inside and pinning my back against the front door. "Hi, I missed you." She whispers, pressing her warm lips against my icy ones.

"I missed you too baby," my eyes dart around the room. "but maybe we should ease your parents into the fact we're together, rather than put on a live porno show the second I step foot through the door." I chuckle, my heart beating hard and warming every crevice of my body now Callie is wrapped around me.

"Nobody is home yet, they went to the shop to get some more food for tomorrow."

Oh, ok then.

I pick her up immediately, listing to her squeal with childlike joy and carrying her up the stairs over my shoulder, using my nose to locate her bedroom like she used to do to me when we were first together. I push open the squeaky door that screams 'I'm Callie's bedroom' purely from the gymnastics posters that litter the walls and I drop her down onto the bed. I lay my body on top of her's and breathe her in, her flowery scent mixed with the general christmassy aroma of cinnamon and spices fill the air around us and I feel strangely at home for a place I've never been to before.

"So," Callie giggles, wriggling under my tickling grip on her waist. "Wanna fuck before they get back?"

"God yes," I groan, dipping my hand into her leggings and pushing my fingers into her warmth.

Maybe this week will be better than I thought.

Chapter 43

Callie

Christmas Eve has always been my favourite day of the year, I prefer it to the big day itself purely because I actually get to relax on Christmas Eve. Christmas Day is always pretty chaotic, cooking with my mum, getting the house ready for guests and throwing out the bundles of wrapping paper that end up strewn across the living room floor. Mum and I have always baked on Christmas Eve, she'd let me lick the bowl clean and I'd sit cross legged in front of the oven, keeping my eyes pinned on whatever was baking away in there. But this year is different of course, Sean got here yesterday but my parents didn't arrive home until late and by that point Sean and I were already curled around each other under my duvet, eyelids drooping with sleep. This morning though is quite different, surprisingly my dad hasn't even asked why Sean is here or why he slept in my bed last night. And right now the two of them are lounging back on our sofa, hockey game blaring out of the TV as they chat about things I don't understand, using terms like lip lettuce which immediately makes me want to close my ears for fear of whatever the hell that means. I'd rather not know.

 I'm in the kitchen with Mum, mixing a bowl of dried fruit into a blob of much too sniff dough, watching in awe as Sean and my dad tip beers to their lips in unison. The damp air around me is making my hair stick to the back of my neck, the strong smell of baked bread and cinnamon laced candles fill the house and I'm 100 percent here for it. The two men on the couch have me in a trance as they comfortably laugh together, Sean's taut arm hanging over the back of the sofa like he's lived here all his life. I'm totally mesmerised by the two of them until my mum comes behind me and gives my waist a loving squeeze.

"So that's him then? The guy you were bawling over not too long ago?" My mum wiggles her eyebrows and I stifle a laugh, all the while amazed that she can decipher every thought that passes through my brain.

I break my fixed gaze from where it rests on Sean and turn towards my mum. "How do you always do that?"

She pats the lump of dough on the counter, watching it wobble. "Mother's intuition baby, now spill, I want to know everything."

I heave a sigh, one filled with equal parts happiness and exhaustion from fighting against the ever growing love I have for this man. "Yeah he's just…" I turn my head back to look at Sean, his dimples deepening as he laughs at something my dad says. "He's everything Mum."

Her hand lands on my shoulder as I tear my eyes away from Sean again. "I can tell honey, I've never seen you so in love before."

"Woah, I don't know if I'm quite there yet Mum," I hold my hands up, watching her sly smile as she kneads the dough roughly, squashing it against the counter.

Obviously I am there, I'm so fucking there and have been for a while now.

A quiet laugh escapes her and she shakes her head. "Oh honey, you're so there." She lifts the huge blob of dough from the counter and drops it into a mixing bowl with a strained huff. "And he is too, trust me."

Daisy Egan

"How can you tell?" I say, taking another peek over my shoulder and immediately catching Sean's gaze on me. His eyes are soft, warm and comforting, watching me like I'm the only person in the room.

Mum shrugs and shuffles past me, bowl of heavy dough in hand. "It's so obvious Callie, just the way he watches you it's…"

"How does he watch me?" My eyes are still trapped by Sean's, like he can hear every word of our conversation his mouth turns up into a smile that makes my chest thump.

"Like he's waiting to take a bullet for you." Mum whispers, planting a kiss on my cheek and leaving the kitchen, oven whirring along with my mind as I process what she just said. I'm not stupid, I know how Sean feels about me, he makes it abundantly clear in his words and his actions. But that part of me that always doubts whether I'm good enough for people is still attempting to fight it's way through the strong wall of self worth I've built since being with Sean. The way his eyes are still locked on mine now only confirms what my mum just said, he gestures with his head for me to join him on the couch, shit eating grin still blazing a fire in my chest as I land in the spot next to him. It takes my dad less than a second to pounce, his demeanour changing when he spots Sean's arm lift over my head and come to rest across my shoulders, hauling me into his side.

His face darkens slightly, stress lines on his forehead deepening. "So, shall we have this conversation now or after dinner?"

My words get stuck in my throat, do I just admit it straight away and deal with his anger or try to deny everything and tell him Sean and I are just friends? Luckily for me I don't have to decide, Sean sits up straight, pulling me up with him.

Daisy Egan

"Look Coach, I'm sorry we kept this from you, we should have told you sooner but Callie was worried about your reaction. She tries so god damn hard to please you and all she wants is for you to be proud of her." He takes a deep breath, his eyes flitting to me for a second. "But we are together, and that's not going to change."

Wow, I think he took my breath away with that speech. Watching him take control like that and stand up to my dad is so sexy, I just want to ride him like a horse. My dad sits taller too and my stomach lurks at the possibility of a full blown argument between the two most important men in my life.

"Well, I can't say I'm not disappointed that you didn't tell me sooner…" his eyes land on me and I shrink into Sean's side a little. "But I understand why you kept it from me."

Ok, what?

My eyes shoot up to my dad's, his ageing features softening under my wide eyed stare. "Really?" I croak and he nods with a small smile. "Wow, ok, well…thanks."

"Callie, you don't need to be worried about telling me things, I won't ever stop you from being with someone that you love." Sean and I tense at the same time, the 'L' word rearing it's head again and making us both shift uncomfortably. "I need you to know too Cal," my dad continues, not sensing the tension thickening around us after he threw out the word love like it was nothing. "I am incredibly proud of you."

Jesus Christ my heart can't take all this up and down, one minute it's beating at a normal rhythm, then it comes to a complete stop hearing the word love fall off my dad's lips so casually and now it's beating at an unnaturally fast pace. I don't think my dad has ever uttered the words, 'I'm proud of you.' Since the moment I was born he's always been pretty hard on me, expecting results and accomplishments to keep himself feeling fulfilled as a father. But those words are pretty much all I've wanted to hear from him my whole life, the weight that lifts itself from my shoulders hearing it leaves me feeling like I might float away.

The tears prick against my eyes, stinging and I quickly sniff them away, swallowing them down. "Thanks Dad, that means a lot to me." I squeak as Sean's arm tightens around my middle, him always reading my every emotion like a book.

Dad slaps his hands down on the arms of his chair and comes to a standing position. "Right, enough of this soppy shit, let's eat."

Sean

"Ow," I groan, rolling away from the annoying pointy elbow that's burying itself repeatedly into my side.

Callie's mouth brushes over my ear. "Wake up please, I'm bored of waiting for you and I've been awake since 6am."

Jesus Christ, what is going on?

I peel my eyes open just as my brain manages to catch up and I remember it's Christmas Day, the best part being that I get to spend the whole day with my girl. I roll back onto my side facing Callie, her eyes bright with childlike excitement, a hint of laziness left in her slightly droopy eyelids. "Merry Christmas Captain," She smiles, her eyelashes fluttering and my dick instantly hardens on command. He's more awake than I am because my mind is still semi conscious from being woken abruptly by my annoying girlfriend a few seconds ago.

I raise my eyebrows, scoffing with disbelief. "Really? You want sex right now? I literally just opened my eyes woman."

Callie purses her pouty lips and my dick responds again. "No…I don't know what you're talking about." Her mouth says she has no idea what I'm getting at but her eyes look sultry as hell.

"You called me Captain, which means you want me to break you in half with my dick." I laugh and she kicks her pointed toes towards my bruised shins. I reach out and grab her ankle, dipping my face to her's and brushing my lips against her open mouth. "No kicking, you little shit." I press a firm kiss to her lips, nibbling delicately on her bottom one and eliciting a sexy groan from deep in her throat. I've been waiting for this morning so I can give Callie the present I've been hiding from her for the past week and there's no way I'm going to let my ever hardening cock ruin this moment. Or her own constant horniness around me for that matter.

"I have a present for you." I smile, landing a soft kiss against her cheek as I climb over her warm, half naked body — that I'm trying desperately not to look at — and reach into my overnight bag. When I locate the small, wrapped square I look back at my girl, who is now sitting up, cross legged and scowling at me.

"Sean Taylor," *uh oh, I'm in trouble.* "I thought we weren't doing presents." Her mouth is twisted into a frown and her eyes are snake like.

I gulp hard, momentarily forgetting that she's five-foot-four and I can pick her up with one arm. She's scary when she gives me that look, the one that she's giving me right now. Luckily for me I know the real her, the one she can't hide when she's around me, the soft, mushy one and I know all I have to do is dig it out from under the fiery demeanour that she wears.

Daisy Egan

I climb back onto the bed, taking her face in my hands and forcing the fire to fizzle out under my gaze. "So you're telling me you didn't get me anything?"

She stutters, looking away from me. "Well, no...I...I mean...I did but—"

"Exactly," I silence her, pressing a fleeting kiss to her lips and stopping her in her tracks. "So shut your pretty mouth and turn around."

She grumbles something unintelligible but does as I say and turns away from me. I pull the ribbon on the box, watching it unravel in my hand before taking out the delicate chain and lifting it over her head, fastening it at the back and pulling her smooth curls out from under it. She peers down at it, twiddling it between her fingers whilst I hold my breath for her reaction. My heart is pounding, nerves prickling the back of my neck and making me sweat as I wait silently for her to say something.

"23?" She squeaks and I can hear the croak of the tears in her throat.

"That's your jersey number."

I grip her biceps and turn her back around to face me. "Yeah, now everyone will know who you belong to."

Her watery eyes widen with sarcasm almost immediately and I crack a smile. "Who's that then? You I suppose?"

I nod, my hand creating a necklace when I wrap it around her throat, the '23' charm dangling below it. "You're learning, good girl." I smash my lips onto her's, hearing her breath hitch as she climbs into my lap, straddling my hips. "I'm the only one who gets to make you come," I murmur against her open mouth as her warm breath fans against my lips. "All over my face and all over my cock." Callie pulls away and takes a jagged breath, pulling her swollen bottom lip between her teeth and looking down at our joined bodies. "Are you turned on?" I whisper, wedging my hand between us and cupping her pussy. The heat is pulsating from her, begging me to dive in and steal a taste.

Callie takes a second jagged inhale. "Everything you say turns me on." She says with a wobbly laugh.

I take that as my invitation to move this to the next level, the level I've been dying to climb to since the second I opened my fucking eyes and looked at Callie's sultry gaze staring back at me. I flip her over, our bodies still joined together like magnets as I pull her shorts to the side and dip my hand inside. I drag my fingers through the sodden mess between her thighs and she claws at my back. Her back lifts off the bed when my fingers enter her, sliding inside her effortlessly as she clenches her perfect pussy around me.

I could actually bust in my boxers just watching her like this.

She screws her eyes shut for a moment and then she tentatively removes my fingers from her sopping heat, watching with a painfully turned on expression when I suck them into my mouth.

"Wait," she pants, still catching her breath from where I stole it from her. "before we do that, let me give you your first present."

"First present? There's more than one?" I smirk, sitting up and readjusting my cock as Callie bends over, showcasing her beautifully sculpted ass.

"Well," she stands, a wrapped velvet box in her hand, not much bigger than the one I gave her. "The second present is kind of for both of us." She winks and I bark a laugh, I like where her line of thinking is headed.

I stand up with her, approaching like she may have a rabid animal inside that box she holds lightly in her palm. Her smile as she watches me take it lights up my whole chest and I rip the wrapping paper off eagerly, my heart thumping fast. I lift the silver, chain link bracelet from it's velvety bed and clamp my lips together, not knowing whether to laugh or cry.

"Callie…" I murmur and her glistening eyes burn a whole through my heart, she's so excited to give this to me, something she knows I've wanted for so long. "You know I've wanted this bracelet for ages."

"That's why I got it for you," she says, her fingers lightly tracing my forearm as I stand there, speechless. "Do you like it?"

My eyes fly up to her's, catching her waiting gaze. "I love it Cal…but it's too much, how much did you spend on this?"

She rolls her eyes, wafting a dismissive hand towards me. "Just say thank you Taylor."

"Thank you baby," I whisper, hauling her body into mine and squashing her with a tight hug that likely blocks her airways.

When I eventually release her, watching her suck in a breathy laugh, I try to resume my earlier conquest of breaking her in half with my dick. But Callie has other ideas.

I try to slide my hand back into her shorts but she wags a finger at me and pushes at my chest. "Hold on, I told you I have one more present for you."

Before I have a chance to respond she whips out of the room like a gust of wind and I'm left standing in the centre of her bedroom, my dick protruding from my boxers. When Callie finally emerges, she's wearing a white, satin dressing gown, one I've never seen before and my dick that was quickly deflating stands to attention again.

My eyes widen. "What's going on here then?" I say as she leans against the now closed door, her eyes hooded with seduction. *I fucking love where this is going.*

Callie shrugs, a sexy smirk pulling at her lips. "You can unwrap *me* now."

Fuck. Off.

"You're serious?" I croak, my cock now straining against the cotton, fighting to get to her.

"So serious,"

I practically sprint across the room to get to her, yanking at the silky tie that keeps her body hidden from me and the second the dressing gown falls off her shoulders and pools at her feet I'm totally gone. She's wearing a white set of lingerie, the lace clinging to the curve of her delicious hips, cupping the swell of her breasts and drawing my attention to the apex of her thighs like an 'x' marks the spot. I fall to my knees without thinking, this fucking goddess standing in front of me is mine and sometimes I still can't believe that's the truth.

"Jesus, you're a fucking dream." I whimper, biting my fist and blinking faster than usual to make sure I'm not dreaming all of this. Just when I think I couldn't get any luckier with this woman, she goes and pulls something like this. Callie puts her hands behind her back, crossing one leg over the other and I look up at her, begging her with my eyes to let me have her.

"Do you want to touch me?" She murmurs, her voice so sexy, breathy but teasing all at the same time and I'm fucking living for it. I nod, my throat tight and dry when I try to swallow but Callie simply runs her manicured nails through my mess of curls.

"Beg me then," she whispers and my heart nearly burns a whole through my chest, my dick following suit and trying desperately to escape.

I force a dry swallow. "Please baby," I croak, "please."

Callie's finger lifts my chin, a flabbergasted smile splitting her freckled face. "I was joking Sean."

"I wasn't, get your pants off now." I groan, trailing my fingertips down her milky thighs, stopping at her knees and making my way back up again.

Callie lets out a snicker and I gaze up at her again, inhaling her beauty, her lightly tanned skin, her dusting of freckles, her bright green eyes that make me want to collapse and die from their insufferable beauty.

This girl has me totally wrapped around her finger and she knows it.

"Can I?" I rasp and she nods quickly.

I know why she's so keen the second I remove her thong, the scrappy lace being immediately launched over my head to land somewhere on the ground. Her thighs are practically dripping with need, the heat radiating from her pussy, begging me to fill her. And trust me, I intend to do nothing else for at least the next hour.

Daisy Egan

Chapter 44

Callie

"Callie? Can you hear me?"

"Yeah Dad, I can hear you. What's up?" I mutter, trying to tie my shoelaces as I wedge my phone between my shoulder and ear.

He's quiet for a moment and I can hear him muttering to someone in the background, his tone is making my stomach twist with nerves. I'm sure he's talking to my mum, whom I haven't seen for the last two weeks since we got back to Redwood after the best Christmas break of my life. I've been training all day and my brain needs to rest just as much as my body, but I'm sensing in my dad's tone that he's going to ruin any plan of relaxing that I had for the rest of the evening before I have to drive four hours to the bottom of the country.

"I think maybe you should come home for the weekend, just to spend some time with your mum." He mutters and I hear a door close, muffling my mum's irritated voice even further. I couldn't decipher anything she was saying, but I could hear the warning and frustration towards my dad in her tone.

"I just saw her two weeks ago…" My words are coming out weak because the truth is I'm scared. I'm scared about what this means, is he saying her condition is worsening? And if he is then why doesn't he just come right out and say it. "Is Mum ok?"

My dad heaves a tired sigh. "No, not really Cal, she's going downhill and fast. I suggest you skip that competition tomorrow in Devon and instead come here and spend the weekend with your mum."

I've always known my mum was going to die from cancer, the doctors told us the second time she was diagnosed that it was almost inevitable that it would take her from us at some point. But when I saw her two weeks ago she seemed in great spirits, full of life and bright sunshine as always. I guess that's the thing about cancer though, it can decide to ruin your life at any given moment and you don't always see it coming. My mum is also renowned for pretending she's ok when she's not, putting on a brave face for everyone around her and remaining strong even when she feels weak.

"Let me talk to her," I rasp, forcing a swallow when my throat feels unnaturally dry. I hear my dad sigh, but he knows I'm just as stubborn as my mum so he doesn't bother to argue with me.

The next thing I hear is a wet cough come through the speaker. "Cal, you ok honey?"

I take a breath. "Yeah Mum, I'm fine. The real question is, how are *you*? Dad said you've gone downhill and I should skip my competition this weekend to come and see you."

Another hard cough. "Don't you dare skip that competition Callie Burch, you've worked so hard with those god awful routines and you're going to smash them this weekend, no ifs or buts."

"Mum, are you sure? I can come home and spend the weekend with you."

"No," she croaks, clearly her gravelly throat again. "You go baby, I'm ok don't worry about me."

Daisy Egan

But I do, I do worry about her. I know she's struggling and I can definitely hear the change in her voice from two weeks ago when I saw her. She sounds more frail, more damaged and it's killing me to listen to. However, just like my dad I know not to bother arguing with her, so I reluctantly agree to go to my competition, promising to call her tomorrow night.

Sean

Bang, bang, bang. No answer…shit, did she leave without saying goodbye to me? Surely she wouldn't do that but I haven't heard from her all day and I know she was planning on leaving for Devon this afternoon. I press my ear to Callie's door, listening for footsteps, movement, anything, but all I hear is silence. I try to call her, but her phone rings out before sending me to her voicemail. Fuck, why would she leave for the weekend without saying goodbye to me? That's not like her at all. Did I do something wrong?

I'm wracking my brains for anything that could have upset her when I hear a muttered, "Fuck," from down the hallway. Callie comes stumbling around the corner, four shopping bags overflowing with food dangling from her tiny frame as she struggles against the weight to keep herself upright.

I rush towards her and take the bags from her arms. "Here baby, let me help."

Her hand flies to her chest in shock. "Jeez Taylor you scared me, what are you doing here?"

"I thought you'd gone to Devon and not said goodbye to me." I pout and she strokes my prickly jaw, sighing.

Daisy Egan

"Sorry, no I wouldn't do that. I've just had a shitty afternoon since I finished training." She unlocks her dorm and gestures for me to follow inside.

I dump the shopping bags onto the counter top and follow behind her like a puppy as she turns on the coffee machine, grabbing two mugs from the top cupboard. I can sense the tension in her shoulders without even needing to touch her, I can hear the millions of thoughts whirring around inside her mind, I just don't know what's causing them.

I plant my hands on her shoulders, massaging the knots out of them as she continues making our coffee. "Baby, what's bothering you?"

She spins around, letting her forehead fall to my chest and blowing out a sharp breath. "My mum isn't doing well at the moment. My dad called me this afternoon and said I should skip my competition to go home and spend the weekend with her." I thread my fingers through her soft curls as she continues. "And that only means one thing…he doesn't think she has long left."

Oh my god, I wasn't expecting the conversation to take such a dark turn.

I bracket her jaw in my hands, forcing her to look at me, holding my eyes for a moment before dipping my head and touching my lips to her's. "Do you want to skip the competition to go and be with your mum?"

She shakes her head, her hands lightly resting on my waist. "Mum forbade me from skipping it, you know what she's like, stubborn as hell."

"Like someone else I know." I smile and I see Callie's mouth pull up at the sides.

She swats at me and turns back to the coffee machine, pressing the button on the top and watching the steaming liquid filter into the mug. The piercing aroma fills the air and I breathe deeply, trying to keep my mind on anything but the fact that Callie's mum could die soon.

"Do you want me to come with you this weekend? I don't have any games." I say, tipping my face to kiss her bare shoulder as she mixes the piping coffee and hands it back to me.

"No Sean it's ok, but I appreciate the offer." She smiles mildly at me, fluttering her eyelashes innocently and I just want to stitch her to my skin so she never has to be without me.

She's the strongest woman I've ever known, she doesn't need me but I know I make her life better. That's not me being cocky or arrogant either, I've seen the change in her like everyone else has since she met me. But I decide not to argue with her over coming to Devon, letting her have her space if that's what she needs, I know she'll call if she needs me.

I leave Callie's dorm around 8pm after cooking a meal for Molly, Anais and Callie before they all make the long drive down to Devon. She'll be back on Monday after her competition weekend and I already can't wait for her to get back…maybe I have attachment issues, or maybe I'm just madly in love with this girl. I don't know how much longer I can wait to tell her how I feel, the words almost tumble off my tongue every time I'm around her and I can feel how close I am to just blurting it out one of these days. I'm currently lying on my bed, one arm resting behind my head and the one tapping away at my phone, watching the time tick by as I wait for my girl to text me that she got to her hotel in Devon safely. There's no chance of me sleeping knowing she's still on the road, the drive taking her just over four hours which means she won't arrive until after midnight.

The time is coming up for midnight now and I'm waiting with bated breath for her to message me, telling me she's ok and that she arrived safely. She's sharing a room with my sister Lois which I know she's nervous about as the two of them haven't spoken much since the panic attack incident when Lois inadvertently found out that Callie and I are together. I did text my sister earlier this week to warn her about being nice to my girl whilst they were sharing a room for the weekend. Did she reply? No, of course she didn't, she can be a brat sometimes but the truth is she has a heart of solid gold under that tough skin of her's. I'm just hoping sharing a room will force them to reconcile and not let my relationship with Callie come between what was a strong friendship.

Ping!

"Thank god for that," I mutter to myself as I open the text message from Callie.

Callie:

'I've just checked into my room, Lois isn't here yet so I think I'll just go to bed, the drive took it out of me. I'll text you in the morning, goodnight. X'

Sean:

'Oh come on, I don't even get a tit pic before you go to sleep? I waited up for you to make sure you got there safely, I think I should be rewarded for being the best boyfriend ever. X'

A few minutes go by with no response and I assume she's had enough of me for one day and gone to sleep. But after a moment my phone pings again, this time telling me I have a picture waiting for me. My cock is hard before I even open it, eyes widening with disbelief when I see a full screen view of Callie's round, perky tits. Her skin is golden tanned, tiny freckles splattering across her torso, up to the swell of her breasts. Damn, I just want to suck her nipples into my mouth and feast on her soft skin. It's going to be a long weekend without her.

Chapter 45

Callie

Competition days are always go, go, go. From the second I open my eyes it's an adrenaline rush, the flipping of my stomach as I watch my teammates compete, the surge of endorphins when I land that difficult dismount I've been trying to nail for ages. I love competing, it's in my blood to be ravenous for a win, claws out the entire time but also laser focus turned on and able to think of nothing else but smashing my routines. I'm currently top of the leaderboard, Anais nipping at my heels with only two points less than me and Lois following after. The team event is not until tomorrow, so for today at least I'm competing against some of my closest friends, but it's all part of the sport. We don't take losing personally and learning to lose graciously is a huge developmental milestone in elite sport, it's just as important as winning gracefully. I drop down onto the bench at the side of the floor area, stretching my calves before I have to go and complete my last and least favourite piece of all, vault. As I push my heels into the carpet, leaning down and flattening my chest against my shin — that's now littered with purple bruises from falling off the bars yesterday — I feel someone sit down beside me. When I glance up from my stretch I see Lois fiddling with her fingers, biting anxiously at her nail as she watches the scoreboard, waiting for the judges to determine her fate.

"You did well Lo, don't stress." I mutter, pulling out some tape from my bag and re-strapping my ankle before I have to start my least favourite vault move ever.

She's still biting at her nails when I sit up straight, still feeling the very heavy tension between us that I'm desperate to shift. When she got to the hotel last night I was already sleeping and we were up and ready by 6am this morning so I've not had chance to try and clear this stale air between us.

"Lois come on, please talk to me. Look, I know you're mad that I'm dating your brother but I can't help it, he was going to have me whether I liked it or not." I try to hide my growing smile when I think about Sean, as always he's making me blush without even being here.

Lois' score flashes onto the board, moving her into second place and her face lights up along with a muttered, "Thank god," before she turns back to me with a deep sigh. "I'm not mad at you Callie, I'm just hurt that you kept it from me."

I sigh now too, knowing she's totally right. "I know, I'm sorry. I just didn't want you to think badly of me for being with someone like Sean, who is known for his hobby of flitting between women like they're flavours of ice cream."

Lois titters. "That's one way of describing my brother,"

"I really like him Lo, please don't let this come between us."

She pats a hand on my bare thigh and stands up, reaching her hand down to help me to my feet too. "It doesn't change our friendship Cal, I still love you and hey, I guess one day you could be my sister-in-law." She grins and my stomach does it's own little backflip. I'm not sure if it's a good backflip or not.

"Erm, I'm not sure that's on the cards just yet Lo," I laugh and she nudges my shoulder, gesturing to Ellen who is stood waiting for me at the vault, hands on hips and eyes like a snake.

I huff and kiss her cheek. "Better go before Ellen gouges my eyes out." Lois pats my ass as I move past her, yelling after me, "Go and smash it Cal!"

Oh, I intend to.

I'm well and truly fucked when I get back to my hotel room and not fucked in a good way like when Sean has broken me with his 9 inch dick. No, I'm fucking exhausted, mentally, physically, emotionally. I dump my bag on the ground, making a mental note to sort all of my sweaty shit out later and sink back onto my bed. Lois lands beside me, pulling out her phone and beginning to scroll through her messages from today. We both groan with exhaustion, a hint of frustration laced through both of our guttural sighs after the competition ended with neither of us collecting a gold. After I fucked up my vault I was dropped to second place, Lois pushed to third and Anais following in fourth. Ellen was pissed to say the least, but not as pissed as we were at ourselves for not coming top of all the universities like we usually do. My phone screen is filled with messages when I turn it on, not having had chance to look at it since 8am when we started warming up this morning. The first name I notice is of course Sean's, I scroll through his many messages of support from this morning, the latest one from only an hour ago asking me to call him when

I get back to the hotel. Just as I'm about to hit the call button, desperate to hear my favourite voice, I notice my dad has tried to call me a few times today too. My stomach sinks and before I have chance to think too much into what this means, he calls again. I answer immediately and can hear the thumping of my heart in my ears as I wait for him to speak.

"Callie why haven't you been answering your phone? I've been trying to reach you all day." He says, so quietly it's making my skin itch with anxiety. Usually if I'd ignored his calls all day he'd be yelling, scolding me for not being at his beck and call. But his voice is totally foreign today, a soft, raspy sound there that I don't think I've ever heard before.

I clear my throat. "I was at my competition Dad sorry, everything ok?"

It's not, I can already feel it deep in the pit of my stomach.

Then there's a silence on the other end of the phone, a silence so heavy I feel like it might crush me. I can hear him breathing, stuttering and uneven as he waits, for what I don't know but I can't bear this any longer so I mumble quietly, "Dad?"

He inhales a long breath. "Cal, I'm so sorry to have to do this over the phone but…"

"No," I gasp, my lungs closing in on me and my ears prickling with heat, waiting for the words to fall from his lips, the words that will make me want to curl up in a ball and die.

"I'm so sorry honey," he chokes on his tears, "but she passed away this morning."

My ears are ringing, my head burning as the red hot flames crawl up my neck like a wildfire, spreading to every crevice of my skin and lighting me up like a house engulfed in flames. My eyes instinctively flood with tears, my vision a total blur as they roll down my cheeks in a heavy stream, leaving a trail of ice on my burning skin. I hang up the phone without saying another word, grabbing my chest where it feels like my heart might fall out of it.

Lois twists her face to look at me, seeing the tears and sitting up straight. "Cal, what's wrong?"

I collapse into her, gripping her t-shirt so hard I'm worried I might tear a hole in it, she holds me as I weep and god, do I weep. I scream a low, throaty bellow as she hugs me tight, my entire body feels like it's made of jelly, my legs and arms totally numb. When my mum's beautiful, childlike grin enters my mind is when I totally lose it, rolling away from Lois and curling up in a ball, lying on the bed in the foetal position and rocking myself repeatedly as I sob with pain into my knees.

How can this be happening? How can she just be gone? Just like that. I saw her two fucking weeks ago and she was fine! I don't understand, I don't understand anything right now.

I don't know how long I'm in that position but I do hear my phone ringing on repeat for what feels like days. When I finally feel able to lift my head from where it's almost crusted to the pillow with tears, I see Lois sitting on the other side of the hotel room drinking a glass of water and watching me like a hawk.

When our eyes meet she stands up and approaches me, tenderly laying her hand on my arm as I sniff with the still trickling tears. "Callie, I'm so sorry, I saw the text from your dad when you were asleep." *Did I sleep? I don't remember sleeping.* "He's tried to call you...so has Sean."

Sean. I need him, right now, I need him.

I sit upright. "Where's my phone?" I croak, my voice hoarse and dry.

My throat hurts, my head hurts, everything hurts, especially my heart. Lois immediately retrieves it from her back pocket and puts it into my outstretched hand. I nod in thanks and unlock the screen, finding Sean's number and pressing it with shaking hands.

Lois stands up from the bed. "I'll give you some privacy Cal."

She leaves the room just as Sean picks up the phone, his voice full of pride and excitement, the total opposite of how I'm feeling. "Hey baby, I heard you totally smashed it today, I'm so proud of you."

I can hear the grin in his voice and for a split second the usual warmth spreads through my chest. Until the blazing fire returns and makes me want to die again.

I sniffle, speaking through my tears. "Can you come here?"

He falls silent for a beat and then whispers, "Are you crying?" I hear him shuffling around but I don't respond. "Tell me what happened, tell me now Callie." His voice is stronger now, that usual protective instinct wading through his deep tone.

I choke on my tears again. "My mum she…" *God, I can't say it out loud, it's too painful.* "She's gone Sean." I wail, dropping my phone onto the bed beside me and burying my soaking wet face into my hands, sobbing loudly.

"Shit," I hear Sean murmur, my phone still laying on the bed beside my knee. "I'm coming baby, I'll be four hours ok?"

He hangs up before I can reply but I don't care, all I care about is that he's coming. I don't think I've ever been so desperate to be in his arms than I am now, I need him to hold me so tightly I can forget just for a moment that my heart has been ripped from my chest and stamped into the ground in front of me. I need him here and fast.

Chapter 46

Sean

Shit, shit, shit. My brain feels like there's a cloud of fog hanging over it, preventing me from being able to think clearly. I've been swerving in and out of cars down the busy motorway for just under four hours now, my satnav says I have twenty-five minutes to go until I'm at the hotel but I'm determined to be there in half the time. I haven't stuck to the speed limit for more than five minutes of the entire journey here and yet the time seems to be dragging by so slowly, it's driving me fucking insane. Fifteen minutes later when I round the bend and the hotel comes into view I feel my heart beat normally for the first time since I spoke to Callie earlier. I still can't believe this is happening to her, my poor baby, all I want to do is wrap her up and keep her heart caged in my own chest forever so nothing can ever hurt her like this again. I slam my car door shut, sprinting towards the double doors and walking straight past the reception desk. My face must be totally thunderous right now, as the young, mousy girl on reception simply watches me pass her with wide eyes, not even attempting to stop me barging inside. I press the button in the lift, taking me up to the top floor of the five story building and listening to the echoing sound of my feet stomping along the silent corridor towards Callie's room. I count the numbers in my head, 104, 105,

106, 107, finally 108. I lift my fist to smash it against the door but I stop
myself, imagining the delicate state my girl must be in and deciding a light
tap will suffice.

The door pulls open just a crack and my sister's face appears in the gap.
"She's in a state Sean, she's just been laying on her bed in silence, she
won't say a word to me." Lois' eyes are soft with sadness, powerless to
help her friend and I consider reaching out and giving her a hug. But then I
remember my girl needs me and she's waiting.

"Let me in Lo," I half plead, half demand and she immediately nods,
opening the door wider and dragging me inside by the pocket of my grey
hoodie.

It takes me only half a second to scan the room and find Callie curled up in
a ball in the centre of the bed, just like Lois said. She looks like a small
child, holding herself together like her limbs might fall off if she lets go of
her vice like grip around her knees.

"Baby," I murmur and Callie sits up fast, twisting her body around and
crawling across the bed towards me.

Her eyes are the first thing I notice as she scrambles closer, climbing me
like a tree and wrapping her legs so tight around my middle I can barely
suck in a breath. Her face is sunken, her eyes a deep purple underneath
from the onslaught of tears and I feel my heart breaking as I hold her,
hearing her sob uncontrollably into my shoulder. My solid arms encircle
her like armour, fighting to protect her from any pain she's feeling.
Unfortunately that pain isn't caused by something physical, something I
can fight off and protect her from, it's emotional, it's in her heart and all I
can do is hold her. Knowing I can't take away this pain for her is the most
difficult part, every one of my instincts is screaming at me to do

something, stop this feeling for her and take it for myself, but I can't. I
sigh into her neck, breathing in her warmth and her flowery scent, the
thick sadness hanging over us.

"Baby, I'm so, so, sorry." I whisper, so only she can hear.

She gives me a tighter squeeze, her arms clasped around my neck and her
face nuzzling deeper into my shoulder as her gut wrenching sobs continue.
I must hold Callie like that for at least half an hour before carrying her
over to the bed and laying down behind her, stroking her hair in a robotic
motion as I try to collect my scattered thoughts. Her sniffles quiet down
after a while and I pepper light, barely there kisses on the back of her neck
and shoulder, wrapping my body around her's as her breathing deepens
and slows. When I know she's deep in sleep I get up, Lois still hovering on
the chair in the corner of the room, pretending to be engrossed in her
phone when I know she's really been watching me in awe since I got here.

Lois sighs. "She's broken isn't she?" She whispers, tilting her head
towards my sleeping girl.

"Yeah, she is. But I'll fix her, don't worry." I murmur, heading for the
door, desperate for a breath of cold air in my lungs.

"Hey Sean, can I ask you something?"

"Sure," I whisper, conscious of waking Callie if we talk too loudly.

Lois swallows, like she's nervous. "Are you serious about her?"

I nod immediately. "Yeah, I am—"

"Because if you're just fucking around," she interrupts me, pointing a
warning finger in my direction.

"I'm in love with her Lo…" I look back at Callie, curled up like a sleeping
kitten. "Like I'm really fucking in love with her."

"Well, good. Because she may act like an angry cat most of the time but inside she's very squishy and vulnerable." Lois still has a warning glare plastered on her face which only makes me chuckle, these two tiny women love to give me shit and act like they could pin me to the ground when we all know I could pick them both up with one pinky finger.

"I know Lo, I've seen every side of her and that's why I can't leave the girl alone, I'm obsessed."

"Have you told her that you love her?"

I shake my head, eyes falling to the ground with embarrassment. "No, not yet. I wanted to wait until she was ready, I'm still not sure she's there yet." Lois snorts a quiet laugh behind her hand. "You stupid fucker," she laughs again. *I would consider smacking her if she wasn't a girl.* "She's obviously in love with you too."

Lois isn't the first person to say how obvious mine and Callie's feelings are for each other, maybe we're both being stupid, like we're scared of three little words. Well, I'm not scared of them, I'm fucking dying to say them to her, say them with my whole chest and mean every single syllable. But I know Callie was reluctant to give me a chance when we met and I've spent our whole time together doing all I can to prove that I can be good for her, to prove that I can commit to one woman, if that woman is Callie.

Lois sighs and stands up, planting a hand on my shoulder. "Sean, you're the only person she wanted today, she didn't want me or Molly or her dad...only you." Lois smiles tenderly and my heart pounds with excitement. "Trust me, she's in love with you."

Well shit, my little sister is smarter than I thought. Maybe Callie and I are both holding back for no reason, why can't we both be honest about our feelings for each other? I know it's fear on her part, fear of rejection and eventual abandonment. But for me it's been about patience, or so I thought. I thought I was waiting for Callie to be ready but maybe that's been my mistake all along, maybe she's needed the reassurance of me telling her I love her first, for her to feel confident enough to say it back. I'm going to tell her, not right now when she's grieving but when she's feeling more like herself again, I'm just going to say it. I'm going to tell her how every time I look at her my heart flutters, every time she laughs or smiles my chest feels tight and how I love her with my entire being. I'll tell her how I've never loved anyone before and I will never love anyone else the way I love her.

Chapter 47

Callie

I'm pretty sure my heart is no longer in my body, I don't know who has it but it's certainly not me. I hope to god it's Sean because at this point I'm almost certain he's the only one who can take care of it and stop it from shattering into a thousand pieces. Maybe it's already shattered, I don't fucking know, I don't know anything right now other than the intense, aching pain I feel in the centre of my now empty chest and the desperation I feel to be attached to Sean at all times. It's the only thing keeping me in one whole piece, having him hold me is the only thing that is stopping me from totally falling apart and considering things I've never dreamt of doing before, none of them good.

When I peel open my dry eyes, squinting under the much too bright light of the hotel room, the first thing I notice is the piercing coffee aroma that's invading my nostrils. Usually I'd be straight out of bed and hunting for the source of the mouth watering smell, but today all I can feel is the cold spot behind me where Sean was. I flip myself over, scanning my aching eyes across the small hotel room and thankfully I spot him quickly before the panic sets in. He's sitting in the chair that Lois made her home in last night, his caramel eyes full of worry as he rubs the back of his neck, muttering quietly as he talks on the phone. I clear my throat and his eyes

spring up to meet mine, softening with empathy as he takes in my
dishevelled look, my face twisted into a painful frown.

"I gotta go, I'll call you back when I've spoken to her." He mutters and
places the phone — which I now see is mine — onto the desk he's sitting
next to, rising to his feet and coming to land next to me on the bed. His
arms haul me against his chest, cradling me in his lap like a baby and I
push my nose into his hard chest, inhaling his comforting woodsy smell
mixed in with the coffee that floats around the room.

I swallow down the tears that are teetering on the edge of my eyes. "Did I
dream it? Or did it really happen?" I stutter, one single tear escaping down
my cheek and landing on Sean's forearm.

He squeezes me tighter into him. "I'm sorry baby," he sighs, dipping his
forehead to lean against my damp cheek as I sniff back the remaining
tears. I'm not going to spend all day crying today, I refuse to crumble into
a total mess when I know my mum would have hated to see me this way.
The irony is that I've known this day was coming for a while, I thought I'd
managed to get my head around it to some degree, but the way the news
hit me yesterday was like a fucking bulldozer falling from the sky. Luckily
Sean was able to catch it before it landed directly on top of me, crushing
me under it's weight and taking me away from him forever.

Sean sits me up, my legs straddling his waist as he tucks a lock of hair
behind my ear tenderly. "Do you want to go home today? I can take you."
He murmurs, thumb running across my cheekbones where the trail of my
previous tears still sit. I shake my head and he lets out a breathy sigh. "I
won't push you Cal, but I really think you should see your dad."

I know he's right, the man is always right and he is one of the most level
headed people I've ever met, but I don't know if my heart can take the

pain of seeing my dad today. I know it's the right thing to do, we need to be a support for each other in times like these but to be brutally honest I don't think I have anything left to give my dad. It's not secret that the two of us have never been close and just because we mended some bridges at Christmas doesn't mean we're suddenly going to be hugging and crying all over each other. The only person I want to comfort me is Sean, he's the only one who can do it properly, the only one who actually makes me feel better when I'm in his arms. But this isn't just about me and I know that, my dad must be broken too, just as much as I am. I feel a responsibility to be there for him, unlike me he has nobody else to comfort him or be with him whilst he grieves.

I sit up straighter, Sean's hands running up my bare back under his t-shirt that's draped over me. "Ok, I'll go, but I don't want to stay overnight. I want to go back to Redwood tonight, to see Molly and sleep in my own bed."

Sean nods. "Whatever you want to do baby, that's what we'll do. I totally get it if you want to stay at the dorm tonight with Molly, I can drop you off after you've seen your dad."

I lift my head fast from where it had dropped into Sean's neck. "You… you're not going to stay at the dorm with me tonight?"

I need him to stay with me, I can't sleep alone.

"Oh, I thought you meant you wanted to just stay with Mol tonight," a small smile lifts his lips, "of course I'll stay with you, you know I never want to be away from you, especially when you're delicate."

"Hmm," I hum, burying my face into Sean's neck again and letting him smother me as he huge arms wrap around my waist.

The drive to see my dad is painfully long, mostly because I just stare out of the window the entire way there, Sean's hand running up and down my thigh as he drives in silence beside me. I know he's giving me the quiet space I so desperately need to process everything that's happened, I appreciate it but I kind of wish he'd say something. I wish he'd rattle on about hockey or his family or something that would keep my brain busy and focused on something, anything other than the same sentence that keeps spinning around inside it. I'm never going to see my mum again.

"Cal," Sean shakes my shoulder gently and my eyes flutter open, I don't even remember falling asleep. "We're here baby."

Shit, shit, shit, I don't want to be here.

I stretch my arms above my head, my spine cracking after sitting in the same twisted position for hours. Sean's hand finds my chin, raising it and forcing my tired, sunken eyes to look at him.

"Want me to stay here so you can—?"

"No," I cut him off, not needing to hear the rest of his sentence to decide that I most definitely can't go in there without him. "I can't go alone."

We walk up the cobbled path together, Sean's large hand enclosing mine in it's warmth before his other fist lands with a soft thump against the front door. I feel like I'm holding my breath when the door finally creaks open, my dad's sullen face appearing behind it. He gestures for us to enter, not saying a word and closing the door with a click behind us. My hand tightens around Sean's, our fingers interlocked in a unbreakable hold as I watch my dad shuffle uncomfortably, not knowing what to say. I get it, I don't know what to say either, so instead I peel my hand out of Sean's and take a few steps across the hallway to my dad. I hook my arms around his neck and hug him tighter than I ever have before. To my surprise I feel his arms around my middle without hesitation, holding me close to him. A spluttered sob cracks through his throat and my own dam bursts before I can stop it, now here we are doing exactly what I said we never would, holding each other and crying. The shared grief is like a magnet between us that never existed before, something drawing us to each other, the way we empathise with how the other one is so utterly broken as ourselves.

We hold each other for a long minute before breaking apart, the second we let go of each other I immediately gravitate back to Sean, nuzzling into his side and dipping my hand under the back of his t-shirt, planting it firmly against his warm skin as he drops a kiss to the crown of my head.

"Do you guys want to stay for dinner? I can order a takeout?" Dad sniffs, wiping his wet eyes roughly with the back of his hand.

I nod, looking up to Sean who is smiling tenderly down at me. "Yeah, sure Dad,"

My dad nods, a warm smile tipping his lips although he keeps his eyes on the ground. "Great, let's sit."

I look to Sean for reassurance again and as usual he's already looking down at me, his chocolate gaze fixed on me like I'm the only thing he sees. "You're everything to me," he whispers, eyes locked onto mine as I stand there speechless for a moment, my heart faltering under his intense stare. Sean's face splits into a bright grin and his hand lands on my lower back, steering me after my dad towards the living room. My heart flutters when I replay his words in my head and I want to shout how much I love him from the rooftops, but I guess today isn't the day for that when the crack that split my heart yesterday is far from healed. The first thing that hits me as Sean and I land on the sofa is the strong smell of my mum in here, maybe this is where she was the other day when my dad called and I could hear her scolding him in the background. I feel the tears pricking my eyes again but I force them back down, drowning them and forcing a sad smile onto my face as my dad makes eye contact with me for the first time since we got here.

"Is there anything you need me to help with, like with the…the funeral?" I croak, swiping at the moisture pooling in my eyelids.

Fuck, how I am supposed to go to the funeral?

Sean, reading my mind as usual, gives my thigh a reassuring squeeze. "I can deal with that stuff, you both need to take some time to be with your feelings, let me handle the admin."

I take his hand in mine and let my body fall to the side, cuddling into him when his arm comes around me as my dad watches with a smile.

"Keep a tight hold of that," he gestures to the two of us, "both of you. I hope you both know how lucky you are to have found each other, don't take it for granted." He sighs, the sullen look weakening his usually hard exterior as he reaches for the remote, turning on the TV and filling the heavy silence.

Chapter 48

Sean

We don't arrive at Callie's dorm until almost 11pm, the silent walk down the hallway is making me itch with the urge to say something, but I don't know what to say or if I should even be speaking right now. These past two days have likely been the hardest of Callie's life and I'm not sure whether I should be keeping quiet, giving her the space to be inside her own head or trying to drag her back to earth with me by keeping her mind distracted. I take hold of her hand as she twists her key in the lock and she flashes me a quick, forced smile. As the door creaks open Molly jumps up from the sofa immediately, her eyes wide with worry for her best friend as the blankets she was wearing tumble to the ground.

Molly takes two long strides across the room to Callie. "Oh Cal," she tips her head in sympathy and Callie blubbers, spluttering and trying to hold back the assault of more tears, but she can't hold them in and she bursts. Molly hauls her into a hug, rubbing her back and squeezing her tight as she cries.

"I'm so sorry Cal, I'm so sorry." She murmurs, holding my girl tightly as she fights to control her tears. I want to reach over there, take her back and be the one to hold her when she cries but I know she needs this moment with her best friend, the one who was here long before me. When they eventually pull away, Molly rubs her thumbs under Callie's eyes, mopping up the moisture and cradling her face between her manicured hands.

"I love you, anything you need you let me know ok?" Molly says softly and Callie nods in response, swiping the back of her hand across her tear streaked face.

Callie sniffs. "Thanks Mol, I love you too." She whispers dryly, her throat tight and hoarse. "I'm going to my room."

I nod when she twists her face to look at me, trying to force a smile of my own for her sake before she picks up her bag and trundles off down the hallway, her shoulders low.

I sink down onto a barstool and let my head fall into my hands. "Jesus Christ," I huff, a deep sigh leaving my lips. "What a weekend this has been,"

Molly slides a cup of hot coffee across the island to me and I return her empathetic smile.

"I know this is a stupid question but," Molly pauses, pushing her blonde waves back from her face. "How's she been?"

"Not great, as you can imagine, but she's tough." I sigh, sipping at the liquid gold and revealing in the warmth trailing down my dry throat.

"I can't believe you drove four hours to be with her when she needed you," Molly says and I look up at her again, her eyes are bright with gratitude this time. "I mean, I know you're like boyfriend of the year or whatever but..." she glances over her shoulder, making sure Callie can't overhear what she's about to say. "I think even Callie was surprised you came running the second she called for you."

I let out a quiet, disbelieving laugh. "I would have walked there if she needed me Mol,"

Molly nods, face crumpling with deepening thought as she stirs another cup of coffee that I assume is for Callie. "I'll make your guys some food in a minute, I'm sure you're hungry."

"It's ok, you don't have to do that. We actually ate with her dad a couple of hours ago but maybe she'd like some ice cream if you have any."

Molly immediately dips down below the island so she's out of sight, rummaging in the freezer before holding up Callie's favourite ice cream flavour — cookie dough — with a triumphant grin. She slides it across the island too, two spoons following it's path to me and I quickly pocket them.

"You staying with her tonight?" Molly says, handing me the piping hot mug of coffee to take to my girl.

I nod. "That's ok right?"

Molly smiles brightly at me, nodding too. "Of course it is, like I said, you're who she needs right now."

Fuck yes I am, I fucking love that.

When I walk into Callie's bedroom, coffee in one hand and ice cream in the other, the spoons clattering around in my pocket, I see my baby curled up on the bed. Her hair is sprawled out over the pillow behind her, emerald irises hiding behind her closed lids as her chest rises and falls at a steady pace. It's moments like this when I just look at her and think, how the hell did I get so lucky? From almost the first second I spotted her in that penalty box it's like I knew something was different, it was a different kind of attraction, like a magnetic force pulling me to her. Then when she rejected me I was even more hooked on her, desperate to change my fuck boy ways and prove to her that I can be everything she needs. I just want to put her in my pocket and keep her safe, I want to do everything life has to offer with her, experience every new thing with her.

I sit down beside her, lifting her floppy arm and placing it over my middle
as I shuffle my own arm under her neck and bring her closer to me.

She stirs slightly, eyes fluttering open and in a groggy voice she whispers,
"You have ice cream?"

I breathe a quiet laugh. "Yeah baby, I have ice cream, you want some?"

"God yes," she replies, sitting up and rubbing her tired eyes with the heels
of her palms. "You got my favourite." She smiles, her freckled cheeks
drawing my attention as always, she's so painfully beautiful.

"Of course I did…" I snicker, "well, Molly actually handed it to me from
the freezer but—"

"You would have chosen this flavour anyway, because you know it's my
favourite." Callie cuts me off and digs her spoon into the tub of frosty
goodness, jamming her full spoon into her mouth and cringing at the cold
as it hits her tongue.

Her mouth is packed with ice cream as she murmurs, "You know me so
well and I love that."

I fucking love it too.

Before I can even blink her lips land on mine, cold and sweet from the ice
cream and I suck them into my mouth, fighting my way in with my tongue
and lapping up any remnants of milky sweetness that's left. She's hungry
for me, probably hoping this will make her forget about her grief even if
it's only temporary and I'm more than happy to help her feel good, even if
it's only for tonight. Her hands are in my hair, pulling me closer, my own
hands in a bruising hold on her hips as I hoist her up into my lap. I feel like
I haven't kissed her like this for years when in reality it's only been a
couple of days, but she's like a drug to me, without her I'm shaking with
addiction. The warmth of her pussy is apparent the minute she's straddling

my waist, grinding on me, desperate for any kind of friction she can get as our tongues battle for dominance. My palms slide up her waist, following the curve of her torso before stopping on either side of her face and reluctantly pulling her lips off mine.

"Baby, are you sure?" I pant, watching her eyes wash with confusion and rejection. "I'm just checking you definitely want to have sex right now, I don't want you to regret it tomorrow."

Callie huffs a laugh and pulls my hands from her face. "Don't be ridiculous Sean, I'd never regret it with you, no matter what the circumstances."

Do I say it now? I really fucking want to say it now.

"Callie, I…"

Callie's face twists in confusion again, but this time impatience is definitely there too. "You what Sean? Come on please just say whatever you want to say so you can fuck my brains out."

I shake my head with a laugh and the urge to say those three words disappears again, this isn't the right time, it's like it's never going to be the right time with this sassy mouthed girl I chose. Instead of saying anything else I flip her over so her body is under mine, fully intending on doing exactly what she wants, fucking her brains out. She claws at my back, pulling my t-shirt over my head and launching it somewhere behind me.

"I need you to make me forget," she breathes into my mouth as I run my palm under her t-shirt and locate her hardened nipple. "Not forever, just for tonight,"

I nod, inhaling her sweet smell. "I can do that,"

I hum as her hand tracks the length of my torso, dipping inside my grey joggers and wrapping perfectly around my cock. Her palm fits over me like a glove, slipping up and down in a motion that could easily make me come all over her hand right now. But I'm desperate to be inside her like I always am, so I pull away, sitting up and undressing as she does the same. We're like animals, ravaging each other's bodies and taking exactly what we need from the other. No matter how many times I fuck her, kiss her, hold her, it will never be enough to satisfy me, I'll always need more. She rakes her hands through my curls, kissing me hard as I line myself up at her soaking wet entrance, running my fingers through her moisture and watching her back lift off the bed with pleasure before I sink myself into her. She's so hot, so wet and the sensation is almost blinding, her pussy tightens around me as I move in and out at a steady pace.

"Fuck Sean, that feels so good," she wails and I cup my hand over her mouth, her eyes pinging up to mine.

I clamp my lips together to hold back my laugh. "Molly is next door, I don't think she needs to hear that."

Callie laughs too, for the first time since her life was turned upside down. "But you do…need to hear that I mean."

Fuck yeah I do.

I smash my lips down onto her's again, slipping my cock in and out of her faster, harder, everything she murmurs into my ear. Before I even have chance to flip her over, push into her from behind and see the break taking view that is Callie's ass jutted up to the sky in front of me, I can feel my dick twitch inside her. She drains me totally dry, her pussy squeezing every last drop of come out of me and I collapse on top of her, taking only a moment to catch my breath before lowering myself down to her still dripping pussy. Her own wetness isn't the only thing seeping out of her now though, so I grab a tissue and clean the mess up that I made inside of her. She tries to sit up but I push her back down, confusion washing over her beautiful, freckled face.

"You think I'm going to just please myself and forget about the fact you didn't get to come?" I laugh, "Do you know me at all?"

"Oh," Callie muses, lying back and burying herself deep into the mattress. "Well, in that case, go right ahead Captain."

Jesus, I fucking love when she calls me that.

I don't hesitate to tease her a bit, trailing my tongue around her throbbing clit but not actually touching it at all, hovering over it, but never making direct contact. After only a few seconds Callie is writhing under me and I can see the growing frustration as I watch her, I know her next move before she even makes it. She huffs and groans, reaching down to grab a fistful of my hair and stuff my face between her thighs. I stifle a laugh and get to work pleasing her, lapping my tongue up and down, sucking her pulsing clit between my lips and tasting her sweetness, revealing in the way only *I* can make her feel.

Her thighs wrap around my face and she groans, "Sean, I'm…I'm…"

I slap my hand over her mouth again. "Come on baby, let me taste you."

That's all I need to say for her to be coming all over my tongue as I lick her clit, soothing to burn from all the nipping and sucking that I did to send her toppling over the edge, watching the orgasm drown her. All I want to do now is wrap my body around her, nuzzle my face into her warm neck and wait for her to fall asleep buried in my chest. Callie has the exact same idea as she twists around to face me, curls tickling my stomach as she sinks her face into me, breathing softly and after only a few minutes she's taken deep into sleep where I soon follow.

Daisy Egan

Chapter 49

Callie

Molly has already left for practice when I wake up and make my way out into the kitchen, leaving Sean asleep in my bed. He has to leave today, I know he does and yet he hasn't mentioned it at all. I'm dreading it, him being gone for a whole month, especially now when I need him more than I think I ever have before. But I have to be strong, keep going on my own and not let myself crumble into a million pieces on the ground when he's not around.

I turn on the coffee machine, the familiar whirring sound blurring the thoughts spinning around in my mind, the coffee smell invading my senses and bringing a wash of peace with it for a moment. Through the noise of the machine I don't hear the padding of Sean's footsteps as they approach me from behind, so when his huge arms come around my waist I jump a little, before letting out a relieved breath when his usual woodsy scent cocoons me.

He plants a kiss in the crook of my neck. "Morning beautiful, how are you feeling?"

"You know what? I'm actually feeling ok," I murmur, pouring the coffee into two mugs and watching the steam billow up towards the ceiling.

Sean's hands slip down to my hips, holding me tightly and tilting his face around to peck my lips softly before taking the coffee from my hand and sipping at it. I turn around to watch him, mesmerised as always by the way his bare torso contracts, the way his dimples deepen when he catches me looking at him and the way his v-shaped pelvis points towards my favourite part of his body that hides under his grey track pants.

"What time do you have to leave?" I say, a hint of moisture pooling in my eyes at the thought of him going and not being able to see him for a month. He sips at his coffee again and watches me with an uncertain look in his eye.

"I don't *have* to go," he finally says, "I can stay here, if you need me." His voice is so smooth, so sure of what he's offering but he should know me better than that by now, I'd never ask him to miss his most important games of the season for me.

I shake my head immediately. "No, you're going. So what time do you need to leave?"

He's still watching me as he drinks, his eyes never leaving mine like he's trying to read my mind as to whether I mean what I say. Of course I'd love him to stay here with me, he's like my anchor, holding me down when I feel like my soul is floating away from me. But I also know how amazingly talented he is on the ice and how his team rely on him to lead them. He's so good at what he does and I'm so fucking proud of him it hurts, so there's no way on earth I'm going to ask him not to leave, even though my heart is screaming at him to stay.

Sean sighs and puts down his now empty mug in the sink, brushing past me and muttering, "I have to go at 8am, we have a long drive."

He leaves the kitchen without another word and a sinking feeling makes itself known in my stomach, is he mad at me? Does he want me to ask him to stay? I follow after him, pushing open the bedroom door and watching him shove last night's t-shirt over his head.

"Are you mad at me?" I squeak and his eyes spring up to mine, eyebrows scrunched tightly in confusion.

"What? No, baby, why would I be mad at you?" He stands up and moves towards me, collecting my curls and bringing them to hang down my back.

I shrug. "I don't know, it just kind of felt like I upset you a minute ago."

"No, you didn't upset me, I just really don't want to leave and I was kind of hoping you'd ask me to stay so I had an excuse not to miss you like crazy for the next month."

"I mean, of course I don't want you to go Sean but…" I look into his caramel eyes, all of his feelings so clear as they pour out of him and I consider just screaming how much I love him right into his face. "I'll miss you so much," I run my thumbs along his jaw, the scratchy bed of stubble making my fingers itch. "But you have to go, your team need you and hockey is important you."

"Not as important as you Callie," he shakes his head, his warm palms covering mine on his cheeks. "No where fucking near as important as you." He takes a long breath, pressing his lips to mine for a long beat and then collecting his car keys from my side table. "I better leave in a minute, I have to go home and get all my stuff together before I have to meet the team at the rink."

Oh god, he's leaving already.

"Ok, well call me when you get there ok?" I sigh, already fighting off the tears that I'm desperate to stop from spilling.

I know it will only make it harder on Sean if he sees me upset at him leaving, even though inside my heart is dying at the thought of not having him hold me for four long weeks.

"I will," he brackets my jaw again, "and Callie, if you need me to come back, you call."

I let my eyes flutter closed, mainly to stop the tears from spilling and giving away how much I fucking hate this. "I won't ask you to come back Sean."

"Cal," he huffs, shaking his head with exasperation. "Just nod for yes." He smiles and I can't stop the airy laugh that leaves my lips as I nod, doing as I'm told for once.

Sean's dimples deepen and I want to run my fingers over them, but I'm only making this harder for both of us, so instead I let him lead me by the hand towards the front door, where he shoves his feet into his shoes and steps out into the silent hallway.

He turns back to face me, his own expression sullen. "Ok, well, I guess I'll see you in a month then."

He leans his face down to mine, ghosting over my lips for a moment before they crash down onto me. The kiss is intense to say the least but not in a sexual way, it's like everything we both want to say but are too scared or stubborn to, is poured into this kiss. His strong hands are around my waist, holding my body to his like a puzzle piece, lifting my feet slightly off the floor so we're on an equal level. His lips are so soft, so comforting as they move methodically against mine and I never want to stop…but I know we have to, so I reluctantly pull away after a long moment.

"I'll call you tonight," I say, swallowing the words I'm so desperate to launch at him.

Sean nods and turns to leave, planting one last fleeting kiss against my
lips.

As I watch him get closer to the stairs I feel a heavy weight settle in my
chest, like my heart is saying, "What the fuck are you doing?"

Sean has been my absolute rock this weekend, he's done anything and
everything he ever could to make me happy, to support me through thick
and thin and I can't even be honest about how I feel towards him. I've
never loved him more than in this moment and that's why my heart takes
over before my head can catch up.

"Sean!" I yell after him, even though he's no more than 10 metres away
from me.

He spins around, his eyes sad, his face drooping with the longing to stay.
This is it, I have to say it now, I have to tell him.

I take a jagged inhale. "I love you."

Sean's expression immediately transforms to one of surprise, but his eyes
soften and for a moment I think he's going to cry, meanwhile I'm holding
my breath for him to say something. This will be the moment when I know
for sure, he'll either reject me and everything I've been scared of
happening since I met him will come crashing down on me. Or he'll tell
me that he loves me too, I don't know what I'll do if he just walks away.

"I love *you* Cal," he says, his expression pained as he marches back to me,
hauling me up into his arms and hugging me so tightly I can barely
breathe.

But you know what, I don't fucking care, all I wanted was for this man to
love me as much as I love him and now I've heard the words leave his lips
I feel like my knees might buckle from the relief. He didn't reject me, he
loves me too. My head and chest feel so light as he holds me there, his face

in my neck, his arms around my middle as I wrap my legs around his waist like a vice, never wanting to separate myself from him.

Sean lifts his face from my neck, his features still warm and soft. "One kiss Callie, that's all it took." His face crinkles into a smile. "One kiss and I was done, I was yours forever."

My heart feels like it might burst out of my chest right now.

"Forever…" I muse, pursing my lips to hide my growing smile. "That sounds nice."

Sean's face cracks in two, the full force of his dimpled grin hitting me right in the chest. "Hell yeah it does." He presses a tight kiss to my lips and then smacks another to my cheek before grinning at me again. "I can't believe you love me,"

I roll my eyes and wriggle down from his body like a tree. "Yeah, well, don't keep going on about it or I'll take it back." *I fucking love teasing him.*

"Nu-uh," he wags a playful finger at me, "no take backs." He strokes my cheeks with his rough hands and plants one more lingering kiss to my lips. "Ok, I really have to go now before Coach screams at me for being late." I nod, still not wanting him to leave but not being able to ignore the way my whole body now feels lighter than before, when I was carrying around my love for Sean but never letting him have any of it.

"Ok, I love you, be safe." I sigh and his face splits again, bright smile almost blinding me.

He blows out a sharp breath. "I'm never going to get tired of hearing you say that," he leaves a kiss on my temple. "I love you too by the way, incase you were unsure about that." I press my lips together to stop my laugh as he turns to walk away.

"Don't finger yourself too much whilst I'm gone." He warns as he reaches the staircase that will take him away from me for a month.

"Oh, I will." I say, wiggling my eyebrows and electing another deep laugh from Sean.

He shakes his curls, looking at me once more. "I know you will, at least film it and send it to me so I have some good jerk off material."

I flash him a wink and he leaves, his panty dropping grin and his godlike body disappearing down the stairwell as the pit in my stomach widens a little now he's gone.

Daisy Egan

Chapter 50

Sean

Pretty much all I've done since I left Redwood three and a bit weeks ago is mope around and think about Callie. Mainly just replay the moment she finally told me she loves me, it was like the hallway started moving underneath me when she said it, like my mind went foggy for a second and all I could hear was a ringing in my ears. Her face was so vulnerable, unwavering as she let those words finally fall from her lips like it was the most natural thing in the world to say. I can't lie, a few tears almost escaped down my face before I collected myself and instead launched myself at my girl, holding her to my waist and vowing to tell her how much I love her every single day that she'll let me. It made all the months of waiting to say it worth it, I'm so glad I let her say it first, even though I had promised myself I would share my feelings with her once she was moving past her grief. But it seems she didn't need to wait, she was ready to tell me and she did, and since that day it's all I've been able to fucking think about. Luckily I've had enough time between our hectic game and training schedule to call Callie at least once per day, obviously texting her as much as possible through out the day too but it's nowhere near enough to satisfy the constant craving I have for her. Being away from her for all this time is putting me in a shit mood, the thunder cloud that's started following me around is getting closer to bursting every day and I'm at the point now of counting the fucking hours until I can go home. I'm also stuck sharing a hotel room with Nick as Lewis had to stay home, icing his injured leg and Kyle paid for his own room. *Snobby prick.* We're all praying we have Lewis back before the end of the season, but I have to say, it's not looking good for him.

It's coming up for 9pm and I feel like a fucking zombie walking down the hallway to my hotel room, Nick trailing behind me, dragging his bag along the floor. The sound of the leather dragging across the tiles is making me irrationally irritable and I have to crack my neck to one side, squeeze my eyes closed for a moment in order not to punch Nick square in the face. The second we step into our room Nick groans loudly and falls back onto his bed. "Jesus, I'm fucked after that. Coach really spanked our asses after that colossal fuck up of a game."

He's not wrong, we got our asses kicked by the other team today and Coach didn't hold back the fire when he got into the locker rooms after the game. He totally let rip on us but I didn't stand up to him like I usually would, knowing he's clearly still deep in grief and if he wants to take it out on us then I'm happy to receive the wrath of his feelings.

"Maybe you should have kept your eyes on the puck then, rather than constantly scanning the stands for girls you'd like to fuck." I mutter, rolling my eyes out of sight so Nick can't see my distaste. I know, that would have been me too not that long ago, but I guess I've grown up.

"First of all, that's not what I was doing, I have a girl keeping me busy right now" Nick picks at his fingers sheepishly, staying tight lipped about this mystery girl again. "And second of all, you're one to talk. Didn't you get purposefully sent into the penalty box when you first saw Callie, leaving us a man down?"

I huff a laugh and shrug. "Ok, you have a point." *I hate admitting when Nick is right.*

"Exactly, so shut up and sit down so we can play COD for an hour before we both collapse from exhaustion." He says, reaching for my controller and tossing it across to my bed.

"Alright, your charming demeanour has convinced me. Let's see if Lewis is free to join too, the poor fucker has been in that house all by himself for almost a month now."

Nick nods, slipping the headphones over his ears and flicking at his controller, starting a game for us and inviting Lewis to join.

"Come on man, you're so fucking boring." He groans after a moment and I know before I put my headphones on that Lewis has joined and he's likely complaining about being disturbed again.

The man has done nothing but sit on his royal ass at home for the last three weeks and every time we try to call or get him on a game with us he moans that we are interfering with his 'rest' which pretty much includes him jerking off twice a day and watching chick flicks on the sofa like a big girl.

"You two are fucking annoying, can't I be left in peace for more than five minutes at a time without you two boner killers calling me and begging for my attention?" Lewis grumbles through the speakers of our headsets.

I snort a loud laugh, headphones now securely in place. "We're not interested in how many times you tug it per day Lew,"

He huffs something I can't decipher before joining the game and quitting his winging, the three of us quickly becoming engrossed in the TV screen.

Daisy Egan

After about an hour and too many animated bullets coming my way, blood splattering the screen soon after, I'm ready to listen to my stomach's incessant rumbling and eat something. I slide the headphones off, getting up from my cross legged position on the bed and stretching my aching muscles, competing so many times in such a short space of time really takes it's toll on my body.

"Going to grab some food from downstairs, you want anything?" I say, patting Nick on his tattooed shoulder as I pass him, making my way towards the hotel room door.

"Just get me a burger or something please man, I'm fucking starving."

I nod and leave the room, the door closing softly behind me with a click as I step out into the quiet hallway and begin towards the lift.

I pull my phone out of my pocket and check my messages, I have one from Callie that was sent nearly two hours ago.

"Shit," I mutter under my breath as I read her words, telling me how much she misses me and more importantly how much she loves me. *I still can't believe she actually loves me.*

I call her immediately but she doesn't pick up so I shoot her a text back instead, apologising for taking so long to respond and telling her to call me back whenever she can. I of course tell her how much I miss her too and how much I love the fucking bones off her.

When I finally get back to the hotel room my hunger pangs have been overtaken by the tired mist that's clouding my brain. I'm so fucking zonked I can barely see straight and the worst part is that I still haven't heard back from my girl, maybe she's mad at me for not replying to her for two hours earlier. I couldn't blame her if she was, as here I am checking my phone every two-seconds to see if she's responded to me. Each time I see the empty lock screen my heart beats a little quicker with worry that I've upset her and she's sulking with me. Usually I find her sassy attitude and sulking endearing, but not when I'm a shit ton of miles away and I can't force her into a bear hug to pull her out of her mood. I drop the paper bag containing Nick's requested burger and chips into his lap where he sits on the bed, still immersed in a game with Lewis. I can't be fucked to play anymore violent shit with them tonight so I lie back on my own bed, closing my eyes and resting my hands behind my head with a deep breath. I need to talk to Callie before I can sleep, the gaping pit of anxiety in my stomach is widening the longer time goes on without hearing from her. I can barely keep my eyes from drooping as I try my hardest to watch Nick play, fighting to keep my mind awake as I listen to him and Lewis yell to each other through their headsets, Nick's mouth crammed with fries like the pig he is.

After a few minutes of fighting sleep I hear Lewis mutter through Nick's headset, "Someone's at the door so I better go," then the two of them call it quits, Nick turns off the console and lies back against his own pillows with a sigh.

"Are you just as fucked as I am?" I grunt, peeling my eyes open to look over at Nick as he pulls his t-shirt over his head and tosses it to the ground. "Uh huh," he nods, flopping back against the mattress, his tattoo covered stomach contracting. "I'm so ready to go home and chill the fuck out for two weeks."

We have two weeks off when we get home, two weeks of no games and barely any training, I can't fucking wait for a rest.

Ping!

"Oh thank fuck for that," I breathe a sigh of relief, grabbing my phone from the nightstand and reading the text from Callie that appears on my screen.

She's telling me all the things I needed to hear, that she's not mad at me, that she couldn't respond because she was driving and that she can't wait to see me at the weekend.

When the shit eating grin splits my face in two, Nick laughs. "You're wrapped around her fucking finger you know that?"

"Yeah I know," I grin lazily at him, "I fucking love it, and I love her."

Nick rolls over with a fake gag and turns off his light, plunging his side of the room into darkness.

I shoot Callie a reply, asking where she was driving to at this time of night and letting her know she can call me if she wants. I'll have to go out into the hallway to talk to her now that Nick is passed out and already snoring obnoxiously, but I'll do whatever I need to just to hear her soft voice before I go to sleep. The second I press send another ping breaks the silence in the room and makes me jump slightly, shoving my phone under the pillow to try a mute the sound from waking Nick. Luckily the man sleeps like a fucking elephant, a tornado could rip through this hotel room and it wouldn't wake him. I'm surprised to see a text from Lewis when I look down, squinting my eyes into the bright light of my phone screen as it filters through the darkness around me.

Lewis:

'Your girl just showed up at my door, she wants to sleep in your bed tonight, she's missing you man.'

Oh god why is she so damn cute all the time? I just want to wrap that girl in cotton wool and keep her in my pocket. I tap against my screen, replying as quickly as I can.

Sean:

'I fucking love that girl, look after her for me Lew.'

I check Callie's message thread again…no reply yet but she's probably getting undressed and climbing under my duvet, snuggling into the scent that drowns my pillows. My heart beats so hard for her it's crazy that it doesn't spring out of my chest and go running back to Redwood to find her. Only five more days until she's back in my arms, and she doesn't know this yet but we're 100 percent spending the entire weekend naked and wrapped around each other. I can't fucking wait.

Chapter 52

Callie

I don't know how I got here, all I know is that I'm missing my 6-foot-4, irritatingly handsome hockey player more than I'd like to admit to myself. I've had to claw out every smidgen of inner strength that I have over the past three weeks without him, navigating my grief as well as missing the only person who can comfort me in the way I need has really taken it's toll on me mentally. The funeral was the absolute worst, standing there next to my dad in the drizzling rain as they lowered my mum into the ground. My hand tensed beside me, searching for Sean's comforting grip when it wasn't there. I just need to feel like I'm near him, even though he's hundreds of miles away right now and won't be home until the weekend. I guess this is how I got here, standing outside his front door and tapping lightly against it with my fist, an overnight bag slung over one shoulder as I shiver on the spot. The January wind is slicing at my bare arms as I shudder, banging slightly harder against the wood just before the door swings open and Lewis stares out at me, a confused expression clouding his eyes. His chestnut hair is blowing as the winter air invades the house, so he quickly gestures for me to come inside. I smooth my curls the minute I step foot into the quiet hallway, Lewis shutting out the icy chill behind me.

Daisy Egan

"Can I stay here tonight please?" I blurt out, my cheeks flushing pink with embarrassment for needing to be here for the night. I know it's clingy of me to need to sleep in Sean's bed when I'm missing him but I don't care. Lewis raises a honey coloured eyebrow. "You know he's not back yet right?" I nod, feeling the heat spreading across my entire face. "Oh," he whispers, "that's *why* you want to stay here, you want to sleep in his bed." *Fucking hell, can every guy at this university just read me like a book or something?*

I sigh, resigning myself to the embarrassment and meeting Lewis' eyes. There's nothing there but a soft understanding and it's then that I remember Lewis having a serious girlfriend last year who broke his heart. The poor guy was depressed for months after she left him, pining after what they had. He's not like his friends, he loves relationships just like I always have, we've always had that in common. Looking into his soft, green eyed gaze right now reminds me that he's probably one of the only people around me that deeply understands how I feel right now and that I don't need to be embarrassed about needing Sean.

"Can I?" I mutter, "Please?" My voice is still quite as a mouse when I speak but Lewis' bright face splits into a smooth smile.

He nods as his smile widens and he shoves his hands into his pockets. "Of course you can," he tips his head towards the stairs, "make yourself at home and I'll be down here if you need anything, can't get up the stairs with this stupid fucking leg." He nods down at the strapped portion of his knee, his toes a light shade of purple from the tightness of the strapping.

"Ok, thanks Lewis I do appreciate this." I smile, heading for the stairs. Lewis titters a laugh. "You and I both know he'd rip my balls from my body if I didn't let you stay here."

Daisy Egan

"Yeah," I laugh, "he probably would, but thank you all the same."

"You know, I never see him happier than when he's with you," *my heart's grown wings again,* "he loves you so much, he's like a lost puppy when you're not around." Lewis chuckles under his breath, raking a hand through his short, brown bristles.

There's my bashful smile coming back with a vengeance, pink cheeks following suit. "He makes me happy too."

"I can tell, he brings out a totally different side of you, one I'd never seen before you guys met."

He's right, he's so right.

I shrug. "I guess I was never really happy before. All those parties were just a way to keep me sane when I was training and dealing with Joel's shit all the time. I never really knew what it was like to be properly loved, even with all my faults…until I met Sean."

Lewis ponders my words and I know he's reminiscing his own failed relationship, but after a beat he simply nods and throws me a lazy wave, heading back to his indented place on the sofa. I head up the stairs, hearing my phone ping after a moment and reminding myself to respond to Sean before I go to sleep, hopefully he can stay awake long enough to say goodnight to me. I pull my t-shirt over my head, digging in Sean's draw for one of his to wear to bed, loving the warm, mushy feeling I get when I slip it over my head and curl up under his covers. His king sized bed swallows me whole as I bury myself in the centre of it, the pillows smothering my face in Sean's manly scent that I want to drink up every drop of. But instead of letting my eyes win the battle and fall closed, dragging me into a well deserved sleep, I check my phone first. Sean's message makes my heart skip as usual and the second I hit send on my reply he reads it, like he was staying awake, waiting for me to respond to him. A moment passes and he hasn't sent anything back so I stuff my phone under Sean's pillow and turn onto my side, letting the thought of sleep overwhelm me as it drags me under. My eyelids are drooping, the smell that surrounds me relaxing every muscle in my body as usual and I just know I'm going to have the best sleep of my life since Sean left almost a month ago. But he has his own plan, which includes waking me from my almost peaceful slumber as my phone starts to ring, vibrating through the pillow and giving me an unsolicited face massage.

"Hi you," I croak, my voice already rough from my near sleepy state.

"Hey baby, I'm so glad you're still awake I was trying not to fall asleep so I could talk to you. I'm out in the hallway so I don't wake Nick, although to be honest the man snores like a fucking elephant so he'd probably sleep through a little bit of phone sex anyway." He murmurs, his sexy voice making my stomach burn with desire.

I breathe a muffled laugh. "We're not having phone sex Sean and I'd love it if you'd hurry up and come home so you can actually fuck me, playing with myself is getting pretty boring." I smirk to myself, knowing that I can get him going so easily.

"Yeah well, you still haven't sent me that video you promised me," he huffs, "I don't know how I'm expected to jerk it without some sort of motivation and nothing makes me fucking hard anymore other than you, I think you've broken my dick."

I laugh, imagining him leaning back against the wall in the hallway with that bright smile across his face as he talks to me, his torso contracting as he laughs, his dimples deepening and his arms flexing a he moves the way he does. Fuck, I'm so damn horny without him.

"There's nothing broken about your dick," I hum softly, desperate to turn him on as much as I am even though there's not much either of us can do about it right now.

"Hmm," he muses, still a smirk to his husky voice. "You're right about that, I'll show you when I'm home in…" he pauses, "ninety-six hours."

I blow out a tired breath, not only tired for sleep but exhausted from constantly missing Sean. "I miss you," I sigh, "I can't wait another ninety-six hours,"

"I know baby, it's fucking awful being away from you, I can't concentrate on the ice either, not when I'm missing you so badly."

We talk for a while longer, going over our plans for the next few days which mostly consist of counting the minutes until we can see each other and trying to keep busy. Sean has a few more games before they come home and I can tell by the way his voice drags when he speaks about it that he's struggling with the exhaustion of so many games jammed so close together in his schedule. He has two whole weeks off when he's home and I intend to stay within a metre of him for as much of those two weeks as I can.

I don't get much sleep even though I'm painfully tired, so when I wake for the fifth time at 6am I decide to just give up on chasing sleep and get up, tiptoeing down the stairs to make a coffee in silence. Lewis is sleeping on the couch right now considering he can't get up the steep staircase to his room with the state of his injured leg, so I try extra hard not to wake him as I make my liquid gold. Taking the first sip and proceeding to burn my bottom lip however isn't a good start and I try to let the curse that slips from my lips escape as quietly as possible, but Lewis sits up straight from his position on the sofa. He digs into his eye sockets with the heels of his palms before squinting over at me as I hold my hands up in apology.

"Shit, sorry I didn't mean to wake you," I grimace, "I was trying to be extra quiet but the coffee was so fucking hot it burnt me and the curse just fell out of my mouth before I could stop it, I'm sorry."

Lewis shakes his head, a lazy grin plastered across his face. "Don't worry about it, I've been tossing and turning all night anyway, this sofa is really uncomfortable." He plants his hands on his lower back, twisting his body and cracking the achy bones with a groan.

"Yeah," I mutter, "I was tossing and turning too."

"Being in Sean's bed not good enough to help you sleep?" He muses, standing up and grabbing his own mug from the highest cupboard.

I shake my curls, tucking a handful behind my ear. "Not really, it was better than being at the dorm but…I just want him back now." I sigh, sipping at my coffee again and enjoying the warmth as it glides down my throat.

Suddenly Lewis' expression changes to one of deep thought, like he's contemplating a crazy scheme and when his eyes find mine again he says, "hey, I have an idea…"

Chapter 53

Callie

I'm on a plane, a fucking airplane and it's only been four hours since I got out of bed. Lewis is a great guy, so fucking great and he's an amazing friend to Sean but maybe this idea of his was a bit bananas for a random Tuesday morning. He knows I'm missing Sean, desperate to see him yada, yada, yada but I didn't expect him to offer to pay for my plane ticket to surprise him in France today. It's no secret that I'm pretty much broke 99 percent of the time, I've never shied away from that fact, never hidden it from people but I certainly don't expect handouts from anyone. The truth is Sean could have bought me a plane ticket himself, his bank account is bulging at the seams and he's often overly generous, especially towards me. But his efforts to persuade me to travel to France for the month with him were shot down when I told him how busy I was with training and competitions. What I accidentally — or not so accidentally but don't tell him that — forgot to mention was that I didn't have anything on during the last week of his trip. I kind of thought it would be pointless flying out there for one week and I definitely underestimated how much I'd be missing him. So here I am, half an hour from landing in Bordeaux on a Tuesday morning and my boyfriend has no idea that I'm coming. I know he has a game at midday today so I booked my ticket in the taxi that Lewis practically shoved me into at 7am this morning, insisting Sean and I both need this. He's right, we do need this, we need to see each other and my chest is fluttering continuously when I picture the way his face is going to look when he sees me waiting outside the rink for him.

My leg won't stop bobbing up and down when I finally find my bag and get into a taxi, taking me directly to the rink. My nail has found it's way to my mouth as it always does when I'm nervous, my teeth taking tiny pieces out of it as I watch Bordeaux fly by the window. By the time I actually make it to the rink it's only fifteen minutes until the game starts and my chest is thumping with anticipation, just being in the same room as Sean after almost a month away from him is giving me an anxious stomach ache. I shuffle past a few people, apologising under my breath and land in my seat with a sigh just as the guys all start sliding onto the ice, one after another. Then he comes into view, just after Nick as he glides onto the ice, looking painfully hot with a panty dropping grin plastered across his face. I know other girls will be thinking the exact same thing as I am right now, god I want him to fuck me until I can't walk, but I don't care who else is looking at him because he's always only looking at me. Not right now of course, as he has no idea I'm even here watching him. He flies across the ice like a bullet through the air, zipping in and out of his teammates towards the goal, passing to Nick and flying around the back of the net — a tactic he often uses to confuse his opponents — and takes the puck back from Nick, smashing it into the goal within the first five minutes of play. The arena erupts, everyone on their feet cheering my guy on as he flashes a smile at his team, they clamber on top of him, enveloping him in a huge brawl of a hug. He takes several pats to the back and pucks to the shins for the remainder of the first period, scoring one more goal ten-seconds before the whistle sounds. I'm so fucking proud of him I could burst and as he makes his way off the ice, Kyle hangs a loose arm over his shoulder, glancing up and making brief eye contact with me, throwing me a wink and pushing Sean off the ice ahead of him.

I had to text Kyle on the way here to let him know I was coming, he's the only one of Sean's teammates that I trust and I needed him to keep my plan in action. Kyle will bring Sean out of the rink after the game and take him towards the docks where I'll be waiting for him. There was no way I could ask Mac or Nick to pull this off, they'd be fucking useless and Kyle is Sean's best friend, the only guy he really likes on the team aside for Lewis of course.

When the third period comes around Redwood are three nil up and absolutely dominating the ice, the tension in the air is worsening, becoming thicker and heavier the longer time goes on and the other team can't get even one measly goal in. Kyle is catching their every attempt with his eyes closed and the rest of the guys are lapping up the electric energy in the arena. The minute the whistle blows to indicate the end of the game one of the French defensemen start on Sean, shoving him back into the boards. The two of them have been toe to toe pretty much the entire game and the smoke is now puffing out of the French guys ears, a string of unintelligible French curses flying out of his mouth as he dives on Sean. The two of them rip off their gloves and helmets as they collide with each other, fist flying, spit and blood following as it splatters to the ground, decorating the ice like paint on a blank canvas. I simply roll my eyes and reach for my phone as it begins to vibrate incessantly in my pocket. Don't get me wrong I love when Sean fights, it turns me on and my vagina always does a little dance, excited to get some action herself later. But I know he can look after himself so I never stress when the blood starts leaping through the air, I've watched him fight enough times to know he has it under control.

Molly's name flashes onto my screen and I accept the call, keeping my eyes on the fight. "My man is fighting again."

"You sound awfully calm about that," she muses, a popping sound telling me she has a mouth full of gum. "Getting used to the whole hockey wag life are you?"

I huff a laugh. "Yeah, I kind of like the fighting," I look back to Sean as he's carted off the ice, swiping a smear of blood across his face with the back of his hand. "Screw that, I fucking love it."

Damn, he looks so sexy with sweat dripping down his face like that.

"It's hot as balls right?" Molly chirps, cackling when I audibly groan low in my throat as I watch Sean shaking out his hair and leaving the ice with blood smeared across his cheek. "Anyway, you need to start taking me to more games with you, you're not a good friend." She muses, popping her gum loudly again. "You've been depriving your best friend of watching hot, sweaty, godlike men throwing punches at each other."

I clear my throat dramatically, standing up from my seat. "Do you want my boyfriend? Because if you do we may have a problem."

"Ha!" Molly barks, "You wish Cal, I just like watching them roll around together."

"Horny bitch," I mutter with a laugh as I make my way out of the stadium into the icy breeze.

Daisy Egan

"Says the one who has sex with her boyfriend three times a day, every day." She teases and I don't even bother to deny it. I mean we don't have sex three times a day, that's a bit of a stretch but it's true that there's nothing I love more than letting that hunky man break me in two with his dick.

I tell Mol I'll be home at the weekend and promise to take her to at least one hockey game a week from now on to make up for apparently being a shitty best friend, depriving her of watching sexy men punch each other in the face.

When I finally get around to the docks at the back of the stadium my legs are shaking from the freezing air swirling around me. Maybe that's part of the reason I'm shaking but I can't deny how nervous I am to see Sean, I have no idea why but my chest is compressing so much I can barely breathe as I lean against the railing waiting for him. I've been so caught up with nerves since the moment I got here that I have barely had chance to look around me. The scenery is beautiful, the water below me sparkling blue and although the air is frosty, that doesn't stop the sun from blaring down on me. I let my mind wander for a moment, dreaming of summer and letting the rays warm my face, that's when I hear them, two very familiar voices muttering to each other as they round the corner and come into view.

.

Chapter 54

Sean

"What the fuck are we doing round here man? I just want to go home and shower, I smell like a fucking wet dog." I groan as Kyle drags me towards the docks, my body aching from the fight I just won. I don't like to brag but I fucked that guy up, it's his own fault for starting on me, he should have known better.

The docks are beautiful, the crystal blue water sloshing under our feet as we walk across the iron railed bridge towards the other side. I still don't know what the fuck we're doing out here, Kyle said he had to show me something in private. At first I thought he might whip his cock out and show me how big it is or some weird shit like that but not sure why he'd choose such a public place for it.

Kyle shoves me in front of him as we reach the end of the bridge, the sun glaring in my eyes. "Just shut the fuck up and look."

He points towards the railing on one side of the docks and I squint my eyes, desperately trying to see through the blazing sun.

And that's when I realise exactly what I'm seeing…or more like, *who* I'm seeing. Her dark curls flow down her back so effortlessly, her freckled cheekbones and her bright emerald eyes staring directly into mine. That fucking smile cracks her face too, the one I live for and I'm stuck to the spot, my throat sticky, stopping any sound from breaking free.

I turn to Kyle. "Did you…?" How did…?"

Kyle pats my shoulder once and nods towards Callie. "Go and get her man, she's waiting for you."

I look back at my girl, standing there next to the railing, her face soft and warm when mine is frozen in surprise. I force my legs to move even though they feel like jelly, wobbly and unsteady as my strides turn into a run. I bound towards her like an overexcited puppy and as her face becomes clearer I remember exactly why I fell in love with her in the first place. She's so excruciatingly beautiful, her skin pink from the wind and her wild curls fanning her cheeks. She's so fiery but mushy all at the same time and her heart belongs to me and me only. I feel the happy tears prickling my eyes as I crash into her, hauling her into my arms, lifting her body up to mine and inhaling every drop of her fruity smell. Her arms hook around my neck, her thighs around my torso and her whole body tightens around me, like she wants to lock us together. I don't think I've ever missed anyone as much as I've missed her this past month so I hold her in my arms so tightly, breathing her in.

I nuzzle my face deep into the warmth of her neck. "My baby," I breathe, wrapping my arms around her middle and sucking in a lungful of her scent. "Fuck, I missed you."

Her legs tighten around me. "I missed you too," *god I've missed her voice.* She brings her face round to mine, pressing our lips together in a soft but hungry kiss. My fingers wrap through her curls just as her hands wrap through mine, our mouths moving methodically against each other and her taste is driving me fucking crazy.

"I love you, I fucking love you, do you know that?" I moan against her soft lips as she devours me with her touch.

She nods and breaks the kiss. "I know that and I love you too, so much Sean, I couldn't wait to see you."

I plant my lips on her's again, sucking her bottom one between my teeth and swiping my tongue across it gently, listing to a moan rumble in her throat which makes me immediately hard. The taste of her tongue is making me insane with need, I just want to be inside her for the next week, never stopping, never taking a break. Her mouth is so familiar to me, so comforting like the parts of her that are buried the deepest are handed over to me when we kiss.

"God baby, your lips taste like home." I whisper and Callie's light, airy laugh permeates the private bubble around us.

"You're so weird," she titters, rubbing along my jaw with her thumb.

I hum as her fingers brush against my neck and I bury my face back into her shoulder, I could just stay here forever, holding her like this. But more than anything I want to take her back to my hotel room, take all of her clothes off and fucking worship her until my dick is too numb to work anymore.

As if she's read my mind she dips her mouth down to my ear, her breath tickling my neck. "Wanna go back to your hotel?"

"Hmm," I hum, letting my forehead land on her's softly. "I can't wait to feel every single inch of you."

The drive back to my hotel is too fucking long, the scenic views that whiz past us doing nothing to distract me from the fact that I have Callie's hand in mine, my other hand firmly planted on her thigh. I can look at nothing but her, watching the way she stares out of the window in awe at the sparkling water that passes by. Her eyes are bright with wonder when she looks at me, catching me staring and letting a knowing smile tug at her lips as we pull up outside my hotel. I practically yank her out of the taxi, dragging her up the stairs and into my bedroom before Nick can get back from the restaurant the team have gone to for celebratory drinks. I couldn't give less of a fuck about celebrating anything but the fact my girl is here and she's all mine for at least the next hour until Nick comes back and ruins my fun. I'm dying to take this slow, having not made love to her in almost a month I just want to feel every inch of her, taking my time and relishing in how she feels wrapped around me. I want to touch every part of her soft, milky skin and run my hands all over her but I'm also like a starving lion that finally caught a gazelle, and I'm fucking desperate to tuck into my meal. Callie feels more tense than usual when I lay her down on the bed, her clothes long gone and her naked body stretched out like a goddess in front of me. Her green eyes don't hold mine like they usually do, the intensity there but something clouding it in the way they flicker around the room, like she's nervous. I can't for the life of me work out why her muscles are tight with tension though, why I can't capture her eyes like I usually can.

I cover her body with my own, lightly lifting her jaw and forcing her to look at me. "Hey, you doing ok there?"

She nods and swallows hard, taking my pulsing cock in her palm and sucking every worry out of my mind when her hand moves around me like that.

"Ah, fuck Callie that's so good," I groan against her collarbone where I slap open mouthed kisses, occasionally sucking hard at the skin and leaving my mark on her.

I reach between us and caress her clit, making her arch off the bed and claw at my back like she always does when I tease her, pinching the throbbing bud between my fingers and massaging it softly. I push my cock into her and she sucks in a sharp breath as I stretch her out, trying to be as gentle as is humanly possible when all I want to do is fuck her so hard my dick falls off.

Suddenly Callie's eyes flash with uncertainty and she shoves at my chest. "Wait, wait, wait…"

I pull out of her immediately, moving my painfully hard cock away from her opening and stroking her cheek as the worry overtakes her expression.

"Hey," I whisper, "do you want to stop? Just tell me and we'll stop."

She shakes her head, biting at her already half eaten finger nail. "I'm just nervous."

"You never need to be nervous with me Cal, I know it's been like a month since we—"

"It's not that." She cuts me off and I rake her hair back off her face. "I love you now," she murmurs, finally catching my gaze. "So, this feels different."

Ah, I get it.

"Well," I half chuckle, keeping one hand on her jaw. "I wish I could say the same, but I've loved you for a long time."

"How long?" She squeaks, her eyes wider than they were just a moment ago.

I clear my throat, unsure whether to tell the truth. "Since we had sex," I mutter, hoping she'll mishear me, but of course, she's like a bloodhound, so she heard every word and she's quick to snap back at me.

"The *first* time?" She gasps, her eyes fighting through the wall I'm using to hide my vulnerability.

I nod sheepishly and her hands are on my face before I can blink, her expression soft with understanding as her green pools pin me in place.

"Why didn't you tell me?"

"I wasn't sure if you were ready to hear it so Lewis said to wait until you said it first."

Callie slaps a hand to her forehead and scrunches her eyes in angst. "God, you two are so fucking stupid. You should have told me how you were feeling."

I take her hand from her head and kiss her palm, holding it's warmth to my cheek. "Well, I'll just make sure to tell you every single day from now on."

Callie giggles. "Can you fuck me now please?"

There goes my dick again, obeying her orders the moment they leave her lips.

"Your wish is my command," I say against her soft lips, pressing against them and pushing my cock back inside her where I intend to keep it for as long as possible.

Chapter 55

Callie

Sean made love to me every day this week, he kicked Nick out of his hotel room every night and respectfully railed me into his mattress, whispering things like, "Fuck, I love you," and "you look so god damn beautiful when I'm fucking you."

That man makes me constantly weak in the knees but I'm never more in love with him than when he's expressing his feelings, opening his heart to me and telling me exactly how he feels. I don't need to be with someone who makes me guess what they're thinking, Joel was like that and it's something I never want again. Luckily for me Sean is opposite in every way, always making his feelings for me clear and making me feel loved like I never have before. He scratched an itch in my chest that I never knew was there and he continues to scratch it every day, keeping my heart satisfied and pumping with love and need for him.

That's what I need to focus on today as my legs shake with nerves just like the first time I was in this situation, meeting Sean's parents for dinner after their trip to Italy. They arrived back two days ago and immediately asked to see Sean and I for a catch up. They made me feel so comfortable last time I met them and I was most certainly flung into *that* encounter with no prior warning whatsoever. Sean was amazing at trying to keep me calm, holding my nerves in his warm palm and caressing them slowly, stopping my heartbeat from going into overdrive and exploding straight from my chest. This time feels different though, with both of our feelings out in the open and so much having happened since I last saw Sean's parents I'm not exactly sure how to feel today.

My heels click clack across the laminate flooring of the restaurant, my ankle length dress flowing with me as I move as closely to Sean as is humanly possible. My hand is cocooned inside his huge one, his thumb creating robotic circles against my palm as we walk towards a private table in the back of the semi-busy restaurant.

It's a Sunday afternoon and the atmosphere in here is so different to the last time we came for dinner. Mostly families crowd the space, the noise of children chatting and crayons clattering to the ground makes my heart happy and most importantly numbs the nerves I feel buzzing around in the pit of my stomach. The thin satin of my dress swishes against my freshly shaved legs, the material tickling my skin where the dress slits up one of my thighs, showcasing my pale skin. God I need a spray tan soon, I'm sick of being the colour of a milky bar.

"Hey you two!" Sean's mum beams, standing up and greeting us both with a hug.

My fluttering heart calms even more when her arms come around me — Sean tightening his grip on my hand — and I relax into her embrace. Sean's dad simply nods at us both, a man of few words as he is and gestures for us to take a seat opposite them. We get to talking immediately, them filling us in on their amazing trip to Italy, describing the snowy peaks and the golden sands to us but I imagine it's even more beautiful than what I'm picturing in my head when I listen to them. Judith is sparkling with excitement as she talks but even more so when she listens to Sean explain everything that's going on in our lives. Her face almost bursts with anticipation when Sean gets to the part when I surprised him in France a few days ago, her chin resting on her fists like a child as her bright eyes flicker between the two of us.

When our food finally arrives my stomach is screaming at me to shove it down my throat as quickly as possible. I haven't eaten a single thing all day because of the nerves, the mere thought of food this morning was making my stomach churn uncomfortably. But now I'm fucking ravenous and I have to remind myself not to demolish the entire plate like a starved animal. I can feel Sean's eyes on me as I tentatively take the first bite, letting my eyelids flutter closed momentarily as the peppery sauce hits my tongue and I fight to hold back my pleasure filled groan. It takes me only minutes to clear my plate even when I purposefully try to eat as slow as I can, keeping my beady eyes on everyone else and their pace as all of our plates slowly become more and more empty. The only thing left now is a smearing of sauce and a couple of abandoned vegetables between us as we all sit back with tight stomaches.

"So," Sean's mum starts, taking a long gulp of her wine. "When are you two getting married?"

I choke on my own drink, coughing and sitting upright in my chair as Sean pats at my back. "Sorry," I croak, still trying to clear my throat of bile as Sean's hand rubs circles on my skin.

I can tell he's holding back a laugh, likely a cocky one at the fact his mum assumes I'd want to marry him. That man likely believes every woman on earth wants to marry him, it's a pity he'd be 100 percent right.

Sean chuckles under his breath. "I don't think Callie is quite there yet Mum."

What? What the hell does he mean 'Callie isn't there yet'? What about him? He can't possibly already be thinking about marriage right? He's a crazy fucker.

"And you are?" I whisper, still swallowing down the lump of utter shock that's lodged in my throat.

Sean simply nods, grinning at me. "Whenever you are baby."

Ok, what the fuck is going on today?

By the time we leave the restaurant my head is spinning and I'm not sure if it's due to the sheer amount of red wine that I drank or the fact that Sean's intention of marrying me is now out in the open. I'm only 21 and to be totally honest marriage is never something I've even allowed to enter my mind before, fear of rejection has always ruled me and so the thought of someone ever wanting to commit their life to me was a silly idea that was never even to be considered.

We follow Sean's parents back to his childhood home and when we get inside Sean insists we head straight up to his bedroom. I can see by the twinkle in his eye that he thinks he's about to get lucky, but if he knows me at all he'd know that never in a million years would I have sex with him whilst his parents are downstairs none the wiser. He leads me up the grand staircase, my eyes still adjusting to the brightness of the house, almost the entire downstairs is made of glass, the huge windows covering the place from floor to ceiling and letting the sunlight pour in. Sean pulls me down the hallway behind him as I stumble on my own feet, unable to do anything but stare at my surroundings before he hauls me into the last room on the right and closes the door behind us. My face cracks into a smile when I realise I'm in his bedroom, the walls are covered in hockey posters, so much so you can barely make out the shade of paint hiding behind them. The king sized bed in the centre tells me Sean's always been a huge guy, even when he was just a teenager living here, he told me once how he hit 6 foot when he was only thirteen and I can totally believe that now. He drags me over to the bed and my eyes continue to trail around his room in awe, the carpet is pristine, white and crystal like, gleaming back at me. When I finally look over at Sean — who surprisingly hasn't tried to remove any of my clothes yet — he's wearing a sheepish smile on his face, his dimples deep and beautiful as always.

"This is weird," I let out a breathy laugh, unsure where to look next. "It's like being inside your brain."

My eyes continue their path around the room, taking in every detail and falling even more deeply in love with Sean the more I look around at his bedroom. I can't explain it but, it's just so…him. When I turn my face back to his he's simply staring at me, wonder and adoration clear in his caramel eyes.

"I'm so in love with you," he says and my heart kicks into gear, battering my ribcage as I suck in a sharp breath followed by a light laugh.

"I know," I smile arrogantly, teasing him. "I'm great aren't I?"

Sean barks a laugh of his own, a snort mixed in there too. "Yeah baby, you really are great."

He tips his face to place a delicate kiss against my lips, his mouth moulding to mine in the way it always does, like it was made for me.

"I know what my mum said back there scared you," he whispers, breaking the kiss and planting a firm hand on my thigh.

"It didn't scare me," I stutter, but Sean presses a finger to my lips to stop me.

He shakes his head, eyes soft and understanding. "Don't lie to me baby, I know it scared you and that's ok."

Why can he always read my mind like that? It's so fucking weird but I guess I secretly love it. It's like I don't always have to say how I'm feeling, the man just knows.

"I guess it did take me by surprise," I smile and he returns with his own. "But it also kind of sounds…nice."

Sean's face widens with surprise. "Really?" I nod and his face gleams with happiness. "Well, that's great because I really want to marry you Callie." He takes my face in his huge hands, thumbs caressing my cheekbones.

"Not yet though Sean, I'm only 21." I say as softly as I can, desperate not to hurt his feelings, but to my total relief his face doesn't split in pain or sadness, he nods, a look of understanding and agreement clear in his eye.

"One day though? Promise you'll marry me one day?" He whispers, lips now hovering over mine as his hands trail down my face and land on either side of my neck.

"Yeah Sean, I promise."

"That's good," he grins, dimples making my heart beat faster as always. "Because if you said no I would just keep pestering you until you changed your mind anyway." His smile is so wide that my stomach reacts, flipping in all directions as I look into his sparkling eyes.

"Huh," I raise my eyebrows, sass lacing my tone. "You mean like you did to win me over in the first place?"

"You always wanted me," he scoffs, "even in the beginning when you pretended like you didn't."

He flexes his bicep, squeezing it and making the veins pop as the inside of my thighs become increasingly slippery. I can't let him know that though, the arrogance still isn't lost on me, no matter how long he's been my boyfriend.

He plants a fleeting kiss to his solid bicep and flashes me a dimpled, toothy grin again. "Who could resist this?"

"Watch it Taylor," I point at him sternly, swallowing the laugh that tries to bubble up my throat. "You're on thin ice right now."

THE END

Acknowledgements

To be honest I don't really know where to even start with thanking people, there are so many of you that unknowingly contributed to this book and for that I'm eternally grateful.

I guess I should start with my amazing fiancé who never tires of me tapping away at my laptop and moaning that I don't have enough time to write whilst staring at a blank word document. He's accepted this new path of mine with nothing but support and love, I don't even have the words to express how lucky I am to have him.

My mum, who always reads my books even though she doesn't usually like romance, but will sit through spicy chapter after spicy chapter to show her unwavering support for everything I do.

One of my best friends, Nerissa. You read my work and cringe through the sex scenes, but you read them anyway and I love you for that.

To the ice hockey romance book club on TikTok and Instagram, I love the enthusiasm you've shown for Sean and Callie before you even had chance to meet them.

And of course to every single person who has ever read anything I've written, just thank you, from the bottom of my heart.

Follow me on instagram for updates on future books: @daisyeganauthor

Daisy Egan

Printed in Great Britain
by Amazon

42700432R00229